THE ROCKING R RANCH

THE ROCKING R RANCH

TIM WASHBURN

WHEELER PUBLISHING
A part of Gale, a Cengage Company

LIBRARY OF CONGRESS CIP DATA ON FILE.
CATALOGUING IN PUBLICATION FOR THIS BOOK
IS AVAILABLE FROM THE LIBRARY OF CONGRESS.

ISBN-13: 978-1-4328-8101-6 (softcover alk. paper)

Published in 2021 by arrangement with Pinnacle Books, an imprint of Kensington Publishing Corp.

Printed in the United States of America
1 2 3 4 5   24 23 22 21 20

Dedicated to
Isabelle Kathleen Chandler
and
Graham Karson Snider
The second wave of the next generation.

CHAPTER
1

There was no hint of the approaching dawn when Cyrus Ridgeway pulled his rifle down from where it hung over the door and made his way outside, dropping wearily into one of the half-dozen rocking chairs that dotted the long front porch of their two-story home. He leaned the rifle against the house and sat back. Now at sixty-four, Cyrus had spent a majority of those years outside and on a horse and he didn't sleep well anymore. Too many aches and pains and something else — an ever-present worry that gnawed at Cyrus like a lingering toothache. And more than once he had cursed his ancestors for staking a claim to this land that, over the years, had absorbed a river of Ridgeway blood.

It's not that the ground under their feet wasn't fertile, because it was, the grass growing knee-high during the summer months and fattening the Ridgeways' ten thousand head of cattle. And it wasn't the climate, either. The area received adequate rainfall and most days were sunny and warm. No, what irked Cyrus was the location. Set hard against the Red River in northwest Texas, the Rocking R Ranch spanned for as far as the eye could see across more than forty-five thousand acres of relatively flat terrain. If it had been any other river it would have been acceptable. But not this river. And his contempt didn't have anything to do with the quality or quantity of water that flowed through her banks. In fact, it didn't have much to do with the river at all. No, his annoyance, disgust, and loathing stemmed from what was on the *other side* of the river — Indian Territory.

The Territory was home to a conglomeration of Indians, many of whom would rather slit your throat than look at you. And Cyrus thought he probably could have tolerated that if it was just the Indians he had to worry about. But it wasn't. There was more, much more, that kept him up at night. A lawless place, Indian Territory was also home to a large assortment of cattle rustlers, horse thieves, murderers, robbers, and would-be robbers, con men, swindlers, scoundrels, crooks, and many other nefarious no-gooders with evil on their minds. If Cyrus had a dollar for every stolen cow or horse, he would be rich — or rather — richer than he already was. His children and their families who lived on the ranch insisted the occasional losses should be chalked up to the cost of doing business. But that didn't sit well with Cyrus, who was a firm believer in protecting what was theirs, no matter the cost. And he'd gotten most of the stolen stock back over the years, with the thieves often paying a steep price for their transgressions when they found themselves at the end of a short rope that was tied to a tall tree.

Cyrus heard someone stirring around inside and listened to the footfalls, trying to decipher who was about to horn in on his quiet time. With a big family and four other homes on the place, it was difficult to know who was sleeping where on any given night. Most nights, a grandchild or two would slink up to his house after dark, well after Cyrus had already turned in. He didn't have to listen long to identify the footsteps as belonging to his wife, Frances. The door squealed when she opened it and stepped outside.

"What are you doing sitting out here in the dark, Cy?" she asked as she took a seat next to him.

"Can't sleep."

Frances reached out and put her hand on his back. "What's worrying that noggin of yours so early this morning?"

"Nothin' but the usual worries." Cyrus glanced in her direction. The moon glow was bright enough to see her profile and hints of her gray hair but not her individual features. And that was okay because Cyrus had them memorized by now, especially her blue eyes.

"That shoulder bothering you again?"

"Nah. Just can't sleep." Cyrus was a bear of a man at six-three with strong, powerful shoulders from a lifetime of hard work. He'd packed on a few extra pounds over the years and his once-dark hair was now mostly gray. With a full beard and mustache, he had started trimming it shorter after Frances teased him about looking like Santa Claus.

Frances removed her hand from his back and leaned back in her chair. "It's about time you let the boys carry some of the load."

"What about the girls, Franny? They not get a say in it?"

Cyrus and Frances had produced seven offspring, four of whom made it to adulthood — two sons, Percy and Elias, along with two daughters, Abigail and Rachel, the youngest. All now had families of their own and lived on the ranch.

"That'd probably be up to Percy. Shouldn't he get more say in who does what since he's the oldest?" Frances asked.

"Maybe," Cyrus said. "But I don't reckon any of it's writ in stone. And you're liable to stir up a passel of trouble if you ain't careful."

Frances clucked her tongue. "Decisions need to be made, Cy. We're not getting any younger." Tall at five-eight, her once-red hair was now gray and, lithe and lean as a teenager, her body was a bit stiffer but, remarkably, she still wore the same size dress as back then and still filled it out in all the right places.

"I ain't dead, yet," Cyrus said, a surly tone in his voice. "Besides, might be best to let the kids figure all that out when we're gone."

"Talk about stirring up trouble," Frances said. "I won't have my family ripped to pieces over this cattle ranch. We need a plan."

"What do you care? You'll likely be dead, too, fore it comes to that."

Frances sighed and pushed to her feet. "I'm going to put on some coffee."

Cyrus watched his wife's silhouette disappear into the house. His preference was to keep the ranch intact for the future generations, but Frances had mentioned a couple of times through the years that they should divvy it up and give it to the kids. "Over my dead body," Cyrus grumbled as he thought about it. Every time he pondered the situation, he ended up with a stomachache. The original Spanish land grant the ranch was founded upon had been in his family since Texas was still called Mexico, and Cyrus had added to their holdings over the years, buying up the farms and ranches of those who grew tired of fighting the Indians and the outlaws that drifted across the river. He'd worked too hard to make the ranch what it was and if the children wanted the land divided, they were going to have to wait until he was dead.

Cyrus wiped the sweat from his brow. August in this part of the country was hot, muggy, and miserable and those were the nighttime weather conditions. The same conditions existed during the day but were intensified about tenfold. The sun wasn't even up yet, and Cyrus was already damp with sweat. Thinking about the heat, a weariness crept into his bones. It didn't matter if it was scorching hot or finger-freezing cold, there was always work to be done — horses to be broken, cattle to be branded, corrals to be fixed, and on and on, all while keeping a watchful eye for marauding Indians, cattle rustlers, or others who might want what wasn't legally theirs. Sometimes Cyrus wished he had listened to Frances and moved to San Antonio when they were younger. And they might have if his two older brothers who were set to take over the ranch hadn't been slaughtered by a roving pack of Comanche savages while Cyrus and his new bride had been on a horse-buying trip to Saint Louis. Their deaths sealed Cyrus's fate because he was the last of the Ridgeway boys. But all that was years ago — time that had slipped away, year after year, and, once Frances started having kids, leaving the ranch hadn't made any sense at all. Now here it was, 1873, and Cyrus knew his dead carcass would be buried up on the little knoll where they buried his brothers and all the children who had died way too early.

Frances returned a while later, handed her a husband a cup of coffee, and retook her seat just as the first rays of the sun stretched across the landscape. They sat in silence for a few moments as the orange orb peeked over the horizon. They had positioned the house so that they could watch the sunrise on the front porch and the sunset on the back porch. Hearing the clop of horses, Cyrus sat up and reached for the rifle he'd brought outside and then relaxed when the night riders rode past on their way to the bunkhouse.

"Good thing they weren't renegades," Frances said, "or they would have been on us before you could lever a shell into that rifle of yours."

"Hearin' ain't what it once was," Cyrus mumbled. "Maybe you ought to be the lookout since you still got all your faculties."

Frances chuckled. "Oh, Cy, you're doing just fine. Don't you think I'd have told you if trouble was headed our way?"

"Don't need my wife to tell me when there's trouble a-comin'. My damn eyes still work just fine." Cyrus turned to look at his wife. "We eatin' breakfast sometime today?"

Frances chuckled again. "Don't get all riled up, Cy. We all have our shortcomings." She stood and leaned over to kiss her husband on the cheek. "You'll always be my protector. What are you planning for the day?"

"Me and Percy and a few others are gonna track down them rustlers who stole them

14

two steers yesterday afternoon."

"Aren't you getting a little old to be traipsing off after outlaws?"

"Like I said, I ain't dead yet. 'Sides, can't let them rustlers go unpunished or word would get out and we'd be robbed blind."

"And if you find them?"

Cyrus took a sip of his coffee then said, "Hang 'em, I reckon."

CHAPTER
2

A short distance down the road from the main house, Abigail Turner walked through her dark house and into the kitchen, trying to recall the dream she'd just had. She struck a match and lit the coal oil lamp and stoked the fire, adding more wood from a small stack beside the stove. The dream involved a carriage, a man, and a large city, possibly Saint Louis. But try as she might, she couldn't recall any of the details of who was involved or what she might have been doing. And the last time she had been in Saint Louis was years ago, before she'd met her husband, Isaac, and settled down.

As the last fragment of the dream frustratingly faded from memory, Abby stepped out the back door and walked to the outhouse to relieve herself, then filled a pan with water from the well and returned to the kitchen, the sweat already running down her back. Wetting a dish towel, she wiped her face and under her arms and then gathered up her long, red hair and used a strip of fabric to fashion a ponytail. Abby was tall like her mother and had also gotten her mother's red hair and blue eyes, but that's where the similarities ended. She had her father's larger frame with wide shoulders, larger hands, and she wore a size nine shoe. Abby wasn't chubby or fat although she looked larger than an average woman. She called it being big-boned. With her hair off her neck, she already felt cooler. After putting on a pot of coffee, she grabbed her sourdough starter from an overhead shelf and began making biscuits.

Over the years a succession of cooks had paraded through the Turner home, yet none ever quite lived up to Abigail's expectations. So now, much like her mother, Abigail was responsible for a majority of the cooking duties and usually begged for help only for special occasions or holidays. Her sister, Rachel, however, had run through a long line of cooks before she got tired of that and settled on the last person she'd hired and she rarely, if ever, ventured into the kitchen of her house next door. Abigail couldn't decide if her sister had a less discerning palate or if it was just plain laziness. Knowing Rachel as well as she did, Abby suspected it was the latter.

In addition to the main house where her parents lived, she and her three siblings had constructed four other three-room homes that formed a horseshoe-shape with the main house at the center. Although they all shared a huge backyard, there was a good deal of distance between the houses and that allowed for a modicum of privacy while also creating a fairly strong defensive position. If marauding Indians rode up to the rear of the homes, they'd face the cold steel of a dozen rifle barrels. And around front, the semicircle arrangement allowed a single shooter at the main house an almost unlimited field of fire to keep any intruders at bay.

Her husband, Isaac Turner, walked into the kitchen, pulling his suspenders over his shirt. "Biscuits ready?"

Her hands covered in flour as she mixed the dough in a bowl, Abigail said, "Do they look ready?"

"You don't gotta bite my head off."

"Why're you asking if you can plainly see they aren't ready?"

Isaac poured himself a cup of coffee. "I got work to do."

"Work your butt up the ladder and roust the kids."

"You wake up mad?" Isaac asked before taking a sip from his cup.

"Yes, and I'm likely to stay that way."

"One more reason to get out of the house," Isaac mumbled as he stepped out of the kitchen. Rather than crawling up the ladder to the sleeping loft, he shouted upstairs for the kids to get up.

Abigail pursed her lips and blew a stray strand of hair off her face. "You tryin' to wake up everybody on the ranch?"

"I expect they's already up. What's got you so riled up? Cookin'? I tole you to hire another cook."

"It wouldn't hurt you none to learn how to make biscuits."

"Okay, I'll make biscuits and you go traipsing after your pa all day." Isaac had sandy blond hair and he and Abby were the same height. Wiry and lanky, he might weigh 140 pounds if he put on his coat and stood in the rain for an hour. Being about the same size as Abby, they had often argued about who would win if they ever got into a real fight.

A clatter arose from overhead as the three children climbed out of bed.

"Where are you going?" Abigail asked.

"Hunt down them rustlers that stole them two steers."

"Does two less steers really matter?"

"It surely does to your pa."

"If he says *jump* do you ask how high, too?"

"Don't start, Abby." Isaac pulled out a chair at the table and sat.

"Have the law take care of it."

"What law? You know there ain't no law round here except your pa."

Raised voices interrupted their conversation when an argument erupted upstairs. She raised her eyes to the ceiling and shouted, "Hush up and get down here." She turned back to her husband to say something else but was interrupted by footsteps pounding down the ladder. Their oldest daughter, thirteen-year-old Emma, appeared first. "Emma, you and your sister go gather the eggs," Abigail said.

"Ugh," Emma moaned. "Can I go to the outhouse first?"

"You can. But if you want to eat, I need the eggs."

Emma grabbed the hand of her sister, seven-year-old Amelia, and dragged her outside as Abigail, using a spoon, dolloped the biscuit dough into an iron skillet and slid it into the oven. She pulled a large pan from the shelf overhead and started slicing bacon into it. She glanced over at Isaac.

"What about the ranger that was through here a few days ago?"

"Charlie Simmons? Hell, he's too lazy to wipe his own ass. Claims he's lookin' for rustlers but he ain't."

"Momma, Pa said a bad word," ten-year-old Wesley said as he entered the kitchen, his hair looking like a bird's nest.

Abigail wiped her hands on a towel and smoothed Wesley's hair down. "Hush up. We're having grown-up talk. Now go do your milkin'."

Wesley groaned, grabbed the bucket, and headed outside.

"Why're you all the sudden so concerned about us trailing after a couple of cattle rustlers?"

Abigail stirred the bacon around the pan. "Did I say I was concerned?"

"Why ask all them questions, then?"

"Because you'll be gone who knows how long leaving me here to wrangle the kids."

"Send 'em up to your mama's for the day."

"What makes you think she wants to wrestle our rascals? She'll be swamped with Percy and Mary's bunch once Percy rides off with you."

"What's wrong with Mary? She feelin' poorly again?"

The bacon done, Abigail carried the pan

21

over to the table and set it down. "What do you mean, 'again'? She's been feeling bad for months. Might not hurt for you to take a good look around once in a while."

"Hell, I can't keep up with my own family."

"Thank you for makin' my point. Anyway, Mary has something bad wrong with her. Says her eyes get blurry and she hurts all the time. Claims she's so stiff sometimes she can hardly move."

"Shoot, I'm stiff as a board after bein' in the saddle all day, too," Isaac said.

Abigail, on her way back to the kitchen, stopped midstride and glared at her husband. "Sometimes I wonder why I married you."

The kids eventually returned with the requested items and Abby scrambled the eggs and carried the pan to the table and sat.

Eating was an act of warfare in their home, and as her family mowed through breakfast like it was the last meal they ever expected to see again, Abby nibbled the corner of a biscuit, waiting for them to finish so she could get on with her day.

Once her family had eaten everything in sight, Abigail added a fresh batch of biscuits to a basket, along with more bacon and scrambled eggs she'd hidden in the oven, and asked Emma to take the food over to Percy's house. Then Abby dived into the cleanup and was in the middle of wiping out the cast-iron skillets when Isaac returned to the kitchen carrying his bedroll. Tossing it on the table, he grabbed his gun belt from the coatrack by the door, and strapped it on, eager to try out his newly purchased pistol. He pulled it from his holster and looked at it — again. The Colt Single Action Army revolver — the Peacemaker — was a new type of weapon and had just been released from the manufacturer earlier in the year. There was no more packing powder and ball into each of the pistol's cylinders — with the Colt all Isaac had to do was drop in six .45 caliber metallic cartridges and he was ready to shoot.

"Why do you even bother with a pistol?" Abigail asked from the kitchen. "You can't hit anything with it."

Isaac frowned. "Can, too. Amos give me some pointers."

"Blind leading the blind," Abigail said. "If you want to learn how to shoot, you'd be better off talkin' to Percy."

"Why? 'Cause he rode with the Rangers

for a spell? That don't make him a crack shot."

Abigail shrugged. "Suit yourself."

Angered by his wife's pessimism, Isaac shoved a couple of boxes of ammunition into his saddlebag, slung it over his shoulder, grabbed his rifle and his bedroll, and walked to the front door. With his hand on the latch, he paused for moment, hoping his wife would at least offer parting words or give him a hug before he left. But after a few moments of silence and no movement on Abigail's part, he pushed the door open and stepped out into the dawn. "Damn that woman," he muttered as he walked toward the barn.

While saddling his horse, Isaac's mind drifted repeatedly to his wife. Things hadn't been good between them for a while now. They were cordial to each other — mostly — but a man had his needs and Abigail had been less than cooperative. Yes, the birth of Amelia had been hard for Abby, but that had been seven years ago. Since then, their bedroom encounters had been few and far between and Isaac didn't know if Abby was afraid of getting pregnant again or if it was something more. He had even thought about broaching the subject with Abby's sister, Rachel, yet for one reason or another hadn't. Probably because he knew what his sister-in-law's answer would be — *Tie it in a knot and quit pestering your wife.* Besides, he thought, the chances of the story getting back to Abby were high and if she found out Isaac was talking about their private business, he'd catch eternal hell. With no easy answers available, Isaac climbed aboard the now-saddled horse and shoved his rifle into the scabbard. With a cluck of his tongue and a touch of his spurs, he steered the six-year-old bay gelding out of the barn.

Emma had named the horse Blaze because of the slash of white on his forehead and not because of his speed. However, Blaze had a comfortable gait and was Isaac's preferred choice for long rides. And with his stubborn father-in-law, a long ride was almost assured.

CHAPTER
3

Percy, the oldest of the four Ridgeway siblings, felt conflicted as they worked to cut a few extra horses out of the ranch's herd for the trip. Feeling guilty about leaving his wife, Mary, in such a terrible state, a part of him was looking forward to a day or two away from the house to clear his mind. The last few weeks had been extremely difficult, and the doctor was doing all he could, but it was clear to Percy that his wife's condition was worsening. Physically, Mary no longer resembled the woman he had married and, the hardest part to accept, her once-active mind was dulled by an unending supply of laudanum that barely eased her pain.

Percy returned to the task at hand and spurred his gray mare into the horse herd to cut out a paint horse he enjoyed riding. Riding along beside the paint, he strung out a lasso with his rope and tossed it over the mare's head, pulling her to a stop. Nudging the gray closer, he rubbed the paint's neck and talked to her in a low, soothing voice. Most of those on the ranch thought Percy was crazy for choosing to ride mares, often citing their tendencies to be bad tempered and meaner than hell. But Percy found them companionable and gentle as long as they weren't in heat. He led the paint mare over to the horse wrangler for the trip, Luis Garcia.

Luis was a short, compact Mexican man who had been born south of the border and had eventually migrated north. Percy thought he was one hell of a hand and Luis could ride anything on four legs. He shook his head as he grabbed the rope and said, "Wouldn't hurt to pick out a gelding, Percy."

Percy grinned and he suddenly realized that was the first time he'd felt a spark of happiness in a long while. "Always been a lady's man, Luis." He nodded at the paint. "That mare is as gentle as a kitten."

"Might be, but kittens turn into cats and most are meaner than hell," Luis said. "Some'd scratch your eyes out just for spite."

Percy widened his eyes and pointed at his face. "Still got two good ones." Percy laughed as he turned his horse. Tall at six-three, Percy had his father's dark hair and his mother's lean frame. Rangy and strong, his smooth and graceful movements often appeared effortless to others and he was smarter than most, allowing him to quickly adapt to any situation. With wide-set shoulders that tapered to a narrow waist, Percy disliked shaving and only accomplished the task every couple of weeks when he got tired of the stubble.

Deciding the two horses would be enough, he rode toward his father, who was sitting his big white gelding, Snowball, watching the men pick out their mounts. A big man needed a big horse, and Snowball was one of the largest saddle horses on the ranch, measuring over seventeen hands tall. Percy reined to a stop and said, "What happens if these rustlers turn out to be a couple of Comanches?"

Without turning, Cyrus said, "Don't matter. A thief's a thief."

Percy, continually frustrated by his father's unbending will, said, "You willing to start an Indian war over a couple of steers?"

Cyrus turned to look at his son. "What would you do? Just let 'em ride off with them cattle with no punishment? We do that and we won't have any cattle left fore long."

"I'm not sayin' we do nothing. But hangin' a couple of Comanches might not be too smart on our part. Might spark a shootin' war."

Cyrus turned and looked off to the west, toward the heart of what was still Comanche territory, a scant few miles away. "Injun war's already a-brewin' and it ain't got nothin' to do with cattle." He turned back to Percy. "Besides, it ain't Comanches. Wilcox claims the rustlers headed north, across the river. Might be Injuns, but it ain't Comanche. Far as I know, ain't many of 'em on the reservation."

Percy sagged in the saddle a little. Moses Wilcox could track a gnat across a desert. And if he said the rustlers went north then they went north. And just about every time they'd ridden into Indian Territory bad things had happened. "So, we're headed north?"

"Looks like," Cyrus said. He pulled out his pouch of Bull Durham and began rolling a cigarette. As if reading Percy's mind, he said, "Ain't my favorite direction of travel, neither. But ain't much we can do about it." Cyrus licked the edge of the paper and ran his finger along the seam before putting the cigarette in his mouth. He pulled a match from his pocket, flicked the head with his thumbnail, and lit up. As the smoke curled out of his nostrils, he watched as the last of the hands rode in with their preferred mounts.

"Eli staying back?" Percy asked.

"Yep, as usual," Cyrus said. "Boy ain't got a lick of fight in 'im." He took another drag from his cigarette and the smoke danced around his bearded mouth when he said, "I don't know where I went wrong with that boy." He shrugged and said, "Anyways, I hope you brought plenty of ammunition." He spurred the big gelding forward without waiting for Percy's reply.

Percy paused, mentally calculating how much ammo he had packed in his saddlebags. He had two boxes of .44-40 cartridges for the new Winchester rifle and two boxes of .45s for the new Colt Peacemaker he bought recently to replace his older Colt Model 1861 Navy. Percy decided if they were going to need more ammunition than that they might ought to stay home.

CHAPTER
4

Rachel Ferguson, the youngest of the Ridge-way siblings, sat at the table, sipping a cup of coffee as the cook cleaned up in the kitchen. This cook, an older Mexican woman named Consuelo Ruiz, had lasted longer than any of her predecessors and by a far margin, now coming up on her sixth year of cooking and cleaning for the five members of the Ferguson family. Consuelo was a mournful woman, and, in the beginning, Rachel had a small measure of sympathy for her situation — all five of Consuelo's children had died before reaching adulthood — but time and the constant hardships had eroded even that.

That's what life on the frontier was like, Rachel thought as she stared at the oily surface of the coffee in her cup. The day-after-day drudgery dashed the smallest of dreams, leaving Rachel feeling hollowed out. This was not the life she'd yearned to have. There were no grand galas or crowded society dinners where she and her husband, Amos, could rub elbows with those in the upper echelons of society. No, the closest thing the Fergusons got to a party were the Sunday potluck dinners her mother occasionally organized for the ranch hands and their families with a rare neighbor or two thrown into the mix. The same faces — the same stories that were told and retold until Rachel could recite most from memory.

There had been occasional moments of joy over the years, but Rachel's enjoyment dimmed nearly to extinction with the death of their youngest daughter, Elizabeth, four years ago. Some kind of fever, the doctor had told them. Then the doctor had the gall to tell them they were lucky the disease hadn't spread to other members of the family. Rachel hadn't *felt* particularly lucky when they buried Liza in that deep, dark hole on that cloudy, cold day.

Rachel's thoughts were interrupted when Amos stepped back inside the house. He grabbed his gun belt from a peg by the door and strapped it on. "I guess we're heading out," he said.

Rachel's gaze drifted from the coffee cup to the scrapes and gouges on the table's surface. "Okay."

"Don't know when we'll be back," Amos said as he stood by the door.

Rachel traced a deep scar on the tabletop with her finger. "Guess I'll see you when I see you, then." Out of the corner of her eye, she watched her husband as he shook his head and exited. Over the years, cracks had developed in their relationship, but Elizabeth's death had irrevocably shattered the last remaining remnants of their marriage. Now they coexisted out of convenience and Rachel often wondered if she'd sold herself short by settling for Amos Ferguson just because he happened to pass through at a time when she was being urged to wed.

It's not that her husband wasn't handsome because he was — tall and broadshouldered with dark hair and deep-set blue eyes — and he was a good father to their children. But their marriage had never come close to the type of relationship her parents enjoyed. Her mother and father often touched each other — a hand on an arm, an arm around the other — in an unconscious display of their affection for each other. Something that had rarely happened among the Fergusons, either privately or publicly. *Maybe my parents are the ones with an abnormal relationship,* Rachel thought as she pushed to her feet and returned the cup to the kitchen. *Maybe this was what marriage was supposed to be.*

Rachel provided a few instructions to Consuelo then made her way out to the front porch, taking a seat in one of the rockers. The perfect mixture of her mother and father, Rachel had long, dark hair, blue-green eyes, and lush, full lips. Tall at five-nine, she was long-legged and had all the right curves in all the right places. In total, she was a looker and knew it.

Even though the sun was still low on the horizon, the heat was already building and a trickle of sweat dripped down Rachel's back. In the distance she could see the men heading north and she wasn't surprised to see Amos riding at the back of the pack. And riding beside him was Isaac, as usual. They rarely took the initiative in anything they did, often following the lead of others. Yes, her father was the alpha male around the ranch, but just once she'd like to see either Amos or Isaac grow a spine and stand up to Cyrus. But that was probably a lost cause, she thought, because her own two brothers were also spineless when it came to confronting their father. Rachel and Abigail had no such qualms, often telling their father exactly what they thought, much to their mother's consternation.

Rachel turned to look at the barn and saw her three children walking back to the house. Seth, the oldest at twelve, was shuffling along, his shoulders slumped in disappointment as he followed Jacob, who was ten, and Julia, now their youngest, at seven. Seth's body language suggested Rachel was in for a long day. No doubt he felt slighted for not going on the trip and she silently cursed Amos for leaving her to deal with it. Rather than take his son aside to explain the dangers that might lie ahead, Amos most likely uttered his refusal and left it at that.

"Ma, when's Pa coming back?" Julia asked, stepping onto the porch.

"No idea," Rachel said. "I want you and Jacob to go inside and read three chapters of your books."

Julia shrugged. "Okay." She loved to read and could spend all day wrapped up in her books.

"I don' wanna read," Jacob complained.

"Too bad," Rachel said. "You need to keep up with your schoolin' while your aunt Mary's sick."

"That book's stupid," Jacob whined.

"Choose another one," Rachel said. A reader herself, she made sure the cabin was

35

filled with books of all types. "Why don't you try that new book, *Twenty Thousand Leagues Under the Sea?*"

Jacob thought about it for a moment. "What's it about?"

While describing the book to Jacob, Rachel spied Seth out of the corner of her eye as he silently shuffled onto the porch, his cheeks still damp from the tears. He slouched into one of the chairs and rested his chin on his chest.

"And there's a giant sea monster," Rachel said as she arched her arms up and clawed her hands, grabbing at Jacob.

Jacob giggled and squirmed away from her grasp. "I might take a look," he said between giggles.

"Go on, then," Rachel said, playfully swatting him on the butt as he walked by and stepped inside.

Rachel settled back in the rocker and she and Seth sat in silence for a few moments, both staring at the distance. Rachel's gaze drifted surreptitiously to her son, waiting for the inevitable onslaught of unanswerable questions. Seth didn't disappoint.

"Why, Ma? Why won't they let me go with 'em?"

Seth hadn't hit his major growth spurt yet and he was a smallish, thin boy with sandy blond hair and large ears that his head hadn't caught up to yet.

"Are we going to go through this again?" Rachel asked, turning in her chair to face her son.

Seth angrily swiped at the fresh track of tears sliding down his cheeks. "I'm old enough."

"No, you aren't. There's nothin' but trouble across that river," she said, pointing toward the water. "It's not even safe for your pa or the rest of them."

Seth stood abruptly. "I'm tired of bein' treated like a baby," he shouted before stepping off the porch.

"Seth, you come back here," Rachel said, her voice stern.

Seth stopped, turned, and looked at his mother for the first time. "I'm done talkin'."

"Oh, you are, huh? In that case get your butt over to the corral and get to work helping your uncle."

Seth and Rachel joined in an angry stare-off and she mentally ticked off the seconds, waiting for him to turn away first as he always did. But, to her surprise, she was the first to break eye contact and that troubled her. His determined defiance now could be the harbinger of years of difficult battles ahead. She pondered a response that would reassert her authority and fell back on the old standard — issuing orders. "Go on, now. You're wastin' time."

Seth glared at her a moment longer then turned and walked away without saying a word. For Rachel that was even more unsettling, and she immediately felt a need to call him back — to repair the damage before it had a chance to take hold. But she didn't. And that was something she would soon regret.

CHAPTER
5

Riding through land granted by treaty to the Kiowa, Comanche, and Apache tribes in 1867, Cyrus raised his hand and called the group to a halt as Moses Wilcox studied the ground, searching for the rustlers' trail. Percy pulled out his pipe and filled it with tobacco as he watched Wilcox work.

A tall whip-thin man in his late forties, Wilcox had scouted for the army for years until he called it quits when the soldiers turned their focus from war among the white men to killing or capturing Indians. The child of a white man and a full-blooded Chickasaw woman, Wilcox was raised among the Indians and didn't much like pointing out his distant kinfolks for the army to slaughter. He joined up with the Rocking R four years ago and stuck.

Percy flared a match and lit his pipe as Wilcox climbed back aboard his horse.

"The rustlers look to be headed up toward

Fort Sill," Wilcox said. "Could be they're plannin' to sell them steers to the army."

"Not with my brand on 'em, they ain't," Cyrus said. "Just the two of 'em?"

"Yes," Wilcox said. "And they're riding shod ponies."

"Probably stole them, too," Cyrus grumbled. "Still don't mean they ain't Injuns."

Percy took a draw from his pipe then said, "If they're smart, they'll change the brand. Make the *R* a *B* or hit it with a three-quarter circle and they'd have the Circle R brand."

"When's the last time you heard of an outfit called the Circle R round these parts?" Cyrus asked. "Or a Rockin' B? Them soldier boys are smarter than that."

Percy turned to look at his father. "Might be smart enough to see a good deal, too. A couple of steers at about half what they're worth?"

Cyrus looked up at the sun high overhead, sweat trickling down his face and into his beard. "It's hotter'n hell and we're wastin' time with all this speculatin'. Things fall our way, we'll likely be home fore dark. Let's ride." He spurred his horse into a walk.

The terrain was flat and the few trees, mostly blackjack oaks and cottonwoods, were bunched along the banks of the small creeks that cut through the landscape. What the place lacked for trees, it made up for it with the number of insects flying about. Grasshoppers by the hundreds fluttered up at each clop of the horses' hooves. And if they weren't flying, they were perched in the grass and weeds, rubbing their hind legs in a symphony of fast clicks. In addition to the constant noise, gnats swarmed, flies were thick enough that they matted the horses' rumps, and the mosquitoes were merciless, attacking any hint of bare skin. But for Percy, this was all too familiar.

After leaving the ranch at the age of seventeen to see what was beyond the horizon, Percy drifted south, visiting the young city of Dallas for a spell before moving on, searching for what, he didn't know. The one thing he did know was that he wanted to see the ocean, and his travels led him to Houston then down to Corpus Christi, never staying in one place more than a week or two. As his grubstake began to dwindle, he moseyed up to Austin to see the capital of their new state. And while there and desperate to find work, Percy, a good shot with a pistol and a rifle, signed up as a new recruit for the Texas Rangers in 1851. It didn't take him long to figure out shooting at bottles and cans was much different from shooting at another human who was shooting back. But under the tutelage of Ranger Captain William (Bigfoot) Wallace, Percy had learned, and learned quickly, as his unit skirmished with Comanches, Apaches, and Mexican bandits. And over the years and through many battles Percy became a highly skilled warrior and a dead shot with either rifle or pistol. Members of his troop had boasted that Percy was the most lethal man in Texas. Not that it mattered much to him.

Startled from memory when a grasshopper jumped on his hand, Percy flicked it off, tapped his pipe on his leg to empty the ashes, and slid it into his saddlebag. He pulled a handkerchief out of his back pocket and mopped the sweat from his face. The heat was oppressive, and the tall, browned stalks of grass stood undisturbed. It was unusual not to have some type of breeze and when it didn't exist it was noticeable. Percy shifted in the saddle, trying to find a more comfortable spot. When he turned to check their back trail a moment later, he spotted a dozen riders off to the east and headed their way. He spurred his horse into a trot and rode forward to consult with his father.

"Think they're looking for trouble?" Percy

asked his father as he eased his rifle out.

"Naw," Cyrus said. "I'm bettin' they're Montford Johnson's boys. Looks like some Injuns and Mexis without a white man in the bunch."

"How does that make 'em Johnson's men?" Percy asked.

Cyrus looked over at Percy. "Montford is a full-blood Chickasaw and he struck a deal with the Kiowas and Comanches, tellin' them he wouldn't hire no white riders to herd his cattle. I hear them savages do a fair job of lettin' him be 'cause of it."

The riders drew to a stop about twenty yards away and Percy and Cyrus rode forward to meet them. Cyrus studied the group then smiled and pushed his hat back. "How you doin', Joe?" he asked the leader of the group.

"Good, Cyrus. You?" Joe asked as he removed his hat and wiped his brow with the sleeve of his shirt. "It's hotter'n half-price day at the whorehouse."

Cyrus chuckled. "That it is."

"Whatcha doin' up this way?" Joe asked as he put his hat back on.

"Lookin' for a couple of rustlers. Stole two of my steers. You ain't seen 'em, have ya?"

"Nope, but someone stole two of our

horses day before last and we ain't seen hide nor hair of 'em."

"Probably your horses the rustlers are riding," Cyrus said. "Bastard thieves." He uncorked his canteen and took a swallow of water then pointed that canteen at Percy. "Joe, this here's my oldest boy, Percy. Percy, meet Joe Twofeathers. He's been ridin' up in these parts forever."

"Nice to meet you, Joe," Percy said.

"Likewise," Joe said. "I heard the name afore. Rode with the Rangers for a spell, didn't ya?"

Percy nodded. "Been a while." He pushed his rifle back into his scabbard and said, "Only thing I hunt after now is a few stray cattle or a rustler or two on occasion." Although Percy had ridden across the river and into Indian Territory many times, it wasn't his favorite place to loiter. His motto was to get in and get out as quick as possible.

Joe shifted in his saddle. "I wish you'd do a little more manhuntin' while you was up here, Percy. All kinds of bad folk ridin' round these parts."

"Not my job anymore," Percy replied. "Most of them will likely meet a bad end if they keep at it long enough. There's always someone meaner and tougher."

"I guess you're right, there. It can't be too soon for some of 'em." Twofeathers turned to Cyrus. "Ride with a keen eye, Cy. Comanches and Kiowas is all riled up."

"Ain't they always?" Cyrus said.

"Not like this," Twofeathers said. "Scent of blood's in the wind. I can smell it."

"What's their issue this time?" Percy asked.

"Hell, 'bout half of 'em's starvin'. Indian agent's always cuttin' their rations. And a hungry man will get real damn mean right quick," Twofeathers said.

"Hell them Comanches are born mean. Sounds like they's just lookin' for an excuse to go raidin', if you ask me," Cyrus said.

"Maybe so," Twofeathers said. "But some of 'em are hurtin', for sure. Gonna be hard to keep 'em here if they's hungry all the time."

"They stealin' your cattle?" Cyrus asked.

"Mr. Johnson gives 'em a few here and there. Helps to keep the stealin' down some."

"All right, Joe, we'll keep an eye out," Cyrus said.

"If you find our horses drop 'em by on your way back. See you around, Cyrus. Nice to meet ya, Percy." Twofeathers and his men turned their horses and rode off.

45

"Think there's anything to what he's sayin'?" Percy asked.

"You surprised the government backed off on a promise they made?"

"No, not really," Percy said. "I reckon them treaties ain't worth the paper they're written on."

"Nope. And that goes for both sides. Let's roll."

CHAPTER
6

It had been a few hours since her argument with Seth, and Rachel was still concerned there had been a fundamental shift in their relationship. Deciding to walk down to the corral for some emotional mending, she stood, grabbed her short-brimmed sombrero off a peg by the door, and stepped out of the hot house into a furnace. The sun was merciless and, paired with the high humidity, it was suffocating. Rachel was drenched with sweat before she made it twenty feet from the porch. Gnats swarmed, cicadas hummed, and even the chickens had gone in search of shade.

Stepping into the shade of the barn, she nodded at two of the ranch hands who were busy mending saddles and walked on through to the corrals beyond. The stink of fresh cow manure hung like a blanket over the chewed-up dirt and a half a dozen horses stood, swishing their tails, in a skinny spot of shade at the far end of the corral. Trying to ignore the smell, which she'd always hated, she climbed up the fence rails and scanned for her son.

Her brother Eli had a calf snubbed to a post in the center of the other corral and, while two other ranch hands held it down, another stepped over with a red-hot iron and branded the Rocking R symbol on the calf's left-rear flank. The calf bawled and snot flew as it swung its head, trying to get up while the mama cow stood on the other side of the fence, looking through the rails and bellowing. The scent of singed flesh reached Rachel's nostrils as one of the ranch hands holding down the calf notched its ear then pulled off the rope. The calf lurched to its feet and stood on unsteady legs for a moment before moving off. Rachel walked over to the other corral, climbed the rails, and shouted, "Eli, where's Seth?"

He took off his hat and used it to dust off his chaps as he walked over. He put the hat back on and propped a foot on a fence rail, his dirty shirt sagging with sweat. "I saw Seth ride out early this morning. He had his rifle, so I assumed he was going hunting."

"Oh no, no, no. He didn't go huntin', damn it. He went chasin' after his pa."

"Why would he do that?" Eli asked.

"He was mad they wouldn't let him go along with them. You have to go after him, Eli."

"Why? I assume he'll return home if he doesn't find them or they'll send him home if he does."

Rachel said, "That's a lot of assuming, Eli. And you know Seth's never ridden across the river before."

"He can follow a trail, can't he? I presume even a twelve-year-old boy could follow the trail of a group of mounted men rather easily."

"I'm sure he can. But if he doesn't come home, how are we going to know he caught up to them and something else bad hasn't happened? That whole place is infested with some of the vilest people to ever walk the earth."

"Now who's assuming?" Eli asked.

Rachel climbed down from the fence. "You know what? Forget I asked. I'll go find him myself," she said as she turned toward the barn, fuming. She wasn't really surprised by Eli's hesitation. Elias hated conflict and he fancied himself a scholar after going back East to college, thinking he'd leave ranch life behind. He got his degree, but then he floundered around for a couple of years until their father derailed the money train and he was forced to come home.

"Stop, Rachel," Eli shouted.

Rachel whirled around. "What? You change your mind?"

"You're not riding off by yourself."

Rachel stomped back toward the corral. "I will if you won't. I swear, Eli, you're 'bout the biggest coward I ever seen."

"Think what you will, but this is not an issue of bravery or cowardice. It's simply an issue of time." Eli sighed and looked off in the distance a moment before turning back to look at Rachel. "What if Seth arrives back home after I leave? I could spend all after-noon searching for something that isn't there."

"Well, Eli, I reckon a grown man could follow the trail of seven men and a boy on horseback."

"Touché." Eli looked down at the ground and nudged a dirt clod with the toe of his boot. As tall as Percy at six-two, Eli was much thicker and heavier, having gotten a good dose of his father's genes. Not to be outdone, his mother had contributed her fair share, too, giving Eli her red hair and blue eyes and, with it, the pale skin that was so susceptible to the sun. Eli never left the house without his hat and kept his lower face shaded with a well-groomed beard and mustache. He looked up at his sister and said, "Perhaps I'll ride out for a look."

"Not by yourself. I don't want to have to send someone out to look for you, too," Rachel said.

Eli shot her an angry look. "I'm a fine navigator but I suppose Winfield Wilson could accompany me."

"Good choice. One of you needs to be able to shoot a gun and Win can shoot the wings off a fly. Plus, he can read sign almost as good as Wilcox."

"Your assumption that gunplay might be involved is based on what exactly?"

"I have no idea what you're liable to run into but having Win along would ease my mind some. In fact, it'd probably be a good idea if you left your pistol home and took that scattergun of yours. Not much aimin' involved with that one."

Eli's cheeks reddened with anger. "I'll decide which weapons are best to take. And, I have to say, you are vastly underestimating my shooting abilities."

"Maybe so but I'm not goin' to stand here and argue your pistol prowess, Eli. Seth's already been gone too long."

CHAPTER
7

Forbidden from riding north into Indian Territory, Seth was now traveling in unfamiliar lands. It wasn't much different from his side of the river — it had the same flat terrain, the same gnarly branched blackjack trees bunched along the creek banks, and the same tall clumps of blue grama grass — but what made this side different was the fact that he was now trespassing on land owned by the Indians. And when he thought about that, his heart rate accelerated a bit. He soon gave up on trying to remember any of the landmarks and focused his full attention on following the trail left by his father's group. It wasn't a difficult task because the tracks were still relatively fresh. The few times he had trouble were when the group ahead hit a patch of rocky ground or had crossed a creek and drifted downstream before riding back out. But with a little practice he was able to pick up the trail and continued on.

Heat waves shimmered in the distance and, as soupy as it felt, Seth knew a summer storm wasn't out of the question. And storms in these parts could boil up quickly and, just as quick, turn into violent, lightning-infused monsters. He glanced up at the sky and didn't see any storms forming, but he knew it was early yet. He nudged the bay gelding with his spurs to quicken the pace. Although he didn't really like storms, his main fear was the possibility of the trail being washed away and not being able to find his way back home.

He looked up and spotted a grouping of teepees in the distance and adjusted his course to avoid them. Seeing Indians was nothing new for Seth. Living where they did, Indians came and went, trekking back and forth across the ranch land almost on a daily basis. Most were peaceable and more than a few would stop by the main house to trade leather goods or hides for groceries or something they needed. And if they were really hungry his grandpa would trade them a steer or an injured cow in exchange for some work he might need.

But Seth was also well aware that there were other types of Indians nearby — the ones who would kill or kidnap him in an instant. And the biggest problem with that, as far as he was concerned, was that you couldn't tell the difference between a friendly Indian and an Indian with bad intentions. The only way to know if they were friend or foe was to wait and see their reaction and by then it was usually too late. To compensate, Seth's intention was to avoid all Indians, period. And that was hard to do because he was currently riding through lands owned by the worst of the worst — the Kiowas and the Comanches. From the stories he'd heard, the Comanches were the meanest Indians to ever ride the earth.

Thinking of the Comanches and the possibility of a storm popping up had Seth worked into a lather. *Why would they care about a twelve-year-old boy?* But then his mind drifted to the stories of Comanches kidnapping other children and the horrors they'd faced. And he'd even overheard some of the ranch hands talking and they'd said the Comanches' favorite forms of torture often began with some combination of fire and knives and ended with severed body parts. And as Seth thought about that, fear spider-walked down his spine and he twisted in the saddle, searching the area for lurking Indians. None were visible, but that didn't necessarily slow his heart rate any because everyone knew an Indian could sneak up on you without making a sound.

Seth tried to force his mind to think about something else and he focused his attention back on the trail, hoping — praying — he'd catch up with his father's group sooner rather than later. But try as he might, he couldn't keep his mind from clicking back to the Comanches. He thought he recalled his father saying that most of the Comanches, or at least the most dangerous ones, were not and had never been on the reservation, but he couldn't remember if it was them or another tribe. And there was a big difference between a Comanche and a Cherokee.

Reining his horse down into a small creek, he was surprised to find water. This time of the year most of the smaller creeks ran dry and the Red River slowed to a trickle. His horse dipped his muzzle into the water and drank deeply and then Seth rode up the far bank and attempted to pick up the trail on a patch of rocky ground. His father's group appeared to be heading almost on a straight line, but he didn't know if they had a particular destination in mind or were simply following the rustlers' tracks. He loosened the reins and let the horse set the pace as he studied the ground, which soon transitioned from rocky to sandy, allowing Seth to pick up the trail again.

When he glanced up at the sky again an hour later it looked like a storm was forming out to the west. He watched it a moment as the clouds boiled and billowed, growing larger by the minute as the updraft pushed the top of the storm ever higher into the sky. It was fascinating to see, and Seth could've sat and watched it all day if he'd been anywhere else. But not here in enemy territory, especially with the threat the storm posed to Seth's plans. If the rain washed away the trail, he'd be in a pickle.

Having never seen a map of the area — if one even existed — he had no idea of what might lie ahead. So far, he hadn't seen any houses, or trading posts, or anything else that would indicate a specific location. Maybe that grouping of teepees was what was called a town up in these parts, Seth thought. Didn't seem right to him. Those Indians could pack up their tents and be gone before dark, leaving nothing but open space in their wake. And it was strange to think of it that way. Seth's grandfather's grandfather had lived on the land where they now lived, a succession of Ridgeway families all tethered to that one location.

From the looks of things up here, it appeared the Indians didn't much care about putting down roots or anything else that would result in any sort of permanent place. And, as Seth thought about that, he began to understand why the Indians were so difficult to keep on the reservation. It was as unnatural to them as it would be for him and his family to pack up and move, then move again, and again, and again. They were two entirely different worlds, and, for a moment, Seth envied the Indians. They got to go where they wanted when they wanted, and for a boy who hadn't been much beyond the ranch, that was a powerful thing.

Seth's thoughts were interrupted momentarily when he spied a trio of riders headed his way. Though still too far away to discern much about them other than their clothing, that was enough for Seth to know they weren't Indians. He sat a little easier in the saddle as his horse plodded forward, the distance between him and the three riders diminishing. He was hoping they could give him the lay of the land or what might lie ahead and, if not, it was time for him to turn back for home before the storm hit.

But what Seth would soon discover was

that skin color and clothing were irrelevant when judging a man's intentions.

CHAPTER
8

Eli Ridgeway muttered a curse word or two as he and Winfield Wilson rode single file up a game trail on the north bank of the Red River. Most of his vehemence was directed at his sister Rachel, the rest reserved for the building storm clouds to the west. He was concerned the rain would wash out the trail and he was also concerned about their own safety. No man liked to be atop a horse during a lightning storm and if it started hailing it would beat them all to hell. Eli spurred his horse into a lope and Win matched him then rode on ahead to take the point. Eli could read sign, but Win could read it and tell you who was riding which horse and how it had been since their last meal.

Eli slipped his watch from his pocket to check the time and grimaced. They might have six hours of daylight left and Seth had at least a four-hour head start. Eli loosened the reins and let the horse set the pace. The pony he was riding, a black-and-white paint, was native to Texas and could gallop all day and not give out. But it was never a good idea to let a horse run for long periods of time, despite their capability. In this country a man never knew when his life might depend on his horse's swiftness and stamina. Eli's only complaint about this particular horse was that he was a little shorter than most and the stirrups, and his boots in them, got dragged through the tall grass. But he'd take that, knowing his mount was sure-footed and an overachiever.

Thunder rumbled off to the west and Eli glanced up at the sky. A majority of the time the storms in the area moved from northwest to southeast and there was a chance this one could pass behind them. And that's all Eli could hope for, knowing Mother Nature could be a bitch when she wanted to be.

Win slowed his horse to a walk and Eli did the same, easing his horse forward to ride side by side.

"Bunch of redskins off the reserve," Win said out of the corner of his mouth. "Ride through here in the winter and all these small creeks would be crowded up with teepees." With disgust on his face Win surveyed the area. He had no qualms when it came to killing Indians, and Eli knew why. As a young boy, Win had been working out in the field with his father when a Kiowa war party rode up on them. The Indians killed and mutilated his father and they held Win captive for two months before a trader ransomed him and returned him to his mother.

"They'll never stop the Indians from migrating back and forth," Eli said.

"You're right," Win said. He bent over and spat a stream of tobacco juice onto the ground. "Ought to wall off the whole damn territory and let 'em all go at one another." Win steered his horse toward a game trail and followed it down to a small creek and both men let their horses drink under the shade of a large cottonwood tree. "Guvmint give them all this land and they don't do a damn thing with it," Win said, obviously not finished on the subject of Indians. "We ought to take it back. A feller could graze a bunch of cattle up here."

"If we confiscate all of their land, where do you expect them to reside?" Eli asked.

"Six feet under works for me," Win said. "The sonsabitches."

Eli glanced up at the sky again and, eager to change the subject, said, "Think the storm is going to miss us?"

Win shrugged. "If we're lucky." He surveyed the chewed-up ground and picked up Seth's trail again.

"With all of those hoof prints, how do you know we're following Seth?"

Win looked at him like he was a greenhorn. He pulled his horse to a stop and pointed at the dirt. "Tell me what you see."

Eli studied the ground for a moment then shook his head. "A bunch of horse tracks."

Win shook his head. "I'm amazed you can find your way home. Look yonder," he said, pointing to a hoof print ten feet away. "See that track right there?"

"I see it. What about it?"

"That there's Seth's horse. The left, back shoe was put on a tad cockeyed."

Eli rode forward for a closer look. "Well, if it is, it isn't skewed much."

"Don't have to be, if you knowed what you're lookin' for." Win shook his head, disappointed with Eli's poor tracking abilities.

"What else does that track tell you?"

Win touched his spurs to his horse's ribs to get him started. "We've gained some ground on him."

"How much?" Eli asked as he started his horse moving.

" 'Bout an hour or so, I reckon." Win put his horse into a lope and Eli did the same, dejected they hadn't made up more time.

Eli looked up at the approaching storm again. The dark, rain-filled clouds were scudding across the sky and moving directly overhead. A bolt of lightning lit up the gathering gloom and a rumble of thunder rolled across the prairie. They were now on borrowed time.

They came to another small creek and Win and Eli charged down the bank, splashed across the water, and raced up the far bank. Three hundred yards farther, Win slowed his horse and walked it in a circle as he studied the hoof prints. After a moment or two, he reined his horse to a stop and looked up at Eli. "There's three new sets of tracks in here around Seth's horse."

"Shod ponies?"

"Yep. Don't mean much, though, with all the horse thievin' the Injuns do." Win turned his horse and rode east for a bit as Eli watched. After a moment, he returned, his narrow shoulders slumped. "There's four horses headed due east."

All thoughts of the approaching storm were pushed from Eli's mind. Although he already knew the answer, he had to ask. "Seth one of them?"

Win nodded and looked up at the approaching storm. "Let's see how far they go before we lose 'em."

They rode hard due east for another ten minutes before their luck ran out. Fat raindrops splattered the ground for a moment and then the storm unleashed a deluge of water. Win and Eli slowed their horses to a walk and dug out their slickers, crestfallen that Seth's trail was already gone.

CHAPTER
9

With the storms having passed on to the east, Emma Turner decided to take advantage of the break in the weather and headed down to the river to pick some blackberries that grew wild along the bank. That was the excuse she gave her mother, but what she really wanted was some time alone, which was something hard to come by when you lived around four other families.

Red-haired and blue-eyed, Emma's thirteen-year-old body was undergoing a transformation. Her breasts were budding out and her woman's monthly misery had rudely surprised her last month and, as a tomboy, she didn't know what to think about all of it. Not that she had any choice in the matter. She had a couple of friends who were close to her age who lived east of the ranch and they were already talking about men, marriage, and settling down — all things that Emma had never really considered before. And even if she did think about it the pickings were slim. Available suitors weren't flooding the ranch to court her. Not that she wanted to be courted. But was that what was expected of her? she wondered. Settle down in a few years and start pushing out babies? That held very little appeal for Emma, who had dreams of seeing a little more of the world beyond this ranch along the river.

"Ouch," she muttered when her finger snagged a thorn. She stuck her finger in her mouth to suck away the blood as she glanced up at the sun descending toward the horizon and tried to judge how much daylight was left. Maybe an hour or so, she decided as she moved down the bank to another thicket of blackberries. Her mind continued to churn through the new, confusing thoughts invading her brain. *Maybe this is what Ma was talking about when she said being a grown-up was hard.* As far as Emma was concerned, being a grown-up didn't appear to be much different from being a kid. They all worked hard.

The water in the river was up after the thundershower and the muddy current churned with a mess of tree limbs, brush, and other discarded items that had dropped into the river upstream. Emma was just hoping the onrush of water would scour away the millions of mosquitoes that called the river home. She moseyed a little farther down the bank to another patch of blackberries as her mind drifted back to her dilemma. Her mother, Abby, always stressed the importance of education and Emma had dreams of going to college back East one day if she could find a college that took girls, that is. And she had made her wishes clear to anyone who would listen. So, marrying and starting a family had zero appeal to her. Maybe someday, but that someday was a long way off.

Hearing the snick of a horse's hoof hitting a rock, Emma glanced up and dropped her basket of berries. She was surrounded by four Indian braves, their bodies and ponies painted for war.

"He-hello," Emma stuttered. She pointed toward the ranch buildings and brought her hands to her chest and said, "My home."

The dark-skinned braves, painted with black and red clay, were dressed only in loincloths and moccasins as they edged their horses closer, never saying a word. Emma backed down the bank and they formed a circle tight around her, blocking her path. She saw no avenue of escape, so she did the first thing that came to mind.

Emma screamed, took a breath, and screamed again.

The nearest Indian leaned down and grabbed Emma around the waist and pulled her onto his horse as easily as if he was plucking the bloom off a rose. Emma screamed again and began hitting, slapping, and scratching — anything to get away. The savage wrapped his arms around her, pinning her arms to her body. Emma started kicking her legs and screaming, trying to break the Indian's grip, but it was impossible. The Indian calmly steered his horse up the bank as Emma continued to scream and kick. She heard the Indian behind her laughing and that enraged her. She twisted one way and then the other and made no progress. Then she started kicking the horse — in the head, in the shoulders, anywhere she could bury her heels, and the horse plodded onward, unconcerned that she was kicking him as hard as she could. Her voice raw, she tried to scream again, and it came out as a croak. She paused, took a breath, and quickly calculated her options.

Trying a new tactic, she let her body go slack, hoping the Indian would loosen his grip, and all he did was squeeze her harder. Rearing back her leg, she slammed her heel down on the horse's right ear and he didn't even flinch. She pounded her head against the Indian's chest over and over again and all he did was laugh. Knowing there were unspeakable horrors ahead if she didn't get free, she tried squirming out from beneath his grasp again but it was like she'd been confined in a small box.

Tears coursed down her cheeks as the savages kicked their horses into a gallop, the ranch buildings growing smaller in the distance.

CHAPTER
10

Having seen no sight of the cattle rustlers and, with their trail now washed away, Cyrus, Percy, and the rest of the men rode into Fort Sill as the sun settled on the horizon. Cyrus led them over to the trading post and the men climbed down and tied their horses to the hitch rail. Despite the recent storm, a group of Indians were banging their drums and dancing on the parade grounds.

"If they's doing a rain dance, it worked," Cyrus grumbled to Percy.

"Looks like somethin' has them irritated," Percy replied as he brushed past his father and stepped up on the post's porch. He removed his slicker and took off his hat to shake the residual water off.

Built along the Medicine Creek near the Medicine Bluffs, Fort Sill was a fairly recent addition to the string of frontier forts the army was building to clamp down on the marauding Indians who were raiding new settlements along a line that ran from Mexico to the Dakotas. The white man's westward expansion demanded something be done about the Indians despite the fact the Kiowas, Comanches, and Apaches had roamed that territory for hundreds of years. Marching under the banner of Manifest Destiny, the white settlers believed their cause justified and inevitable, and the sooner the savages were subdued and put where they belonged, the better.

Of course, the Indians thought differently and thus, the continuing conflict.

Fort Sill was laid out in squares with the parade ground serving as the centerpiece. Situated around the square were the trading post, quartermaster's storehouse, the blacksmith, stables, bunkhouses, officers' quarters, and, opposite of where they were now, the headquarters for the post commander.

From his place on the porch of the store, Percy took a moment to survey the area. Although called a fort, there were no exterior walls, moats, or anything that might slow an approaching army, which seemed strange to Percy, who had visited his fair share of forts over the years. And the inhabitants of this fort were also different from most. Fort Sill was a menagerie of humanity. In addition to the multitude of different

Indian tribes, including different bands of the same tribe, the fort was also home to the U.S. Army's 10th Cavalry Regiment, one of two cavalry regiments reserved exclusively for black enlisted men. Better known by their Indian name, the Buffalo Soldiers were a seasoned group of hard men presently under the command of Lieutenant Colonel John "Black Jack" Davidson, a man who had visited the ranch many times over the years and whom Percy considered a good friend.

"Isaac, you and Amos keep an eye on the horses," Cyrus said as he stepped up onto the porch. "Them Injuns'll steal 'em in a heartbeat." Cyrus glanced at Percy. "You comin' in?"

"Naw," Percy replied. "I'm goin' to mosey over to headquarters and get the lay of the land from John. We stayin' here for the night?"

"Might as well. River'll be up with all this rain. Ask John if there's a place we can bed down."

"I will. Think the trader has any whiskey hidden away?" Percy asked.

"Doubtful," Cyrus said, looking at the Indians celebrating on the parade grounds. "Them Injuns would cave the door in to get at it."

Percy stepped off the porch and threaded his way through the Indian gathering on his way to Sherman House. The structure was a large, two-story rectangular building that featured a long porch that fronted the first level and four chimneys, each located in a corner of the building When he arrived, Percy opened the door and entered the foyer, where a private was manning the reception desk.

"Evenin'," Percy said. "Colonel Davidson in?"

"Who's askin', sir?" the private asked. The young man was trim and fit with closed-cropped frizzy hair and eyes as blue as the sky.

"Percy Ridgeway."

"I'll check, sir," the private said as he stood and headed down the hallway toward the back of the building.

Percy had worked around and with black men all of his life, but never as a slaveholder, like many of his fellow Texans. He couldn't abide one man thinking himself superior to another based on skin color or anything else. And despite tremendous pressure to join his fellow statesmen in fighting for the Confederacy, Percy had refused, as did all the men at the Rocking R. That refusal was based partly on their beliefs and the other part was that they already had plenty on their plate trying to keep the Indians from killing them or stealing everything they owned.

The private returned and said, "Follow me, sir." He led Percy down a long hall and out onto the back porch, where Lieutenant Colonel John Davidson was standing near a couple of chairs, a bottle of brandy and two glasses situated on a small table between them. Davidson shook Percy's hand and waved to the opposite chair and both men sat as the private retreated. A coal oil lamp flickered on the opposite end of the porch, drawing a horde of insects and casting a wan light that washed over the two men. Davidson poured, and the two men clinked glasses. Percy drained his glass in one long swallow and said, "What are the Indians celebratin'?"

Davidson poured more brandy into Percy's glass. "Got a couple of Kiowa chiefs locked up in the stockade. Appears to have made some members of their tribe angry."

"You goin' to turn 'em loose?"

"Not up to me, but I hope not."

"Why? Afraid they'll start raidin' again?"

"Of that, I have no doubt," Davidson said. "General Sherman is fit to be tied. I have a feeling a day of reckoning is quickly approaching, though." Davidson drained his glass and refilled it.

"How quickly?"

"Spring, maybe. The buffalo herds are already thinnin' out. Once their food source is gone, they won't have any choice but to return to the reservation."

"Still a lot of buffalo roaming the plains," Percy said.

Davidson glanced over at Percy. "I didn't say the Indians wouldn't need some persuadin'." He took a sip of brandy and stared out into the darkness for a few moments. Known for being a stickler for details, Davidson was thin-framed and had a long mustache that extended well beyond his face, along with a narrow goatee. "I'm tired of Indian talk. What are you doin' up this way?"

"Tryin' to track down a couple of rustlers."

Davidson arched his brows. "Your father's idea?"

"How'd you guess?"

"How many cattle are you running down there?"

"About ten thousand head at last count."

"And how many cattle were stolen?"

"Two."

Davidson smiled. "Ole Cyrus won't give

an inch, will he?"

"Nope," Percy said. "We lost their trail in the rain, so I guess they got away this time, much to my father's dismay." Percy took a long pull from his glass and then said, "What's life like commandin' a Negro regiment?"

Davidson turned slightly in his chair so that he could look at Percy. "I'll tell you, Percy, the vast majority of them are illiterate, but they're some of the hardest-workin' troops I've ever been associated with. They might not be book smart, but they damn sure know how to fight. And I'll take a fighter any day. They seldom complain about anything and I've had troops do nothing but complain about all sorts of things. So, all in all, they're a fine group of soldiers and their skin color doesn't make a damn bit of difference."

"I'm assumin' you know what others call you?" Percy asked.

"Black Jack? Yeah, I heard. Nicknames don't mean a damn thing to me." Davidson pulled a couple of cigars from the pocket of his unbuttoned army tunic and offered one to Percy, who accepted. Davidson flared a match and lit both, fanned the match out, and refilled their glasses. Taking a long draw from his cigar, Davidson settled back in his chair. "Although I've been to the ranch several times, a report of a recent raid down your way got me to wonderin' about somethin'."

Percy blew out a stream of smoke and said, "What's that?"

"With all the Indian depredations that have happened in Texas over the years, the Ridgeway clan remains relatively unscathed. Why do you think that is? I know that wagon you had built is one hell of a deterrent but that can't be the only reason, can it?"

Percy shrugged and took a deep draw from his cigar. "Call it mutually assured destruction, John, or maybe mutual respect. As you know, we're not short on firepower and the Indians have learned over the years that we fight back, and our response is often swift and deadly. We take a firm but fair approach with them, and if we leave them alone, they generally do the same with us. And if they're hungry we'll cut out a steer or two for them on occasion and we've traded with a lot of them over the years."

Davidson rolled his cigar between his fingers and tapped off the ash. "They don't steal from you? They'll steal anything not tied down around here."

"They're a thievin' bunch, for sure, and

you've gotta nip that in the bud in a hurry or they'll steal you blind. We lose a few cattle every year to 'em, but it's an unsubstantial number in the bigger picture of things."

"Yet you're up here chasin' after a couple rustlers who stole two steers."

Percy shrugged. "That's part of the nippin' in the bud I was talkin' about."

Davidson smiled and took a sip of brandy. "You can talk about mutual respect, but I don't know, Percy. The only signs of Comanche respect I've seen was when they had a loaded gun pointed at them."

"Like I said, we're not short on firepower. Lawrie Tatum still the Indian agent round here?"

"Nope. Moved back to Iowa after resigning his post at the end of March. Got a new fella now. Name's James Haworth, another Quaker, like Tatum. What he knows about Indians, I don't know. Seems to want to befriend them all and doesn't want the military involved in Indian business."

"How's that workin' out for you?" Percy asked as he took another draw from his cigar.

"Not worth a damn," Davidson said as he tossed the nub of his cigar onto the porch floor and ground it out with his boot. "I don't know why they keep bringin' these Quakers in an attempt to pacify the Indians. Haworth had the gall to ask me to remove the guard from the provision's warehouse as a show of trust."

"Did you?" Percy asked.

"I did. A group of Kiowas went in and stole everything there was to steal. Then he thought having a guard wasn't such a bad idea. I'll tell you, Percy, the only way we're goin' to get a handle on this Indian situation is by the use of force, and the sooner, the better. Sheridan and Sherman are in agreement, but they can't get the folks in Washington to agree. Let the Indians take a few more scalps and I guess we'll see what happens." He turned and looked at Percy. "In the meantime, I'm just hopin' one of them is not yours."

"Me, too."

CHAPTER
11

Having lost Seth's trail in the rain, Eli and Win continued riding through the growing gloom, hoping to stumble upon him. Despite the recent rain, the heat was back in full force and only added to the misery of riding around in wet clothing, where everything rubbed in all the wrong places. The slickers they had donned proved useless against the deluge and did a better job of trapping the heat, which was the last thing either man wanted, so off came the slickers.

Win led them across Cache Creek and onto a broad plain that spread far ahead into the growing darkness. Crickets chirped, cicadas buzzed, and the mosquitoes were as thick as flies in an outhouse. All they could do was keep traveling east, hoping to find some sign of Seth or a fresh trail.

Before it got too dark to see, Win pulled his horse to a stop and climbed down for a closer look at the ground. He walked a wide circle, his eyes searching the grass for bent stalks and the sandy areas for faint impressions that might have survived the rain. Spotting something, he knelt down for a closer inspection. "Found something. Looks like we're headed the right —"

A distant gunshot shattered the stillness.

Eli turned his head, trying to pinpoint its origin as the shot echoed across the prairie. "Sounded like it was due east of here. Not sure of the distance."

"Half a mile or more," Win said as he climbed back on his horse.

Eli spurred his horse into a trot as he scanned the horizon. A little further along, he spotted the yellow-orange glow of a campfire and slowed his horse to a walk. They rode as close as they dared without knowing the particulars and stopped, slipping down from their horses. After sliding their rifles out, they tied their horses to a small bush and crept closer. It appeared to be four people, one of them tied to a tree. Eli didn't know if it was Seth, but he had a sinking feeling that it probably was.

Win moved off to the right, angling to get behind the group, and Eli followed. When they were about twenty yards away, they stopped and squatted down to survey the scene. Three older men were standing

81

around the fire, hooting and hollering as they passed a whiskey bottle around, and tied to the tree was Seth. Eli couldn't make out specific details, but it looked like the men had roughed him up some. For what purpose, Eli didn't know. But three men against one small boy was far from a fair fight.

It was full dark now and the place the men had picked to build a fire was surrounded by high grass, making it difficult to see much of what was going on. It looked like there was a small creek on the other side of the fire and Eli was wondering if it might be a better approach, when Win leaned over and whispered in his ear, "Let's move closer."

Eli nodded and both men stood and crept forward about fifteen yards and squatted back down. It didn't help much with the line of sight, but it did allow them to hear some of what was going on. Most of what they heard were alcohol-fueled stories with no hints about why they'd abducted Seth. And Eli could draw no logical conclusions from the scene before them. Why three white males, who looked to be in their late forties or early fifties, had taken Seth and tied him to a tree and then all but ignored him was mystifying. Then Eli's mind dove to a deeper, darker place searching for answers, and a gear clicked another gear and he had a probable answer. It would explain why they were getting liquored up before starting, and Eli couldn't bear to think what would have happened to Seth if Rachel hadn't convinced him to go looking for her son.

The next series of events happened so quickly and were so insane that Eli and Win couldn't have anticipated them and therefore didn't have time to react.

One of the men walked over to Seth, loosened the rope, and turned him around, and then pulled his pants down and held him while another man pulled a branding iron from the fire, walked over, and branded Seth on the butt.

As Seth's cries of anguish and pain filled the night, Eli's anger flared hot. Win turned and said, "I'm gonna kill them sonsabitches." Win pulled back the hammer on his rifle and stood, tucking the stock tight to his shoulder. He fired and one of the men jerked around and fell. Win was already levering another shell before Eli could get to his feet.

The other two men tried to make a break for the creek, but in their drunken state, couldn't do much more than flounder around. Eli raised his rifle, sighted down the barrel, and squeezed the trigger. The nearest man dropped like his legs had been cut from under him. Eli felt no remorse as he levered another shell and looked down the barrel for the third man, the hot blood surging through his veins. Off to his left, Win fired two quick shots and just like that it was all over. The other men never got off a shot. Win pulled his pistol and walked over to make sure the three men were dead while Eli hurried over to Seth.

"Seth," Eli said as he slowly approached. "It's Uncle Eli, Seth. It's all over now." Eli grimaced at the burned skin. "Okay, Seth?"

Seth whimpered.

Eli gently pulled Seth's pants up, untied the rope, and slowly turned Seth around and knelt down so he could look in his eyes.

Tears were streaming down Seth's cheeks. "Why . . . would . . ."

Eli wrapped his arms around him. "Shh, you're safe and that's all tha—"

His words were drowned out by Win's pistol shot.

"It's okay," Eli said. "They won't be hurting anyone ever again."

Seth nodded his head against Eli's chest.

When the crying finally slowed to an occasional sob Eli asked Seth if he could walk.

"I reckon so . . . but not sure . . . I can sit a . . . horse."

"Don't worry about the horse right now. But we do need to get away from here."

Seth nodded.

Win came over and squatted down next to Eli and said, "We need to git gone."

"I know," Eli said as he stood and took Seth's hand. "Win, grab the horses and Seth and I'll mosey on along behind you."

Win kicked out the fire, grabbed Seth's horse, and went after the other two horses.

They walked west for a good hour or so, trying to put some distance between them and the three bodies. Eli had no idea who they had been, nor did he care. And if they had families or loved ones concerned about their whereabouts that was just too damn bad.

Seth was limping from the pain and finally — mercifully — Win led them through a small copse of trees and into a clearing near the creek they'd been following. Win unrolled a bedroll and Eli knew it would be too painful for Seth to sit. "Lie down on your stomach, Seth."

Seth nodded and lay down on the blanket. Both men unsaddled the three horses and hobbled them so the horses could graze and drink from the creek without fear of them running away. Eli retrieved a bag of jerky from his saddlebag, grabbed his canteen, and offered both to Seth before taking a seat next to him. Seth refused the jerky but he eased up on his side and took a long draw from the canteen as Win gathered wood for a fire. Eli pulled off his still-wet shirt and spread it out on the grass to dry.

The night was hot and muggy, and they certainly didn't need a fire for warmth, but Eli did need the light to better examine Seth's face. As they waited for the fire to take hold, Eli dug around in his saddlebag, looking to see if he had anything to give Seth for the pain, and came up empty.

"Why did they do that to me, Uncle Eli?"

Eli suspected the branding was one part of a larger ritual that he and Win had interrupted and could only guess what the men had in store for Seth. But three men, a bottle of whiskey, and a young boy was a recipe for all types of deviant behavior. But telling Seth that would open the door to more questions Eli had no interest in answering.

"Evil lurks among men, Seth. And there is no viable answer to that question. Just take comfort in knowing they'll never do it again."

"But why me?"

"You were simply at the wrong place at the wrong time, Seth. They chose you because you were available at a time when they were seeking to fulfill their evil desires."

Seth thought about that for a few moments and then said, "I'm glad you and Win killed 'em. You sure they're dead?"

"Rest assured, they're dead," Eli said as he pulled a rag from his saddlebag and dampened it with water from the canteen. "Roll up on your left side, Seth, and let me examine your face."

Seth rolled onto his side, and Eli gently cleaned his face. "You have some scrapes and some bruising but no deep lacerations."

"Lacerwhat?" Seth asked.

"Lacerations. Cuts." Eli scooted back and said, "You can lie back down now."

As they settled in for the night, it finally dawned on Eli that he'd killed his first man and he wondered if he'd have to deal with mental recriminations later because, at the moment, he felt no remorse whatsoever.

CHAPTER
12

Abigail Turner was getting worried. It wasn't unusual for Emma to stay out after dark catching fireflies with her older cousins or whatever else they could find to do to occupy their time. But she couldn't remember Emma ever staying out this late. Although she had been trying to allow Emma more freedom, staying out until eleven p.m. was going too far. She pulled a lantern off a peg near the door, lit it, and stepped out into the dark night.

Abby decided her first course of action was to check her mother's house, hoping Emma had decided to stay over. When Abigail reached her parents' house, she climbed the steps up to the porch that fronted the house and eased the front door open. Over the years, as the Ridgeway clan grew more prosperous, additions were made to the main house and it now contained six bedrooms, a parlor, the main living area fronted by a large fireplace, and a large kitchen. Hoping not to wake her mother, she shifted the lantern to her left hand so that her body would shield most of the light.

Stepping lightly across the yellow pine floors, she walked toward the rear of the house, where three of the bedrooms were, the others, upstairs. Despite her best attempt at being quiet, she heard her mother say, "Who's there?"

"It's me, Ma, Abby," she said as she walked toward her parents' bedroom in the far back corner of the house.

There was a rustle, a squeak, then the sound of feet on the floor. "What in the world are you doin' prowlin' around the house in the middle of the night?" Frances asked, stepping out in the hall as she belted her robe.

"Lookin' for Emma."

"She's not here, Abby. When's the last time you saw her?"

"At supper. Have you seen her since then?"

Frances shook her head. "No. I saw her earlier in the day. Think she might have decided to spend the night with one of her cousins?"

"Not without asking. She knows better than that."

"Check the barn?"

"Not yet. Thought I'd try here first."

"Let me put on some shoes and I'll help you look," Frances said. She ducked back into her bedroom and returned a moment later, wearing a pair of moccasins an old Ponca woman had given her.

Abby followed her mother through the house as her mind spun with possible locations where Emma might be. The bunkhouse was off-limits to any and all children and there were several other shacks scattered across the ranch, but none close enough to walk to. That left the barn, or the other three houses owned by her brothers and sister. Abby's mind returned to the present when her mother reached above the fireplace and took down the double-barrel, ten-gauge shotgun.

A tingle of dread raced down Abby's spine. "What are you thinkin', Ma?"

"I'm not," Frances said. "And don't you start thinkin' about a bunch of bad things, either. The shotgun is in case we run into varmints while we're lookin'."

Abby started biting the nail on her right index finger, a nervous habit she'd had since childhood.

"Quit bitin' your fingernails," Frances scolded. "We'll find Emma." Frances didn't need to check if the shotgun was loaded — it remained that way at all times. She walked over to a shelf by the front door and grabbed a few extra shells and slipped them into the pocket of her robe. "Think we need another lantern?" Frances asked.

With her apprehension about Emma's welfare on the verge of spinning out of control, Abby said, "No, let's just go." She grabbed her lantern from the table and hurried toward the door. She stepped out into the darkness, and Frances followed behind. "I don't even know where to start," Abby said.

"We'll start at the barn and work out from there," Frances said in an even voice, trying to ease her daughter's worry. "Emma has to be here somewhere. We'll find her."

"I'm goin' to wring her neck when we do," Abby said angrily.

After searching the barn and the surrounding area outside, they found no sign of Emma. Frances and Abby checked the smokehouse just in case and went house by house, inquiring about Emma's whereabouts. They'd looked everywhere they could think to look and there was still no Emma.

After being awakened, Eli's wife, Clara, and Rachel joined the search and they now had three lanterns burning.

"Let's pause for a minute and think this through," Frances said as she grabbed Abby's arm and pulled her to a stop.

"We can't stop," Abby shouted as she yanked away from her mother's grasp.

"We're not stopping, Abby," Frances said. "We'll search all night if we have to, but we need to be smart about it."

"We need more people," Rachel said. She walked over to the bunkhouse and knocked on the door to roust the ranch hands and then walked back.

"Where haven't you looked?" Clara asked.

"We've looked everywhere I can think of," Frances said.

"Is it possible she fell asleep somewhere?" Clara asked.

That was a question they all pondered for a moment.

"Outside?" Abby asked.

Clara shrugged. "Maybe. It's miserable inside. Maybe she found a cool place to lie down and fell asleep."

While they were talking, Frances's mind clicked through possible places Emma might be. The ranch was a big place and they'd have to wait until daylight to mount a full-scale search if she couldn't come up with another idea. Then she hit upon something. "Emma said something this morning 'bout making a blackberry pie. Let's check the blackberry patch down by the river."

Abby turned to look at her mother. "You can't pick blackberries in the dark."

"I know, but maybe she's hurt and can't make it back to the house."

Abby picked up her lantern and started walking. "Let's go."

"Wait, Abby. Just a moment, please."

Abby stopped and began gnawing on her fingernail again.

Frances looked back over her shoulder and shouted instructions to the men now spilling out of the bunkhouse.

"Now we can go," Frances said. "Everyone, spread out and form a line."

Once everyone was situated, they began walking toward the river. They all shouted Emma's name repeatedly and all they heard back was silence. Although the sun was long gone, the heat it created was still present and they were all sweating. And the lanterns didn't help, their heat only adding to the misery. They walked all the way to the berry patch with no sightings of Emma.

Jesse "Stringbean" Simpson, ranch foreman, held his lantern close to the ground, looking for sign. "Everyone, take it slow and easy," Jesse said. "We don't want to clutter the ground up in case we find somethin'."

Abby and the rest of the group continued shouting for Emma as Jesse worked his way into and through the brush, studying the ground.

"Found something," Jesse shouted.

Abby rushed over. "Where is she?"

Jesse stood and handed a basket to Abby. "Found that basket and a bunch of spilt blackberries."

"This is my basket. Where's Emma, Jesse?" Abby shouted, on the verge of hysteria.

"Don't know that yet, Miss Abigail." He picked up his lantern and slowly backed away. "Ya'll stay there for a minute while I do some lookin'." With the lantern held low and his eyes focused on the ground Jesse stopped, walked sideways for a bit, then turned and walked west for about a hundred yards before returning. When he looked up, his face was pinched with worry.

"What is it?" Abby asked.

"Looks like four ponies rode right through here," Jesse said.

"Shod or unshod?" Frances asked.

Jesse looked at the ground for a moment then looked up and said, "Unshod, ma'am."

Abby let loose a wail that pierced the night as she sank to her knees.

Rachel hurried to her side and knelt down, wrapping her arms around Abby as Frances took charge, telling Jesse to gather the men and saddle up the horses, praying they weren't too late.

Abby shook out of Rachel's arms and lurched to her feet. "I'm goin'," she shouted as she bulled in between Frances and Jesse. She looked Jesse in the eye and said, "Saddle my horse, please."

"Ma'am, we're going to have to ride hard and fast if we have any hopes of catchin' them Injuns," Jesse said.

Abby took a step closer to Jesse. "I can ride as good as anyone on this ranch. She's my daughter and I'm going."

Frances saw Jesse looking at her for help and she stepped forward, putting an arm around Abby, and, with a firm hold, steering her away. After a short distance, Frances stopped and turned to face her daughter. She reached up and gently placed her hands on either side of Abby's face. "I know you're hurting, but you have to let the men handle this. Jesse is right — they need to ride hard and fast and they can't do that if they have to worry about protecting you, too."

Tears rolled down Abby's face, wetting her mother's hands. "She's needs her mother."

"You've got two other children who also need their mother. You have to let the men do their jobs. When Cyrus and the others get back, they can take up the hunt, too. We'll get her back if we have to move heaven and earth."

Rachel stepped over to join her mother and sister. "We're burning time and every second counts, sis. Let the men handle it."

Abby wiped her nose with the back of her hand and offered the tiniest of nods.

Frances gently thumbed away Abby's tears before letting her hands drop. She looked over at Jesse and the other men and said, "Saddle up. We'll pack some provisions while you men get loaded up."

Rachel took her sister by the hand and led Abby back to her house. Frances offered a few more instructions to the men and offered them bonus pay for their pursuit then she and Clara followed Rachel. Inside, Frances put on a pot of coffee then she and Clara began gathering supplies for the men.

A few minutes later the men, six in all with the others away, stopped by the house. Clara and Frances carried the supplies outside and the men divvied them up and stuffed them down their saddlebags. Frances stepped over, grabbed Jesse by the elbow, and steered him out of earshot. "Jesse, this is hard country and it takes hard men to get the job done."

Jesse nodded and said, "Yes'm."

Frances lowered her voice and said, "I have only one request."

"What's that, ma'am?"

"I want you to kill every one of those filthy savages who kidnapped Emma."

Jesse looked off into the dark for a moment, then turned to look at Frances. "What if it be Comanches?"

"I don't give a damn what they are," Frances said.

"All of this is assumin' we find them. Ain't no guarantee of that," Jesse said. "They could be thirty, forty miles away by now. We got no idea how long the girl's been gone."

Frances spent a moment considering Jesse's suggestion. She wasn't impractical, and Jesse had made some good points, but it was a helpless feeling standing around while her granddaughter was getting farther away. The horses snorted and stomped, impatient to get on with their duties now that they were saddled. Frances glanced up at the faces of the men that were just visible in the halo of light produced by the lantern. They looked determined, willing and able to take up the chase, but was that the right course of action? Her thoughts were interrupted when Jesse spoke again.

"And to tell the truth, ma'am," Jesse said as he waved a hand at the other five riders, "none of us left here are worth a damn at reading sign. Wilcox would be who you'd want."

"Wilcox isn't here," Frances said.

"No, ma'am, he ain't. We're mounted and ready to ride, ma'am. Just give the word."

Frances was torn. Every minute that Emma was gone mattered. But she also knew making a hasty decision and sending the men off on a foolhardy mission could end up costing lives. She clasped and unclasped her hands, unsure of what the right decision was. Sending a telegraph to Fort Sill to alert Cyrus and the military about the kidnapping wasn't an option because there were no telegraph lines running to the fort and even if there had been, the closest telegraph office was in Dallas, a hundred miles away. After a few more moments of thought Frances, as difficult as it was, made her decision. "Jesse, would you pick a man to ride with you, then head north to find Cyrus and the others and tell them what's happened?"

Jesse mulled that over for a moment. "I will, ma'am." He turned and looked at the men. "Clay, you're with me. Everyone else, unsaddle your horses and get some shut-eye."

The men dismounted, unloaded the supplies from their saddlebags, and Jesse and Clay Hendershot picked up some jerky and stuffed it into their bags. Both men mounted up and Jesse looked down at Frances and said, "Might be best to keep a close eye out in case them Injuns come back."

"If they do," Frances replied, "I'll give them an up-close look at my ten-gauge."

"I 'spect you will," Jesse said before spurring his horse forward.

CHAPTER
13

Emma was physically and emotionally numbed as the four Indian ponies thundered across the plains, the savage's grip on her never loosening. They had been riding for hours with no stops and — more important — no opportunities to escape. And Emma was planning to escape or die trying. During the long night, thoughts about her fate tormented her mind until, through sheer willpower, she finally tamped them down. If they were going to kill her, they would have already done so.

But Emma also knew some fates were worse than death.

As the sky began to lighten, heralding the coming dawn, the Indians rode down into a small creek and allowed the horses to drink. The Indian holding her, whom she named Big Nose, finally loosened his grip and elbowed her off the horse. Emma hit the ground hard and her breath rushed out in a whoosh. She curled up in a ball as she tried to get her wind back as the four Indians moved upstream from the horses and drank from the creek. Once she regained her breath, she glanced around to mark the Indians' location and scrambled to her feet. She was desperate for water, but her desperation to escape was more urgent.

Emma had no idea where they were in relation to the ranch. West Texas was immense, and she could be miles from civilization, but that didn't dampen her urge to run. After a quick glance to pin their location, Emma took a deep breath and charged up the creek bank. She heard the Indians laughing as she grabbed on to a sapling and pulled herself over the top. She pulled up short when she discovered the wide-open prairie extended for as far as she could see, with no signs of civilization in any direction.

That's all Emma got to see before the Indians were on her. The Indian who had grabbed her ripped off all of her clothing and threw her on the ground. Emma cried when he began his assault and that earned her a beating, the brave repeatedly slapping her. By the time the third Indian knelt on the ground and lifted his breechcloth, Emma was resigned to the fact that she was powerless to stop them. She squeezed her eyes shut and let her mind drift, flashing on images of her family, wondering if she'd ever see them again or even if they'd want her after this. But those thoughts were too painful to ponder so Emma turned her mind to the gnarled branches of an old post oak tree that shaded a portion of the creek. She focused on tracing the branches from the trunk to their tips, with not a foot of straight in any of them. Some twisted up, some down, the others this way and that with apparently no predetermined path. A lone tear formed in her left eye and drifted across her face and into her hair before the Indian on top of her could see it.

Eventually — finally — their appetites were sated. Emma looked down to see her thighs covered with her own blood and before that thought could register, her captor grabbed Emma by the hair, dragged her down to the creek, and rolled her into the water. Emma looked up to see the other three savages cutting her calico dress into shreds, each taking a piece of material and tying it around their heads like victors of a conquest. In the back of her mind she was hoping — praying — that they'd maybe let her go now that they got what they wanted. But, as she suspected, an Indian pulled her up by the hair, threw Emma over his shoulder, and tied her to one of the horses they'd stolen somewhere along the way. Naked as the day she was born, tears streamed down Emma's cheeks as the Indians mounted up and, leading her horse, rode up out of the creek.

Emma winced in pain with each step of the horse. To add to her misery, the sun was now riding high in the sky and she could feel her pale skin already roasting and knew she'd be burned and blistered by the end of the day. The Indians kicked the ponies into a gallop and each lunge of the horse sent shockwaves of pain radiating through her body. If she hadn't been tied to the horse, she would have gladly jumped off and been content to die where she fell.

Through sheer force of will, Emma mentally suppressed the pain from raging to a level just below unbearable and tried to focus on her captors. She still had no idea which tribe the four Indians called home, or if it even mattered. Due to the location of the ranch, it could be any of a dozen tribes, but judging from their brutality Emma was thinking they were either Apaches, Kiowas, or Comanches. Not that there was a whit of difference between the three — all were known to be sadistic and all took pleasure in devising new ways to torture their captives. The only thing that kept her from going crazy was that she knew her grandfather had a good relationship with a good number of tribes and his contacts could possibly lead to a quick recovery. Before she could give that further thought, her mental wall collapsed, and a wave of intense pain washed out any other thoughts.

CHAPTER
14

With the rustlers' trail gone for good, Percy, Cyrus, and the rest of the group had rolled out of Fort Sill at daybreak. Now it was midmorning and the horses were lathered up and the men were drenched with sweat. Yesterday's brief storm had not only muddied the ground, it had elevated the humidity level to agonizing levels, making the journey home miserable. Unaware that Emma and Seth had gone missing, the men weren't in a hurry, fearing if they pushed the horses too hard, they'd ruin them. As it was, the men were switching mounts every couple of hours, making good use of the extra horses they'd brought along, all in an effort to keep the horses fresh in case they encountered a group of marauding Indians. And that wasn't out of the question with the Comanches presumably on the warpath.

Percy glanced forward and spotted two men running their horses hard toward them.

Still too far away to learn much about them, he slid his rifle out of his scabbard. "Two men ridin' hard our way," he told the other men. Other rifles were drawn as Percy surveyed the approaching riders, his horse walking steadily forward.

"Them boys're gonna kill those horses," Cyrus said. "They ought to be horse-whipped."

"I expect they've got a reason," Percy said. "Let's hope there's not a pack of wild Indians coming up behind them."

When the two riders drew closer, a tingle of dread crept down Percy's spine.

"Hell, that's Jesse and Hendershot," Cyrus grumbled. "I've a mind to fire their asses on the spot."

The two men reined their horses to a stop and before Cyrus could say anything, Jesse looked at Isaac Turner and said, "Injuns kidnapped your oldest girl, Isaac."

The blood drained from Isaac's face and his shoulders slumped. "When?"

" 'Bout dark, yesterday. Found the tracks of four unshod ponies and they're headed west."

"So not reservation Injuns?" Isaac said, his voice barely audible.

"Unless they done circled around, no," Jesse said.

"How many men you got trackin' them?" Cyrus asked.

Jesse studied the ground for a moment then looked up at Cyrus and said, "None. Miss Franny told me to ride up here and find ya. The girl had probably been gone for hours fore we found the tracks." Jesse looked at Amos and said, "Seth ain't with you?"

"Why would Seth be with us?" Amos asked.

"He rode off after you yesterday mornin'."

Amos was momentarily taken aback. "Do what?"

"Seth rode out not long after ya'll rode out. Miss Rachel sent Eli and Win out to fetch him."

"So he's back home?" Amos asked.

"No, sir," Jesse said. "They still ain't back."

Not one to dawdle with a bunch of questions, Cyrus Ridgeway was a man of action and he began barking orders. "Eli and Win can handle Seth, maybe. Wilcox, take Amos and Isaac with you to see if you can cut the Indians' trail. Percy, you, Jesse, and Hendershot head back to the ranch and hitch up the wagon. It'll slow us down but we're going to need it. Load on some more ammunition and, Percy, tell your ma to pack enough supplies for a couple of weeks."

Cyrus gave little thought to consoling his daughter Abigail, nor did Isaac appear to give much thought about consoling his wife. And there was no question about which wagon to hitch up, because they all knew which one Cyrus was referring to.

Cyrus looked at Jesse. "Any idea which band of Injuns took her?"

"Didn't find no arrows or nuthin', but I'm bettin' Comanche since they rode west." Jesse thought a little longer then said, "Could be Apache, though."

"Two feathers of the same bird," Percy mumbled.

"They're all nasty and mean," Cyrus added. "Jesse, you and Hendershot trade out for fresh horses." He glanced at the position of the sun to gauge the time and guessed it was somewhere around ten in the morning. "We're burnin' daylight."

"What are you, Luis, and Arturo goin' to do?" Percy asked.

"We're going back to Fort Sill. I'll report Emma's kidnappin' to the army and the Indian agent then we're goin' to roust some of them redskins and see if we can maybe find out where their kin is camped. A bunch of the Injuns speak a little Spanish so Arturo or Luis can help with that." Cyrus paused a moment to mentally calculate the logistics of everything. The wagon was going to slow everything down, but that couldn't be helped. "Jesse and Clay, I want you two to hang back at the ranch and keep an eye on things. Try to get the rest of them calves branded so we can start a drive up north to the railhead. For the rest of you, we'll meet in two days where Wildcat Creek feeds into the Pease."

The men were starting to ride away when Cyrus rethought his strategy. "Wait," he shouted. "Percy, you rode all over this country when you was rangerin'. You might ought to go with Wilcox, Isaac, and Amos. Each of you grab an extra horse to take along with you."

"Who's going to get the wagon?" Percy asked.

Cyrus looked at the two Mexicans he employed. They were good men and would stick to a task until it was done, regardless the circumstances. "Arturo, you and Luis go get the wagon. Jesse and Clay, you help 'em get her hitched up. I'll ride back to Fort Sill myself."

"Sí, patrón," Arturo Hernandez said.

"Make sure you get plenty of ammo," Cyrus ordered, "and tell Señora Frances to pack some grub."

"*¿Dos semanas?*" Arturo asked.

"*Sí,*" Cyrus replied. "Could be longer, but who the hell knows." Cyrus, usually a very decisive man, was having trouble wrapping his mind around who needed to go where. He shifted in the saddle, feeling the pressure of time slipping away. The major sticking point was trying to decide the best use of Percy's skills. And guarding the wagon would be paramount. "Scratch that. Percy, you go with Arturo and Luis to get the wagon. Tie on a couple of water barrels, too. I got a feelin' we're headed into dry country."

"Okay," Percy said, an exasperated tone in his voice. "We set now?"

"We're set," Cyrus said. "See ya'll in two days."

The men separated and rode off in three different directions. Percy and his crew rode hard toward the ranch, arriving early in the afternoon, after changing horses several times during the ride. The men stripped their saddles from the worn-out horses and Percy asked Hendershot and Jesse to round up the wagon team and some fresh mounts. As they dispersed to saddle fresh horses, Percy headed toward his mother's house to ask her to pack up some grub. On the way, Abby and Rachel came outside to meet him and fell in step beside him. Abby looked as if she hadn't slept a wink since Emma had disappeared.

"Where's everybody else?" Rachel asked.

"Most went west to see if they could cut the Indians' trail. Pa rode back to Fort Sill to report Emma's kidnappin' and to see if he could dig up some information about who might have taken her."

"What are *you* doin', Percy?" Abby asked. "You're going out to help find her, aren't you?"

"Yes. I came to get some supplies and to grab the wagon."

"What wagon?" Rachel asked, then she answered her own question. "Oh, *that* wagon."

"Yes, *that* wagon," Percy said. He looked ahead to see his mother stepping down off the back porch of the main house.

"How long are you goin' to be gone?" Rachel asked.

Percy shrugged. "Pa's planning on a couple of weeks."

Abby reached out her hand and pulled her brother to a stop. "I want to know what you think, Percy. You've ridden out to that part of the country."

Percy really didn't have time for all these questions, especially when he didn't have

111

any answers his sister would want to hear. He knew how difficult the task ahead of them was. The area they were heading into was a sea of nothingness that stretched for hundreds of miles in all directions. Looking for a single band of Indians was going to be like looking for a single needle in a barn full of them. "I don't know, Abby. I can promise you we'll do everything we can."

Percy awaited the arrival of their mother and she slipped an arm around her son's back and squeezed a hug.

"What do you need me to do, Percy?" Frances asked. She had lived long enough on the frontier to know exactly what was going on.

"Need some grub, Ma, and plenty of it," Percy said. "We'll hunt game for meat, but we could sure do with some flour, coffee, and whatever else you think we'll need."

Frances looked at her two daughters and said, "Grab anything you can from your two kitchens and bring it to the house. Don't worry if you're runnin' low because I'll send somebody to Red River station for supplies later."

Once Rachel and Abby were out of ear-shot, Frances put a hand on Percy's arm and said, "I know you don't know how long you'll be gone, but you need to spend a mo-

112

ment with Mary before you leave."

"How is she today?" Percy asked, his face crinkling with new worry.

"Not good, son. She can't get out of bed."

Percy looked off in the distance for a long spell. "You'll watch after the kids?"

"Of course," Frances said.

Percy blew out a long breath. "Okay. Let me get the wagon squared away and I'll look in on her."

Frances patted her son on the arm before turning for home.

Percy, as hard as it was, turned his mind back to the task at hand. He walked around to the side of the barn and slid open the wide door. Inside was *the* wagon. Built by the Peter Schuttler Wagon Works Company out of Chicago, the wagon had oversized wheels, a beefed-up frame, and a bed that was designed to float the river crossings without wetting the contents. And it was those contents that made this particular wagon so special. It was the equalizer that kept any marauding Indians at bay.

Mounted at the front of the wagon, with a 360-degree field of fire, was a Gatling gun. A hand-cranked rotary cannon, the gun's six rotating barrels could spit out two hundred rounds per minute. The original gun shipped with a forty-round, gravity-fed magazine that slipped into a slot at the top of the gun. The Ridgeways increased the rate of fire by adding a drum magazine that held two hundred .50 caliber rounds. And if that wasn't enough to get the job done, there was an even more sinister weapon mounted on the back of the wagon — the M1841 mountain howitzer. Loaded with canister shot, the weapon could blast 148 .69 caliber lead balls in a single firing. It was like a hundred sawed-off shotguns firing at the same time. The effective range of the weapon extended to hundreds of yards, but the closer, the deadlier. At two hundred fifty yards, the howitzer could level an enemy with lethal precision. The Indians were mighty afraid of the Gatling gun but they were absolutely terrified of the mountain howitzer.

After what seemed like forever, Jesse and Hendershot returned, leading the mule team and driving some fresh horses out in front of them. Luis and Arturo worked quickly to harness the four mules and they pulled the wagon from the barn.

Percy leaned over the rail and counted the cases of ammunition stored aboard. By his estimation, they had enough ammo to wipe out all the Comanches currently walking the earth.

CHAPTER
15

Seth was unable to sit a horse with his blistered bottom so the three of them — Seth, Eli, and Win — were making slow yet steady progress heading back to the ranch afoot. Leading their horses, the three started around daybreak and were now in sight of the Red River. There had been no discussion about who the three men Win and Eli had killed were or where they might have been from. Dead was dead, and the rest of that stuff didn't matter. Eli thought they were lucky they came along when they did because he had no doubt the three men had other devious deeds in mind. And if they'd tried to do whatever it was to Seth, how many other children had endured the same? Not anymore, Eli thought.

The water level in the river was up slightly from yesterday's brief shower, but it was little more than ankle deep in most places with a few deeper pools thrown into the mix. Eli didn't know who'd given the stream its name but whoever it was had nailed it — the water was muddy and brackish, and so salty it was unusable most of the year. What the riverbed lacked in water, it more than made up for it in the amount of quicksand which littered the entire Red River basin. It would suck a cow or horse in so deep the only way to get them out was to put a rope on them and pull them out. Luckily, the three avoided any quicksand and a couple of water moccasins sunning on the sand and crossed safely.

As they were climbing up the far bank and back onto ranch land, Eli's heart stuttered when the roar of gunfire shattered the silence. The quick *tat, tat, tat, tat* could be only one thing — the Gatling gun. The three turned their horses loose to find their own way back to the barn and quickened their pace, weaving through a thick stand of blackjacks, not knowing if the ranch was under attack by a swarm of warring Indians or a roving pack of ruthless raiders. When the weapon didn't sound again, Eli and Win glanced at each other, confused. They paused at the tree line and scanned the surrounding area. A large swath of land around the ranch buildings had been cleared of all trees and brush to allow for a wider field of fire and the only thing Eli could see were the heat waves shimmering in the distance. There were no clouds of dust indicating a group of invaders and the gun hadn't sounded again. Hoping younger eyes might be sharper, Eli leaned in close to Seth and whispered, "See anything?"

Seth shook his head. "I reckon they're just horsin' around."

"I hope you reckon right," Eli said. He led the other two out of the woods. Hugging the tree line just in case, the three worked their way around to the side of the barn and saw Percy bent over the Gatling gun.

"What the hell, Percy?" Eli asked as they walked over to the wagon and stopped.

Percy stood and said, "Makin' sure the gun's workin'. I see you found Seth, proving miracles can still happen."

"Funny," Eli said. "Are you anticipating an all-out assault on the ranch?"

When Percy didn't immediately answer, Eli asked the question again.

Percy shot his brother a glare and climbed out of the wagon. Percy winced when he saw Seth's bruised face, but he'd wait to get the story from Eli. He ruffled Seth's hair and said, "Why don't you go tell your ma you're back so she'll stop worryin'."

"Are you goin' to shoot the gun again?"

Seth asked, his eyes alight with excitement.

"Shootin's over. Now, go on, your ma's worried sick," Percy said.

Seth hung his head and limped toward home. Once he was out of earshot, Percy looked at Eli and Win and said, "Indians took Emma sometime last night. We're headed out to look for her."

"Which Injuns?" Win asked, his mustache and beard so thick you couldn't see his mouth move.

Percy stared off in the distance for a moment, then refocused his gaze on the two men. "Comanche or Kiowa."

"Not a hair's difference between them," Eli said. He looked down and nudged the dirt with the toe of his boot for a moment then looked up at his brother. "You've heard the horror stories of what they do to their captives."

Percy sighed. "I know. Only hope is to find her quick."

"Wagon's gonna slow us down," Win said.

"Can't be helped," Percy said.

"Want me to accompany you on the search?" Eli asked.

"No," Percy replied. "Best you stay and keep an eye on the place." He nodded toward Jesse and Hendershot who were busy with the wagon and said, "Them two are stayin' back."

"What do ya need me to do?" Win asked.

Percy pondered the question for a moment. Win was a hell of a tracker, much better than he was, but the two Mexicans could cut sign almost as good as Win could. However, Win had fought in his share of Indian scrapes and was deadly with a rifle in his hand. "Probably be best if you went along, Win," Percy said. "The more eyes lookin', the better. Accordin' to Colonel Davidson the Comanche are gettin' mighty frisky."

"Why doesn't Davidson do something to address the problem?" Eli asked.

"Army's goin' to but he didn't know when," Percy said. "I reckon he's got his hands full keepin' what Indians he does have corralled."

"Ought to take their damn horses away," Win said. "That'd keep 'em from ridin' off."

"That's his problem to worry about," Percy said. "We got our own problems." He looked at Eli and asked, "What happened to Seth?"

Eli told Percy what had happened, including Seth's branding.

"Jeezus," Percy said under his breath. "Where are those three bastards now?"

"They remain right where we found

119

them," Eli said. "You can rest assured they will never abduct another child."

Percy nodded. "Good. Any idea of who they were?"

"No, nor do I particularly care," Eli said. "When are you leaving?"

"As soon as I can get things squared away," Percy said.

"What are the odds of quickly finding Emma?" Eli asked.

"Not good," Percy replied. "It's wide open country out west and finding anything will be a damn chore, much less a bunch of sneaky Injuns on the run." He pushed his hat back and wiped his sweaty brow with his shirtsleeve. "I need to go do a few things before leaving." Percy issued instructions about what he wanted done and turned for his house. He walked by the corral to see if either of his two sons, Chauncey or Franklin, were around but he saw no sign of them. Probably out fishing, he thought. Walking up the stairs to the front porch, Percy paused, took a deep breath, and pushed through the door.

"You're back," his sixteen-year-old daughter, Amanda, said. Tall and willowy with long dark hair and blue eyes, she was the spitting image of her mother when she had been young.

"Not for long," he said, leaning down to kiss Amanda on the cheek.

"Goin' out to look for Emma?"

Percy nodded. "How you holdin' up?"

"I'm scared, Papa. That coulda been me out there."

"Can't live your life running scared all the time. How's your ma?"

"She ain't gettin' any better."

"She *isn't*."

"You say *ain't* all the time," Amanda said.

"Doesn't mean I want my kids sayin' it."

Amanda rolled her eyes and Percy smiled before shuffling toward the bedroom they'd added on three or four years ago when things got too tight. The curtains were drawn, the room dark. Percy had met Mary Blalock in San Antonio at the tail end of his time with the Rangers. And she had been a beauty with long dark hair, blue eyes, and a wicked sense of humor. But the person now lying in the bed in front of him bore little resemblance to the woman he'd met those many years ago. Percy inhaled a deep breath and released it before stepping into the room.

"Mary, you asleep?" Percy asked.

"You back already?" Mary asked, her voice slow and slurred by laudanum, a powerful drug derived from dissolving opium powder in alcohol.

"Yeah, but I have to head back out." Percy stepped over to the window and cracked the curtain open a tad so that he could see.

"Emma?" Mary asked.

"Yes," Percy replied as he took a seat on the edge of the bed. He reached out and covered Mary's hand with his own. "How are you feelin'?"

"Poorly. Can't use my left arm at all."

Percy had brought in doctors from all over, but none could say with any specificity what was ailing his wife. The most common response was that Mary might get better or her condition could continue to worsen. *Thanks very much,* Percy had thought at the time. "Want to try and get out of bed to walk around a bit?"

"I can't, Percy. My eyes . . . are so blurry . . . can't hardly see and . . . can't feel . . . my left leg at all."

The two sat in silence for several moments and Percy's mind drifted to the task ahead. The odds of finding Emma were long, but knowing his father, they would ride to the ends of the earth before even thinking about riding home.

"Percy?" Mary said, drawing Percy away from his thoughts.

"Yes?"

Mary withdrew her right hand from under his and reached out, placing a hand on Percy's gun belt.

"You have . . . your pistol?"

Percy had a pretty good idea where this was going. "Yes."

"Please . . . I beg you . . . please . . . shoot me. I can't stand this . . . misery," she said, with a feeble tug of his gun belt.

It was a request Mary had made before and Percy knew she was in agony, but he couldn't bring it upon himself to kill his wife and the mother of his children. "I can't do it, Mary."

"Then leave me . . . your pistol and I'll . . . do it myself."

Percy stood and leaned over and kissed his wife on the forehead. "I can't do that, neither." Percy turned and walked out of the bedroom and then out the front door, tears streaming down his cheeks. He'd debated the issue a thousand times in his mind and, if it had been just the two of them, he might have done it. But Amanda had been the one caring for her mother and the thought of asking her to help clean up the aftermath of a bloody suicide by gun was more than Percy could tolerate.

Percy stopped, dried his eyes, and returned to the house. He stuck his head in the door and asked Amanda to step outside for a moment and she did. "Mandy," Percy said, "your ma's in terrible shape."

"I know that," Amanda snapped. "I'm the one takin' care of her."

"I know, and I appreciate it mightily." Percy paused, trying to frame the next few statements in his head. After a moment or two he said, "Where do you keep the bottle of laudanum you've been givin' her?"

"On a shelf in the kitchen."

"I want you to leave the bottle on her bedside table," Percy said. "And when that one runs out, put a new bottle out and just keep doin' it."

"Until when?" Amanda asked.

Percy took a deep breath and released it. "Until it's over." Expecting anger, tears, or outright hysteria, Percy was astonished when Amanda simply said, "Thank you."

Father and daughter hugged and that was when the dam broke, Amanda's tears wetting his shirt. Percy rubbed her back and talked to her. The last two years had been a hellish nightmare as Mary's health declined gradually enough that hope for a recovery lingered, stretching on for months. There was no such hope now.

"How long are you . . . goin' to be gone?" Amanda asked between sobs.

"A couple of weeks. Could be longer. I ain't got any idea how long it's going to take."

Amanda lifted her head and looked at her father. "You said 'ain't.' "

Percy smiled a small smile. He rubbed her back and said, "I gotta go."

With one final squeeze, she broke the embrace and stepped back, wiping the tears from her cheeks. "Find Emma, Papa."

"We will, however long it takes. If I don't make it back in time, you tell your uncle to put your ma up on the hill with your brother and sister."

Amanda nodded.

With a heavy heart, Percy turned and headed for the wagon.

CHAPTER
16

Rachel Ferguson was thumbing through an old issue of *Harper's New Monthly Magazine* when she glanced outside to see Seth limping toward home. She tossed the magazine on the table and rushed outside and wrapped her arms around him, anger coursing through her body at the obvious beating Seth had taken.

Seth burst into tears and buried his face in his mother's chest. When the sobbing subsided, Rachel stepped back and held Seth at arm's length. Her heart broke to see his battered face. She wanted to ask a thousand questions, but instead, took Seth's hand and led him back to the porch, deciding Seth needed to tell the story at his own pace. Rachel took a seat on one of the rockers and Seth attempted to sit down then immediately jumped back to his feet.

"What's wrong?" Rachel asked.

Seth loosened his belt and pulled his pants

down far enough to expose the *X* branded on his left buttock.

All thoughts of allowing Seth to tell the story flew from her mind and she lurched to her feet, trembling with rage. "Who did that to you?!"

"Three men. They're the ones who roughed me up, too."

"Where are these bastards?"

"Uncle Eli and Win shot them."

"Good," Rachel said, the sudden rage dropping back to a medium simmer. She stepped in the house, grabbed a pillow, and returned, placing it on the rocker's seat. "Sit."

Seth gently eased down on the pillow as his mother retook her seat. "What else did they do to you?" Rachel asked.

"Slapped me around, then burned me with the brandin' iron."

"Nothing more?"

"I reckon that was enough."

Rachel breathed a sigh of relief. "Were they Indians?"

"No. White fellers about Pa's age. They was drinkin' whiskey."

"Bastards," Rachel muttered. "Well, they deserved what they got. How'd you run into them?"

"I saw 'em riding toward me. Didn't

nothin' seem unusual about it. I was hopin' to ask them if they'd seen anything of Pa's group, but when they rode up and stopped, the meanest of the three grabbed the reins out of my hand."

"Why didn't you just jump off your horse?" Rachel asked.

"And go where?" Seth asked, his voice tinged with anger. "A man afoot ain't no match for three armed men on horses." He stared at his mother a moment. "You act like it's my fault."

Rachel took a deep breath, wanting to tell him if he hadn't ridden off nothing would have happened. But she didn't. "You sure they didn't do anything else to you?"

"How many times you goin' to ask me that?" Seth asked. "Ain't being beat up and branded enough?"

Knowing that some people were capable of the most vile, deviant behavior, Rachel was hoping her son was telling the truth and that nothing else had happened. "I'm just glad you're home safe now."

"When's Pa comin' home?" Seth asked.

Rachel shrugged. "Who knows how long it'll take them to find Emma."

Seth looked away then did a double take. "Where's Emma?"

"You didn't hear?"

"No, but I heard Uncle Percy shootin' the Gatling gun. I wondered why. What happened to Emma?"

"She was kidnapped by Indians last night."

Seth hung his head. "Oh no."

"They'll find her," Rachel said with more conviction than she felt. "Now, go inside and wash up and put on some clean clothes."

Seth pushed unsteadily to his feet. "Which Injuns took her?" he asked.

"Don't know yet," Rachel lied. "Now go on." She didn't have the heart to tell Seth that it was most likely the Comanches. Everyone along the frontier knew what happened to Comanche captives. They'd all heard the horror stories. And Seth needed to focus on healing rather than wonder what tortures his cousin might now be enduring.

Seth limped into the house and Rachel stewed. If Amos and the others hadn't gone off on a wild-goose chase after rustlers, she thought, things probably wouldn't have gone sideways. "Damn him," she muttered.

CHAPTER
17

Emma wanted to die. Not figuratively, but literally — a bolt of lightning out of the blue, an arrow to the heart, or a broken neck from a fallen horse — any of those would be welcome relief from the excruciating pain pulsing through her body. Still tied to the horse, her pale skin was blistered, and she was sitting in a mixture of her own bodily fluids — blood, urine, and feces. And having ridden endlessly for hours with no water, her tongue was swollen with thirst. She would have begged them to stop, but she knew what would happen if they did.

Emma winced in pain with every lunge of the horse. To her it felt like her insides were going to fall out and deep within her, it felt as if something had torn loose. What it was she did not know, but she was still bleeding, and the constant pain felt like someone had placed a burning coal deep in her stomach. During the very brief periods when the pain subsided to a dull ache, Emma worked to remove the rope encircling her wrists. She thought it a futile task because even if she were somehow able to free her hands, they were now so far beyond civilization that escape was impossible.

Big Nose, the name she'd given to the savage now leading her horse, never once glanced over his shoulder to check on how she was doing or even to acknowledge her presence. Not that she wanted him to. The less they thought about her the better.

The area they were riding through would appear as a blank space on a map. There were no towns, no houses, no man-made structures of any kind — a vast open space where a person could ride for hours and feel like they hadn't gone anywhere at all — the big empty. Occasionally, when they came to a patch of soft ground, the Indians would slow and rein their ponies first one direction then the other in an attempt to throw off any pursuers. A few seconds of random riding would add hours to those tracking them. Emma had also noticed that when they were leaving a stream or creek, the braves would always choose an area of rocky ground to make their exit. How her father and grandfather would ever find her was something that weighed heavy on her mind.

Thinking of creek crossings only heightened Emma's desperation for water. She was so parched she could barely swallow, and her thirst was exacerbated by all the blood she'd lost and continued to lose. Finally, around midday, they came upon a wide muddy river and the Indians herded the stolen horses into the water and allowed their mounts to dip their muzzles in for a drink. Big Nose and the others made no move to dismount and Emma worried they wouldn't allow her an opportunity to drink.

Emma's fears were put to rest when Big Nose rode his horse into the middle of the stream and pulled Emma's pony up beside him and untied the rope, pushing her into the stream. The four savages laughed as Emma sputtered back to the surface. She splashed the water with her hands and shouted a string of obscenities, but in truth, the water felt glorious, cooling her blistered skin and her chafed inner thighs. Emma rode the gentle current as it pushed her downstream and, once she quenched her thirst, began plotting an escape. Trees lined both sides of the river, but they were sparsely spaced and unsuitable for hiding. She didn't know what the Indians would do if she tried to escape again and, despite what she'd been telling herself throughout the long ride, she came to the sudden realization that she didn't want to die. Not here and not now. She had too much life left to live and if she could just hold on long enough, her grandfather and father would come.

After gently scrubbing her torso clean, she swam for the far bank where the Indians waited, not knowing if she would be molested again or if the four savages had some other form of torture in mind. As she got closer, she began feeling for the river bottom with her feet, found it, and walked out of the water.

Humiliated because of her nakedness, she crossed her arms over her chest to cover her breasts. The Indians laughed and then Scar, her name for the meanest of the four with a knife wound on his cheek, walked over, yanked her hands down, then latched on to her right breast and squeezed with all his might. Emma's knees sagged with the pain, but she refused to submit and stood her ground, looking the Indian in the eye as he squeezed and twisted her breast. It felt like someone was stabbing a hot poker into her chest and it took everything Emma had to not cry out. Finally, one of the other Indians said something and Scar gave one final squeeze and smiled before turning her loose. Then just as quick, he grabbed her by the hair, pulled her to the ground, pulled up his breechcloth, and assaulted her. Once the other three had another turn, Emma, bleeding freely again, was tied onto a fresh horse and the journey through hell continued.

CHAPTER
18

Cyrus rode back into Fort Sill ready to stomp a mudhole in someone's ass and then walk it dry. As he approached, a pack of cur dogs began barking and snarling at his horse and he was sorely tempted to pull his pistol and send them back to their maker. But he didn't and, instead, steered toward the Indian agency building and dismounted. He arched his back in an attempt to stretch out the kinks and then wrapped the reins around a hitching post and stepped up onto the porch.

The recently constructed building was a square, two-story clapboard structure with two long porches fronting the building, one on each level. Indians of all types — squaws, kids, men young and old — lazed about in the heat, no doubt, Cyrus thought, waiting for a handout. He hadn't always felt this way about the Indians, but after a lifetime of scrapes over stolen livestock or attempts to drive him from the land that was right-fully his, Cyrus now thought the only good Indians were the dead ones. He opened the door, stepped through, pushed his hat back on his head, and shouted, "Who's in charge here?"

A short, balding, portly man waddled out of a nearby office and said, "That would be me."

Cyrus walked over to look the man in the eye, his spurs jangling with every step. "Who're you?" he asked.

"James Haworth, the Indian agent for this facility."

"Where's Tatum?"

"He resigned in March. To whom am I speaking?"

"Cyrus Ridgeway. I run a spread down south of here. You a Quaker, too?"

"That's not relevant, sir." Haworth shuffled back a step. "How may I help you, Mr. Ridgeway?"

"Some of your thievin' savages run off with my granddaughter."

"They aren't my Indians, Mr. Ridgeway. We're here merely to help them integrate into our society."

"Layin' around on the porch? That part of your integratin'?"

Haworth sighed. "Sir, I don't want to get

off on the wrong foot with you upon our first meeting." He waved a hand at the door to his office. "If you'll come in, I'll be glad to write up all the details."

"What good's that goin' to do?"

"Well, it will allow me to pass on the pertinent information to traders, other tribes, and anyone else that might have business with the Indians."

"I want to talk to some of your thievin' Comanches."

"Sir, they're not — never mind. I'd be pleased to introduce you to some of the Comanche members and will also provide you with an interpreter, but I need a few more details about the kidnapping before we proceed."

Cyrus brushed past Haworth and entered the office the man had just exited. When Haworth didn't immediately follow, Cyrus turned and looked at him and said, "Get your pencil."

Haworth sighed, entered his office, and worked his way around the desk, taking a seat in his chair. He opened a drawer, pulled out paper and pencil, and set to work as Cyrus sat. Over the next fifteen minutes, Cyrus passed on all the relevant information about who and where, as Haworth dutifully wrote it down.

"I'll pay whatever ransom it'll take," Cyrus said.

Haworth laid his pencil on the desk and leaned back in his chair, resting his hands on his ponderous belly as he steepled his fingers together. "Mr. Ridgeway, we've recently instituted a new policy of not paying ransoms for Indian captives."

"I don't give a damn about your policies," Cyrus said. "If I find out you had a chance to ransom my young'un and don't, I'll shoot you right between the eyes."

Haworth squirmed in his seat and dropped his hands to the arms of the chair. "I don't appreciate being threatened."

Cyrus pulled off his hat, mopped his face with a red handkerchief, put the hat back on, and leaned forward, giving Haworth a hard stare. "Ain't a threat, sir. Ask around. I'm a man of my word."

Momentarily flustered, Haworth quickly changed the subject. They discussed who might have taken the girl and where Emma might now be. "If I find out they've snuck back onto the reservation, you're goin' to have a passel of trouble."

"I'll make inquiries, but I don't think they'd return here right after taking a new captive."

Cyrus pushed to his feet.

"Where are you going, Mr. Ridgeway?"

"You said we're making inquiries. Let's go."

Haworth remained seated. "I need to give some thought to who best to approach."

"How 'bout we start with the first Comanche we see? Every minute you spend in here thinkin' is another minute of torture my young'un's facin'. You know what these savages do to their captives. Get your ass up and let's get goin'."

Still, Haworth sat, and Cyrus's anger flared red-hot. "You're 'bout as worthless as tits on a boar hog. I'll do my own askin'."

That got Haworth to his feet. "Mr. Ridgeway, there's a right way to do this. Please don't enflame the local Indian population."

"Screw the local population. Most of 'em are a bunch of thievin' murderers." With that, Cyrus exited the office and made his way outside. He paused a moment to think then decided to pay a visit to Davidson to tell him about the kidnapping and to put some pressure on him to send out a patrol. But Cyrus's immediate plans changed as he walked past the trading post, where a man was loading a buckboard wagon with supplies. Cyrus, whose eyesight wasn't what it once was despite what he told his wife, thought he recognized the man, but he hadn't seen him for three or four years. Walking across the street, Cyrus shouted, "Charlie Goodnight?"

The man dumped his load into the wagon and turned. "Cyrus Ridgeway, how the hell are you?"

The two men shook hands. "Last I heard you was up somewhere in Colorado," Cyrus said.

Goodnight pushed his hat back on his head. "Yep, still there, but hopefully not for long. Gonna do a little scoutin' around down this way while I'm here."

"Thinkin' about running some cattle round here?" Cyrus had met Charles Goodnight back when Goodnight worked as a ranger and scout for a troop of Texas Rangers.

"Maybe. Don't know yet. The army needs to get these Indians squared away fore I can do anything."

"I'm glad you said that," Cyrus said. He went on to explain the details of his granddaughter's kidnapping.

When he finished Goodnight asked, "You talk to the Indian agent?"

"Far as I can tell," Cyrus said, "he ain't much good for nothin' but sittin' on his ass. You been around the Injuns, Charlie. Any idea who'd know anythin' about where my young'un might be?"

Goodnight thought about it a moment. "Yeah, I do." He looked up at the sky and said, "But it'll be dark before we could get there. How about you hitch your horse to my wagon, and you can camp with me. Get a fresh start in the mornin' and I'll take you out to meet Kicking Bird, a Kiowa chief."

Cyrus hated the thought of losing more time but prowling around in the dark up in these parts could get a man dead real damn quick. "Sounds like a plan."

CHAPTER
19

Sitting at the kitchen table alone, Abigail was absently watching the dust motes drifting about in a slash of sunlight cutting through the front window. She was working overtime to tamp down thoughts of what might be happening to her daughter Emma, but it was a losing battle. Amelia and Wesley, her two youngest, were with her mother or playing with their cousins. Abby couldn't muster the energy to go outside to find out. And it was approaching suppertime, and she had no appetite nor any inclination to even think about rustling up some grub.

Abby sighed, stood, and shuffled over to the rocker in front of the fireplace and sat. Percy and others had set out a little earlier in the war wagon, but she knew the difficulties they faced and also knew it would be days or even weeks before she heard anything. She turned and picked up a pair of pants that needed mending from a basket on the hearth, held them in her hands a moment, then tossed them back. Then she picked up a book she'd been reading before Emma's abduction and the words ran together on the page. Tossing the book on the floor, she rubbed her face and wondered, why now? Why did the Indians, who usually cut a wide berth around the ranch, come in and kidnap her daughter? Every savage in the Territory knew her father gave no quarter.

The only thing that made sense was the four Indians were a bunch of young bucks who didn't know the Ridgeways fought back — blood for blood. Even if they did know, would that deter them from harming Emma? Those questions piled on top of a hundred others, but they were all unanswerable and wondering about them was only going to drive her crazy. Instead, her thoughts turned to her husband, Isaac. If he hadn't gone chasing after those rustlers, she thought, he'd have been home, and Emma would never have been kidnapped. Or that's how she reasoned it. Just one more thing to add to her list of things Isaac had or hadn't done.

Several times she'd thought about quitting the ranch altogether — take the kids and move down to San Antonio or even

Galveston or anywhere where she wouldn't have to look over her shoulder every single minute of every single day, wondering if a group of Indians or a gang of outlaws were riding up with no good on their minds. But she hadn't and, now that her parents were growing older, the prospects grew dimmer. Already tired of sitting and getting hot inside the breezeless house, Abby pushed to her feet and shuffled toward the front door, thinking she probably should find out where her other two children were.

Being outdoors wasn't much of an improvement. The heat settled around her as she stood on the porch — an unescapable misery that simply had to be endured. As sweat trickled down her spine, she surveyed the distance, but there was no sign of Amelia or Wesley. In fact, there was no sign of much in the way of humanity at all. Cows and horses, yes, but the late afternoon sun beating down upon the earth had driven everyone else to shade. Abby stepped off the porch and headed for Rachel's house, unsure if she was up for much conversation.

At Rachel's, she knocked and entered without waiting for an answer. That was how it was for all of them. Any hope of privacy was long gone. Rachel was sitting on the sofa thumbing through an old catalog from a jewelry store in New York City. She looked up when Abby entered and stood to greet her, opening her arms wide. Abby collapsed into her sister's embrace.

"How are you holding up?" Rachel asked as she rubbed Abby's back.

"Barely," Abby said. She felt like crying but her well of tears was as dry as the dirt outside. She shuffled over to an arm chair and sat as Rachel returned to her seat.

"I'm afraid Emma will be all hollowed out inside. That's the way all the Indian captives are when they come back."

"You don't know that," Rachel said. "Emma's a strong girl."

"Not strong enough to fight off a bunch of savages," Abby said.

"Have you eaten anything today?"

"Not hungry." Despite her answer, Rachel turned to look at Consuelo in the kitchen and nodded.

Abby was apparently going to get a plate of food whether she wanted one or not.

"How's Seth?"

Consuelo walked over, gently rubbed Abby on the shoulder, and handed her a plate of leftover biscuits and bacon.

"Three men roughed him up and then had the gall to brand him with a brandin' iron."

Abby turned to look at her sister, her brow arched in surprise. "What?"

"The bastards branded a big ole *X* about the size of a four-inch square on his butt."

"Why?" Abby asked. She broke off the edge of a biscuit and put it in her mouth.

Rachel shrugged. "No idea. Seth said they were drunk."

"No excuse to do that to a twelve-year-old boy." Abby broke off a little more of the biscuit and chased it down with a slice of bacon. "Did Pa send someone up to exact some revenge?"

Rachel shook her head. "No need. Win and Eli took care of it."

"What do you mean, 'took care of it'?"

"They shot the three men."

"Eli?" Abby asked, her eyes widening in surprise.

"I know," Rachel said. "Eli's always been slow to anger, but once he's a-burnin' there's not much you can do to stop him."

"Any idea who they were?"

"Nope. Don't care, neither. They got what was comin' to them."

Abby picked up the remainder of her biscuit and paused, turning to look at her sister. "I hope those savages that took Emma get the same punishment. I wish Percy would start that Gatling gun and not

146

stop killin' Indians until they were all exterminated." Abby tossed the rest of the biscuit in her mouth and chewed. "Seen Amelia or Wesley?"

"Yep. Down at Ma's house with my two youngest. She's got Percy and Mary's kids, too."

"Bless her." Abby picked up the last piece of bacon, doubled it over, and put it in her mouth. The two sisters sat in silence as Consuelo puttered around the kitchen. After a few moments, Abby said, "I can't stop thinkin' about all the bad things that might be happenin' to my Emma."

"You ain't gonna stop, either. But you can't let it eat you up. They're gonna find her."

Abby looked at her sister and said, "That part's botherin' me, too. What exactly are they goin' to find when they do?"

Chapter
20

Riding toward the southwest, Percy and Winfield Wilson were ranging out a half a mile in front of the wagon, trying to cut the trail of Indians who'd taken Emma. Leaving late yesterday afternoon had been a mistake because they hadn't made it far before darkness had overtaken them, forcing them to make camp at the eastern edge of the ranch. Back in the saddle at daybreak, they were now detouring around a large southerly bend in the river rather than having to cross it twice. It was out of the way, but it was better than taking a chance on burying the war wagon in a patch of quicksand. So far there had been no sign of the Indians' trail and they weren't really expecting to find anything until their course turned more north and west. Win was thinking they might pick up the trail somewhere around the area where Wildhorse Creek fed into the Red River — three hours ahead if they were lucky.

Arturo Hernandez and Luis Garcia were manning the wagon and all four had their heads on a swivel. This was dangerous territory and it would become much more treacherous the farther west they rode. Comancheria is what the whites called it but the Comanches called it home after driving the previous natives out of the area generations ago. Bordered on the east by white settlements and the picket line of frontier forts, the area stretched north to the middle of Kansas and Colorado, south to the Rio Grande, and west all the way to the Pecos River in New Mexico Territory — an area covering over ninety thousand square miles. And trying to find anything in such a vast area was damn near impossible.

The specially built wagon wasn't the fastest form of transportation, but it was a marvel of engineering. In addition to the two swivel mounts for the Gatling gun and mountain howitzer that allowed a 360-degree field of fire, the builders had assembled a quick-release canvas cover that could be released in seconds with a push of a spring latch.

And the wagon wasn't the only thing the Ridgeways had bought from the Peter Schuttler Wagon Works Company. Inside the second story of the main house back at the ranch was another marvel of engineering. It was a uniquely designed platform that could be raised and lowered through a hatch in the roof. This wasn't a platform that was slapped together with scrap two-by-fours, it was engineered to precise specifications and armored with thick timber around the bottom half that shielded a majority of the operator's body from enemy fire. In the center of the platform and, mounted on another swivel head, was the ranch's second Gatling gun. The unit could be deployed in under two minutes and had been used — so far — a total of two times. The only weakness in the design was the threat of an enemy torching the house, but with that weapon it was highly unlikely anyone would ever get closer than five hundred yards, well outside the reach of torch throwers or flaming arrows.

A couple of hours later the four were closing in on the area where Wildhorse Creek fed into the Red. Much like a snake trail in the sand, the Red twisted and turned, the water seeking the path of least resistance. And after hours of riding, the group was only about twenty miles from the ranch as the crow flies.

Win was about a half a mile ahead when

Percy looked up to see him riding back toward the wagon. He rode out to meet him.

"Four riders just rode down the north bank of the river," Win said.

"Headed this way?" Percy asked.

"Don't know yet. But they'll be on us quick if they are."

"Let's drift back to the wagon just in case."

Win and Percy's worst fears were realized when the four riders rode up the near bank and headed directly toward them. The four men appeared to be white or of mixed race and they stopped about twenty yards away and fanned out in a line until they were abreast. Percy and Win sat easy in their saddles while Arturo, sitting on the wagon seat, pulled his shotgun onto his lap. The clothes of the four men facing them were worn and dirty and all looked to be hard men, their holstered pistols in plain view. After a general overview of the group, Percy took a moment for closer study of each individual while mentally calculating how the scenario might play out. The man in the center was packing two pistols, their butts pointing forward. His mouth was hidden behind a face full of black whiskers and his long, greasy hair snaked out from under his black, flat-crowned hat. Percy pegged him as the leader and decided if this encounter escalated to gunplay he would have to be eliminated first.

Percy's assumption that the man with two pistols was the leader was affirmed when he was the first to speak. "Got you a mighty nice wagon there."

"Thank you," Percy replied. "We're mighty fond of it."

"I bet you are," the man said. He stood tall in the saddle and craned his neck one way then the other, trying to get a look inside. "Whatcha got in there?"

Remaining cool and calm and with his hands resting easy on the pommel of his saddle, Percy said, "That's none of your business."

"What if I make it my business?" the man with two pistols asked as the other three strangers laughed.

"Where you fellers from?" Win asked, joining the conversation.

"Got a place up in the Territory."

"That's mighty strange," Win said. "I thought white folks couldn't do that."

The leader smiled and said, "I ain't say it was permanent." The man then turned his gaze on Arturo and Luis, who remained seated in the wagon. "You two Mexis get on down, now."

Their only response was Arturo's cocking of the two hammers on the double-barrel shotgun. The two clicks were loud in the silence.

"We're not looking for trouble," Percy said. "Best you ride on."

The leader smiled again. "Well, looks like trouble done found you."

Percy locked eyes with the leader and said, "What's your name, pardner?"

"Why? Don't matter none."

"It does to me," Percy said.

"Why's that?"

Percy continued to stare. "Because I always like to know the names of the men I kill."

The man broke eye contact first, and Percy could see his Adam's apple bob up and down when he dry-swallowed. But Percy knew the man thought of himself as a gunhand and was unlikely to back down. Flexing the fingers of his right hand Percy waited. He wore his pistol on his left hip with the butt facing forward for a right-hand cross-draw. He studied the man's body language, waiting for the tell.

"Well," the man said, "I don't much care 'bout names." The man made a show of counting the assembled men and said, "Looks like a square fight to me."

With his gaze still centered on the man with the two pistols, Percy spoke out of the side of his mouth and said to Win, Arturo, and Luis, "I'll take the two on the right. Other two are yours."

The man in front of Percy dry-swallowed again, and the other three strangers shifted in their saddles. Win applied a little more pressure. "You fellers can ride on now and we'll let it be." Win turned to look at the man with two pistols and said, "You might fancy yourself a gun hand, but I'll tell you, my friend, yer takin' yer last few breaths on this here earth."

"Is that so, old man?" the stranger said.

Win nodded and said, "Yes, sir. I reckon it's up to you if this here's the day you want to die."

One of the other strangers found his voice and said, "C'mon, Wade. Whatcha goin' to do with that wagon?"

"Shut up, Charlie," the man now known as Wade said.

"Might ought to listen to your friend, Wade," Percy said. "But either way you're wastin' our time." Percy saw Wade's body tense when he reached for his gun. In one fluid motion, Percy pulled his pistol, cocked the hammer, and fired before Wade's pistol could clear leather. Re-cocking his revolver,

Percy pivoted to the second man, wondering in the back of his mind why he hadn't heard the shotgun. The answer came when his eyes fell on the second man, who had his hands up. In fact, all three had their hands held high. Percy eased the hammer down on his pistol and slid it back in his holster. The next sound heard was Wade's body slipping off his horse and thumping to the ground.

"You can lower your hands," Percy told the men. "I want you to ease your pistols out and toss them as far as you can into the field." The three remaining strangers complied then Percy ordered them to do the same with their rifles. Once the men were unarmed, Percy said, "Tie your man on his horse and get."

The three men climbed down from their mounts and went about their task. It was a struggle for them to get the body lifted up and slung over the saddle, but they did and quietly remounted. "What about our guns, mister?" the man known as Charlie asked.

"You can ride back and pick them up later."

Charlie nodded. "But, mister, I gotta warn you, Wade's got some mighty mean kinfolk."

"So do I," Percy said. "I've got a warning for you, too. All three of you. I don't tolerate thievin'. If I ever see any of you again, you better be reaching for your pistols. Now get."

The three men reined their horses around and rode off. Once they were far enough away that they couldn't return quickly to gather their weapons and bushwhack Percy and the others, they restarted the wagon and continued on their journey.

There was some talk later on about which was faster — the three men reaching for the sky or Percy on the draw.

CHAPTER
21

The next morning, about eight miles east of Fort Sill, Charlie Goodnight turned his wagon off the main trail and steered toward a V-shaped bend in Medicine Creek. Wooded on both sides, the oak, walnut, and elm trees provided abundant shade — a welcome relief from the blistering sun. As they rounded the bend and broke into the clear, the hair on the nape of Cyrus's neck stood at the first sight of the Indian lodges that lined both sides of the creek and stretched for as far as the eye could see. Cyrus turned to look at Goodnight, his brows arched in surprise. "How many Injuns are up in these parts?" Cyrus had spent a lifetime living around Indians, but he'd never seen so many teepees in one place.

Goodnight shrugged and said, "There's a passel of them, that's fer sure. Probably be three times this many come wintertime."

"Jesus Christ," Cyrus said in a low voice.

"There's enough Injuns here to kill all the whites 'tween here and San Antone."

"Probably right," Goodnight said, without a hint of concern in his voice. "Most of 'em are just plain tired of fightin'."

Cyrus waved a hand at the lodges spread out before them. "These all Kiowa and Comanche?"

"These here are mostly Kiowa. There'll be a few others in the mix, maybe an Apache or two, maybe a few more from other tribes. You damn sure won't find any Tonkawas anywhere around here."

"Why's that?" Cyrus asked.

"These here tribes will kill a Tonk as quick as they see 'em." Goodnight pulled on the left rein and the two-horse team veered to the left, around a grouping of trees as the Indian dogs started up a ruckus, barking and snarling and running around. "Know what a cannibal is, Cyrus?"

"A man that'll eat another man?"

Goodnight nodded. "Yep. Tonks got a taste for human flesh."

"That's just downright disgustin'."

"Don't seem to bother the army much. Got a big bunch of Tonks workin' as scouts. Think that's another major reason these here Indians don't like 'em much."

"This Kicking Bird we're goin' to see, he

a chief?"

"Yep. Kiowa. The wild Injuns don't like 'im much, either, but he pretty much calls the shots round here when it comes to Kiowa doin's."

They rode in silence for a few more minutes before Goodnight steered toward a larger teepee set off a short distance from the others. At the sound of the approaching wagon, a short, squat, bowlegged Indian threw back the cover concealing the opening to his lodge and strode out. His long dark hair was parted in the middle and gathered into two pigtails on either side of his head, and he had a large nose that dominated his other facial features. He smiled when he saw Goodnight. Returning the smile, Goodnight said something in the chief's native language and Kicking Bird replied. Cyrus had no idea what was said, but he looked around and didn't see Indians drawing back their bows.

Goodnight and Kicking Bird continued to speak, and, after a few moments, Goodnight turned to Cyrus and said, "The chief has invited us into his lodge."

Cyrus tipped his hat to Kicking Bird and whispered out of the side of his mouth, saying, "I ain't eatin' his grub."

"Might have to if you want to get out of

here without bein' scalped," Goodnight whispered back before they both climbed down from the wagon.

Goodnight made the introductions using a mixture of Kiowa and sign language. Kicking Bird looked at Cyrus and said in broken English, "You Heap Big Guns."

Cyrus smiled. "That's me." Cyrus chuckled that the Indians had given him a name.

Kicking Bird laughed and led them into his lodge. Both men took off their hats before entering, hoping good manners would lead to an abundance of information. It took a moment for Cyrus's eyes to adjust once inside, but the smell wasn't as unpleasant as he thought it was going to be. There was a slight gamy odor mixed with the scent of unwashed bodies, yet that was masked somewhat by the aromas of sage and woodsmoke. The fire pit in the center of the floor was cold and it appeared most of the cooking was taking place outdoors. Buffalo robes were stacked around the outer perimeter and Cyrus assumed that's where the chief's squaw or squaws slept.

Kicking Bird sat down cross-legged on a large bearskin and invited Goodnight and Cyrus to do the same as he began adding tobacco to a long, thin pipe that was about two feet long and had a small bowl at one end. Cyrus's knees popped and cracked as he sat, and he was hoping he was going to be able to get up again. As he looked around more, he wondered why the Indians didn't build some furniture or something. But the more he thought about it he began to understand why — it would be difficult to move, and the Indians were frequent movers.

Kicking Bird was taking his time filling the pipe and Cyrus, feeling time slipping away, wanted to tell him to hurry the hell up, but he didn't, wanting to leave with all of his hair intact. Finally, the pipe was filled to the chief's liking and he pulled out a match, lit it with a flick of his thumbnail, put the pipe in his mouth, and touched the match to the bowl of tobacco. Blowing the match out on his exhale of smoke, the chief passed the pipe on to Goodnight, who took a deep pull before passing it on to Cyrus. After taking a puff, Cyrus handed the pipe back to Kicking Bird, eager to get the conversation started. But he was disappointed when the chief seemed content to sit and smoke.

Cyrus looked over at Goodnight and gave a shrug.

"Patience," Goodnight said in a low voice.

After a few more moments, Goodnight

and the chief began talking and, judging from their laughter, Cyrus knew they weren't talking about anything important. Goodnight relayed some of what was said, and Cyrus nodded and smiled for the chief's benefit. Eventually, Goodnight's tone turned serious and Cyrus leaned forward, knowing they were now getting to the heart of the matter. Goodnight pointed at Cyrus as he talked with the chief. The chief responded and Goodnight turned and translated. "He says he can't believe any Indian would be foolish enough to take one of your kin. He said you and your family are well known among his red brothers."

"Well, it happened," Cyrus said. He nodded at Kicking Bird. "He have any idea where my young'un is?"

"Not there, yet," Goodnight said before turning back to the chief and continuing their conversation, their hands moving quickly to sign, bridging the language gap.

There was a rhythm to Kicking Bird's words that, in other circumstances, Cyrus might have found soothing. But not today. The chief droned on for a few more minutes then stopped as Goodnight translated. "He says it must have been a group of young braves who didn't know about you and your family."

Cyrus was tired of the runaround. "I don't give a damn who it was. I want to know where I can find the bastards."

Sensing Cyrus's tone, Kicking Bird stiffened.

"Easy, Cy," Goodnight said in a low, even-tempered voice. "There's a certain way of doin' this."

Cyrus spent a moment tamping down his anger and said, "Okay."

Goodnight turned back to Kicking Bird and continued their discussion. Whatever he said had an effect because Cyrus saw Kicking Bird relax again. As their discussion continued, Cyrus thought if he had his Gatling gun and cannon, he'd get an answer right damn quick.

Kicking Bird stopped talking and Goodnight looked at Cyrus.

"Does he know where my young'un is?" Cyrus asked.

"Maybe," Goodnight said.

CHAPTER 22

Emma's misery continued as the Indians and their ponies raced across the plains. Adding to her despair was the hunger that gnawed like a bad headache. She hadn't had anything to eat since her last supper . . . back at home. And that thought launched a flood of memories, and fresh tears sprang to her eyes. She didn't care if the Indians beat her for crying again or not. She'd beg them to run her through with one of their lances if she thought her request would be granted. But she knew it wouldn't — she was chattel to be sold or traded to the highest bidder.

A glimmer of hope appeared on the horizon, in the form of a dust trail, the only signs of humanity Emma had seen since being captured. She had no idea what it was, but it had to be better — much, much better — than her current situation. Big Nose hadn't tied her hands as tight as he'd had every time before, probably thinking any escape out here in the big nowhere would be futile. Emma looked around to make sure the Indians weren't watching her and began working to free her hands. The pain, the agony, the hunger, were all pushed to the back of her mind and thoughts of escape moved to center stage.

Emma knew the Indians had seen the dust trail because they immediately changed direction, adjusting their course to intercept the source of the dust trail. Working furiously on the knots binding her wrists, Emma began plotting her escape route. But an awful thought struck her — what if it was just more Indians? Perhaps the tribe her four captors belonged to? Emma worked hard to vanquish that from her mind. Her luck couldn't be that bad, could it?

As they drew closer, the Indians slowed the ponies to a walk. As they topped a rise, Emma's hopes soared — it was a pair of freight wagons! Emma doubled down on her efforts. Even if she couldn't get free there was hope that whoever was driving those wagons would be able to barter — or maybe even fight — for her freedom. When they were within a half a mile of the wagons, the Indians changed course again, now heading for a ravine that ran parallel to the trail. From the looks of things, the freight haulers were unaware they were being pursued by four Indian braves painted for war. They hadn't yet altered their course, nor had they whipped their teams into action.

Success. Emma now had her hands free, but she held the rope tightly around her wrists to avoid suspicion. The only hiccup she could see was if the Indians decided to tie her to a tree before the upcoming encounter with the wagons. Or, horror of all horrors, what if the Indians decided to avoid the wagons altogether? Emma couldn't even comprehend the results of that scenario. Trying to force an encounter, she began shouting as loud as she could.

Big Nose, leading her horse, immediately pulled her mount forward and backhanded her across the face. The blow stunned Emma and she immediately tasted blood. But that didn't stop her. She shouted again, as loud as she could. That bought her a roundhouse right from Big Nose, and her head slumped to her chest.

Emma opened her eyes. Her head pounding and her ears ringing, she had no idea how long she'd been out. She worked her jaw to see if everything was functioning as it should be and found that it was. Next, she checked to make sure her hands were still free and discovered they were, the untied rope still wrapped around her wrists. Did she dare open her mouth to scream again? That was a question that required more thought. If she yelled again the Indians might well kill her. *But isn't that what I wanted only moments ago?* Emma didn't think the people on the wagons could hear her anyway, so she held her tongue. And with freedom so close, getting killed now would be extremely unfortunate.

The Indians put the horses into a gallop as they continued down the ravine. They were now riding in rough country. The enormous seas of grass had been replaced with a rocky, hilly, barren terrain cut through with numerous dry ravines and, from what Emma could tell, there was no source of water in sight. And that made her thirstier, if that was possible. The horses had not been watered in hours, but they didn't seem to be any worse for wear because of it. As for the four savages, nothing appeared to bother them — not the lack of water or food and not the lack of sleep. They just kept going, and going, and going and Emma finally understood why they were such a difficult enemy to defeat.

After a while, the Indians brought the

horses to a stop and Scar jumped from his mount and, crawling on his belly, slithered to the top of the ravine. While he was doing that, Big Nose pulled her horse forward and Emma braced for another beating. Instead, he grabbed her by the hair and pulled her close, shoving a piece of rawhide into her mouth. He whispered something in Comanche that Emma didn't understand, but from his tone, she judged it to be a threat.

After a few moments of looking, Scar wormed his way back down, stood, nodded his head, and remounted his horse. The braves began preparing their armaments as Emma looked on. She was at a critical point of her escape plan — would the Indians take her along on their raid? If they didn't take her, she would not be able to alert the wagon drivers of her presence, eliminating any hope of a rescue. And if the wagons were to flee from the Indians, Emma thought there would be no way she would ever catch up to them before the savages recaptured her.

Once Big Nose was satisfied his weapons of war were arranged to his liking, Emma's worst fears were realized when he led her horse over to a large tree and tied the rope securely around the trunk. Emma's brain immediately went into overdrive, calculating a new escape plan. She estimated that it was maybe two or three hours before darkness and if she could get away, she just might have a shot at eluding her captors.

The Indians walked their mounts toward a game trail that led topside and turned up the path, pausing when they were just below the rim. Emma silently urged them on. The quicker they were gone, the quicker she could implement her new plan. Moments later, with a loud whoop that sent a tingle down Emma's spine, the Indians charged up out of the ravine. Emma tossed the rope that had bound her hands to the ground and began working out how to free her horse.

CHAPTER 23

Cyrus's legs were going to sleep as he sat in Kicking Bird's lodge waiting for Charlie Goodnight to get the details of where his granddaughter might be. He desperately wanted to stand up and stretch, but he didn't know if that would be an insult that would cost him his life. He'd been around Indians all of his life but never *with* them. Kicking Bird paused his narrative and shouted out something in Comanche. Cyrus moved his hand a little closer to his pistol, ready for whatever might happen. The one quick decision he made was that he wasn't dying alone. A moment later a squaw lifted the flap and stuck her head in. The chief muttered something, and the squaw disappeared. Cyrus relaxed, or got as relaxed as he could get surrounded by hundreds of Indians.

Kicking Bird restarted the conversation using a mix of Kiowa and sign language.

The chief appeared to be an honorable and honest man, but Cyrus knew looks could be deceiving. Kicking Bird might be a hospitable host one day and then he could just as easily head south on a raid the next, killing, raping, and stealing from white settlers all over Texas. It happened repeatedly and Cyrus didn't know if the Indians relished the killings or if they were a byproduct of their ultimate quest to steal as many horses as possible. Money — greenbacks, coins, or gold — held no allure for the Indians. Their primary wealth was determined by the number of horses they owned.

Goodnight responded to something the chief said then turned to look at Cyrus. "He thinks a group of Quahadis may end up with your young'un."

"Now we're gettin' somewhere," Cyrus said. "Where can we find these Injuns?"

Goodnight posed that question to the chief, who responded, saying, "Llano Estacado."

Cyrus didn't speak much Spanish, but he understood what the chief said and groaned inwardly at its implication.

"You catch that?" Goodnight asked.

"Yeah," Cyrus said. "We'd have a better chance findin' 'em if they were on the moon." Cyrus nodded at Kicking Bird and said, "He narrow it down some?"

While Goodnight attempted to extract more information from the chief, Cyrus ruminated on the task ahead. The Llano Estacado was a vast expanse of nothingness. Treeless and waterless, it was inhospitable to both man and beast. A scattering of sun-bleached bones in the sand would be the only indication that someone had attempted to traverse the remote region and failed. For the Comanche, all that space was their fortress. Luck would have to be on their side, Cyrus thought, if they had any chance of finding Emma. Cyrus's thoughts were interrupted when an extremely attractive, young, light-skinned Indian woman threw back the flap and stepped into the teepee. Cyrus thought she might be the prettiest Indian gal he'd ever seen, but despite her beauty, he cringed when he saw what she carried — three bone bowls steaming with some type of stew.

Kicking Bird patted his chest and pointed at the woman and said, "Me, Topen."

Lucky bastard, Cyrus thought, if he got to bed down with that woman every night. Goodnight said something to the chief and he replied. Goodnight translated. "Her name is Topen and she is Kicking Bird's daughter."

Okay, maybe not so lucky, Cyrus surmised, thinking every buck in the tribe was probably sniffing after her. If he had to guess her age, he'd peg her at sixteen, or a year or two on either side of that.

Topen offered a small bow and passed out the bowls to the three men. Cyrus glanced at his, trying to determine the contents without offending their host. He held the bowl up to his nose, took a sniff, and was surprised to find the aroma enticing. It smelled much like the stew his wife made and contained some of the same ingredients — meat and root vegetables combined in a broth. Cyrus's main discomfort stemmed from questions about the specific species of meat the Indians had used for the meal. Strictly a beef eater, he would dine on venison or buffalo on occasion, but drew the line there. He refused to put squirrel, snake, armadillo, or opossum anywhere near his mouth. Another sticking point to eating was that Topen hadn't brought anything with which to eat the stew. That was soon resolved when Kicking Bird dug into his bowl with his hand. Goodnight followed suit, and Cyrus sighed and plucked a chunk of potato from the lukewarm broth and tossed it in his mouth.

Apparently, dinner conversation was not

something the Indians indulged in. The chief remained quiet as he gulped down stew by the handfuls. Goodnight didn't seem to be concerned, his hand in constant motion between bowl and mouth. Cyrus, tamping down his apprehension, popped a chunk of meat in his mouth and chewed. It was a bit tough, but otherwise tasted fine. Cyrus tried some more, then more until his bowl was empty and he slurped down the remaining broth. He set the bowl aside and wondered if he should even ask the question but felt compelled to do so. He looked at Goodnight and said, "Stew's pretty good. Was that buffalo we was eatin'?"

Goodnight slurped the rest of his down and then said, "Nope."

"Well, what was it?" Cyrus asked.

"Dog," Goodnight replied.

Cyrus's stomach roiled and he muttered a curse word or two. Goodnight laughed and said something to the chief, who also began to chuckle. "First time eatin' dog, Cyrus?" Goodnight asked.

"I wish to hell I hadn't asked, now," Cyrus said.

Goodnight laughed again. "Ah hell, Cy, ya couldn't tell a difference, could ya?"

Cyrus didn't reply and instead muttered another string of curse words that elicited

174

another round of chuckles from Goodnight and Kicking Bird. Eventually the chuckles died, and the three men got back down to business. Cyrus asked, "Did the chief narrow it down any?"

"He seems to think the Quahadis might be camped somewhere 'tween the Canadian and Arkansas rivers," Goodnight said. "I know that's not a lot to go on but it's all you're gonna get."

"Who's the big chief for the Comanche that might could tell us more?" Cyrus asked.

"There ain't one," Goodnight replied. "The tribe ain't got no big chief or much of anything else. They ain't got no type of structure like we got. The individual groups'll have a chief of sorts, but they pretty much all do what they want."

"Well, hell," Cyrus said. "Maybe they ain't got no big chiefs, but somebody's got to make the decision of when to move camp and where to. Who's runnin' that show for this here group we're talkin' about?"

Goodnight posed the question to Kicking Bird. The chief answered and Goodnight translated. "He thinks it's probably Quanah Parker."

Cyrus reared back in surprise. "Cynthia Ann Parker's boy? Weren't you in on the raid that rescued her?"

Goodnight nodded. "That's him. And yes, I was there, a lot of good it did. Should have left her with the Indians."

CHAPTER
24

Emma's hopes soared when she heard gunfire echoing across the prairie. If the wagon drivers could kill her Indian captors all of her problems would be solved. That thought quickened her efforts. She untied the rope that bound her to the horse and kicked her mount in the ribs to get him to walk forward so she could free the lead rope from the tree. When the horse didn't move, she kicked again, this time harder, and the stubborn horse refused to move. Emma didn't know if she could get back on the horse if she had to climb down to free the rope. *Would the horse move with the rope untied?* There was only one way to find out.

Emma climbed down from the horse and nearly went to her knees when her feet touched the ground. Her legs were weak and sore. She rubbed and kneaded the outside of her thighs to get the blood moving and eventually recovered enough to limp forward and untie the rope. Giving the rope a hard jerk, she finally got the horse moving. *How do I get back on?* Emma scanned the area around her and quickly formulated a plan. Leading the horse over to the side of the ravine, Emma climbed up the bank until she was even with the horse, gritted her teeth, and jumped. The jolt of pain when she landed on the horse's back was so intense, she had to bite her lip to keep from crying out. "Oh God . . . oh God," she muttered as the pain radiated all the way up her spine and down to her toes. Inhaling a series of deep breaths, the intense pain slowly receded to the all-too-familiar dull ache and she grabbed a handful of the horse's mane and tapped her heels against his ribs. The horse began to walk, and she steered it toward the game path that led out of the ravine as more gunfire reverberated across the plains. *Please, please let the Indians be dead.*

When the horse was topside and on firm footing, Emma changed her plan again. The wagons were her only real option for escape. She nudged the horse into a gallop and immediately regretted it. Every stride was torture, but she clamped her jaw shut and let the horse run, listening for more gunfire and hoping she could catch up to the wagons before they were too far away.

She quickly picked up the wagon tracks and followed them, her brain buzzing with thoughts of freedom as she fought to stay on the horse. The rope they'd used to tie her on was behind her and inaccessible, and it didn't take her long to discover that riding a running horse bareback across a long stretch of ground was much more difficult than riding a walking horse bareback from the barn to the river back home.

Looking ahead, she still didn't see any sign of the Indians or the wagons and she hadn't heard any more gunfire. *Could the Indians already be dead?* It was too much to hope for. Feeling a burst of intense pain, Emma glanced down to see she was bleeding again. She tugged on the horse's mane to slow him, but the horse continued to run. Trying again, she pulled with all of her strength and shouted, "Whoa, whoa!" and it had no effect. She doubted the horse understood English, but Emma was at her wit's end and the pain was becoming unbearable. Switching tactics, Emma focused on controlling the horse with her legs. She squeezed her thighs as tight as she could and the horse thankfully — finally — slowed to a walk. She and the horse wouldn't cover as much ground, but the relief from the constant bouncing was instant.

Now that she understood how better to control the horse, she turned her focus to finding the wagons and her saviors. But the farther she went, the more doubt crept in. Should she turn the horse around and ride as hard as she could to get away? She hadn't seen any hint of civilization in two days, and worse, she hadn't seen any sign of water since the last time they stopped. How far would she get without water? Not far, she decided. Her best chance — her only chance — for escape lay with the men driving the wagons. Topping a small rise and looking ahead, her heart plummeted, and any hope of a rescue vanished in an instant.

Emma rode forward slowly, and the scene told the story. Tears leaked from the corners of her eyes as the horse plodded onward. The four white men — her four liberators — were dead, their bodies acting as pincushions for a volley of arrows. All had been scalped and all had been mutilated. The savages had disemboweled two of the men, their entrails scattered upon the hard, barren ground. The other two wagon masters had fared no better. Their limbs had been chopped off and tossed about, the blood still draining into the earth. The scent of death was heavy in the still air and the savages' lances dripped with blood.

Emma's horse came to a stop next to the other Indian ponies that were tied to the wheel of one of the wagons. Her four captors were covered in blood as they searched the wagons for plunder. Big Nose looked up and grunted. If he was surprised to see her there, he gave no indication. Emma sat her horse and cried, all hope of escaping vanquished. One of the other braves she'd named Shorty because of his diminutive stature, climbed down and began uncoupling the two teams of horses. The Indians were in a celebratory mood, laughing and talking to one another in their harsh language. Emma's sadness quickly transitioned to anger. Swiping away the tears, her gaze swept across the ground, searching desperately for discarded weapons. If she could find a gun, she'd dismount and blast them all to hell. But to her deep dismay, there wasn't a single weapon in sight — probably already scooped up by the Indians, Emma thought. To them, rifles and pistols were even more precious than captives.

She began to wonder which was more important to the Indians — her or the contents of the wagon? She rolled that thought around for a minute as she glanced at the position of the sun, to get her bearings. With only a couple of hours before sunset, the sun was ahead of her and to her left a bit, meaning behind her was east and civilization, or as close to east as she was going to get. But how was she going to find her way? *Follow your own trail, dummy.* She decided that would work and wished she'd thought of it earlier.

She swiveled her gaze back to the wagons. The Indians were leisurely opening crates and poking through the wagon's contents, like they had all day to accomplish their task. Which they likely did, now that Emma thought about it. The savages weren't paying any attention to what she might be doing and she might well be a tree if there were any within a hundred miles of where they were.

Turning, she looked at the rope still attached to her horse and wished she had it in front of her for a handhold. If she was going to make her escape, she'd have to ride all out until either the Indians gave up or caught her, or an arrow pierced her back. But her success was also dependent upon her horse and if he faltered, what then? Emma's thinking became clouded with a stream of negative thoughts. *What if my horse does go down? I'd die for sure. No way a person could walk all the way back to civili-*

zation. Then another thought rowed across the stream of negativity and all of her thinking distilled into a single question — *Do I want to stay and be abused by the savages for however long or do I want a shot at freedom?* Emma scooted back on her horse until the rope was in front of her, and she began loosening the knot. When the rope was loose, she eased it forward and tied it tight around the pony's girth. Now she had something firm and stable to latch on to.

Glancing over at the wagons again, she checked the Indians' progress. They were busy unspooling rolls of bright fabric like children on their first visit to the store. Emma looked longingly at a stack of blankets packed into the second wagon, thinking how much more comfortable her ride would be if she could get her hands on one, but she wasn't willing to risk it.

Emma took a deep breath, lazily turned her horse around, and then buried her heels in the horse's ribs. The pony went from full stop to full gallop within seconds and Emma wrapped her hands around the rope and held on. Glancing back over her shoulder, dread raced down her spine when she saw Big Nose jump from the wagon and onto his horse. She turned back to the front and urged her horse on.

Well, whatever happens, at least I tried.

CHAPTER
25

Back at the ranch, Abby was pacing the front porch of her sister's house, having no idea her older daughter was on the ride of her life. The same thoughts circled through her mind over and over again like an endless loop. And it was hard not to think those thoughts when everything she'd heard about Indians and their captives was one long horror story. Abby had no appetite and could barely summon enough will to continue functioning. Rachel was working hard to make sure Abby stayed engaged, offering encouragement or reassurance that all would be well in the end. But Emma was her daughter and the bloom of life had been about to unfurl to a whole new world for her.

A fresh set of tears began to wind down Abby's cheeks and she wondered if Emma's chances for a normal life had been snuffed out. How would she ever find joy again when she'd been victimized by some of the vilest savages on the planet? Abby then made a vow to herself that when Emma returned, she would do all she could to help her daughter heal even if that meant leaving her husband and ranch life behind.

Wiping her cheeks, Abby stepped off the porch and headed for her parents' house. Her mother wouldn't be able to make everything magically disappear, but she was the emotional rock that everyone in the family leaned on. As Abby shuffled across the sunbaked ground, her feet kicked up clouds of red dust that hung suspended in the still air. Sweat trickled down her back and her worn dress clung to her like a wet blanket.

However, she noticed none of this.

She did glance toward the corral to see her son, Wesley, helping with the branding, but even that barely registered. In the back of her mind she knew she had to buck up and get on with it, despite Emma's predicament. But that was much easier said than done. Abby sighed and pulled her long hair off her neck and tied it with a strip of leather she wore around her wrist for such purposes.

Loss and despair were not new sensations for any members of the Ridgeway clan.

Abby and Isaac had lost two children in back-to-back years. Her third child, John, died at six months old, unable to survive the harshness of the frontier. And while she was still grieving for John, disaster struck again after the birth of their fourth child, also a boy, whom they christened Charles. And his death was more painful than John's only because he lived long enough to establish a personality, laughing and cooing until the night he died at the age of nine months.

Yes, despair was not new for Abby, but with Emma it felt like someone was clawing her insides out. People often said there was a certain affinity mothers had for their firstborn and it was no different for Abby. How Isaac felt she did not know, and she hadn't seen him since Emma's abduction. He certainly hadn't rushed home to console her or to reassure their children that their father was going to make everything all right again. No, he'd just done what he was told to do and that angered Abby. If she thought of him as an object, she expected he'd be a tree — a person could touch it and it was always there, but other than its ability to survive, the tree was devoid of any real expressions. A person can't converse with it, argue with it, or interact with it in any form other than by touching it. And, Abby thought, that pretty much summed up her husband.

Stepping onto the front porch of her parents' house, Abby paused to take a deep breath. Inside would be laughter, joy, and happiness. That's just the way it was at her mother's house. And it had always been that way, other than the few times Frances had allowed sadness to linger for a day or two. But, never any longer than that. Life was too precious and short to dwell on the past, was what her mother always said. Abby eased open the door and stepped inside. Her mother was sitting at the kitchen table playing some type of card game with Percy and Mary's two boys, Chauncey and Franklin, and Abby's youngest, Amelia. Her mother spotted her and rose from her seat. She ruffled Franklin's hair on the way past and stepped up close and wrapped her arms around her daughter. Abby sagged against her mother, trying to let the tension and worry drain from her body, but it was a lost cause.

Frances, who refused participation in any type of pity party, said, "Want to play cards with us?"

Abby gave her mother a final squeeze and stepped back. "Maybe I'll just watch." Abby glanced at her nephews at the table and asked in a whisper, "How's Mary?"

Frances shook her head. "No change."

Abby nodded. She walked around the table, giving each child a hug, and took a seat. Her mother returned to her seat and resumed the card game. They were playing slapjack and it wasn't long before they were back to laughing and having fun. In addition to the games, Frances would intersperse funny stories and it wasn't long until Abby was sucked into the fun.

Abby marveled at her mother's strength and resolve. She never once bitched or complained about much of anything, and her only knock was that she was as stubborn as a ten-year-old mule. Abby remembered a few years ago when her father wanted to sell a portion of the ranch to a group of Irish investors. Frances put her foot down hard, and her father quickly overcame his urges. And her mother knew the ranch business, Abby thought, probably better than her father and she was never shy about nosing into negotiations over cattle or horse prices, much to the other party's chagrin. What her mother and father had, Abby often surmised, was a real and true partnership, which was fairly unusual, given the time. Abby had interacted with other couples over the years and in a majority of those relationships the women played a subservient role to that of their husband's. But not in their home while growing up. Yes, her father would often grumble about it until, days later, when he would grudgingly agree that his wife's instincts had been spot on.

Abby was spurred from her reverie by a knock on the door. A moment later, her niece Amanda stepped into the room. Her cheeks were tear streaked, her hands were trembling, and her voice tremored when she asked her grandmother to come outside. Abby stood and followed, knowing that Amanda's mother — her sister-in-law Mary — had reached the end of the trail.

Outside, Amanda burst into tears again. Abby reached out her right arm and Frances her left, and they pulled her into a tight embrace.

"Papa told me . . . to let . . . to let Ma have . . . have all the . . . laudanum she . . . she wanted," Amanda blubbered.

"Your papa was right," Frances said. "You didn't do one thing wrong, honey." With her free hand, Frances gently cradled Amanda's face in her hand and looked her in the eye. "You. Did. Nothing. Wrong. Your ma was sufferin' somethin' terrible. She's now free of all of that."

Amanda nodded and sobbed. Eventually the crying slowed to a stop, and Amanda dried her eyes. She took a couple of deep breaths then whispered, "What am I going to tell my brothers?"

"They knew the end was near," Abby said in a soft, quiet voice. "But we'll go in and tell them together. Is that all right?"

Amanda nodded again.

"Good," Abby said. "We'll make it through this." As the three headed inside, Abby wondered if the words sounded as hollow to them as they did when similar words were told to her. Then thoughts of Emma's capture crashed down on her and she had to hold on to the doorframe to keep from sagging to her knees.

CHAPTER
26

Cyrus's stomach convulsed when they stepped out of Chief Kicking Bird's tent and into a pack of Injun dogs who were sniffing around an old squaw who was scraping the rancid meat off the inside of a buffalo hide. He worked hard not to gag at the smell, hoping not to offend their host. Kicking Bird shouted something in Comanche and the dogs scampered away, their tails between their legs. That helped to quell Cyrus's urge to vomit.

The chief and Goodnight conversed for a few more moments and Goodnight turned to Cyrus and said, "The chief wants to know if you brought him any presents."

"Well, hell," Cyrus muttered. "What's he want?" he asked Goodnight.

Goodnight shrugged. "I guess anythin' you got extra."

"I'll tell you one thing I ain't got and that's any more patience."

"Easy, Cy. He's helped you out. Got any coffee or sugar?"

"Yeah, I got a little," Cyrus said.

"Give it to him. You can stop at the trading post and get some more before headin' out."

Cyrus mumbled a curse word or two, walked over to his horse, and untied the flap on his saddlebag. He was mildly surprised to find his horse was still there, knowing that the Injuns would steal a horse right out from under you. He pulled out the remainder of his coffee and sugar and returned to Goodnight's side. "Do I gotta kneel, too?" he asked out of the side of his mouth.

"No. Just hand it to him so we can get the hell out of here," Goodnight said.

Cyrus handed the parcels across and the chief took them and offered a small bow before passing them on to one of his squaws. Cyrus and Goodnight shook hands with Kicking Bird and headed back to the wagon. Cyrus looked around the camp, hoping to steal one more glance of Topen, Kicking Bird's beautiful daughter. Cyrus could never imagine himself coupling with a squaw, but her looks sure got his loins buzzing, despite the circumstances of their visit. Then the sudden thought of Frances going after his private parts with a butter knife

193

obliterated all thoughts of Topen. Cyrus and Goodnight climbed aboard the wagon and Goodnight started the team forward. There was no way Cyrus was going to mount up and ride away from their current location — he liked what was left of his hair too much.

Goodnight and Cyrus talked cattle, cattle prices, and the difficulty of ranch life as they lumbered back toward the main trail. Fortunes were presently being made in the cattle business and all it took was a few thousand head of cattle, a dozen cowpunchers, and the will to drive those cattle north to the new railhead in Ellsworth, Kansas. Cyrus and his crew had driven three thousand cattle — mostly steers — north last year and he cleared $37,000 after expenses. His hope was to do it again this year, but that all depended on the outcome of their search for Emma.

"You know this feller Quanah Parker?" Cyrus asked.

"No, but I hear he's a wily and tough redskin," Goodnight said, steering the wagon around a patch of muddy ground.

"Ain't they all? You'd think bein' a half-breed would take some of the fight out of 'im."

"He might be a half-breed, but he was

raised Injun. Killin's all he knows."

"I'll show him a thing or two about killin' if he's got my young'un," Cyrus said. "I'll put a bullet right 'tween his eyes even if he's half-white."

"He'll have a bunch of Injuns with 'im."

"Don't matter."

Goodnight arched his brows in surprise and said, "How many men you takin' with you?"

"Ain't the number of men that matter."

"Well, hell, Cyrus. You draggin' that war wagon of yours along with you?"

"Damn straight. I only need one man on the Gatling gun and another on the cannon. A couple of rounds with them guns and the Injuns'll be begging me to quit."

"I've gotta say, you're pretty wily yourself."

"Probably not wily enough. I'd pay you well if you wanted to act as a guide for us."

"Can't, Cyrus. Got stuff I gotta do before headin' back north."

"You sure?"

"Yeah. Sorry."

"Well, it didn't hurt to ask."

The two men chatted all the way back to the main trail, where Cyrus took his leave. He covered the eight miles back to Fort Sill and dismounted at the trading post to

195

restock his supplies. Cyrus stuck a fist against his lower spine and arched his back. The thought of spending the next couple of weeks in the saddle only made his back ache more. He pushed his hat back on his head, pulled a handkerchief from his back pocket, and mopped the sweat and dirt from his face. As he returned his handkerchief to his pocket, Cyrus spotted a large, handsome black stallion tied to another hitching post at the far end of the store's porch. He walked over and studied the horse for a moment, wondering whom it belonged to. That question was answered shortly after Cyrus entered the store.

A tall, broad-shouldered man with long, dark hair, a droopy mustache, and wearing buckskin pants was standing near a long, narrow counter, a new Colt Peacemaker in his hands. He was wearing his flat-crowned, wide-brimmed black hat, tall leather knee boots, and a blue-checked flannel shirt with a red neckerchief tied loosely around his neck. Cyrus walked a little closer, but not too close. Walking too close to the man at the counter could cost a man his life. Stopping a few feet away, Cyrus got a look at the man's two ivory-handled Colt Navy 1851 revolvers tucked into a sash around his waist, the butts of the pistols pointing forward. "You ain't thinkin' about gettin' rid of them old Colts are you, Bill?"

The man looked up slowly and smiled. "I'll be damned if it ain't Cyrus Ridgeway." He laid the pistol on the counter, stuck out his hand, and they shook.

"How ya doin', Bill? Last I heard you was workin' as a lawman up in Abilene."

Wild Bill Hickock shrugged. "Yeah. Ain't nothin' last forever, Cyrus. Except you and your big spread down there south of the river. How's Frances?"

"Still alive and kickin'. Whatcha doin' down this way?" Hickock had stopped at the ranch many times on his travels through the area. It was one of the few places Hickock could go and let his guard down.

"Doin' a little scoutin' for the army and workin' as a guide for some rich Russians wanting to hunt buffalo on occasion."

"Can't them Russians find the buffalo all on their own? Damn, it can't be that hard."

"Ain't the buffalo they's worried about, Cy. They're scared to death of bein' scalped by an Injun."

Cyrus chuckled and leaned against the counter. The two men caught up on recent events for a few moments. Hickock was a legend all across the country, mostly due to his own making. Bill had never been one to shy away from a magazine or newspaper reporter, and Cyrus didn't like that part of him, but they'd been friends for a long time.

"Heard you was doin' some actin' with Bill Cody."

Hickock frowned. "Tried it for a spell and didn't much like it. Thinkin' about driftin' up to the Dakota Territory when I finish up down this way."

"Sounds cold to me, Bill. You been out scoutin' lately?"

"Some. Why?"

"Lookin' for an Injun named Quanah Parker."

"So's the army. He's a hard one to find."

"Any ideas?"

"How far west you been, Cy?"

"Only as far as I needed to go. I hear it's rough country. Percy went out that way when he was rangerin'."

"How's Percy?"

"Gettin' older like all of us. Tell me what you seen out there."

"You can travel forever and you'll feel like you ain't goin' nowhere. That's what protects the Comanches and Apaches. All that space. It's about the most unfriendly place I've been. Not just 'cause of the Injuns, neither. Water's scarce and the weather can turn on you lickety-split. You've got your work cut out for ya, Cy."

Cyrus rolled that around in his mind for a few moments then said, "Wanna earn some extra money? I'll pay you well to act as our guide."

"Can't, Cy. Meetin' some duke of somethin' outa Russia at the railhead in Kansas this time next week for a buffalo hunt. Percy'll be with ya, won't he?"

"Yeah."

"You're in good hands, then. Ain't much changed out there in the last few thousand years or so."

The two chatted another few minutes then shook hands again. "Take care of yerself, Bill," Cyrus said.

"I'm tryin', Cy. Ain't so easy sometimes. Someone's, usually the young studs, always wantin' to try their hand with me."

Cyrus wanted to say that he was partly to blame for that, but he didn't. "Well, Bill, keep them pistols of yours oiled up."

Hickock smiled. "First thing I do every mornin', Cy."

Cyrus and Hickock parted and Cyrus quickly purchased the supplies he needed and stepped outside. After stowing the goods in his saddlebag, Cyrus untied his horse, put his left foot in the stirrup, and groaned as he pulled himself up. He turned his horse and rode away from the fort, wondering how long it'd be before his old friend ran up against a gun slinger he couldn't beat.

CHAPTER 27

Emma had a new pain and it resided in her right breast. Her ride for freedom had ended abruptly when Big Nose caught up to her before her horse had gone a hundred yards. To show his displeasure, he had grabbed her right breast — sunburned and already blistering — and pinched and twisted until Emma almost passed out from the pain. Now bruised and already swelling, her breast ached something fierce and, with her hands retied, she couldn't rub it to try and soothe the stinging, burning pain that radiated all the way up to her jaw. Emma knew the pain would eventually fade, but what wouldn't fade away was her extreme thirst. The Indians had refilled their water skins from a barrel on one of the wagons and, as further punishment, guzzled water in front of her, without offering her one tiny sip.

She thought she saw a look of pity wash

across Shorty's face and she filed that away in her memory for future use. The braves tied some of the unspooled colorful fabric to their horses' tails and remounted their horses. Each had a freshly taken scalp dangling from the belts that were used to hold up their breechcloths and the braves had donned some of the clothing they'd taken off the bodies of the dead wagon drivers. Big Nose had on a large sombrero on which he'd tied a long strip of bright red fabric that draped down behind him and fanned out across his shoulders. The four savages looked like devilish fiends who'd just ridden straight through the gates of hell and up to the surface of the earth.

The Indians walked their horses away from the massacre site without a care in the world. They drove the mules from the wagons into their growing herd of stolen horses and pushed them out ahead, allowing them a chance to graze at a slow, easy pace. Big Nose was leading Emma's horse and Scar, the evilest of the four, dropped back beside her and reached across with his left hand and started fondling her breasts. Emma allowed him the luxury for a few seconds and then she opened her mouth and clamped down on his forearm. She dug her teeth in until she tasted blood and then, like a dog with a snake, she jerked her head violently from side to side until a large chunk of skin and tissue tore free in her mouth. Scar was screaming and jerking on his horse, trying to free his arm as Emma looked up, smiled a bloody smile, took a deep breath, and spat the clump of skin and tissue onto his lap.

Enraged, Scar yanked the lead rope out of Big Nose's hands and reeled in her horse until Emma was only a foot away. He reared back his right hand and punched Emma in the mouth. Stars exploded in Emma's brain and she wobbled and would have fallen if not tied on, but Scar wasn't done. He pried her mouth open and shoved the piece of skin deep into her mouth then clamped her jaw shut with his palm and reached two fingers up and pinched her nose closed until she could no longer breathe. With no other alternative, Emma swallowed — or tried to. Her mouth was so dry she didn't have enough saliva to wash it down and the flap of tissue hung up in her throat. She couldn't open her mouth and she couldn't breathe, and within seconds, she began to panic. *Is this how it's going to end?* she wondered. She tried shaking her head, but Scar's grip was like a piece of iron strapped across her jaw. She tilted her eyes down to see if Scar was still holding the lead rope and discovered he wasn't. She kicked out her legs and rammed her heels into the horse's ribs as hard as she could and the pony jumped forward, breaking Scar's grip.

Emma was free of Scar, but she wasn't out of the woods yet. She coughed and hacked, trying to dislodge the chunk of skin. With her hands tied, she was unable to stick a finger down her throat to make herself vomit so she tried swallowing over and over again, but the obstruction remained. Emma felt her horse moving and looked up to see Scar pulling the lead rope again. He hauled her up close again as blood ran in rivulets down his arm. Once again, he jammed her lower jaw shut with his palm and pinched her nose closed. Instead of fighting this time, Emma locked eyes with Scar and sat as still as she could. She refused to give him the satisfaction he was seeking. Emma did not blink, and she did not move, despite what her brain was telling her to do. After a minute of this, Emma's lungs were screaming and darkness was creeping into the outer edges of her vision. She didn't know how long she had before she passed out or died, but she was determined to keep her eyes locked on Scar's. Out of the blue, someone shouted something in Comanche and Scar held her gaze a moment longer before turning to look at whoever had shouted. Scar replied, saying something, and then there was more shouting from the other side. It was Big Nose's voice, but she had no idea what they were saying. Emma's shoulders sagged and she could feel herself slipping away. Scar shouted something else, turned to sneer at Emma, and finally loosened his grip.

Emma sucked in air through her nose and began coughing and hacking again. She was back in the same predicament — unable to swallow Scar's chunk of skin and unable to cough it up. She was afraid the obstruction would slide lower in her throat and completely close off her airway. She tugged futilely at the rope binding her wrists and shot angry glares at her captors. Finally, Crooked Finger, so named because the tip of his pinky finger turned inward, nudged his horse forward, held up his water skin, and dribbled some water into Emma's mouth. It was just enough to allow her to swallow, and she did, Scar's skin and tissue included. She nodded at Crooked Finger then, in a taunt, opened her jaws to show Scar her empty mouth. She had no doubt that if given the okay, Scar would torture her mercilessly before killing her. But she didn't think that would happen — yet. She was much too valuable alive.

Scar angrily bound his wound with a piece of cloth and the Indians started their horses off, Big Nose back in control of her horse. Crooked Finger's dribble of water did little to quench Emma's immense thirst, but she was hoping he'd offer more later. Emma wondered if the Indians had found any food in the wagons because, if they did, they certainly hadn't shared any with her. But Emma's hunger was way down the list of her present ailments. Her breast still ached, her skin felt like it was on fire, and Scar's fist had split her bottom lip wide open and she could feel the warm blood dribbling down her chin and neck.

Despite her misery she couldn't help but celebrate her one moment of triumph when she had bitten down on Scar's arm. She'd have to keep her eye on him for the rest of her days in captivity, although there was little she could do to ward off any punishment he decided to dole out. The only thing she could do would be to curry more favor with Big Nose, who appeared to be the leader at this particular time. She didn't know if the roles would change among the four savages or if there were certain hierarchical standards they adhered to. Not that it mattered to Emma as long as Scar wasn't the one calling the shots.

After walking the horses for a while, the Indians kicked their ponies into a lope. Scar and Shorty pushed ahead and started the herd of stolen animals moving at a more rapid clip. Emma had no idea how long they planned to run the horses, but they obviously had a destination in mind. To her, the last mile looked exactly like the next mile and what the Indians were using for navigational guideposts remained a mystery. The only good thing she had going her way was that Big Nose had tied her so tightly to her horse that she was no longer bouncing up and down. It didn't necessarily make it any less painful, because her thighs were rubbed raw, but she was hoping it would aid in slowing or stopping the blood that continued to leak from inside her.

Glancing up, she spied another — larger — dust trail off to her right. As far as she knew it could be a herd of buffalo or a pack of wild mustangs although that thought did little to dampen the surge of hope that flooded her brain. It was large, whatever it was, and Emma began envisioning what it might be. *A posse coming to my rescue? Or maybe it's the army out on patrol? Maybe more freight wagons and more people?* But then another thought struck her. *My captors surely have to have seen it by now and they aren't taking any evasive maneuvers. Why is that? Wouldn't they be looking for a place to hide out like they did last time?* It had Emma stumped as the Indians rode on seemingly unmoved by the dust cloud's presence. Emma was riding behind Big Nose and couldn't see the expression on his face, but if he was unaware of the situation, Emma certainly wasn't going to be the one to tell him. The more she thought about it, the more confused she became. *Unless . . . no . . . no . . . no. It can't be. Please, God, not that!* But it was the only thing that made sense and Emma's heart plummeted at the thought. *Please, God, don't let it be that. Please?*

Despite her mental pleadings, Emma's worst fears were realized moments later when Big Nose and the others started whooping it up as a very large contingent of painted-up savages rode into view.

CHAPTER
28

Other than the one discussion of who was quicker — Percy on the draw or the men reaching for the sky — Percy deemed the matter closed and there was no more talk about the conflict. Despite what Percy said to the others, he did spend a few moments mulling over the situation. That man hadn't been Percy's first kill and over the years there had been others at different times and different places, but it had been a long time since Percy had been in a gunfight. The last had been seven or eight years ago when he got the drop on some rustlers and one foolishly went for his pistol. That one ended the same as this one — a man dead while Percy walked away unscathed. But Percy didn't consider himself a gunfighter and he knew there were plenty of men faster than him and that didn't bother him one iota. He wasn't out to make or maintain a reputation and he took life only as it came. If that involved gunplay, then fine, but if it could be avoided, he was all in. Life was hard enough without looking over his shoulder all the time — at least any more than they all did where they lived — wondering if someone was going to come gunning for him. As far as he was concerned, the fewer people that knew Percy Ridgeway existed, the better.

With the wagon along, the pace never got beyond a walk and Percy estimated they'd covered about seven miles since daybreak with a whole lot more to cover if they were going to make the rendezvous point in time. Win was riding about a mile ahead, cutting sign. So far, they hadn't been successful in finding the trail of Emma's captors, but Percy wasn't too worried. It hadn't rained since the day of Emma's kidnapping and if the rain held off, the trail would be there.

There was one matter that did cause Percy some concern — he wondered if they were making a mistake not to have invited a few friendly Indians along. There was a reason the Rangers and the army employed Indian scouts and that was because nobody knew more about the surrounding territory than those who'd lived in it for years. Yes, Percy had been born on the ranch and grew up there, but they had never strayed far from home and, other than the few times he traveled out this way with the Rangers years ago, he knew there had to have been changes. Not drastic ones, because the landscape had remained basically the same for an eternity, yet they could expect subtle changes and some, such as dried-up water holes, could prove deadly. He took some comfort in the fact that Wilcox had traveled all over this harsh ground when he was working as a scout, but even with all of his experience no one knew the land like the natives who'd migrated after the buffalo herds for thousands of years. Percy decided all of the worrying was giving him a headache and it was all water under the bridge now anyway.

Glancing ahead, he caught sight of Win in the distance and he was standing in his saddle and waving his hat. Probably not a good thing, Percy thought as he spurred his horse into a lope. He covered the distance quickly and reined his horse to a stop. "What'd you find?" Percy asked.

Win pointed at the ground and said, "Fresh sign not more than a couple of hours old."

Percy studied the ground for a moment and then looked up at Win. "How many you figure?"

"Fifty, sixty, maybe."

"A mix? Women, braves, and kids?"

Win shook his head. "Nope. That there's a war party. Looks like they're headed south. More'n likely lookin' to do a little raidin'."

"What are the odds there are more comin' and they'll cut our trail?"

"Don't know," Win said. "Probably ought to keep a close eye out. I doubt they'd tangle with us oncet they got a look at what was in the wagon. But a man don't ever know for sure. Could circle back and try to pick us off around dark. That'd be how I'd do it if I was a Injun."

"Well, there ain't nothing we can do about it but keep goin'," Percy said. "Ride north a ways to see if you can spot any dust trails."

"I will, but I'm mighty partial to what hair I do got left. You hear me shootin' you get that wagon there quick."

Percy smiled. "Will do, but I'm hopin' there isn't any shootin'. I'd just as soon not tell 'em we're here."

"Me, too," Win said. He turned his horse and rode off and Percy took a long look around before drifting back to the wagon.

"*¿Qué pasa con él?*" Arturo asked.

"Injun tracks," Percy replied.

"*Magnífico,*" Arturo muttered facetiously.

"¿Reciente?"

"About two hours old, accordin' to Win."

Arturo mumbled something else that Percy didn't catch. "We'll be okay, but you need to be ready to man that gun at a moment's notice."

"Sí, jefe," Arturo said.

Percy let the wagon roll by then rode back about a quarter of a mile to check their back trail. He didn't see anything, but that was of little comfort — you never saw an Indian coming until they were on top of you. Especially with the Comanche. The planet hadn't seen anything like them since the rule of Genghis Khan. They had driven the Apaches out, scattering them all over hell and gone, demolished the Spanish army, and made Mexico their own playground. To build a buffer between themselves and the Comanche, the Mexican government had offered free land to anyone who had wanted to settle down and start a homestead. Four thousand acres free for the taking and, sure there might be some Indians around, but that's just the cost of doing business. Offer anything for free and people would flock to the place, and it had been no different with the offer of free land. Americans had arrived in droves and the Mexicans wondered if they'd made a terrible mistake, but then the raids started, and every tiny step west was followed by a rapid retreat to the east, the line of westward expansion never moving more than a mile or two at any given time.

Yes, the Comanches might be Indians, but they were in a category all of their own. They viewed *all* outsiders as the enemy, killing and mutilating the men, raping and killing the women, and hauling the orphaned children back to their lairs for indoctrination into the Comanche way. But old Father Time has a way of catching up and much like the way they drove the others off the land, they, too, were now facing annihilation as the westward expansion pressed ever onward. Percy didn't know how it would all play out or if there would be any Comanches left alive to see the final outcome. Not that he was all that worried about it. His only concern was getting Emma back and if that required killing a few Comanches, then so be it. He took one more long look around at their back trail, turned his horse, and spurred her into a lope to catch up to the wagon.

CHAPTER
29

Frances had asked Jesse and Eli to dig a grave in the family plot while she tended to Mary's body. She had thought about asking Abby and Rachel to help but decided they had enough on their plates at the moment. Besides, Frances had done this more times than she wanted to count. That's just the way life was and as the matriarch of the family she often took it upon herself to prepare a body for burial. She dipped her small towel into the bowl of soapy water, wrung out the excess, and gently cleaned Mary's face. Frances had no idea what Mary's affliction had been, but her once tense and contorted limbs were now finally at rest. She couldn't recall anyone else in the family who had suffered with the same disease and she wondered if it was something passed down on Mary's side. That thought spurred worry about Mary and Percy's children, her grandchildren, and she hoped the three never contracted whatever this illness had been.

Once Mary's face had been cleaned to her satisfaction, Frances picked up Mary's brush and began brushing out her long, dark hair. Parting it down the middle, she arranged it so it fell softly on either side of Mary's narrow face. Before her illness, Mary had been a very beautiful woman and had been fun-loving and amiable, and Frances knew her son had adored her. In fact, they all had. But the last two years had been a living hell for Percy and the children as Mary's health began a downward spiral. The last few months were the worst as larger and larger doses of laudanum were needed just to take the edge off her immense pain.

But all of that was over now and Frances was sad that Percy wasn't there to see his wife finally at peace. Once Mary's hair was acceptable, she pulled the blanket up to the top of her shoulders and stepped back for a final look before opening the bedroom door.

Nine-year-old Franklin was the first to enter. To Frances, he looked the most like Percy and he stepped over and grabbed his grandmother's hand as he stared at his mother. He was trying hard not to cry so she pulled him close.

"She looks so peaceful," he said.

Twelve-year-old Chauncey was the next to enter the room. He shuffled across the floor and stood next to his brother. He favored his mother with his dark hair and blue eyes, and he spent most of the time looking down at his shoes, which was all right with her. If he didn't want to look at his dead mother, he didn't have to.

Amanda was the last to enter. Her cheeks were red from crying, but her eyes were dry now. Frances thought the expression on her face was more one of relief than sadness. She had borne the brunt of her mother's illness and if she could overcome her feelings of guilt Frances thought she'd be okay. Amanda stepped over to the bed, leaned down, and kissed her mother on the forehead. She stepped back, and Franklin walked hesitantly forward, leaned down, and quickly pecked his mother on the cheek.

Chauncey remained rooted in place at his grandmother's side.

"Your mother is now pain free," Frances said in a soft voice. "She's gone on to a better place." Frances was unsure if the better place she was speaking of existed, but the words were a comfort to her grandchildren. She'd let them decide for themselves if they wanted to believe in a supreme being.

Amanda nodded as fresh tears bubbled up and wound down her cheeks. After a final glance at her mother she turned and walked out of the room. Chauncey followed shortly after, but Franklin lingered a little longer, his gaze locked on his mother's face. Frances knelt down and wrapped her arms around him and whispered, "It's okay to be sad."

He offered a tiny, hesitant nod and then burst into tears. She held him tight while he cried. Nine was a hard age for boys and the death of a parent was monumental. Frances knew this because she'd lost *her* father when she was young. Not as young as Franklin and her circumstances had been different — her father's death was sudden — but she knew grief was universal no matter the age. As Franklin continued to cry, Frances found her mind drifting to her son Percy and her own death. She didn't know when that day would come, and she didn't spend a lot of time worrying about it, but Percy had turned into a stoic man who was reluctant to reveal his real emotions and, now with Mary gone, so, too, was Percy's one outlet to unburden his most private thoughts. She did not want her son to become a bitter, detached man who trudged through life only because he had to.

Franklin sniffled and wiped his eyes before looking at his grandmother. "Are we gonna bury her now?"

"I think we'll wait until sunset," Frances said. "Do you think your mother would have liked that?"

Franklin sniffled and nodded. "Yeah, she would."

Frances stood and took Franklin's hand, led him from the bedroom, and pulled the door shut. She'd come back later to wrap Mary's body in a clean, white sheet before the burial. The mood inside Percy and Mary's house was somber, which was to be expected, but Frances didn't want the children moping around the house the rest of the afternoon. She glanced at the clock on the mantel and decided they had three or four hours until the burial. Frances asked the boys if they wanted to go outside to play and both nodded, the relief apparent on their faces as they scampered out the door.

Amanda exhibited no such exuberance and, instead, sat down wearily on a wooden chair at the dinner table. Frances grabbed another chair, pulled it close to her granddaughter, and sat. "I know what you're thinkin'," Frances said.

"You don't know," Amanda said, rubbing her index finger along the ridges of a deep gash in the table.

"I do know." Frances reached out and covered her granddaughter's hand with her own. "Look at me, please."

Amanda lifted her head and looked Frances in the eyes for a second before averting her gaze to some spot on the far wall.

Frances waited patiently until Amanda looked her in the eye again. When she did, Frances said, "You did nothing wrong."

Amanda quickly looked away again and Frances waited. What she really wanted to do was grasp her granddaughter by the shoulders and try to shake some sense into her, but she knew that was the wrong approach. So, she waited.

"I shouldn't . . . I shouldn't have done it," Amanda stuttered, still staring at something on the far wall.

"Done what?" Frances asked. "Did you force your mother to drink the laudanum?"

"Of course not."

"Was it her decision, then?"

Amanda wiped a stray tear from her cheek and looked at Frances. "Yes."

"That's right. It was your mother's choice."

"But I shouldn't have put the full bottle on her nightstand. Pa asked me to do it and I should have . . . should have . . . said no."

"Can I ask you a question?" Frances asked.

Amanda was back to staring at the wall. "I guess."

Frances put a hand on her granddaughter's chin and gently moved her head until they were looking at each other. "If your mother could have gotten out of bed to get her own laudanum don't you think she'd have done the same long ago?"

"Maybe," Amanda said. She tried to avert her gaze again, but Frances was having none of it. She gently moved Amanda's head again, forcing her to look at her.

"There's no maybe about it. Your mother was suffering terribly. And I would make the same choice if I was in her predicament. We shoot animals to put them out of their misery and I sometimes wonder why we don't do the same for our loved ones. Your mother was not going to get better and she'd had enough. She was brave to do what she did."

"But the Bible —"

Frances put her finger to Amanda's lips. "— doesn't matter," Frances said, finishing Amanda's statement. "No one knows what happens when we're gone, but I do know your mother is no longer suffering. And that's all that matters. Does that make sense to you?"

Amanda wiped away another tear and nodded.

"Good. Put all that other nonsense out of your mind. What happened today was what needed to happen. And we'll not talk about this foolishness again. Agreed?"

"Agreed," Amanda said, just barely loud enough to be heard.

Frances leaned forward and kissed her granddaughter on the forehead. "I'm kinda hungry. Let's go see what we can find in my kitchen. What do you say?"

Amanda nodded. Frances stood, linked arms with Amanda, and groaned as she pulled Amanda out of her chair. "Either I'm getting too old or you're getting too big for me to do that much longer." She wrapped an arm around Amanda's back and ushered her out of the house.

After supper, Frances slipped outside and told Eli and Jesse to bring the wagon around then continued on to Percy's house to prepare Mary's body for burial. Over the last few months Mary had hardly eaten, and she'd withered away to almost nothing. It wasn't much of a chore for Frances to get the sheet under her. Once that task was completed and the body was somewhat centered in the middle of the sheet, Frances wrapped one side over and tucked the excess under the body. She then draped the other side of the sheet across and spent some time neatly folding the material a certain way before securing it closed with a single safety pin. Once Frances was satisfied, she exited the house and asked Eli and Jesse to carry the body to the wagon.

The rest of the family began gathering by the wagon as Jesse climbed up onto the seat and took the reins. The two-horse team started off at a walk and the family fell in behind the wagon. It was a solemn procession to the family burial plot, which resided on a slight rise and was shaded by a large cottonwood tree. Eli and Jesse removed the body and carried it over to the gravesite, where two ropes had been stretched across the hole and would be used to lower Mary into her final resting place. Frances gathered up Mary's three children and held them close as Eli returned to the wagon to retrieve the little-used family Bible.

The cemetery represented all the sadness the Ridgeway clan had endured over the years. Buried there were grandparents, parents, aunts, uncles, husbands, and wives, but the saddest were the children who were called away too soon. It was a place Frances didn't visit very often because she'd lived through most of it. She and Cyrus had already picked the spot where they were to be buried together, but neither was in a big hurry to get there. If Frances had her way, she'd be buried in an unmarked grave, so no one could mourn over her. Life was hard enough to be fretting about those already gone.

Eli returned, took his place beside Clara, opened the Bible, and began reading the 23rd Psalm as the sun settled on the edge of the world. When he finished the sun was dipping below the horizon, painting the clouds a pink and purplish hue, and casting long shadows across the hallowed ground where Ridgeways had laughed and cried, loved and fought, and lived and died.

CHAPTER
30

Cyrus's back tingled as he threaded his way around the various Indian encampments that stretched out along the creeks and rivers near Fort Sill. He knew they were allegedly "friendly" Indians, but he couldn't shake the feeling that some young brave was going to practice his archery skills with his back as the target. And — worse still — were the large number of dogs that roamed around and through the various camps. He wondered which lucky dog would end up in tonight's supper pot.

An hour out from the fort, Cyrus realized he'd forgotten to tell Colonel Davidson about Emma's kidnapping. He stopped his horse and debated if he wanted to ride back. If he did, he'd have a bed to sleep in, but it would also put him and the search further behind. Deciding Davidson would hear the news from the Indian agent, he spurred his horse forward.

With only three hours of daylight left, Cyrus wanted to get clear of the Injuns before even thinking about bedding down for the night. His best guess was that he'd be at the stated rendezvous point by midafternoon tomorrow — if he didn't hit any snags, and that was never a sure thing in this part of the country. He hoped that the Rocking R brand displayed prominently on his horse's left hip would help to alleviate any scrapes he might encounter. If Kicking Bird knew who he was and knew he wasn't a man to be trifled with then it was likely that many of the other Indians knew who he was, too. Or that's what he hoped anyway. From the way it looked, most of the Indians he'd run across so far weren't much interested in the lone horseman riding through their part of the world. But he also knew that could change as quick as the weather did around these parts.

The more Cyrus thought about bedding down out in the open and on the hard ground, the more his back ached. He glanced up at the position of the sun, calculated when it might set, and then clucked his tongue and tapped his horse with his spurs to put Snowball into a lope. A giant horse, Snowball's stride ate up the ground. If he could cover enough miles before dark, he could drop in on an old friend — a friend who had a spare bed and a Mexican cook who was making Cyrus's mouth water just thinking about her cooking. Despite his increased pace, Cyrus maintained strict situational awareness, his right hand never straying far from the butt of his pistol.

After riding for a while in a southwesterly direction, Cyrus crossed the Red River at the point where it turned back north and he felt a little safer now that he was back in Texas. At his current location he was about forty miles west of the ranch. The area he was riding through was wide open with no hint of civilization. That was all thanks to the Comanches and Apaches who constantly raided and frequently killed any settlers who were brave enough to venture that far west on the plains. One of the exceptions was Dan Waggoner, a man who'd ventured into these parts in the early 1850s. But even the Waggoners weren't immune to the Indians. Dan, his wife, and son, W. T., had settled a little farther south down on Catlett Creek when they first arrived, but that didn't last long. The Comanches took exception and, rather than looking over their shoulders every minute of every day, the Waggoners chose to move north to Denton

Creek, a tad bit closer to civilization. It wasn't until a couple of years ago that the Waggoners moved a third time to their current location on the Wichita River — the place Cyrus was now aiming for.

It wasn't long before Cyrus began seeing cattle with the familiar reversed three-D brand and he knew he was close. Dan and his crew had driven a large herd of cattle north to Kansas a few years ago and he had walked away with $55,000 in his pocket. With that money they began buying land and now had a nice spread. Not nearly as large as the Rocking R, but Cyrus had no doubt that Dan's spread would become as large as his own place and maybe larger. Dan was a shrewd man and, from what Cyrus knew about the son, it was obvious the apple didn't fall far from the tree.

The sun was settling low on the horizon when he came in sight of the Waggoner home. Cyrus hadn't been there in quite some time and it looked as if Dan had wasted neither time nor money making very many improvements and the house hadn't changed, either. It remained the same square, single-floor, boxlike structure and Cyrus thought Dan had probably left everything that way on purpose. It would be easier to flee without losing too much sleep about lost possessions if the Indians went on the warpath again. Five or six fine-looking horses prowled around in the timber-built corral adjacent to the ramshackle barn, the D-71 brand on their left front shoulders barely visible in the fading light. Cyrus didn't know why Dan used two different brands — one for the cattle and one for the horses — but he figured he must have a reason. Could be family related, Cyrus thought. His sons-in-law, Isaac and Amos, also used different brands on their horses than on their cattle although they all ran in the same herd with the Rocking R animals. Whatever the answer about the different brands, it didn't make a damn bit of difference because everyone in this part of the country knew who owned what.

As Cyrus rode closer to the house, a man stepped out on the porch. It was too dark to determine who it was, but the silhouette of a rifle barrel pointing at him was readily visible. The man was way too small to be Dan Waggoner and Cyrus thought it might be one of Dan's cowpunchers or maybe the young black boy that had once been Dan's slave when he first moved to Texas.

"Who's there?" the man shouted from the porch.

"Cyrus Ridgeway," Cyrus shouted back.

He saw the rifle barrel drift down until it was pointing at the ground and he sat a little easier in the saddle. "Who am I talkin' to?"

"It's me, Cyrus. Tom. How ya doin'?"

"I'll be better when I get off this horse." William Thomas (Tom) Waggoner, Dan's only child, had grown since the last time Cyrus had seen him.

"Climb on down," Tom said. "Leave your horse there and I'll have one of the hands take care of him."

"Much obliged," Cyrus said as he climbed down from the saddle. He took a moment to stretch his back and then walked up the porch steps to shake Tom's hand. "How old are you nowadays?"

"Just turned twenty-one."

"Hell, I already had a wife and a kid and another in the oven when I was your age. How come some gal hasn't scooped you up yet?"

Tom chuckled. "Women are pretty scarce around here. Besides, Pa keeps me too busy to do much lookin' around. Whatcha doin' down this way?"

"A group of Injuns took one of my young'uns. I aim to get her back."

"By yourself?" Tom asked, an incredulous note to his voice.

"No, I'm meetin' up with the others

tomorrow. Your pa around?"

"Yep. We're just sittin' down to a late supper. Come on in." Tom stepped over to the front door, opened it, and waved Cyrus through. Dan was sitting at the dining room table when he spotted Cyrus coming through the door. He smiled and stood, stepping over to shake Cyrus's hand. A tall, beefy, dark-haired man, Dan sported a full beard that was now more gray than black.

Dan pumped Cyrus's hand. "Been a long time, Cyrus."

"It has been, Dan. Good to see you. Hope you don't mind me bargin' in."

"You ain't bargin' in, Cy. You're always welcome here."

Dan's second wife, Sicily Ann, who was about half Dan's age, stepped out from behind the stove and walked over, giving Cyrus a hug. "How's Frances?" she asked, stepping back.

"Meaner than ever," Cyrus replied.

"You hush, now. That woman has a heart of gold."

"I reckon she does," Cyrus said. He looked at Sicily's flour-spattered apron and tried to hide his disappointment when he asked: "What happened to Gabriela, your Mexican cook?"

"She went back home," Sicily said. "Her

231

mother was sick." She saw the look of despair that briefly washed across Cyrus's face and laughed. "She left me her recipes, though."

"That's good," Cyrus said. "My mouth's been watering the last ten miles or so."

Sicily laughed again. "Have a seat. I've made a fresh pot of coffee and supper'll be ready in a minute."

Dan returned to his seat and Cyrus worked his way around the table and dropped into the chair opposite him. Tom chose a seat at one end of the table and they settled in as Sicily appeared with three steaming mugs of coffee, which she handed to the men. The three talked cattle prices, horses, and the weather for a few moments and then all talk died when Sicily placed a platter of steaming tamales down on the table. She retreated back to the kitchen and returned with a large pot of pinto beans, a plate of fresh corn tortillas, and a jar of freshly made salsa. As was typical, the men started eating before Sicily could get all the food on the table. Long, drawn-out meals were reserved for the city folk. Out here on the frontier, food was fuel. Cyrus grabbed a tortilla, filled it with beans, added a heaping spoon of salsa, rolled it up, and took a big bite. As he chewed, he noticed everyone around the table had stopped eating and was staring at him with grins on their faces.

Cyrus found out why a second or two later when he chomped down on a slice of pepper that set his mouth afire. He managed to swallow what was in his mouth and then he croaked, "Water, please."

Everyone laughed as Sicily stood, hurried into the kitchen, and returned with a cup of water. Cyrus swallowed it in one gulp and set the empty cup on the table. His face felt flushed and his eyes began to water as a fresh bead of perspiration popped on his forehead. "Coulda warned me," he mumbled. His tongue felt large and thick in his mouth.

"Hell, Cy, wasn't time to warn ya," Dan said, his smile spreading from ear to ear. "We got a new type of pepper up outa Mexico. They're a tad bit warm."

Cyrus coughed and said, "That's puttin' it lightly." He unrolled the tortilla, spooned most of the salsa off, and resumed eating. He swallowed that bite and said, "That's the hottest thing I ever put in my mouth. I don't know how you eat it."

"You get used to it," Tom said. "It takes a while."

"I bet," Cyrus said. He went easy on the salsa for the rest of the meal and the heat in his mouth finally subsided. Once the plates were cleared away, the three men pulled the makings out of their pockets and began rolling cigarettes. Once they were rolled to their satisfaction, Dan struck a match and lit all three.

Dan exhaled a cloud of smoke and said, "Tell us more about your young'un that's missin'."

"Ain't a lot to tell," Cyrus said. "She's Isaac and Abby's oldest daughter, Emma. Best I can tell from askin' around, I need to be lookin' for an Injun named Quanah Parker. Know him?"

"Know of 'im," Dan replied, the smoke curling out of his nostrils. "I hear he's a hard one to find and damn near impossible to catch. I s'pose the same could be said for all those wild Comanches."

Cyrus took a puff from his cigarette and blew out the smoke. "Seen any Comanches round here the last coupla days?"

"Nope. But, hell, you can't tell any of them Injuns apart so we treat 'em all as hostile until we know different. Even if they be friendly I don't want them around here eyein' my livestock, so we got us a shoot-first policy round here. I reckon that's why the Injuns are skittish 'bout comin' round too much. And I gotta couple of hands that could shoot a stinger off a wasp and Tom here ain't too bad a shot hisself. My eyes ain't so good anymore."

"I gotta lot that ain't good anymore," Cyrus said. "And I'm a might older'n you. Got any ideas 'bout where I could find this particular Injun?" Cyrus snubbed out his cigarette on a tin plate full of smashed cigarette butts.

"Out west is all I know, Cyrus," Dan said. "Somewhere out there in the big nowhere." He leaned forward and stubbed out his cigarette on the same plate Cyrus had used.

"I don't know even where to start," Cyrus said. "I got a man cuttin' sign, but you know how the Injuns are. They'll split up a half a dozen times somewhere along the way."

"I'd bet they were out somewhere along the Canadian or maybe further up west along the Pecos. Look for the buffalo. The Injuns won't be very far behind."

Sicily, carrying a bottle of hard-to-find Hennessy cognac and four glasses, returned to the table. She sat, poured two fingers in each glass, and passed them around, reserving one for herself.

"You didn't have to break out the good whiskey for me, Dan," Cyrus said.

"Don't matter. Gotta drink it sometime and you bein' here is cause enough." Dan lifted his glass and said, "To findin' your young'un."

The four touched glasses and they gulped down the contents. Cyrus put his glass on the table and turned to look at Sicily. "Didn't know you was a whiskey drinker."

"This is cognac. There's a big difference compared to that bathwater they sell in the saloons." She held up the bottle and asked, "Want more?"

Cyrus slid his glass over and she splashed in more cognac then added more to her own glass. "Dan, Tom, want more?"

Dan leaned forward and pushed his glass across the table. "Can't have you two drinkin' alone."

Tom followed suit and this time they sipped instead of guzzled.

"You beddin' down here?" Dan asked.

"If that's all right with you," Cyrus said.

"Be fine," Dan said. "Take the room in back." Dan pushed to his feet. "I'm beat. Cyrus, I'll talk to you in the mornin'."

"Night, Dan," Cyrus said. He drained his glass, put it on the table, and nudged it toward Sicily as Tom took his leave. "How about a nightcap?"

Sicily poured more into his glass, added a slug to her glass, and corked the bottle. Cyrus wanted to ask her why she and Dan had never had kids but held his tongue. It wasn't any of his business. He drained his glass and pushed wearily to his feet. "I'm too damn old to be settin' a saddle all day. Thanks for the hospitality, Sicily."

"You're welcome, Cyrus. Might want to sleep light."

"Why's that?"

"Saw some Indians way off to the west right before sundown."

"Dan said they were skittish about comin' round here."

"We've been lucky lately, but you never know what they're thinkin'."

"Great," Cyrus mumbled as he made his way to the back of the house and into the spare bedroom.

CHAPTER
31

Darkness enveloped them before Emma could really get a good look at the new, larger group of Indians, but she saw enough to know that they had arrived with captives of their own. Emma saw two small white boys who looked to be brothers and were maybe seven or eight years old, and two other white women who looked to be in their late thirties or early forties — judging age wasn't Emma's strong suit. But, like her, all had been stripped of their clothing, their skin blistered by sunburn, and all had been tied to their horses. In addition, all looked to be as frightened and as miserable as Emma was.

As the pack of savages rode through the darkness, Emma wondered if she'd ever get off the horse again. And then she recalled the abuses she endured when the Indians did dismount, and she hoped they rode all night long. The insides of her legs were chafed raw and the pain pulsed hot with every step of the horse. The taste of blood lingered in her mouth on the few occasions she could generate enough saliva to swallow, and her belly rumbled with hunger. Emma would gladly welcome an arrow to the heart just to end her suffering, but she knew that if she was to die at the hands of the savages, Scar would make it a slow and painful process.

Despite her agony, Emma's head lolled as her pony plodded onward. She hadn't slept since being captured, other than a few minutes here and there, and her mind was foggy as to how long ago that had been. It felt like they'd been traveling for weeks although Emma knew that wasn't the case. Nor did it really matter other than it helped Emma to estimate how long it would be before any rescue attempts could be made. If the family had discovered her absence immediately after it happened, then freedom could be riding only a half a day behind them. But she thought that highly unlikely. It would have been extremely difficult to track the Indians in the dark, so if they started at first light that next morning, Emma thought, then her father and grandfather could be a day or a day and a half behind.

However, the more Emma thought about it the more she fretted. Even if her saviors were only a day — or even two days — away they would be tremendously outmanned now that her little band had joined up with the larger pack of Indians. The only chance they'd have to rescue her would hinge on the willingness of her captors to negotiate. And she couldn't see Scar letting her get away without extracting his pound of flesh. The Indians could hide her somewhere and deny any knowledge of her existence, but even that depended upon the willingness of the two sides to talk rather than fight. Knowing her grandfather, it could be guns blazing before thoughts of discussion ever entered his mind. The word *guns* sparked Emma's brain down a new path of thought. She *did* know her grandfather and she knew he would exploit any advantage he could. And the biggest equalizer was already at hand — the war wagon. It would mean there'd been a delayed start and that Emma was in for more misery, but there was hope on the horizon. All Emma had to do was stay alive.

In the moonlight, Emma saw her horse's ears prick up and he quickened his pace as did the other horses. A few moments later she understood why when she heard splashing in the distance. *Water!* Her hope now was that they'd let her partake. Big Nose, leading her horse, splashed into the stream, and Emma braced for what she knew was coming. Big Nose untied the rope securing her to the horse and pushed her off into the stream. It wasn't more than ankle deep and Emma was momentarily stunned when she thudded to the ground on her back. But not knowing how much time they'd allow, she rolled up on her side and plunged her face down into the tepid water. It tasted awful, but Emma couldn't get enough of it. Her stomach began cramping with the sudden infusion of fluid and she had to slow until the cramping subsided. On the far bank she could see the Indians gathering wood in the light of the full moon and she hoped that meant food.

What she would soon discover was that fire also meant pain.

Emma drank until she could drink no more. Her immense thirst sated, she began to wonder if she could slip away in the darkness and confusion. Before she could get any farther down that road, someone grabbed her by the hair and began pulling her out of the water. Because of the darkness she couldn't see who was doing the pulling, but she had a sickening feeling it was her archenemy, Scar. With her hands still tied, she could do little to defend herself, and all she could do was endure. It felt like the skin at the top of her skull was going to be ripped from her head and she kicked with her legs, trying to ease the strain. In a few moments she was out of the water and was being dragged up the far bank, the brush tearing at her flesh. She could feel the stickers puncturing her skin as she clawed at the ropes binding her wrists. If she could free her hands, she might be able to snag a rock, a limb, a chunk of wood — anything she could use for a weapon.

The pulling stopped as abruptly as it had started, and she was immediately flipped onto her back. She looked up to see Scar's sneering face staring back at her in the moonlight. Using the last of her mental strength, Emma willed her body slack as he began to assault her. Other female screams shattered the silence, and, to Emma, it sounded like a scene straight out of hell. Emma stared at the moon overhead and tried to think of something that would take her mind off what Scar was doing. He paused long enough to slap her across the face and then continued, his hands now clawing her breasts as he grunted in exertion.

Then he was done. He slammed his fist into Emma's stomach, crushing the air from her lungs. As she struggled for air, he untied her hands, flipped her over, and jerked her arms behind her, and retied the rope. Then he slipped a rope around her ankles and drew her legs up behind her until she thought her hips were going to pop out of their sockets. He tied her that way, stood, grabbed the rope, and dragged her toward the fire. Emma wondered where Big Nose was and why he was allowing this to happen. Before she could formulate an answer, Scar dropped her on her belly, knocking the breath out of her again. As she gasped for air, Scar stepped away and returned a moment later with a red-hot stick in his hands.

In the moonlight, Emma could see Scar smiling when he touched the burning stick to the sole of her right foot. For the first time in a long time, Emma screamed. And she continued screaming as he pressed the stick down on the sole of her other foot.

Her screams died when she finally passed out.

Sometime later Emma came to. She was still strung up like a hog being slaughtered, but she was alone. The same couldn't be

243

said for the two older women the Indians had captured. Their anguished screams filled the night. Facedown in the dirt, Emma couldn't see what the savages were doing to them, but she could imagine. Her burned feet throbbed with every beat of her heart and she had to force her head to the side to keep from suffocating. Before passing out again she mentally began devising all the ways she could torture and kill Scar.

CHAPTER 32

That same full moon that was shining brightly upon the Llano Estacado was shielded somewhat here by the leaves of a large walnut tree under which Percy and Win had chosen to camp. They'd picked a wooded spot along Buck Creek, bypassing the larger Prairie Dog Town Fork of the Red River that ran nearby, hoping to avoid any wanderers — Indians, specifically — in search of a place to water their animals. Arturo had driven the wagon behind a thick copse of stunted blackjacks and they had unhitched the team, loosely hobbled them so they wouldn't run off, and turned them out to graze. Unsure if Indians were lurking, Percy had insisted on a cold camp and a rotating schedule of guards.

Now deep in the night, Percy was asleep when he heard a noise that immediately awakened him. He rested his right hand on the pistol he had kept in his lap and tuned his ears to the surrounding landscape. He was stretched on his bedroll, his saddle blanket folded over for a pillow. Then he heard it again. It sounded like the rustle of fabric rubbing against the brush. Percy cocked his Colt Peacemaker and the *click-click-click-click* was loud in the stillness of the night. They were making too much noise to be Indians, but Percy knew there were other threats out there — the family of the man he'd shot earlier slipping into the forefront of his mind.

Percy cocked his head one way then the other, hoping to pinpoint the location if it occurred again. Then a whisper up by his head. "Boss, it's me."

Percy released the held breath and lowered the hammer on his pistol. "Why are you sneakin' around, Arturo?" Percy whispered. He threw back the thin blanket and sat up.

"Vi algo."

"What did you see?" Percy whispered.

"No sé," Arturo whispered.

Percy leaned close to Arturo and whispered, "What do you mean you don't know?"

"Movimi —"

"English, please. My brain's too tired."

"Movement," Arturo whispered.

"Where?"

"Back the way we came."

Percy nodded and whispered to Arturo, "Wake the others."

Percy pushed to his feet and quickly strapped on his gun belt and seated his pistol before walking over to the wagon. He silently cursed himself when he immediately saw their folly. It had been a long time since he'd operated out on the prairie, but this was a beginner's mistake. Yes, the wagon was hidden but the guns were as useless as an unloaded rifle because there was no field of fire. For them to be useful the wagon would have to be pushed out into the open.

Win, Arturo, and Luis walked over to where Percy was standing. Percy mimicked pushing the wagon, and the three men nodded and took up positions. The wagon creaked and groaned when they started it moving, the noise loud in the quiet night. Slowly, they pushed the heavy wagon out to open ground. It wasn't the preferred location, but it was a damn sight better than where it had been. The new field of fire was limited by the trees on the right although Percy thought they'd have about 180 degrees of open area in which to operate. Enough, he hoped. While Percy climbed up in the wagon, the other three men scooted away to grab their rifles. When they returned, Percy directed Arturo and Luis to watch their rear and asked Win to cover the trees to the right. From all that Percy had seen during his Indian-fighting days, he expected all the fighting to occur out in the front. Percy double-checked that the Gatling gun was loaded and ready then settled in for the wait.

Percy didn't want a long, drawn-out engagement and his plan was to nip whatever this was in the bud as quickly as he could. And he hoped to do it without an enormous amount of bloodshed on either side. With that in mind, he leaned down and whispered to Win, "Load some canister shot in the cannon. When they show themselves, aim high enough not to kill anybody and light it up. If that don't work, reload and send 'em to hell."

Win nodded, placed his rifle on the wagon seat, and went to work loading the mountain howitzer. It was the one weapon that remained unloaded until it was needed, because the result of an accidental firing could be catastrophic. Percy studied the sky, searching for approaching cloud cover while pondering the situation. The Comanches were known for raiding while the moon was full, but they used that to their advantage to take their victims by surprise. Would they do the same against an armed enemy who was wide awake? he wondered. He fished his watch out of his front pocket and popped the lid to check the time. They had about three hours until sunrise and if they spent that time standing around waiting for who knows what, they'd all be exhausted when they needed to be at their sharpest. Percy stared into the distance and sniffed the air, trying to catch the smell of smoke. He didn't smell anything and, since he'd been alerted, had seen no signs of movement.

He began to wonder if Arturo was seeing things, but that would be unusual for such a sharp-eyed young man who was known to be as steady as any man on the ranch. Percy decided he had to take Arturo at his word, and he was back to his original question — Would the Indians wait for daylight to attack or would they even attempt an attack? They were a pair of unanswerable questions. The only way they'd know was to wait and find out. Percy thought about sending Win out to cut sign, but that would expose him unnecessarily and he decided against it. Percy decided to seek a second opinion. "Win," he whispered.

"Yeah, boss?" Win whispered back.

"Think they'll wait for daylight before makin' their move?" Percy asked, his voice barely above a whisper.

"Don't know," Win said. "Maybe."

"You're not helpin' me any." Percy made a decision. "You three get some shut-eye. I'll wake you if I need you."

With no arguments from the three, they walked over to their bedrolls and stretched out on the hard ground. Percy doubted they'd get much sleep, but who knew? Percy climbed over the wagon seat and sat down. All they could do now was wait.

CHAPTER
33

Cyrus was up and moving before the Waggoners' roosters even thought about crowing. Thoughts of wasted time had stirred him from sleep. Every second those savages had Emma was another second of possible torture she had to endure and that thought ate at Cyrus like a fresh gunshot wound. He knew what that felt like because he'd suffered several over his lifetime. After dressing, Cyrus slipped noiselessly out of the house and made his way to the barn, where he saddled his horse. After leading the horse out of the barn, Cyrus mounted up and steered his horse west.

The heat hadn't abated much with the darkness and it wasn't long until Snowball had worked up a lather. The full moon was still up, and it provided more than enough illumination for easy navigation. While his mount plodded along, he was still thinking about his granddaughter when a wave of sadness washed over him. Emma had been the one who named the horse he was now riding back when he was a small colt, and he wondered if Emma would be around to name other colts. He immediately wiped that thought from his mind. If he had to search for the rest of his life, he was going to get Emma back, no matter what. And if that meant killing a bunch of Injuns, then so be it.

He leaned forward and patted Snowball on the shoulder and forced his mind to think of something else. He didn't want to contemplate the task ahead because it appeared too daunting. So, his mind drifted to where it usually did when he wanted to think happy thoughts — his wife of over forty years, Frances.

Although his family had a vast swath of land, they never considered themselves rich. Frances Landry, on the other hand, had been born rich, although that played no role in drawing Cyrus's attention. He would have picked her out of a crowd if she'd been dirt poor. He couldn't put it into words why, it was just a feeling he'd had when he met her all those years ago in New Orleans. In town to buy some horses to crossbreed with the wild mustangs roaming across Texas, Cyrus had met her at a dinner hosted by an old family friend. Frances, dealing with the recent death of her father, who had been killed after gunplay erupted during a high-stakes poker game, was understandably melancholy, but when she did smile, it lit up the room. That smile, and his reaction to it, forced Cyrus to extend his stay in the city.

According to the stories Cyrus had heard, high-stakes poker games and whiskey drinking weren't unusual for Albert Landry, Frances's father. The only son of a wealthy tobacco plantation owner, Albert, with little interest in the family business, had moved the family to a large house in the French Quarter, where he whiled away his time with cards, mistresses, and whiskey. When his father died, Albert turned the plantation over to a foreman who oversaw a slew of slaves and, as many at the time had expected, the place eventually went to seed. After Albert's untimely death, the problems of the plantation landed at the feet of Frances's mother, Millicent. Frances quickly grew tired of all of it — her father's death, the plantation problems, the humid weather, the stench that seemed to linger over the city — and all she had wanted to do was to escape to somewhere else. And Cyrus obliged her after a month of courtship.

As Snowball plodded along, Cyrus smiled at the memory. Going from a large, bustling city to the Texas frontier had been a shock to Frances's system, but it wasn't long until Percy had come along, and the new family settled into a routine. He smiled again as he thought about those early years. There were bumps along the way, like most couples, but they'd weathered them. They lost three children to diseases or illnesses, which created periods of extreme sadness, but life was tough and the only thing they could do was pull their boots up and keep moving forward. The plantation's problems eventually landed in their laps early in 1860 and Cyrus and Frances, who saw the writing on the wall as talk of war spread across the country, liquidated everything and split the proceeds with Frances's three siblings. And they'd gotten out just in time because war broke out the next year, crushing land prices all across the South.

After traveling for a couple of hours, Cyrus hit the Pease River just as daylight was breaking on the horizon. Riding his horse down into the water, he let his horse drink his fill then spurred him up the far bank and followed the river west, hoping to strike Wildcat Creek before too long. Thoughts of Frances faded, and Cyrus turned his mind to what might lie ahead. He wondered if Percy's crew and the wagon were at the rendezvous yet or if they would be delayed further awaiting their arrival. Feeling the pressure of time again, he was hoping Wilcox had already scouted the Indians' trail and had some idea of what direction they should go. Thinking of that made him wish he'd made a harder run at Charlie Goodnight. Goodnight knew this country probably better than any white man alive plus he could speak Comanche a hell of a lot better than anyone else in his crew. But there was little he could do about it now. They had whom they had and that was it.

A little farther along, Cyrus's nostrils picked up a hint of woodsmoke. He peered into the distance, searching for signs of a fire, but with daylight coming on and the heat waves already shimmering, any smoke was difficult to see. Not knowing if they were friend or foe, Cyrus rode on, his right hand resting on his thigh, only inches from the butt of his pistol. After riding down into a gully and up the other side, he spotted the flicker of a campfire that looked to be about a half a mile away. Craving a cup of coffee, Cyrus spurred Snowball into a lope.

A few moments later as he drew closer, he slowed Snowball to a walk, recognizing the two men who were sprawled out on their bedrolls, their saddles acting as backrests. Cyrus reined his horse to a stop and climbed down. "You ain't got nothin' better to do than lay around camp all morning?"

Isaac Turner looked up at his father-in-law. "We been waitin' for you and the rest of 'em. What you want us to do?"

"Nothin', I guess," Cyrus said as he looked over at his other son-in-law, Amos Ferguson. "Where's Wilcox?"

"He rode out before dawn. Pour yourself a cup of coffee," Amos said. He knew Cyrus would be cranky after a couple of days in the saddle.

"I aim to, as soon as I get the saddle off," Cyrus said. He untied his saddlebags and tossed them on the ground, uncinched the saddle and slid it and the blanket off the horse's back and let them fall to the ground, then slipped off the bridle and waved his hand to shoo Snowball away. The horse walked away a few steps and began grazing as Cyrus dug his cup out of his saddlebag. He walked over to the fire, poured a cup of coffee, and pushed his hat back as he surveyed the lay of the land. What he saw before him was not much different from what he saw every day back at the ranch.

After taking a sip from his cup, he turned

and looked at Isaac and asked, "Seen any Injuns round here?"

"Nope. Ain't seen a human of any type, except you," Isaac said. "Find anything out back at Fort Sill?"

"Got a name, but even that's a guess I got from a Kiowa chief." Cyrus took another sip of coffee and stared off into the distance again. "You find any sign of the Injuns that took Emma?"

"Found a trail about a mile north of here," Amos said. "Don't know if they was the right Injuns or not. Wilcox says they's tracks all over the place."

"What's the name you come up with who mighta taken Emma?" Isaac asked.

Cyrus walked over and took a seat on the ground next to the fire. "Quanah Parker. Ever hear of 'im?"

"Nope," Isaac said. "But I aim to kill 'im first chance I get."

"He's Cynthia Ann Parker's boy."

"The Indian captive that went batshit crazy when they returned her to her white kinfolk?" Isaac asked.

"The same," Cyrus said. "They say he'll be a hard one to find. Might be out here a spell."

"How long you figure?" Amos asked.

"No idea," Cyrus said, "but I wouldn't make no Christmas plans if I was you."

Chapter
34

Percy had awakened Win, Arturo, and Luis before dawn, so they would be prepared to repel the assumed Indian assault. A good portion of Percy's brain still wasn't convinced there were any Indians within twenty miles of them, but even a small probability of their presence demanded constant awareness. Despite his uncertainty, Percy reasoned that if there were Indians about, they most certainly knew they and their wagon were nearby. Or that's the excuse he used in determining whether his need for coffee outweighed any potential danger — hence the coffeepot now simmering atop the coals of a small fire he'd built earlier.

The deciding factor in his decision came down to the number of Indians who might be in the area. If they numbered four or five hundred or less, he thought they were in pretty good shape. The mountain howitzer alone was like having two hundred extra rifles. But if there were more Indians than that — say, over five hundred — then it came down to a mathematical equation that involved reload times and firing rate. And Percy was too exhausted to do the math, so he estimated their chances as good to excellent for anything less than five hundred Indians, and fair to middlin' for any number over that. Either way, building a fire to make coffee wasn't going to make a damn bit of difference. Percy refilled his cup and returned to his place behind the Gatling gun.

Winfield Wilson carried his cup of coffee over to his place behind the mountain howitzer while Arturo Hernandez and Luis Garcia took up their rifles and positioned themselves on opposite ends of the wagon. Percy took a sip of coffee and said, "No killin' during this first run if they come. I'm hopin' our overwhelming display of firepower will break their will before any blood is shed."

"And if they keep comin'?" Arturo asked.

"I hope it don't come to that," Percy said. "No tellin' how many Injuns they could pull in from the reservations if we're here very long. My goal is to send them on their way so we can get the hell out of here."

Arturo took a sip from his cup then said, "You still ain't answered my question, *jefe.*

What happens if it don't go like you think?"

"Then I guess we aim to kill. Nothin' else we can do about it. But now that you mentioned it, it'd probably be better if you and Luis worked with Win on the cannon. Those two rifles of yours aren't goin' to make much of a difference. Luis, you pack the powder charge and Arturo, you ram the canister shot home. That'll speed up our firin' rate."

Arturo and Luis nodded and moved to the rear and rested their rifles in the wagon bed just in case they were needed in a hurry. Win's job was to fill the firing nipple with gunpowder and then place a musket cap on it that, when struck by the firing hammer Win controlled with a rope, would ignite the powder charge in the barrel. It's a routine they'd practiced sparingly, and Percy was hoping inexperience wouldn't be the deciding factor.

Percy turned his focus back to the area in front of them. He could see a long way and it looked as flat as a table, but Percy knew there were slight dips and rises and a few scattered ravines where the Indians could hide. If there were any Indians, Percy thought. The sky to the east was beginning to brighten and they all knew an attack could occur at any moment.

Percy studied the wagon layout, searching for weaknesses. The two guns were mounted on opposite ends of the wagon to allow a wider field of fire. The only hiccup Percy could think of involved the cannon's position in relation to the Gatling gun, but that would only occur if the Indians decided to flank them on their right, something he thought highly unlikely due to the dense timber over there. The Indians might try to sneak through the trees on foot in an attempt to pick them off. However, in Percy's past battles with Indians, he found them extremely reluctant to dismount from their fleet-footed ponies.

The thought of horses triggered a sudden panic in Percy. He looked across at his three companions and said in an urgent whisper, "We need the horses up here close or the Injuns will steal 'em."

Arturo and Luis jumped down from the wagon, grabbed a handful of ropes, and took off at a run. Percy was kicking himself for not thinking of it earlier and he glanced over his shoulder to check the duo's progress. It was the wagon team he was worried about. Their personal horses were well trained and would come at a whistle and he could hear Arturo and Luis whistling in the distance to call up their mounts. The mules

262

were another matter entirely and it often took a bucket of oats to get them close enough to put a rope on them. Percy did remember Arturo hobbling them last night and he was hoping they hadn't drifted too far.

Percy's thoughts of horses were obliterated a moment later when a cacophony of Indian war whoops shattered the stillness. The eerie sounds launched a waterfall of fear that raced down Percy's spine as he searched the distance for the enemy. "Where are they?" Percy shouted to Win.

Win pointed ahead. "They'll be comin' a-yonder out of that shallow ravine."

The words were no sooner out of Win's mouth when a line of Indian warriors charged over the lip of the gully. That group was quickly followed by another and then another and they spread out in a long line, racing their ponies forward. "How many, you reckon?" Percy asked.

"Coupla hundred, maybe," Win said.

The Indians were still a good distance away, but they were closing quickly. Percy glanced over his shoulder and was relieved to see that Arturo and Luis had secured the animals and were racing back to the safety of the wagon. He turned back to the front and said, "Remember, Win, aim high."

Win nodded. "How close you want 'em before I touch off this here cannon?"

"Two hundred yards ought to do it," Percy said.

The Indians and their ponies were painted for war and Percy could tell they were Comanches by the way they rode. It was if horse and rider were all one entity, fluid and graceful. If the Injuns weren't on a mission to murder them, Percy could have watched them ride all day. Percy grabbed the gun's handle, leaned down and aimed at a spot in the distance, and waited.

When he thought the Indians were close enough, Percy shouted, "Fire!"

The mountain howitzer roared, and a cloud of smoke swirled around the wagon as Percy cranked the handle of the Gatling gun, working the weapon from left to right and chewing up the ground about ten yards in front of the advancing warriors. As Win, Luis, and Arturo reloaded the cannon, Percy paused long enough to see the Indians turning their horses and racing away, just as he had expected. Arturo and Luis shouted their own war whoops as the Indians divided up and raced away.

"Think they'll try again?" Win asked.

"We aren't stayin' here long enough to find out. I'll stay on the gun and you three get the team hitched up."

Within minutes the team was hitched, and the wagon was ready to roll. Arturo and Luis clambered up on the wagon seat and Win mounted up and grabbed the lead ropes of the other three saddle horses. "Roll out," Percy said. He leaned against the seat and swiveled the gun around to keep it lined up on the retreating Indians. For that reason, it had been decided that Win would lead the other horses rather than tying them to the back of the wagon.

An hour later there were no more Indian sightings, but Percy remained in position just in case. He knew the Indians weren't done. Not by a long shot. They were excellent at guerrilla warfare and Percy knew they'd pester them all day, probing for any weaknesses.

He was just hoping they didn't find one.

CHAPTER
35

Rachel jolted awake at the sound of gunfire. She lay still a moment trying to pinpoint the direction the shots were coming from and it sounded like it was coming from somewhere down by the river. She pushed the covers off, stood, and slipped on her robe. Hurrying to the front door, she eased it open and stepped out onto the porch.

Bam, Bam, Bam. The shots were occurring in rhythm, which suggested it wasn't a gun battle or an attack on the ranch. It sounded more like target practice. But who gets up at the crack of dawn for target practice? Rachel wondered. She slipped back in the house, changed into a simple dress, and pulled on a pair of boots. She debated grabbing the rifle and decided against it. Whoever it was, they were going to get a barrage of angry words, not rifle bullets. Rachel exited the house again and stepped down off the porch.

Working her way around the house, Rachel took off toward the river as the shooting continued — *bam, bam, bam* — as quick as someone could cock the hammer and pull the trigger. It didn't sound like rifle fire, so she assumed it was a pistol. A horse nickered at her from the expansive pole corral that had been added onto more times than she could count over the years. Chickens bobbed and weaved around and through her legs, pecking at the hardscrabble earth in search of grubs as the shooting continued.

She wondered if Eli was practicing after she'd recently pointed out his shooting deficiencies, but that didn't sound like her brother, who wore a pistol only to shoot snakes on those rare occasions he ventured very far afoot. She supposed it could be one of the hands who was killing time before breakfast, and that angered her because there was so much to do with half the men on the ranch off looking for Emma. Whoever it was she was determined to put a stop to it — immediately.

Picking her way through a thick stand of scraggly trees, Rachel climbed up over a sandy berm that had formed from millions of years of flooding and put a hand up to shade her eyes as she scanned the shallow river. The gun was now silent, and she didn't know if the shooter had paused to reload or had decided that the fun was over. But as quickly as that thought entered her head, the shooting started again. Listening for a moment, Rachel pinpointed the location to a spot farther down the river and veered that way. Her vision blocked by an outcropping of brush, she could see the gun smoke drifting upward on the light morning breeze as she picked her way carefully across a sandbar, one of thousands that lined the riverbed, and increased her pace.

As she approached the outcropping of brush, she slowed, deciding it wouldn't be wise to sneak up on someone who was probably lost in thought as he or she banged away with a pistol. Rachel leaned forward and took a peek. And what she saw broke her heart. Seth, with one of Amos's old pistols and wearing one of his father's old gun belts, was repeatedly drawing his gun out of the holster and blasting away at a cottonwood tree on the far bank. Rachel leaned back out of sight as her brain clicked through options as the pistol continued to bark. *Do I want to confront him about it? Or should I ignore it and hope it's a phase he's going through?* They were difficult questions and, at twelve, he was at a stage of life where what happens could have lingering effects that could fester for years.

Her first instinct was to a put a stop to it right now — take the pistol and holster away from him and put them somewhere he could never find them. But guns where as ubiquitous as cattle on the ranch and if Seth wanted a gun, he'd find one. That forced her to realize this situation couldn't be about taking something away — he'd already had his dignity and innocence taken away. And whatever she did, it needed to be handled delicately or she risked pushing him farther away. After debating the issue for a few moments, she thought a conversation with her mother would be the best first step. Rachel turned and retraced her steps, climbing back over the berm and picking her way back through the trees. She saw Julia and Jacob, her two youngest, on the front porch, rubbing the sleep out of their eyes, and adjusted her course, walking over.

"Who's shootin'?" Jacob asked.

"I don't know," Rachel lied. "Sounds like someone's practicin'."

Jacob looked up at his mother and said, "Sounds like it's comin' from the river. Didn't you just come from there, Ma?"

Rachel quickly changed the subject. "Did you eat breakfast yet?"

"Miss Connie's making it now," Julia said. All the kids called Consuelo *Miss Connie* because they were unable to pronounce her full name until they were three or four years old and they had to call her something. Miss Connie was what Seth called her and it stuck.

"Where's Seth?" Jacob asked.

Mr. Inquisitive, Rachel thought. But Jacob had been that way since he began talking. "I don't know," Rachel said. "He'll be along any minute, I bet. Why don't you two get washed up for breakfast and I'll be back in a bit?"

"Where are you goin'?" Jacob asked.

Rachel pointed at the main house. "I'm goin' right there for just a teeny tiny minute."

"Why?" Jacob asked. "Aren't you gonna eat breakfast?"

"I need to talk to my mother, kinda like you and I are talking now," Rachel said. "If you'll save me some, I'll eat when I get back." Rachel turned around and started walking before Jacob could ask any more questions. She loved him to death, but he could wear a person down. With sweat already flowing freely, she pulled a strip of ribbon from her pocket and tied her hair up to get it off her neck. The remaining ranch hands were filing out of the bunkhouse, ready to start their workday. Most had lit cigarettes dangling from the corners of their mouths and all carried a mug of steaming coffee. Rachel greeted them and each either nodded or put a finger to their hat to return the greeting. She didn't know the exact number of men her pa hired, but the number always grew this time of the year as the ranch geared up for fall roundup, where they began the process of weaning the spring calves from their mothers. It was also the time of year when other ranches sent representatives to insure the correct brands were being applied to the calves. If the mama cow had a Rocking R brand, then that was the brand placed on the calf and vice versa for the other area ranches whose cattle all intermingled on the open range.

Clearing the bunkhouse, Rachel turned her thoughts from cattle to kids — specifically Seth.

Entering her parents' house through the back door, Rachel made her way to the kitchen, said "Morning" to her mother, who was cooking bacon, and poured herself a cup of coffee.

"Who's out shooting at the crack of dawn?" Frances asked.

Rachel took a sip from her cup, swallowed,

and said, "That's what I need to talk to you about."

"Oh dear."

"Yes, oh dear. Percy's kids stay here last night?"

"Chauncey and Franklin did. Amanda wanted to stay at home." Frances stirred the bacon around in the pan then looked up at her daughter. "Be better if we have that talk before they get up. Seth doin' the shootin'?"

Rachel nodded. "Yep. Down at the river with one of Amos's old pistols and an old holster that's about four sizes too big for him."

"That pistol's empowerment, or so he thinks."

"What do I do, Ma? Take the gun away from him?"

"Don't you dare. If he wants to go out there and shoot every mornin' you let him. It's a way for him to work through things in his own mind."

"And if he starts shootin' something other than trees?" Rachel asked.

"Then we'll have a problem. But I don't think that'll happen. He's got too good a head on his shoulders."

"Should I talk to him more? Try to find out what's really botherin' him?"

"We know what's bothering him, Rachel. He feels humiliated and ashamed. And talking more about it is not goin' to help matters any. Just let him be for a bit and I'll try to spend more time with him."

Rachel took another sip from her mug, while she spent a moment thinking about what her mother said. "Okay, we'll try it your way for a bit."

"Good," Frances said. "Maybe when Amos gets back, he can take the boy under his wing a little more."

"Yeah, like that's goin' to happen," Rachel muttered. "He's got about as much empathy as a tree stump."

Frances's anger flared and she pushed the pan of bacon off the burner and turned to face her daughter. "Rachel, life ain't always sunshine and daisies. We make do with what we have."

Rachel set her coffee cup on the table and looked up at her mother defiantly. "I'm about tired of making do."

CHAPTER
36

Abigail threw back the covers, climbed out of bed, pulled on a robe, and trudged into the kitchen aiming to put a pot of coffee on. But she soon discovered that she had neglected to add any wood to the stove last night and it was now as cold as Christmas morning. Sleep-deprived and exhausted, she stepped out the back door and looked at the stack of wood for a moment before deciding she didn't have the energy to start a fire. Instead, she shuffled around the exterior of the house and dropped wearily into one of the chairs on the front porch. Feeling helpless while Emma endured who knew what at the hands of those vile savages made her nauseous.

The front door swung open and ten-year-old Wesley wandered out, his hair tousled from sleep. Abby turned, offered him a faint smile, then turned back, staring at nothing as Wesley took a seat next to her.

"Ma," he said softly. When his mother didn't respond he said, "Ma" a little louder.

Abby turned slowly, looked at her son, and snapped, "What, Wesley?"

"Never mind," Wesley said, ducking his head as if she was going to hit him.

It took Abby a moment to realize her response was all wrong, and she draped an arm over his narrow shoulders and pulled him close. "I'm sorry, son. Just got a lot of things on my mind."

"I know, Ma. Me, too."

That statement shattered what was left of Abby's heart. Of course Emma's brother and sister would be worried sick about her, but Abby had been so busy wallowing in self-pity, she'd failed to see it. She pulled Wesley closer and said, "I'm sorry for snapping at you. And I know you're hurtin', too."

Wesley looked up at her and she thought he looked more and more like her brother Percy every day. If he had any of Isaac in him it wasn't much. His eyes shimmered and she could tell he was trying his best not to cry. She lifted her hand and gently pulled his head to her chest and he burst into tears. Abby held him, angry at herself for neglecting the needs of her two other children and vowed to do better. After a few moments, the tears tapered off and Wesley wrestled out of her grasp and wiped his eyes.

"When do you think . . . Pa and Emma will be back?" he asked between sniffles.

"Soon, I hope." She knew it could be a long time before they returned, but that was not something she wanted to burden her son with.

Abby and Wesley rocked for a while in silence, each consumed with their own thoughts. A dust cloud hung over the large corral where Eli and the ranch hands were separating the calves from their mothers — the mama cows bawling for their babies and the calves crying out their replies. And for the first time in her life, Abby felt some sympathy for the mama cows and better understood their pain.

After a few moments of listening to the cattle and contemplating the difficulty of the fact that life had to continue on, Abby said, "Are you hungry?"

"Yeah," Wesley said.

"If you'll wake your sister and get the fire going in the stove, I'll go gather us up some eggs."

"Okay," Wesley said as he pushed to his feet and disappeared back inside.

Abby stood and shuffled off to the chicken coop. Looking up when she heard a door slam, she spotted Rachel exiting their parents' house and she gave a halfhearted wave and continued on, knowing her sister would walk over to offer up more consolation. But Abby was tired of being comforted and she wasn't much in the mood for conversation, either. Opening the door to the coop, Abby picked her way around the chicken scat to the roosting box and began gathering eggs. The ranch had one large chicken coop that was available for family use and it operated on a first come, first served basis and Abby was surprised to find a good number of eggs still there. The chickens roamed free most of the day and the coop had a small door where they could come and go that was closed and locked at night to keep predators out.

"How are you holding up?" she heard her sister say.

Abby didn't answer as she carefully placed the eggs into the pocket of her robe. Once she had a dozen, she decided that was enough and stepped back outside. "Who was doin' the shootin' this mornin'?" Abby asked as she pushed open the door and stepped out, closing the door behind her.

Rachel sighed and said, "Seth. Ma thinks I should just let him be. What do you think?"

"Probably should. I can't see that it's hurtin' anything," Abby said as she started walking back to the house.

Much to Abby's consternation, Rachel fell in beside her. "You don't think he'll try to go do something foolish, do you?"

"I don't think so. Those men who roughed him up are already dead."

Rachel glanced up and saw Seth walking back from the river, the gun and holster nowhere in sight. "Here he comes," Rachel said. "He must be hiding the gun somewhere down there. I don't know what to say to him."

"Why do you have to say anything?" Abby asked. "If we're lucky maybe he'll kill a few Injuns."

CHAPTER
37

Seth saw his mother and his aunt jawing as they walked through the yard and he hurried around the house to the back porch, where he waited to hear the front door closing before picking up the milk bucket and heading toward the barn. There was no doubt his mother had heard the shooting and he wasn't up for answering any questions at the moment. In fact, he didn't want to see or talk to anyone at all.

When he reached the barn, he slid open the large rolling door and slipped inside. Every morning one of the ranch hands drove the milk cows into the barn for milking and Seth walked down the row of stalls and spotted one of his favorite cows, Molly, and stopped. Leaning down to see if she had already been milked, Seth was glad to see her swollen udder. He opened the gate and stepped inside. He liked Molly because, unlike some other ornery cows, she rarely kicked, and her milk flowed easily. And that was exactly what he was looking for this morning. His right arm felt like lead and his hand ached almost as bad as his blistered butt. To add to his misery, the repeated hammer cocking had ripped his thumb wide open.

He talked softly to Molly, a red shorthorn with white spots, as he worked around the stall. Longhorn cows didn't produce enough milk to fill the belly of a newborn kitten, so his grandpa had brought in twenty or thirty shorthorn cows years ago to fulfill the ranch's milk needs. Seth knew there was a breeding method that led to continued milk production, but he hadn't spent that much time studying it. And he wasn't spending any time thinking on it today — he was more focused on his shooting mechanics and how to correct his mistakes. He was pretty quick at getting the gun out, but his aim was always off. And if he concentrated on aiming, then the gun was slow to come up. He needed to learn to shoot like Percy, who made drawing and shooting look effortless.

Forgoing the stool since he wouldn't be able to sit on it, Seth nudged some cow dung out of the way with the toe of his boot and knelt down, placing the bucket under

Molly's udder. Working with only his left hand, he grabbed one of her teats up high and squeezed as he gently pulled his hand down, shooting a stream of milk into the bucket. Using both hands, Seth could have milked the cow in about five minutes but operating one-handed was another matter entirely. He couldn't get into a rhythm and he didn't have the strength in his left hand that he had in his right. After twenty minutes he had less than a half a bucket of milk and called it quits. His ma would be angry with him, but Seth decided if she wanted more milk, she could send Jacob, or she could do the milking herself.

Seth grabbed the bucket's handle, mumbled a kind word or two to Molly, and exited the barn. Spotting his uncle Eli leaning against the corral with a cup of coffee in his hand, he walked over and set the milk bucket down.

"How are you feeling, Seth?" Eli asked.

"Okay, I guess," Seth said. "Can I ask you a question?"

"You may."

"Will you teach me how to shoot?"

Eli smiled. "I don't believe you want me for that job, Seth. If you don't believe me, ask your mother. Your uncle Percy would be a much better instructor."

"But Uncle Percy ain't here."

"No, he's not. And *ain't* isn't a word, Seth. Is this a time-sensitive matter?"

"No, not really." Seth looked down and pushed some dirt around with the toe of his boot.

"Is the recent incident the reason for your sudden interest in shooting?"

Seth shrugged. "I don't know. Maybe."

"A weapon in your hand does not make you a man, Seth. For some men, a weapon is a crutch they rely on when they don't know how to resolve a problem with their mind."

Seth's cheeks turned red with anger. "How was my brain going to help me the other day? Huh? You had a gun and used it, too."

"I did. I did not say a person never needed a gun. There are times when the discharge of a weapon is warranted."

"Well, that's why I want to know how to shoot. For the next time."

Eli sighed. "Assuming there is a next time."

"I ain't that old. There'll be a next time."

"No, you aren't that old. And that brings me to my second point — your age. Don't you think you are a bit young to be handling a pistol? Rifles should be the weapon of

282

choice for boys your age."

"No, I don't. And I had a rifle and those men took it away from me."

"Another disadvantage to relying on weapons as your only means of defense."

Seth picked up the bucket of milk and looked up at his uncle. "Thanks for nothin'." He turned and started for the house.

Eli sighed again. "Wait, Seth."

Seth turned and glared at his uncle. "What?"

"Come here, please."

Seth stomped back, the milk sloshing in the bucket.

"Put your bucket on the ground for a moment," Eli said.

Seth complied.

"First," Eli said, pointing at Seth's damaged right hand, "it might be a good idea to find a tight-fitting glove to wear while you're practicing."

"Okay, I can do that."

"And second, the only piece of advice I can offer on shooting is to think of the pistol as an extension of your arm."

"What do you mean?"

"Uncle Percy would be a much better tutor but think of the barrel of the gun as your index finger. You don't necessarily aim, but rather, you point the barrel at your target like you would point at it with your finger. Does that make sense?"

Seth nodded. "I think so."

"I don't know what you are trying to accomplish or what type of scenario you envision, but my final piece of advice is that speed is vastly overrated. Accuracy is of paramount importance. When it comes to gunplay, second chances are a rarity."

"I'm not tryin' to be a gunfighter or anything, Uncle Eli. I just want to learn how to shoot."

"That's comforting and understandable. From what I gather, gunslingers have a very abbreviated life span. Now, you should take that milk to your mother."

"Thanks, Uncle Eli," Seth said. On the way back to the house, he rolled what Eli had said around in his mind. No, he wasn't aiming to be a gunfighter, but if he got to be good enough, who knew what could happen? One thing he knew for certain was that no one would lay a hand on him ever again.

CHAPTER
38

The screams of the two older women had faded sometime during the night, but Emma didn't know if that meant they were dead or whether the savages had simply stopped their torment of them. Either way, they remained quiet as the sun's first rays stretched across the landscape. The Indians had danced some type of dance that involved the scalps taken during their raids and a portion of that dance was reserved for their captives, who were ceremoniously slapped and beaten about their heads and upper torsos in some type of crude ritual. Emma had weathered that, but her feet had ached something fierce all night where Scar had burned them.

However, the one positive — if Emma could think of any positives — was that the ceremony had included food, or something that would have resembled food if it had been cooked. Once the festivities wound down, Big Nose had untied her and had handed her a piece of barely cooked meat that was unidentifiable in the dark. But Emma was hungry, and she had somehow choked it down, the blood running down her chin and dripping onto the dirt. The captives had also been given water, but in insufficient amounts to quench their thirst.

Emma awoke with her mouth as dry as a powder keg. After those few moments of kindness during the night, Big Nose had hog-tied her again and it now felt as if her shoulders were on the verge of separating from her body. And whatever she'd eaten had caused her stomach to revolt and Emma had soiled herself during the night and her own stench was now gag-inducing.

Although awake, Emma hadn't yet opened her eyes. The longer her captors thought her unconscious or asleep, the better. She had tried to talk to the other captives earlier and for her efforts had gotten a whipping across her blistered back with a willow switch. Lying on her left side, Emma slowly opened her right eye to see one of the young boys lying about three feet away. His right eye was swollen nearly shut, but his left eye was open, and he was staring at Emma — or rather staring in her direction. His gaze appeared vacant and whether he registered her presence, Emma didn't know. She summoned a small measure of humanity from the reserve that still lived somewhere inside her, and she smiled, hoping for a response. But none was forthcoming. She could see his chest rising and falling so she knew he was alive. She coughed and when she saw his eye refocus on her, she smiled again. His response was to turn his head, breaking visual contact. Emma took a deep breath, held it for a moment, then released it in frustration. If they — the captives — couldn't band together in the name of humanity, then all hope was lost.

Emma coughed again, and after a few moments the boy turned to look at her. This time he held her gaze and, rather than smile, Emma nodded at him and he nodded back. Progress, Emma thought. She mouthed the words, "hang in there," and the boy nodded again as tears began leaking from the corners of his eyes. Emma felt her eyes watering up and tears slid down her nose and dripped onto the dirt. They weren't tears of sadness, anger, or pain. They were tears of — not joy, there was no joy to be had here — but of relief at having made human contact with another person who had no intentions of doing her harm. And it was the first time she'd felt that since the

Indians had captured her.

Emma turned her head to see Big Nose walking toward her. Although she had no idea what he had in store for her, she felt instant relief that it was him and not Scar. She hadn't seen Scar again after he had assaulted her last night and she thought he had probably been busy partaking in the torture of the two older women. And her emotions were mixed on that. She felt terrible for them, but anytime Scar was occupied elsewhere was good for her.

Big Nose squatted down beside her, and Emma braced herself for whatever might come. Instead, Emma was surprised when he untied her and helped her to her feet. Stiff and sore from being hog-tied all night, Emma took a tentative step forward and winced in pain when her burned foot struck the ground. She paused, inhaled a deep breath, and took another tentative step, determined to walk wherever they were going. The pain was agonizing, but it was much better than being dragged around by the hair. Once her limbs loosened up, Emma clenched her jaw against the pain as Big Nose took her by the elbow and steered her toward the creek. Once there, he mimicked washing himself and nodded toward the water. Emma waded in, the cool water caressing her burned skin. She angled for a deeper pool and sank down up to her neck. First, she drank until she could drink no more, then she began washing the filth off her body. Why Big Nose was being nice was a question never far from her mind. Were they allowing her a chance to clean up in readiness for a human sacrifice? Or was there another sinister reason? She tamped down the questions bombarding her brain and allowed her body to relax.

With the sun up, she could see other Indians moving about. The Indians hadn't erected any teepees, so she assumed this was a temporary resting place. How long they'd stay was an unknown. Emma would prefer to be on the move because the longer they stayed in one place, the greater the risk for further abuse. Then her thinking changed. If they stayed for a while it would give her father and grandfather a better chance to catch up. If they had been persistent — and she knew her grandfather would be — then freedom might be at hand. Or closer, at least, Emma thought. Those thoughts were interrupted when Big Nose shouted something in his native language. Emma looked up and he waved at her to get out. Well, whatever was going to happen was going to happen soon.

Emma swam toward the bank and waded out of the water. Although she would have preferred a bar of soap, she felt clean for once. And she smelled better, too. She prepared her mind for another assault but was surprised again when Big Nose took her by the elbow and led her back to camp, the pain pulsing up her legs from her burned feet. Emma's head was on a swivel, searching for Scar as Big Nose steered her away from the other captives and through a throng of mulling Indians. Emma's body was tensed up, awaiting the blows. But the Indians didn't show much interest and Emma wondered if Big Nose had staked his claim for her and the other Indians had acceded to his wishes. It was confusing. Emma couldn't see Scar abiding any such agreement no matter who said what.

A few steps later, they came to a spot where several Indians were sitting cross-legged in a circle. Big Nose began speaking while Emma stood and studied the faces of the Indians who were assembled. This was some type of council or whatever the Indians called it, which meant one of these men was the man in charge. She watched their interactions with Big Nose and she quickly pegged the Indian with long braids and a bright piece of cloth tied around his neck as their leader. The man had a distinctive face with a knife-blade nose, high cheekbones, and a piercing gaze. After a few moments, he stood and walked over. He examined Emma as if he was studying a horse and his gaze traveled up and down her body. Emma stood defiantly, trying to mask the fear coursing through her body.

The chief spent a long time studying her face then turned to look at Big Nose and said something terse in his native tongue and Emma saw Big Nose flinch. Big Nose leaned down and picked up a stick and drew something in the dirt. Emma was busy watching their facial expressions, trying to interpret what was being said. When the chief looked down at the ground, Emma saw anger wash across his face. Emma's heart accelerated, not knowing what was coming. She glanced down at the ground and her knees sagged a bit when she saw what Big Nose had drawn.

In a patch of dirt of this godforsaken country was a crude drawing of the Rocking R brand.

CHAPTER
39

Having not slept at all the previous night, Percy found it difficult to keep his eyes open as the wagon rumbled across the prairie, even with the threat that an Indian attack could occur at any moment. And that made him angry. He could remember riding for days with no sleep, and, yes, he had been much younger then, but he hated it when people used aging to explain away a weakness. And it wasn't like he was on the downward slide to his last roundup, either. At forty-three he was as healthy and fit as he had ever been so there wasn't any excuse as to why he couldn't keep his eyes open, but he was finding it a nearly impossible task. He wasn't too worried about a surprise attack because Win and Arturo were ranging out far enough to provide early warning. With that in mind, he asked Luis to slow the wagon for a moment and Percy slipped over the side. One way to keep sleepiness at bay, he thought, was to walk.

They were traveling west with an eye on the Prairie Dog Town Fork of the Red River as a guide a half a mile south of them. With the Indians somewhere around and the river a perfect ambush site, Percy had no interest in getting any closer. The area they were now traveling through was devoid of trees other than the ones clumped along the riverbank and the ground was cut up in areas by dry washes — ugly scars upon the landscape created by centuries of rain. In the distance, Percy could just make out a large herd of grazing buffalo through the heat waves shimmering above the sunbaked earth. The buffaloes' being relatively close was a concern because they were the Indians' primary food source. And where you found one, you often found the other. Percy walked a little closer to the wagon in case he needed to hop aboard quickly.

Grasshoppers were as thick as flies in a hog pen and they fluttered aloft by the dozens with each step. Those that weren't flying were busy making noise by rubbing their hind legs against their forewings and, mixed in with that, was the clicking and buzzing of what sounded like a million cicadas. With the noise and the blazing sun, Percy deemed himself sufficiently awake and clambered back aboard the wagon, drenched in sweat. He stepped over the wagon seat and sat down next to Luis, who had a firm grasp on the reins.

"¿Visto indios?" Percy asked.

Luis shook his head. "No indios. ¿A dónde fueron?"

"I don't know where they went," Percy said, scanning the horizon. "But you can bet they're around here somewhere."

"¿Dónde aprendió español?" Luis asked.

"I picked it up here and there. Where did you learn English?"

"Same," Luis said. "¿Cuánto tiempo más?"

"I'm hopin' we make the rendezvous well before dark," Percy said.

The two rode in silence for a while. Luis steered the wagon around a washed-out area, the wagon bouncing up and down with every dip in the terrain. The ride was so rough that Percy was thinking about climbing aboard his horse that Win had tied on at the back. The wagon hadn't been designed for comfort. The initial design called for leaf springs to be installed on both ends of the wagon bed. But after a flurry of letters back and forth between the ranch and the wagonmaker in Chicago it was decided that the springs wouldn't hold up to repeated firings of the cannon. So off came the springs and with it a more comfortable ride. Luis elbowed Percy in the side and nodded down the trail as he brought the mules to a stop.

Ahead, Win was racing his horse back toward the wagon. Percy glanced right and saw Arturo also loping back in. Percy scrambled back over the seat and returned to his spot behind the Gatling gun as both men reined their horse to a stop almost at the same time. Win turned to look at Arturo and said, "You cut their sign out on the right flank?"

Arturo nodded.

"Whose sign?" Percy asked.

Win pulled off his hat and wiped his face with his right sleeve. "I cut the trail of a pack of Injuns that leads down to the river. Can't be more than an hour old."

"Maybe they're waterin' their horses," Percy suggested.

"Don't think so," Win said. "I think they got their eye on that there wagon."

"Well," Percy said, "they aren't gettin' it. Could you tell if it's the same group from this morning?"

"I don't think it is," Win said.

Percy mumbled a curse word or two. "How many in this group?" he asked Win.

"I reckon there's about thirty-five to forty," Win said.

Win and Arturo climbed down from their horses, hitched them to the rear of the wagon, and climbed aboard. "What's yer plan this time?" Win asked. "Might be better if we was to bloody their noses a little."

"We do that, they'll be after us for days," Percy said. He turned to Luis and said, "Let's move. Angle us away from the river."

Luis nodded as he clucked his tongue and slapped the reins. The wagon began to roll as Percy pondered the situation. It was the same situation they'd faced earlier. He really didn't want to kill any of the Indians because their response would be ferocious and lengthy. But on the other hand, their continued presence was a time killer and a nagging worry. "Let's just see how it plays out," Percy said.

"Want me to give them a li'l taste of the cannon?" Win asked.

"Why not," Percy said. "But let's get the horses away from here first."

Arturo took that as his cue, and he wove his way around the guns and untied the horses. Standing on the lip of the bed, he pulled his horse up even with him and threw a leg over the saddle. He led the other horses a good distance away and kept a tight grip on their reins.

While that was happening, the hair at the

back of Percy's neck stood up and a wave of foreboding raced down his spine. Something was wrong.

Very wrong.

And it didn't take him long to figure it out — the two groups of Indians weren't separate units, they were working in concert.

"Stop, Win," Percy shouted as he turned to wave Arturo back to the wagon. But he was too late. An Indian stood up out of the tall grass behind Arturo and loosed an arrow that pierced his back. "They've got us in a cross fire," Percy shouted as Arturo buckled over and slid off his horse. "Win, take the river," Percy shouted as he swiveled the Gatling gun around to cover their right flank. The cannon roared, and Percy heard the canister shot rip through the trees lining the riverbank as he aimed for the spot where the Indian appeared and turned the crank, sweeping the gun from left to right. He spied their horses bolting out of the corner of his eye, but that was the least of their problems.

"Luis," Percy shouted, "drive the wagon over to Arturo."

Luis slapped the reins across the team's rumps and put the mules into a run. It made shooting with any accuracy extremely difficult, but that was the beauty of the gun

— there wasn't a lot of aiming involved because you'd eventually hit whatever you were shooting at if you kept turning the crank. Win was busy reloading the cannon and, with lack of targets, Percy stopped firing.

"Don't see much," he shouted to Win.

"Not much on my side, neither," Win said. "I don't reckon they're stupid enough to mount a charge."

Nearing the spot where Arturo fell, Luis hauled back on the reins and brought the team to a stop. He set the brake and jumped down. It took him a moment to find Arturo in the tall grass and when he did, Percy saw him kneel down beside his friend of many years. Percy jumped into the wagon seat, released the brake, drove the wagon closer. Arturo was facedown and remained motionless as Percy heard Luis mutter a prayer in Spanish. He broke off the remainder of the arrow shaft and rolled Arturo over onto his back. Percy winced when he saw the razor-sharp, steel-headed arrow protruding from Arturo's chest.

"Get him in the wagon," Percy said, "and we'll give him a proper burial when we can."

Luis angrily yanked the remainder of the arrow out of his friend's chest, leaned over and grabbed him under the arms, and lifted him up. He dragged Arturo over to the wagon and Win helped pull the body on board as Percy scanned the area for Indians.

"What's their plan?" Percy asked Win as Luis climbed back up to the wagon's seat with tears dripping from his cheeks.

"They're gonna try and pick us off one at a time," Win said.

Percy handed the reins to Luis. "Get us out of here and keep us out in the open as much as you can."

"Hold up a sec," Win said. "I want to know who we're fightin'." He slid over the side of the wagon and reached down and grabbed the broken arrow and climbed back on.

Luis released the brake and slapped the reins, putting the wagon in motion.

Win spent a moment studying the shaft and the fletching, then tossed the arrow overboard and wiped his bloody hands on his pants.

"Well?" Percy said.

"Comanche," Win said.

Percy gave Win a hard look and said, "We're now shootin' to kill and we're goin' to kill as many of those bastards as we can."

Win nodded and worked his way back to the cannon.

CHAPTER
40

Leaning over to pour another cup of coffee, Cyrus stood when he heard a faint boom from somewhere in the distance. He cupped a hand around his ear and turned his head, listening. A few seconds later, he heard a vague *tat, tat, tat* of what sounded like rifle fire that was almost inaudible. But from the rhythm of the shots he knew it had to be the Gatling gun. He splashed the dregs from his cup into the fire and shouted, "Mount up!" He nudged the coffeepot out of the coals with the toe of his boot and then started kicking dirt on what was left of the fire.

Amos, who was sprawled out on his bedroll and leaned back against his saddle, said, "Where we goin'?"

"To kill some Injuns," Cyrus said as he hurried over to grab his gear. "Now get your ass up and movin'."

Amos pushed to his feet and began rolling

up the tarp he'd been lying on. "What Injuns you talkin' about?"

Cyrus began cramming stuff into his
saddlebags. "What's wrong with your ears?
Percy's crew is shootin' at somethin'."

"I didn't hear nothin'," Amos said.

Cyrus didn't bother to reply. "Isaac, you
and Wilcox gather up the horses and be
quick about it."

"I knew I heard something," Wilcox said
as he and Isaac hurried off without argument.

Within ten minutes, they were mounted
up and ready to ride and all they needed
was a direction. Cyrus knew the sound of a
rifle could travel long distances on windless
days and across flat terrain. He also assumed that Percy and his crew were somewhere between where they were sitting now
and the ranch. With all that in mind, Cyrus
pointed to the east and they set off. Cyrus
steered his horse toward Wilcox and fell in
beside him. "Did you hear it?" Cyrus asked.

"I heard a faint boom, but nothing else,"
Wilcox said.

"How far you think?"

"Four, maybe five miles."

" 'Bout what I figured," Cyrus said.
"Range out a ways and see what you can
find. I got no hankerin' to ride into a bunch

301

of Injuns on the warpath."

Wilcox nodded and spurred his horse into a lope. Cyrus nudged his horse with his spurs and put Snowball into a canter. The other men quickly followed suit. They began pulling their rifles from their scabbards, their eyes scanning in every direction. After riding fairly hard for a half an hour, Cyrus slowed his horse to a walk as did the other men. The worst thing they could do was arrive at an Indian fight with used-up horses. On a normal day, Cyrus would have pushed the pace, but the suffocating heat took its toll on both man and beast.

It wasn't much longer until Cyrus spied Wilcox riding back their way. He was walking his horse and riding easy in the saddle, but he was also busy scanning the ground and the surrounding area. Cyrus assumed from his body language that the threat of an Indian attack was no longer imminent. Spurring Snowball into a trot, he rode out to meet him.

Both men reined to a stop. "Any Injuns?" Cyrus asked.

"A whole passel of them," Wilcox said. "I cut several fresh trails, but I ain't seen nary a one. Percy and his crew are comin' along in the wagon. Injuns been trailin' them for the better part of two days. One of the Injuns snuck up on Arturo while he was ridin' out away from the wagon and put an arrow in him."

"Is he alive?" Cyrus asked.

Wilcox shook his head. "He was dead before he hit the ground."

Cyrus took a deep breath and let it out. "He was a good hand."

"Yep, he was."

The two sat in silence for a moment. Cyrus pushed his hat back, pulled his neckerchief out of his back pocket, and mopped his face as the rest of Cyrus's crew caught up with them. Cyrus wasn't too concerned about an immediate Indian ambush because they were a good distance from the river and clear of anything that could offer the Indians concealment. Even the tall grass had been chomped down by a grazing herd of buffalo that must have recently passed through. So, they sat and waited for the wagon to catch up to them, which it did after a few minutes.

Cyrus and his men turned their horses and fell in with the wagon. Spurring his horse to catch up, Cyrus slowed as he came abreast. He nodded at Percy in greeting and his son returned the nod. "Can't shake the Injuns?"

"Hard to do when you can't go no faster

than a walk," Percy said.

Cyrus looked at Win, who was sitting in the wagon bed next to the cannon. "How many, you figure?"

"Probably a hundred in all," Win said as he scanned the riverbank for hostiles. "They're too scared to make a run at the wagon."

"I would be, too," Cyrus said. "All we can do is keep ridin' the trail. Either they'll get tired of trailin' us or they'll make a move. Ain't nothin' we can do about it." Cyrus swiveled his gaze to Percy. "Lost Arturo, huh?"

Percy's feathers got a little ruffled at the question. "Not a damn thing we could have done about it."

"I didn't say there was," Cyrus said.

"You didn't have to," Percy said. "I could hear it in your voice."

Cyrus turned back to Win. "Grab your horse and you and Wilcox go scout. Isaac, take over the cannon." He knew his son was angry with him, but he didn't give the matter much thought. Anger and sadness were better left to the weak willed. Out here, any thoughts about anything other than doing your job could get you killed in a hurry.

As the wagon continued to roll, Isaac lined up beside it and stepped out of the saddle and onto the wagon. Walking toward the rear, he led his horse around and tied off the reins. Win did the same in reverse and everyone settled in, their gazes constantly sweeping the surrounding terrain. Cyrus and Amos hung close while Win and Wilcox lengthened their distance out to a hundred yards or so as they cut sign.

After the adrenaline rush from the earlier action, Percy's fatigue worsened. He sat down beside the Gatling gun and leaned his back against the wagon seat. He pulled his pipe from his front pocket, filled the bowl with tobacco, stuck it in his mouth and reached for a match before pausing. He was so tired he hadn't been thinking straight. It would be incredibly dumb, he realized, to strike a match while sitting in a wagon full of gunpowder. He pulled the cold pipe from his mouth and dropped it into his shirt pocket. That was, he presumed, the reason the Indians hadn't fired any conventional weapons at them, hoping to capture the wagon intact.

But, Percy wondered, what would the Indians' response be if they realized they had no hope of winning the wagon? As that question zinged around inside his tired brain, he recalled seeing Indians shoot signal arrows that were tipped with gunpowder and hide glue. What were the odds the Comanches would construct their own fire arrows? he wondered. Could that be a glaring weakness they had all overlooked? The gunpowder used to arm the cannon was stored in a tin can with a lid to keep it dry, but how much had been spilled during loading? It was something to consider, Percy thought.

He turned and leaned against the side of the wagon, so he could observe the area ahead and the river at the same time. Thinking the likeliest attack would come from somewhere down by the water, he reached up and swiveled the gun around so that it was pointing in that direction. As the team plodded on, the crunch of the wheels through the dirt was like a ticking clock in a quiet room and Percy found himself nodding off again, his head bouncing off his chest. He opened his eyes and shook his head, trying to clear the cobwebs, but within minutes his head was lolling again. He couldn't remember the last time he'd felt so tired. The nights caring for Mary weren't easy although, with enough laudanum on board, she'd often sleep for long stretches, which allowed him a chance to nap. *I wonder how Mary is?* He opened his eyes and steadied his head. That thought stirred him out of his reverie for good. The old familiar sensations were back in an instant — the constant worry, the clenching of his guts.

But even those thoughts were pushed aside when he heard a loud *thwack,* like something striking wood. He glanced over at Isaac and saw him diving down below the edge of the wagon. Percy flipped over on his belly and ducked his head down. "What was that?" Percy asked.

"You gotta see it to believe it," Isaac said. "Peek over the side."

Percy pulled himself up far enough to steal a look at the side of the wagon and said, "Jeezus, that was close." An arrow was embedded in the wood two inches below where he'd been sitting.

CHAPTER
41

Emma and the Indians were on the move again. The group had split up before starting out and Emma had gotten a good look at the two older women before they were led away. They weren't dead, but they looked like they were or soon would be. With vacant stares, they sat, tied to their horses. Their faces were bruised and swollen, yet that paled in comparison to the damage done to the rest of their bodies. They were caked with dried blood and their breasts were cut up and dripping blood. Emma couldn't even imagine the horrors they had endured. A tiny part of her was glad they had ridden out with the other group.

It was Emma and the two young boy captives who were riding with this group, along with her four abductors, including her archenemy, Scar. Leading the pack was the chief or whom Emma thought of as the chief. She had sensed a subtle change the moment she'd seen the crude drawing of the Rocking R brand scratched out in the dirt. She didn't know what it meant or even if it meant anything. Perhaps the chief was excited about a larger reward or maybe it meant she would be sold at a higher price to the highest bidder. Emma didn't know, and not being able to communicate with her captors was frustrating.

Big Nose was still in charge of her horse and they were riding toward the front of the pack, not far from the chief. Scar, Shorty, and Crooked Finger had been relegated to the back and, again, Emma didn't know if there was a shift in the hierarchical order or if it was simply an aberration. Whatever it was, she was glad that Scar remained at a distance, although she knew she hadn't seen the last of him. She secretly hoped his arm would become infected from her bite and then the infection would spread throughout his body. Scar dying from such an infection would be more than she could hope for. But she knew the odds of that happening were slim.

Her body was stiff and sore from being hog-tied and her feet ached terribly from where Scar had burned them, but the dull pain that radiated from her inner core was what she noticed most. Huge blisters had formed on her shoulders and the tops of her legs and the unrelenting sun was showing no mercy as they plodded onward. The Indians didn't appear to be in any great hurry, and she wondered if they had a final destination in mind. Surely there had to be a place they called home, Emma thought. They had wives and children and brothers and sisters and moms and dads, too, didn't they?

The answer came several hours later as they approached an immense canyon that stretched farther than Emma could see. It was so large that she couldn't fathom the enormity of it. The floor of the canyon was dotted with trees and stretched on for miles in all directions. In the distance she could just make out a ribbon of water that snaked through the area and had no idea that small stream was responsible for what she was now seeing. The canyon's rugged beauty was breathtaking. The sheer rock walls were a multicolored canvas of reds and pinks and whites that Mother Nature had painted over millions of years. The view was almost stunning enough for Emma to momentarily forget that she was captive to a bunch of savages, but she was quickly reminded of that fact when Big Nose yanked her horse to the left as they picked up a trail that descended to the bottom. Emma wondered how her grandfather and father would be able to find her in all that vastness, not only in the canyon but the empty plains surrounding it.

When they reached the bottom, they picked up a game trail and rode for a good while. The junipers were thick up in the draws and prickly pear cacti grew everywhere they could find a foothold. Along the river, cottonwood and willow trees shaded the banks and there were pops of color from the wildflowers that grew up in random locations. In the distance, Emma could here dogs barking, and she thought they were close to the place they called home.

The chief led them around an outcropping of rocks and through a stand of juniper that eventually opened up to a large wide-open space that was sheltered at the back by a sheer cliff that soared high overhead. A line of teepees stretched into the distance and the dogs were barking and weaving in and out among the horses' legs. The women and children came running and, way off in the distance, Emma saw a herd of horses that numbered in the thousands. Not knowing what to expect, Emma tried to prepare herself for whatever might come.

The women ran over and began untying the ropes securing Emma and the other captives. Once free, a mean-faced squaw knocked her off her horse, grabbed Emma by the hair, and began dragging her through the prickly pear toward the teepees. The long, sharp needles stabbed at her blistered skin and Emma felt like she was being dragged through a bed of red-hot coals. She glanced back and saw that the two boys were enduring the same punishment, though not as quietly as Emma was. Their crying and screaming echoed off the canyon walls.

This hadn't been the welcome Emma had envisioned. As they neared a cluster of teepees, the squaw turned loose of Emma's hair and she thought the worst was over. But she was mistaken. The woman was joined by several others and they began whipping Emma with long willow sticks that stung like a thousand wasp stings. She rolled up on her side, curled up, and tried to cover her head with her arms as the old squaws beat her mercilessly, ripping the skin from her body in chunks. Despite the intense pain, Emma was determined not to give them the satisfaction of hearing her whimper or cry. Then Emma heard someone shout and the beating stopped as quickly as it had started.

Emma lowered her hand from her face and saw the chief striding over, his face contorted with anger — or what Emma hoped was anger. He stopped and shouted at the women in Comanche as he angrily waved his hands in the air. Slowly, the old squaws slunk away like a pack of beaten cur dogs. When they were gone, the chief said something else to someone else Emma couldn't see, and then strode off. Emma looked up to see a younger squaw approaching and she immediately curled up in a ball and covered her head with her now-bloody arms again. She tensed up, waiting for the blows to rain down.

Instead the woman knelt down beside her and pulled Emma's right arm down until her face was exposed. She pointed at Emma and grunted something in Comanche. Emma shook her head to signal she didn't understand. The woman pointed again and then curled her index finger — the universal sign for *come here* — or whatever the word was in the squaw's native tongue. The woman stood and put her hands on her hips, waiting.

Emma groaned as she rolled over onto her belly. She muttered a curse word or two she wasn't supposed to know as she pushed up to her knees. Whether she could stand was yet to be determined. Blood dripped from her wounds as she sat back on her heels and took a deep breath. Without moving her head, she cut her eyes one way then the other, trying to see if the two boys were nearby. If they were, she couldn't see them. She hadn't heard them cry or scream in the last few moments and she wondered what that meant.

After taking another deep breath, Emma summoned the last reserves of her strength and wobbled to her feet. She had to grab the squaw's arm to keep from falling and it took a moment or two to steady herself. The squaw pushed Emma's hand off her arm, turned around, and started walking.

"Thanks for the help," Emma muttered as she took one tentative step and then another. She wobbled after the squaw, who appeared to be heading toward a large teepee that was surrounded closely by two smaller teepees. Without turning to see if her charge was making any progress, the squaw disappeared into the larger structure. Emma finally found her stride, or as much of a stride as she could manage after having her feet burned and being hog-tied all night and then tied to a horse all day and finally having been beaten to a pulp. Each step was agony. Running a mental checklist, she couldn't pinpoint any area of her body that didn't hurt. And she had no idea what to expect when she eventually made it to the teepee where the squaw disappeared. She didn't think she was in for another beating, based on the chief's actions. But there were many other ways to inflict pain and, from what Emma had heard, it was something the Indians were expert at.

When Emma reached the teepee, she tentatively lifted the edge of the deerskin flap and took a peek inside. With the bottom of the teepee rolled up to allow for air movement, there was enough light to see the squaw standing near the cold fire hearth, waiting. She didn't have anything in her hands and Emma took that as a good sign. She lifted the flap far enough to slip through and stepped inside.

CHAPTER
42

Rachel sat and studied Seth as he finished up breakfast. Jacob and Julia had already finished and had gone outside to do their chores. At ten and seven, they weren't overburdened with tasks, but Rachel thought it important they do something to learn responsibility. Consuelo was puttering around in the kitchen and Rachel was debating on whether to confront Seth about his new hobby or not. Rachel had noticed that he did most of his eating with his left hand, which was unusual, but she'd already noticed his damaged right thumb.

There were times that Rachel had wished she'd had nothing but girls because the road for boys was full of hairpin turns. Not that the road for girls was a gentle walk through the woods, but boys, and later as men, appeared to be exposed to more dangers. From bucking broncs to rowdy bulls there were so many ways where things could go wrong. And those were just the everyday dangers and didn't include the basic male propensity — some carryover from past ancestors, Rachel thought — to use their fists, or a knife, or a gun to settle an argument. Not to say that girls and later women wouldn't do the same, although they were the exception and not the rule. And damn it, Rachel thought, girls were easier to talk to. She watched as Seth used a biscuit to mop up the residual bacon grease on his plate. Searching for a way to start the conversation, Rachel decided to start with the easiest approach.

"What happened to your thumb?" Rachel asked.

Seth picked up his fork and pushed a biscuit crumb around his plate. "Nothin'."

"It doesn't look like nothing to me. How did you hurt it?"

Seth shrugged as he mashed the crumb with the tines of his fork. "It's just a rope burn."

"Huh," Rachel said. Well, it was going about as well as she expected. She decided to add a little more pressure. "Did that rope also give you the powder burns on the back of your hand?"

As an answer, Seth stood, walked over to dump his dirty plate in the washtub, then stopped by the door to grab his rifle, and walked outside.

Consuelo walked around the table, ran a damp rag across the top, and pushed the chair back in. "Let 'im be," she said, offering her advice.

"Everybody tells me that exact same thing," Rachel said. "What's everybody going to say if he kills someone or, God forbid, gets shot?"

Consuelo waved her damp rag in the air. "Phew, *te preocupas demasiado.*"

"It's my job to worry," Rachel said as she pushed up from the table. She wanted to say that Consuelo would be the last person she'd ask for parental advice but didn't. No sense in starting an argument this early in the day.

Rachel stepped over and grabbed her short-brimmed straw sombrero from a hook by the door and stepped outside. Eli would know how to handle it, she thought. She put on her hat and stepped off the porch. Her dress was damp with sweat by the time she reached the corral. There was little activity and Rachel wondered if they'd taken the branding operation out to the far pastures. She scanned the surrounding area for Seth but didn't see him. Knowing he usually carried the rifle only if he was going out riding, Rachel made her way to the barn. Inside she found Seth saddling his horse. If he didn't want to talk, then fine, Rachel thought.

She walked past Seth like he wasn't there, grabbed a bucket of oats and a rope, and stepped out into the corral. A dozen horses were milling around, and a big black stallion was scratching his neck against the snubbing post. Rachel walked out among the horses, keeping an eye on Big Blacky, as she searched for one of her preferred mounts. A spirited horse who had little use for humans, the giant stallion had a tendency to bite anyone who came within reach. Spotting a roan gelding that she knew had a comfortable gait, she shook the bucket and had to wave away four other horses before the roan dipped his muzzle into the oats. Slipping the rope around his neck, she led him back to the barn.

Seth was just mounting his horse when she returned. "Where are you going?" Rachel asked.

"Don't know yet," Seth answered as he spurred his horse into motion.

"Well, okay, then," Rachel said as he disappeared out the door. After saddling the roan, Rachel steered her horse out of the barn and rode by the bunkhouse, hoping someone was around to tell her where they were doing the branding and if Eli was in the group. But the bunkhouse appeared empty, so Rachel took a guess and rode east. Once clear of the heavily trafficked areas, she began looking for a trail to determine if she was on the right path. An amateur tracker at best, she was hoping to pick up the chuck wagon's trail. As she rode, she occasionally scanned the area around her, hoping for a glimpse of Seth. She didn't think he was riding out to help the men with the branding, but where he was going remained a mystery. And the last thing she wanted was to be caught following him. Maybe some alone time would help him get his mind right, she thought.

She eventually cut the trail of the chuck wagon and adjusted her course. The heat was oppressive, and she pulled the hem of her split skirt up to her thighs to allow her legs to get some air. Her sister always chided her for not riding sidesaddle and Rachel always responded that if she could birth children, she could sit a regular saddle. And Abby would really be horrified if she saw Rachel riding with her skirt pulled up. She knew *modesty* was a word that had never been used in conjunction with her name and that was fine. Not that she was a harlot by any means, but she disliked those people who thought a woman had to be prim and proper at all times. Rachel smiled. How those people would blush at some of the things she and Amos had done in their marital bed. Or used to do, she thought. Then she tried to recall the last time they'd had intimate relations and couldn't come up with the answer. Not that she still didn't have the urge. But she and Amos had drifted so far apart that it felt like a giant, insurmountable chasm ran right through the middle of their bed.

Rachel picked up a hint of smoke and, in the distance, she saw the chuck wagon. It was too hot to run the roan and Rachel let him set the pace. That was okay because she wasn't in a big hurry. She needed her alone time, too. She ran into more and more cattle the closer she got. The calves were sporting new brands and some still had blood dripping from where their ears had been notched after branding. The notching allowed the ranch hands to identify Ridgeway cattle from a distance.

Rachel pushed her skirt down, rode up to the chuck wagon, and climbed down. The cook, Jesus Reyes, was busy making another pot of coffee. A few hands were hanging around waiting for the fresh pot to brew and Rachel looked at each to see if she knew them. Most were hands from other ranches who were there to claim their cattle for their owners. Rachel recognized all but one — a tall, broad-shouldered man who was standing apart from the others. If Rachel had to guess his age, she'd put him in his late thirties or early forties, much older than most cowpunchers. She walked over and stuck out her hand. "Rachel Ferguson."

The man removed his hat and took her hand. "Leander Hays. Nice to meet you, Mrs. Ferguson." He had long, dark hair and a well-groomed mustache and goatee. Rachel noticed all of that during her cursory inspection because it was his gray-green eyes that commanded her full attention.

"Haven't seen you around," Rachel said. "Which brand do you ride for?"

"The state of Texas."

Rachel laughed. "Must be a very large spread. You a Ranger?"

"Yes, ma'am. I was up this way tracking some rustlers and I took advantage of your cook's hospitality."

Rachel glanced at the pistol on his left hip. The butt pointed forward for a right-hand cross-draw, the same way Percy wore his. "I thought they dissolved the Rangers during the war."

"They did, ma'am. Guess the state of Texas couldn't do without us."

Rachel smiled. "My oldest brother was a Ranger at one time."

"I know, ma'am. Percy, correct?"

"Yes. Where's home when you're not out looking for rustlers?"

"I have a small place down on the Brazos that I don't see as often as I would like."

"I bet Mrs. Hays feels the same way."

"My wife died three years ago, Mrs. Ferguson. Probably the reason I don't go back as much as I should."

"I'm sorry for your loss," Rachel said.

"Thank you, ma'am."

"If you happen to venture up where the main houses are, please don't hesitate to stop in."

"Thank you, ma'am."

Rachel turned and walked back to the chuck wagon. It took her a moment to remember why she rode out there. Then she did. "Jesus," she asked the cook, "where's Eli?"

"He's watchin' them brand, Señora Rachel. We having a calf-fry later if you're hungry."

"Thank you, Jesus," Rachel said. "But I think I'll pass." She remounted her horse, took one last look at Leander Hays, and reined the roan around. The branding was taking place about a quarter of a mile away and Rachel could smell the singed flesh and hear the calves bawling long before she rode up. A dozen people were involved, some on horseback herding the calves in, the others roping them and throwing them to the ground so the man with the branding iron could do his work. Another mounted man had his rope unfurled and was using it to keep the unhappy mama cows at bay. Eli was standing off to the side, watching. She walked her horse up to him.

"What are you doing out here, sis?" Eli asked.

"I came to see you. I want you to have a talk with Seth."

"Seth and I have already spoken this morning."

"And?" Rachel asked.

"The situation bears watching."

"Which means what exactly?"

"Seth is at a very impressionable age —"

Eli paused so he wouldn't have to shout over a wailing calf and a bellowing mother cow. After branding and having a notch cut in his ear, the calf, being a bull, had to undergo further treatment. The ranch hand working on him pulled out a knife, slit open the calf's scrotum, pulled out the two balls, severed the connection, and tossed them in a bucket. Rachel curled her lip and her stomach roiled when she thought about them appearing on a dinner plate later in the day. She turned back to Eli. "You were saying?"

"Either what happened to him festers or he'll eventually learn to put it behind him. Time is the only relative variable that will determine the answer."

"Should I confront him? Take the gun away?"

"Learning to shoot and shoot accurately is not a bad thing, Rachel."

"I don't have a problem with that. I do have a problem with him acting like some would be gunslinger. He was down at the river drawing and redrawing his pistol out of the holster over and over again, Eli."

"I don't believe there is a young man alive who hasn't envisioned himself a gunfighter at some point in his life. Rehearsing the draw and shooting at targets is far removed from actually being one. However, if he were to start killing small animals simply out of spite then there might be cause for concern. As I said, the situation bears watching."

"How concerned should I be?"

"As of now, I wouldn't be all that concerned. I believe when his father and grandfather return, he'll settle back into his normal routine."

"That could be a while, but I hope you're right," Rachel said. "Will you keep an eye on him when you can?"

"Of course." Eli pulled a neckerchief from his back pocket and wiped the sweat from his face.

"What's up with that Texas Ranger?"

"I don't know. Jesse said he arrived shortly after daybreak. Why?"

"Just wondering," Rachel said. "Know anything about him?"

"I know his name. Why does he pique your curiosity?"

"We live such sheltered lives that it's sometimes nice to see a new face. Offer him the guest cabin if he's going to be around for very long."

Eli turned and studied his sister for a long minute. "Is there dissension in the Ferguson home that I am unaware of?"

"Why would you think that? I'm just trying to be neighborly."

Eli pulled his pipe out of his pocket and began filling the bowl with tobacco. "I've learned that those who play with fire are often burned. I will not be the facilitator in whatever scheme you are currently concocting in your mind, Rachel." Eli pulled out a match, struck it with his thumbnail, and lit his pipe. After taking a draw he removed the pipe from his mouth and said, "If you're concerned about the Ranger's welfare perhaps you should be the one to extend the invitation."

"I will. Thanks for lookin' after Seth." Rachel put the spurs to her horse and turned back toward the chuck wagon.

CHAPTER
43

Despite the continued threat of an Indian attack and the recent near miss of a Comanche arrow, Percy had finally succumbed to his exhaustion. The creaking and rocking of the wagon, along with the heat, were a perfect recipe for sleep and Percy had drifted off. When he stirred awake a while later, the wagon was stopped down in a small creek bottom and his father was manning the Gatling gun. "What are we doin'?" Percy asked.

Cyrus pursed his lips and spat a stream of tobacco juice over the side then looked down. "Waterin' the horses. You enjoy your beauty sleep?"

Percy pushed himself up to a sitting position and took a quick look around, hoping another arrow wasn't already on its way. "Where are the Injuns?"

"Wilcox thinks they rode on."

"What do you think?" Percy asked.

Cyrus shrugged. "Don't know. But I ain't leavin' this gun until we know for sure. Probably wanted to get on with their rapin' and killin'."

Percy leaned back against the sideboard of the wagon and rubbed his eyes. "How long was I asleep?"

"A couple of hours."

"How long we plannin' to stay here?"

"Depends on what Wilcox finds. Him and Win are out working the ground. But I'd like to stay here till sundown fore movin' on again. Use the dark in case them Injuns are still around somewhere."

Percy threw his leg over the side. "Then I'm going to stretch my legs a bit. Where's everybody else?"

"Diggin' a grave."

A sudden surge of sadness hit Percy right between the eyes when he remembered the events from earlier in the day. "I'm goin' to miss Arturo."

"Can't be helped," Cyrus said. "Build a small fire while you're stretchin'. Need to get some food and coffee in our bellies."

Percy nodded and climbed out of the wagon. Whether his father felt any sympathy — or felt anything at all — for Arturo's loss was a mystery. But it wasn't a discussion he was willing to start. The only time Percy saw his father show any emotion was with his mother and, at that, it was infrequent. Percy cleared those thoughts from his mind, put his hands on his hips, and arched his back, trying to work out the kinks. The wooden wagon bed was even more unforgiving than the ground. Once his back felt like it had loosened up a bit, Percy walked off in search of wood.

Creeks and rivers were scarce out in this part of the country and Percy was trying to recall the name of this body of water from his previous travels. It was too small to be one of the many forks that fed the Red River system so that narrowed it down some, but Percy still couldn't hit on the name as he gathered up an armload of driftwood. He carried it back to an area well away from the wagon and dropped it on the ground. After gathering up some kindling and a handful of leaves, he began making a fire and that's when the name came to him — Wind River. The *river* part of the name was a misnomer, Percy thought, judging that the small stream of water didn't stretch farther than four feet across at its widest point. He pulled a match from his shirt pocket, struck it, and lit the small pile of leaves. Once the kindling started burning, he added on some smaller sticks and once those took hold, added a larger chunk of wood and stood up and went after the coffeepot.

Stepping around to the back of the wagon, he nearly tripped over Arturo's body, which had been wrapped in a blanket and placed on the ground. Another wave of sadness washed across his mind as he grabbed the pot.

"How far west you reckon we'll have to go?" Cyrus asked.

"Probably best to begin our search somewhere around the Palo Duro Canyon," Percy said.

"How far's that?"

"A long ways. With the wagon I figure we'll get there in a week and a half or two. And that's if we make steady progress without any hitches. And that's just to get there. How long it'll take to find Emma's captors is anybody's guess."

"So, what you're sayin' is we'll be gone at least a month," Cyrus said.

"That's what I'm sayin'. And that's if we find the Indians quickly, which is highly doubtful. I know why you're askin', but I don't think we're goin' to get any cattle up the trail to the railhead this year." Percy lifted the lid and started ladling water from the barrel to the pot.

"Gonna have to push some of the cattle

north of the river, then. Let 'em graze on Indian land and hope they all don't get stole."

"Waggoner's been letting his cattle graze up there for years. Might get a tad heated if he finds out."

"He don't own it and he ain't goin' to have any say in the matter."

"Ole Dan's got a temper."

"I spent a night at his place on the way here and he was mighty hospitable," Cyrus said. "I don't see us comin' to blows over grazin' some cattle on land none of us owns."

"Well, he might think different."

"If he raises a stink, we'll worry about it then. That reminds me of somethin' I was gonna tell you."

"What's that?"

"Guess who I run into up at Fort Sill?"

Even though Percy had slept a little, he was still exhausted. "I don't know. President Grant?"

"No," Cyrus said. "Wild Bill and Charlie Goodnight."

"Huh. I didn't know Bill was still alive and kickin'. What's he up to?"

"Doin' a little scoutin' for the army and takin' rich Russians on buffalo hunts."

"That sounds about right. How'd he look?"

"Like he's hittin' the bottle pretty hard."

"No surprise there. What about Charlie? I sure wish we had him along on this trip."

"Me, too. I asked, but he weren't interested."

"That's a shame." Percy walked over and nestled the pot of water in among the hot coals as Amos, Isaac, and Luis came walking back. Luis's eyes were red-rimmed and swollen and Percy felt another pang of grief. He knew Luis and Arturo were cousins and both had come to work at the Rocking R almost six years ago. Percy stepped over and put a hand on Luis's shoulder. "I'm sorry, Luis. I know you two were very close."

Luis rubbed his eyes. "*Gracias,* Percy."

"We'll bury Arturo around sundown if that's okay with you."

Luis nodded. "He'd like that."

Percy patted him on the shoulder then walked back to the fire to see if the pot of water was boiling. It was, and he nudged it out of the coals with his boot and walked back to the wagon to grab a package of Arbuckles' coffee. He ripped the top open, walked back to the fire, and poured some grounds into the pot and let it steep for a few minutes. While he was doing that, Luis climbed up on the seat and backed the team away from the creek. "Amos, you see any sign that the Indians were still around while you were out digging?"

"Nope. But they could hide behind a blade of grass if they was a mind to. Didn't see no tracks, though." Amos leaned his rifle against a tree. "Am I cookin'?"

"Might as well," Percy said. "There's some beans in one of those pots at the back of the wagon that I put on to soak this morning."

Amos grabbed the pot of beans, drained the water off, and added fresh water and some salt and pepper and carried it over to the fire.

Percy took a moment to study the location where Luis had parked the wagon. His dilemma was whether to leave it where it sat or drive it up out of the creek bottom and make camp in a more open area. If the Indians were really gone then he'd much prefer to camp down here in the shade where it was a little cooler. Percy decided to put the decision on hold until Win and Wilcox returned with some answers. Where it was now was an okay defensive position with a heavy stand of timber behind it. The Gatling gun would be able to cover both sides of the creek and any frontal approach and the only weakness was the rear, but a couple of cannon blasts into the timber would be somewhat effective. Percy walked over to the wagon for a different perspective. His father had stepped out from behind the gun and was lying down flat on his back on the wagon seat and rubbing his chest.

"Pull a muscle?" Percy asked.

"Naw," Cyrus said. "My back. What happens when you get old."

"If your back's hurtin' why are you rubbing your chest?"

Cyrus groaned as he sat up. "Had an itch."

Percy stood back where the gun was mounted and surveyed the situation. A couple of junipers encroached on the right side, but it also acted as a screen in case anyone else, other than the Indians, was around. The Indians already knew they were there. Percy looked at his father and said, "I sure would like to get that team unhitched to let them graze a bit. When do you think Wilcox will be back?" Percy asked.

"He'll be here when you see 'im. Coffee ready?"

"Should be," Percy said. "What do you think about unhitchin' the wagon?"

"It'd put us in a pickle if them Injuns showed up. Best wait to see what Wilcox has to say." Cyrus climbed down, wobbled around to the back of the wagon to grab a cup, then headed for the coffeepot. Percy thought his father was favoring his left side as he walked away, and he didn't know if it was a back problem or something related to his hip. Either way, he probably wasn't going to find out from his father, who worked from can't see to can't see most every day and hardly ever complained about his ailments.

A while later, as they were sitting down for supper, Wilcox and Win rode in. Once they were dismounted and had a cup a coffee in their hands, they began to talk.

"The bunch that was pesterin' us rode on south about three hours ago," Wilcox said.

"All of 'em?" Cyrus asked.

"Looked like it," Wilcox said. "Could be a stray or two around but I doubt it."

"Well, I guess we can unhook the team now," Percy said.

"Might want to hold off," Win said. "That be the good news. The bad news is we cut the trail of a bigger bunch of Injuns that looked to be followin' a buffalo herd to the north of us."

"How far away is the trail?" Cyrus asked.

"An hour due west of here," Win answered. "Might want to head out and get past 'em fore any of them drop back south."

"How many Indians we talkin' about?" Percy asked.

"Might near two hundred," Win said. "And there ain't no pole marks, neither."

"Meaning it's all braves," Percy said. "What makes you think they'll drop back south?"

"Don't know fer sure," Win said. "But if any of 'em get a hankerin' to go raidin' they'll ride smack into us."

"Eat up, boys," Cyrus said. "We'll put Arturo in the ground and then skedaddle."

CHAPTER
44

Emma wept. And for the first time in a long time, it wasn't because she was frightened or injured. No, this time the tears were the result of one of the most basic human needs — kindness. Lying on her stomach atop a pile of soft buffalo hides, Emma studied the ground inside the teepee as the Indian woman who had welcomed her inside knelt next to her, gently removing the prickly pear spines from her back and legs. It was the first time since her abduction that an Indian had touched her without malice in mind. And she didn't know if this was a halt in hostilities or a brief interlude, but she wasn't going to think about that.

When the woman finished removing the spines, she used a damp piece of soft deerskin to wipe the blood, dirt, and grime off Emma's blistered skin. After that, the woman slathered on some kind of oil that had a gamy odor with just a hint of mint.

After the oil had a little time to absorb, the woman tapped her on the leg and said something in Comanche. Emma lifted her head, looked at the woman, and said, "I'm sorry, I don't understand." She certainly didn't want to make the woman angry, but she didn't know if she was supposed to get up and leave or what.

The woman must have understood her confusion. She held her hand out and turned it over.

"I get it," Emma said. "You want me to turn over." Emma rolled over on her back and the woman went to work removing the prickly pear spines from the rest of her torso. "I don't know your name," Emma said out loud, "so I'm going to name you Angel because that must be what you are."

Angel looked up but didn't say anything before returning to her task. Emma took the opportunity to closely study her new-found savior. Angel, like all the Indians Emma had seen, had long, dark hair and a prominent nose. However, she didn't have the heavy brow ridge that many Indians did, and she had a more rounded face and her dark eyes were slightly slanted. With full lips, she was lithe and lean and moved with a certain gracefulness. Emma thought she might be the most beautiful Indian woman she'd seen, and she wondered what role Angel played in the tribe. Was she one of the chief's squaws? Or maybe a sister or niece? The chief didn't look old enough to have fathered Angel, but it was clear she had unfettered access to his teepee, if this was indeed his dwelling. Emma was terrible at guessing ages, but she thought Angel was probably in her midtwenties or somewhere close to that. She'd never know for sure because of their inability to communicate. Thinking of Angel's age made her wonder if the Indians adhered to some type of calendar or if they had any concept of time. Did they celebrate life events such as birthdays or anniversaries? It was an unanswerable question. The Comanche world was as foreign to Emma as if she'd sailed halfway around the world and landed in an unknown land.

Angel dipped the deerskin cloth into a small pot of water, squeezed out the excess, and began wiping down Emma's legs. It hadn't bothered her when she had been lying facedown, but it bothered her now. Reaching down, Emma attempted to take the cloth from Angel and got her hand slapped for her efforts. Maybe it's some type of ritual, Emma thought. She lay back and let Angel continue.

Emma switched from studying Angel to studying the inside of the teepee. Three piles of buffalo robes were lined up around the outer perimeter and Emma wondered about that. Was it for the chief and his family? Did Indian children sleep with their parents? Or did the chief have two squaws that lived in his teepee? The only way Emma was going to learn the answers to those questions was through observation. Overhead, someone had strung a rope all the way around the teepee and hung on it were some of the personal items of the inhabitants — a fringed buckskin dress, a pair of deer-hide leggings, and a few blankets that were unneeded this time of year. There was no sign of a chief's headdress or anything that would indicate a higher social status and that led to doubts about her initial assumptions. Maybe the man she thought was the chief didn't live here at all. But the sheer size of the teepee compared to the others had to represent something. Again, Emma thought, she would have to watch and learn.

Turning her gaze to the ground inside, she looked for clues that would tell her how long the teepee had been there. If there had been grass at one time, it was now gone. The ground was hard packed, suggesting this might be a more permanent location for them. After further study, Emma was fairly certain that this particular teepee hadn't been moved in months. She pondered that as Angel rubbed oil across her upper torso. If that was true — if the Indians lived for long periods of time in one place — then her father's and grandfather's odds of finding her increased exponentially.

Emma's thoughts were interrupted when Angel tapped her on the shoulder and grunted something in Comanche. Angel mimicked walking with two fingers on her right hand and Emma assumed that she wanted her to get up, which she did. Pulling the buckskin dress from overhead, Angel thrust it into Emma's hands and said something else in her native tongue. Assuming she wanted her to put the dress on, Emma slipped it over her head and felt instant relief that she no longer had to parade around naked. She let the dress fall and Angel looked at her and laughed out loud. Emma looked down and saw that the hem of the dress was so long it hid her bare feet and she, too, laughed. The dress had obviously been made for a much taller woman or at least a woman who had matured into adulthood. But Emma didn't care. It had been so long since she had laughed that fresh tears formed in her eyes. The dress was beautifully beaded around the neck and along the shoulders and hem and it was evident a great deal of time was spent working on it.

Angel made her way to the entrance and Emma followed, euphoric over having clothing on once again, even if it was too long. Angel lifted the flap and she and Emma stepped outside. Angel pointed to a large, leather, baglike object with a rope handle and mumbled something in Comanche. When Emma didn't immediately move, Angel pointed again, this time more emphatically. "You want me to pick that up?" Emma asked, knowing it was a pointless question. She stepped over and picked up the bag. It had been stitched along the bottom and on one side and had a round hole at the top. Angel picked up another similar bag and started walking. Emma fell in behind her, having no idea where they were going.

They walked through the camp and it wasn't long before Emma noticed something that puzzled her. The men were lounging about or playing a game of some sort that involved dice, while the women worked. Some were cooking, others were scraping hides or were busy doing something. And Emma noticed that even the young boys sat idly about or played while the young girls were busy helping their mothers or were working on other tasks that someone deemed necessary. Age didn't seem to be an issue, either, because even the oldest of the Indian women were laboring at something. It was startling to see, and Emma couldn't understand why the men didn't offer to help or take on tasks of their own. Seeing the stark contrast between male and female duties gave her an inkling of what life was going to be like during her days in captivity.

Emma kept an eye out for Scar as they walked. She didn't know if Angel's gentle cleansing or being allowed to wear a dress entitled her to certain protections or not. But she wasn't willing to press the issue to find out. And if she never saw Scar again it would be too soon. They left the camp behind and as they drew closer to the river, Emma finally understood what the bag she carried was used for. How she was going to carry it back full of water was yet to be determined.

At the water's edge, Angel slipped her dress off and waded out into the water with her bag. Not knowing if she was supposed to follow, Emma hesitated. Would Angel be angry that she'd spent all that time applying oil to Emma's body only to have it washed off in the river? Or had that been some type of ritualistic cleansing that the Indians held as sacred? Emma was momentarily flustered and angry at her inability to communicate, but she had her answers a moment later when Angel waved for her to come in. Slipping her dress up over her head, she laid it gently on the ground, grabbed the water bag, and waded in.

They didn't spend much time luxuriating in the river, but Emma was grateful for the opportunity. There were parts of her body that Angel hadn't cleaned, and it was a welcome relief to be able to clean those and rinse her hair. They each dunked their bags beneath the surface and let them fill before making their way back to the bank. Angel left her bag in the water and climbed out to put on her dress before she reached down and slung the rope over her shoulder. Emma wasn't paying much attention and didn't follow that sequence of events. Grunting and groaning, she got the bag up high enough to get it on dry land and when she set it down, the bag collapsed and all the water rushed out. She tried one more time with the same result. She stopped and ran through the last few images in her mind and finally understood why Angel had done it the way she did. Emma climbed out, put on her dress, and reached over for the handle. She succeeded in lifting it, but within six steps of the river it felt like the rope was going to cut her in half. And there was nothing she could do but keep on trudging.

Angel was long gone, Emma's shoulder was on fire, her right arm was numb, and she was drenched in sweat as she shuffled back into camp. Some of the water had sloshed out, which helped a bit, and she was hoping they wouldn't make her go back and refill it. It angered her that the men who could probably lift it with a single finger sat and watched her struggle. She'd walk over and dump the water on their heads if she thought she could get away with it. But she didn't. Finally, she made it back to the teepee, where she slid the bag's handle onto a pole and pushed it over next to Angel's bag. All she wanted to do now was to sit down for a moment and rest until the feeling in her arm came back. But it was not to be.

After discovering Emma was back, Angel led her over to a large buffalo hide that had been stretched between a square pole frame. She handed Emma a large piece of bone and, using her own piece of bone, demonstrated how to scrape the flesh from the hide. Forced to use her off hand because her right arm was still numb, Emma began scraping. It was easier than carrying the water bag, but she wouldn't classify the job of scraping as easy, especially with such primitive tools. It was hard, dirty work and, as the monotony set in, she couldn't keep her mind from drifting to thoughts of what the reunion with her family would look like. What she couldn't envision was how long it would be until those images became reality.

CHAPTER
45

Although his mother had been white, Quanah Parker did not live like a white man, did not speak the white man's tongue, and had absolutely no qualms about killing every white man he saw. His band of Comanches, the Quahadis, had never affixed their names to a treaty nor spent a minute on the reservation. And if it was up to Quanah they never would. They were the last of their kind and, from his point of view, the only way he would set foot on the reservation was if the army were to defeat them in battle. Something that hadn't occurred yet and Quanah aimed to keep it that way.

None of those particular issues were weighing heavy on his mind as he sat near the river alone, his spot shaded by an enormous cottonwood tree. It was something else that commanded his attention, and he didn't really know what to do about it. And it involved one of the new captives. He wasn't averse to taking captives by any means, be they white, black, Mexican, or even from another tribe. But he'd never had a captive quite like this one. And that was the problem. The easiest way to solve his dilemma would be to kill the captive and disavow any knowledge of her existence. However, he knew people talked and if word got out that the captive had been in his camp when she was killed then Quanah knew he would be hunted to the ends of the earth. And for the same reason he couldn't pass the captive off to another band of Indians or sell her to the Comancheros that came occasionally to trade.

The second easiest thing to do would be to give the captive back to her family. But that, too, had implications. Quanah had no doubt she had endured some hardships because that's the way the Comanches treated all their captives. And he couldn't be angry with the four braves because they were young and had no idea whom they had captured. In fact, Quanah thought he would have probably done the same thing at that age. However, he was a much wiser man now and what had already happened was water down the creek.

Quanah had never met the man his brothers called Heap Big Guns, but he'd seen him plenty of times from a distance and had heard the stories. And none of the stories he'd heard had happy endings if you were an Indian. Quanah knew the types of guns the man had and had seen similar guns in action, but he'd never fought against anyone who had weapons like that, and he had no desire to do so now. To help prevent any possibilities of future conflict with Heap Big Guns, Quanah had ridden by the man's lodge many times and had spent a fair amount of time familiarizing himself with the faces he saw. That's why he had a general idea who the new captive was even before he saw the brand drawn in the dirt.

As an alternative to the already-discarded list of possibilities, he wondered if he could hide the girl long enough for the old man to die. But then he remembered hearing Little Heap Big Guns wasn't any better and he crossed that off the list.

With no easy answers, Quanah switched his thinking. If he could get some of the braves on the reservation to join him, he figured he could put together a fairly large war party of maybe eight hundred braves. And if the old man and his son were already on the hunt, they could attack them and kill them, thereby eliminating the problem altogether. The only problem he could see with that scenario was one of numbers — how many dead would be too many? The big boom gun and the gun of many rifles would be like squaring off against an army of four hundred well-armed soldiers. Some on his side would surely die, but how many? Quanah wondered. The more he thought about it the more he came to realize an outright attack wasn't plausible. It would be a suicide mission and Quanah liked living too much.

With that off the table, Quanah began thinking about the probabilities of a successful sneak attack — an outright ambush that would catch the enemy unaware. The Comanche had been doing that for hundreds of years, but never against the type of firepower they would be facing. And Heap Big Guns had been around a long time, so he wasn't stupid. They would have guards posted through the night, Quanah thought. He did have a good number of braves who could slip into camp and slit an enemy's throat undetected though they were often dicey affairs where a random snapped twig meant the difference between success and failure. And against that old man and his guns, a failure could result in a massive loss of life. Realizing outright conflict with Heap

Big Guns was best avoided, Quanah began exploring other avenues. He stood and set out along the river.

As he walked, his mind swirled and a new thought began to worm its way into his brain. Why did he have to do anything at all? The girl was here and there wasn't anything he could do about it. And his own mother, Narua — whom the whites called Cynthia Ann Parker — had begun life with the Indians as a captive and she'd fared very well for years until the white men forced her away from the only home she'd known. Why couldn't it be the same for this white captive? Quanah wondered. If he and his people could avoid Heap Big Guns long enough, she'd soon come to learn the Indian way. But if that was going to happen, he and his people needed to be on the move to keep some distance between them and Heap Big Guns. Besides, they had been camped there too long as it was. Anyone who knew their current location could have passed it on to the army, who sent out patrols on occasion. And, as an added bonus, it would be cooler if they drifted north a ways.

As he pondered the situation a little longer, he decided that moving on was the best course of action. He turned away from the river and headed back to camp.

CHAPTER
46

Even with her right arm back in action, Emma was still struggling to master the art of hide scraping. Most of her difficulties stemmed from an enormous lack of interest and the rest she blamed on the lack of suitable tools. Her hands were slick with blood and grease and just keeping the primitive tool in her hands was a major challenge. If she focused, she had some success, but she was more interested in learning the everyday nuances of the tribe to better prepare herself for what might lie ahead. Knowing whom to avoid would bode well for her in the future.

Busy watching, her hands stilled, and Emma learned not to make that mistake again when an old squaw walked over and slapped her hard in the face. Emma was so startled all she could do was glare as blood filled her mouth. The woman moved off and Emma spat out the blood. She'd remember that old hag because her ugly face was now seared in Emma's mind. She went back to scraping and made a mental note to always be aware of who was around her at all times.

A short while later, Emma began to hear a murmur spread throughout the camp. Something was happening, but she didn't know what it was. The men were now up and moving and the women suddenly abandoned whatever they were working on. Angel, who'd been working next to Emma, dropped her scraper and hurried over to the chief's teepee. Another old woman walked over, pushed Emma out of the way, and began untying the hide from the frame.

Looking around, Emma's heart plummeted when she saw the squaws pulling the wooden pins that held the hides on the teepee frames. *No, no, no! How are they going to find me now?* Emma was rooted in place as her mind raced. Her first thought was to find somewhere to hide until the Indians left. She turned in a circle, searching for a suitable place as questions bombarded her brain. How long until her father and grandfather arrived? A week? Longer? Could she hang on that long? Then she began to wonder how long the Indians would search for her before they decided to leave. Would it be possible to get lost in the confusion? That question was answered when she spotted Big Nose in the distance. He was walking her way with a short piece of rope in his hands. Emma panicked. *What can I do?* Running wouldn't do any good because Big Nose would run her down like a wolf chasing a week-old buffalo calf.

The only thing Emma could think to do was to leave something behind so that her searchers would know she'd been there. But what? All of her original clothing was gone. She didn't have a single thing left that would identify her. Emma looked around and hit upon an idea. She hurried over to a pile of white stones and knelt down. She looked back and saw Big Nose getting closer and knew she had to hurry. Working quickly, she rearranged some of the stones until they formed a crude outline of her initials. She stood and looked down at her handiwork. The *ET* was clearly visible but whether anyone would ever see them was an unknown. Having done all she could do, she hurried away, hoping Big Nose wouldn't be curious about what she had been doing.

Big Nose walked up, and Emma braced, expecting to be grabbed by the hair again. Instead he grunted something in Comanche and pointed at her hands. Emma turned around and put her hands behind her, hoping her easy compliance would make him forget about what she had been doing. "Are we done with the hair pulling?" she asked out loud. He ignored her and wrapped the rope tightly around her wrists and tied it.

Horses, being driven by the smaller boys, flooded into camp. Emma looked down at her too-long dress and wondered how she'd ever get her legs far enough apart to straddle a horse. And the last thing in the world she wanted to do was take the dress off. Big Nose grabbed her by the arm and steered her over to where they were taking down the chief's teepee. He pointed at the ground and Emma sat and Big Nose wandered off. Angel was busy pulling out the buffalo hides and rolling them up while the old woman who slapped her was disassembling the teepee. Emma didn't know if that was part of the old hag's job or if she had some tie to the chief. Nor did she particularly care. The old bitch could keel over with a heart attack and it wouldn't bother Emma in the least. And, she decided, if the woman struck her again, she was going to hit back, consequences be damned.

Angel stepped over, untied her hands, and pointed at a stack of buffalo hides and said something in her native tongue. Emma walked over, knelt down, and began rolling up the hides. She noticed something she hadn't noticed when they were inside — the hides were full of tiny bugs and a shiver of revulsion washed through her. She had no idea what the bugs were or where they came from and all she could think about was her time spent lying on them. Well, she thought, there was nothing she could do about it now. If she was lucky, she had washed the bugs off in the river.

Looking around as she worked, Emma wasn't all that surprised to see that the women were the only ones doing the packing. In fact, most of the men, including the chief, had ridden off when the decision to move had been made. Where they went was unknown, however Emma had been glad to see that Scar was among the group and that allowed her to rest a little easier. Although he hadn't bothered her since they'd joined the larger group, Emma had no doubt that he wasn't finished exacting his revenge and would attack when she least expected it. Or, she wondered, had the burning of her feet signaled the end of their conflict? No, she decided, he'd want more, probably much more since she'd humiliated him in front of his cohorts.

While Emma was rolling up the hides, she discovered a long, bone-handled bowie knife, a knife similar to what her father carried. She glanced around to see if anyone was watching before she secreted it under her dress. Could this be some type of test? she wondered. Did Angel put the knife there on purpose? Or was it simply overlooked? Emma pondered all of this as she continued rolling hides.

The knife, Emma thought, would be handy to have when Scar decided to seek more revenge, but she couldn't work out a way to conceal it on her person. She didn't have anything on beneath the dress and even if she did, she thought the weapon too large to keep concealed. And she had no belongings in which to hide it. But she thought if she could find a thin piece of rope, it might be possible to wear it around her neck. The dress, made for a more mature woman, was plenty loose in the bosom, but Emma hadn't worn it long enough to know how the deerskin would drape her body when wet or when the wind blew or while riding. Emma's overriding concern was what the Indians would do if they discovered she had the knife. She didn't know how many more vicious beatings she could endure without sustaining permanent damage.

Then her thoughts turned to a darker

place when she recalled the repeated indignities and tortures inflicted on the two older women captives. At thirteen, Emma had her whole life in front of her and she wanted what other women had and that included children. How much more damage could her private parts take before they were rendered useless? For Emma, that was the most disturbing question.

Okay, Emma thought, carrying the knife was too risky. Was there someplace she could hide it among the chief's things that would allow her easy access? Emma sat back on her heels to look and think for a moment. She glanced up to see the old hag giving her the eye, so Emma leaned forward and continued with her task. "You old bitch," Emma muttered.

She could hide the knife among the rolled-up hides and take it out at the new location before they began setting up camp. And if someone happened to find it before she could retrieve it, there would be no connection to her. Emma thought that the best course of action, but before acting, she returned to one of the original questions — was this some type of test? A way to establish trust or to gauge her honesty? Then she thought about it another way. If she did use the knife to maim or kill Scar, what would the ramifications from that be? Would her access to the hidden knife and her deceit require a harsher punishment?

There were just too many unknowns, Emma thought. Her best course of action was to give the knife to Angel. However, before that, she wanted to use it to cut two slits in her dress that would free her legs. But then she hesitated even at that. It seemed like all she'd done today was question herself. She assumed that would get better as she learned the rules. At the moment, she wanted to know if cutting the beautifully beaded dress was allowed or if it was a punishable offense. And it wasn't like she could ask someone. She decided to leave well enough alone and make do. She pulled the knife from beneath her dress and stood. She was careful to turn it so that the handle was pointing forward as she walked over to Angel, who was on her knees, trying to fold the teepee's hide covering. Emma tapped Angel on the shoulder and when she turned, Emma held out the knife. Angel took it out of her hand and nodded.

Emma knew immediately that she had made the right choice. Angel held up a finger and then she turned around and grabbed the hem of Emma's dress. Using the knife, she cut a long slit in the dress and twirled her fingers, signaling for Emma to turn around, which she did. Angel cut a long slit in the back and then, to Emma's immense surprise, handed the knife back to her. Emma smiled and nodded her thanks. She knew then that the hidden knife had been some type of test and she felt good to have passed, despite her earlier scheming. She leaned down, set the knife aside, and helped Angel finish folding the teepee.

With no way to judge time, Emma guessed that only a couple of hours had passed before all the Indians were mounted up and ready to move. Travois had been lashed to the horses and all their gear, the additional poles, and anything that remained was packed on board. To her immense relief, Emma was mounted on her own horse and free of any bindings. As they rode out of the old camp, and with the knife hanging from a small piece of leather and nestled against her chest, Emma took one last glance back to see if her initials were still there and was pleased to see that they were. She'd left her mark and that was all she could do.

CHAPTER 47

Percy, Cyrus, and the others had been on the move for two weeks before they got a look at the Palo Duro Canyon. During that time, they hadn't seen any sign of other two-legged creatures and that had suited everyone just fine because, out here, the probabilities of those creatures being Indians were extremely high. Percy had been here before, but for the others the enormity of the canyon had been a surprise. Now camped near the Prairie Dog Town Fork of the Red River, the body of water responsible for the canyon, they were on high alert for possible Indian activity.

The Palo Duro Canyon wasn't a place you rode into willy-nilly. It took planning and extreme caution. And due to its vast size, it took something they were in short supply of — time. Who knew what horrors Emma had already endured, and those thoughts weighed heavily on all of them, especially her father, Isaac. His initial anger had transitioned to resolve, and Isaac was the one who pushed them onward at a fairly rapid clip. Now that they'd arrived at the canyon the pace had slowed considerably and that made Isaac anxious and irritable. But trying to carefully search a canyon that was 20 miles wide and 120 miles long without getting scalped was a chore.

Until they could get a handle on whether there were Indians in the vicinity, Percy had elected to hide the wagon in a thick stand of junipers as the first step in his careful plan. With the expectation that the search of the canyon could linger on for several days it would have been impossible to keep the team hitched up for the entire duration. Instead, Percy had tied a couple of long ropes to the wagon's tongue, which would allow two riders the ability to pull the wagon out in a pinch. But freeing the mules also created another problem. Knowing the Indians' affinity for stealing horses meant they had to keep someone in camp at all times to keep a close eye on their animals. Being set afoot out there could be a death sentence.

Currently, Wilcox, Isaac, and Cyrus were searching the south rim of the canyon while Win, Amos, and Luis scouted the north rim.

That left Percy back at camp. And that would have been okay if they'd camped anywhere but there. Percy knew from his previous travels to the area that the Indians frequented the canyon often and he knew that some of the tribes considered it a sacred site. That meant he had to be on guard at all times. In addition to constantly scanning for threats, he had to keep track of where the horses and mules were, and doing both took a level of concentration that was exhausting. To help maintain his intensity, he'd consumed a large quantity of coffee and that had soured his stomach, adding to his discomfort.

Deciding he'd do a little scouting around the camp he grabbed a rope and went after his horse, who was grazing a short distance away. His son Chauncey had named the mare Mouse because of her gray coat. An American quarter horse Percy had bought from a horse breeder in Kansas on his last trip up the cattle trail, she could be a tad difficult to catch out in an open field. Not that he could blame her for being skittish about toting him around for a few hours.

After a long look around for approaching Indians, he hid the rope behind his back and walked out to the mare. When he was about six feet away, he stuck his hand out so she could pick up his scent and began talking softly to her. Luckily, she didn't bolt and he slipped the rope around her neck. Once he returned to camp and had Mouse saddled, he rode out and drove the four mules a little closer to camp in case he needed to get the wagon out in a hurry. It wouldn't be a fun job by himself and it might take him a little longer, but he figured the adrenaline dump at the sight of Indians would be enough to get the job done.

Being mounted increased his sight lines significantly. They had set up camp at a spot where another creek fed into the river that cut through the canyon. Other than the stand of junipers that hid the wagon and a few others that dotted the landscape, it was an open patch of ground, which allowed Percy to see an enemy approach with enough time to do something about it. In the distance, the escarpment that demarcated the beginning of the Llano Estacado snaked off to the north and south and it was truly a sight to see. To Percy, it looked as if a giant hand had pushed a big chunk of country up about six hundred feet. The terrain leading up to the ridge was as flat as a flapjack as was the land on top of the mesa. The only thing that separated the two was the steep cliff. Although Percy had seen it before during his travels, it was the starkness of it that made the place unique to just about any place he'd ever been.

Not wanting to ride too far away from camp, Percy decided to ride a large circle around it to check for tracks and to get a feel for the place. They had reached the campsite around dark last night and he hadn't had a chance to get the lay of the land He crossed the small creek that fed into the river and picked up a game trail that led up a rocky slope to a ridge that was part of the canyon. On top, his view opened up significantly. From that vantage point he could see for miles in all directions and he wondered if it would make a better camp location. But the more he thought about it the more he liked the camp's present location. They would be too exposed up on the ridge.

From that vantage point Percy could see how sparse the grass was and, other than the junipers and swaths of stubby mesquite trees, what he'd classify as normal trees were nonexistent other than those down in the canyon. The one thing that wasn't in short supply was cactus, especially prickly pear. It was as thick as weeds around an outhouse in some places, the beaver tail–shaped pads covered with long, angry-looking spines. Mouse didn't appear to like them much and she cut a wide berth around them. Percy took one more long look around before he steered the mare down the ridge and toward the river. Choosing to ride along the side of the river a short distance, he searched the ground for unshod pony tracks. And found some, but fortunately none looked to be recent.

A little farther on he found something that piqued his interest. He stopped Mouse to allow for further study. What he saw were several lines in the dirt. Some were equally spaced with hoof tracks between them and he knew enough about tracking to know what it was — a travois trail. When the Indians decided it was time to move on, they would tie a couple of teepee poles to opposite sides of a horse or dog and then pile on their belongings. What he didn't know was how old the trail was, but Wilcox would be able to look at it and tell them that and a lot more. Percy clucked his tongue to start Mouse moving and crossed the river to search for the trail on the other side.

But the more Percy rode up and down that side of the river the more puzzled he became. If there was travois trail on this side, he couldn't find it. And he knew the

Indians hadn't just materialized out of thin air. The only thing that made sense was the Indians had covered their tracks and that only added to his puzzlement. Why did they obscure their tracks on this side and not the other? Were they in that big of a hurry to depart? He mulled that over as he rode back to camp. Although most thought the Indians uncouth and uncivilized, Percy had learned over the years that they might be uncivilized, but they were masters of deception. With that in mind, he thought the trail he had discovered was probably a diversion. And that sapped his spirits a bit as he climbed down from his horse. He knew finding the Indians was going to be difficult, but that impressed upon him the enormity of their task.

CHAPTER
48

Riding along the south rim of the canyon, Cyrus, Wilcox, and Isaac were searching the interior for any sign of Indians. No one wanted to venture into the canyon and risk running into a crowd of armed enemies. Yes, the canyon was vast, but the sheer, rocky cliff walls that lined portions of the space severely limited egress points. If they got caught down on the floor of the canyon by a large Comanche war party they'd literally have to run for their lives. Cyrus understood that, but he was tired of pussyfooting around. They were burning through time they didn't have.

"I ain't seen an Injun yet," Cyrus said. "I say we ride on down there for a closer look."

"I don't know, boss," Wilcox said. "We cut a lot of sign up here and there's lots of places to hide down yonder."

"You couldn't hide a big passel of Injuns down there without us seein' 'em. Hellfire, we're so far deep into their territory I reckon they'd be camped in the open. And I ain't seein' a bunch of damn teepees, either." Cyrus brought his horse to a stop and Isaac and Wilcox did the same. "Ain't no Injuns, ain't no Emma, fellers."

"Well, we ain't covered all the canyon yet," Wilcox said.

"And I don't want to ride on and take a chance at missin' her if she's here," Isaac said.

"Well, she ain't gonna be sittin' down there by her lonesome, is she? And we can see a lot of the canyon from here. You even seen any smoke?"

"No," Isaac said, "but they would have seen us comin' for miles. Could've snuffed all their fires."

"Okay, I'll grant you that," Cyrus said. "But they couldn't make their whole damn camp just disappear, could they? I know the Injuns can be sneaky sonsabitches, but they ain't that damn sneaky. And you said it yer-self, Isaac. They woulda had riders out and probably woulda seen us comin' for days. I reckon if they were here at all, they're gone now."

"So what do you want to do?" Isaac asked.

Cyrus looked up to gauge the sun's posi-tion then turned his horse and spurred him into a walk. "It'll be dark about the time we get back to camp. I reckon we can talk about it and see what we can get figured out."

As they were riding back to camp, Cyrus kept an eye on the rim on the other side, hoping to signal the other group to head back. If he had been anywhere else, he would have pulled out his pistol and fired a shot in the air. But not here. And especially not with the war wagon so far away. Cyrus didn't know how many Comanches there might be out here in the wild, but he guessed they had to number in the thousands. And firing a pistol to announce their present location might well have caused them to lose their hair.

With all the open space around them, there was a persistent breeze but all it did was stir around the heat. Add in the fact that the horses hadn't had a drink since morning when they left camp and Cyrus didn't think they could do more than walk the horses back. He was slightly concerned about being caught out in the dark although he knew that cut both ways, either as an advantage or a disadvantage. What concerned him more was Percy's situation. Keeping an eye on things was easy to do in daylight. Not so much at night. Cyrus checked the position of the sun again and judged they probably had an hour before full dark.

Back at camp, Percy fished out his watch and popped the lid to check the time. If it didn't cloud up, he thought he might have half an hour before it became too dark to see. He had built a small fire at the base of a small ridge that was sheltered from sight by a couple of mature juniper trees. Nestled in the coals was a fresh pot of coffee and another large pot of beans with some shredded beef jerky mixed in. As Percy worked around camp, he had the sudden feeling that he was being watched. And not by friendly eyes, either. His hackles up, Percy's movements became determined and precise. He turned his head slightly and took a quick peek at the wagon. It would have to be pulled out if it was going to be of any use. With his right hand he reached up to make sure his pistol was seated and scanned the surrounding area with his eyes, searching for his rifle. He spotted it leaned up against the front of the wagon and he judged the distance. He figured it would take him three long strides to grab the rifle and another second to have it up in a firing position. So, five, maybe six, seconds, he thought. Doable. But what he really wanted was the wagon.

Mouse was still saddled but he didn't know if she had the strength to pull the wagon out by herself. The ropes affixed to the tongue would be easily accessible, so Percy walked through the remaining steps in his mind. If, and it was a big if, Mouse could pull the wagon by herself then he calculated the entire maneuver would consume somewhere close to thirty seconds. That gave him a good idea of how long it would take, but the most important variables were unknown — how far away the enemy was and their exact location.

Percy shook his shoulders to loosen them and walked nonchalantly toward his horse. There was some concern that his father and the rest of the crew would be in the line of fire, but Percy assumed they would get to cover as soon as the first shot was fired. Or that's what he hoped. He wouldn't be able to operate freely if he had to expend any mental energy on their welfare. When he reached Mouse, he talked softly to her as he grabbed the reins. He walked through the steps again in his mind. He had tied a loop at the ends of the ropes so he'd have to pick up those, slip them over the saddle horn, and then slap Mouse across the butt and hope she could do the job while he raced over and jumped behind the Gatling gun. There were so many ways it could all go wrong but trying to fend off an attack by himself without those weapons would be madness.

Percy slowly walked Mouse over to the wagon. He grabbed his rifle and eased it up on the wagon seat. He made sure his knife was easily accessible because he would have to cut the ropes to free Mouse so she could get out of the line of fire. A thousand other thoughts bombarded his brain and he took a deep breath to clear his mind. A cluttered mind could get a man killed. Pulling the horse around until she was facing away from the wagon, he lined her up as best as he could and tried not to think about what would happen if Mouse failed to move the wagon. After bending down to pick up the ropes, he slipped them over the saddle horn and checked the saddle to make sure it was cinched down tight as his eyes scanned for threats.

He still hadn't seen any sign of the enemy and he was working on instinct, although he'd learned over the years that he had been right more often than not. Taking a moment to rethink everything, he pulled the ropes from the saddle horn, took out all the slack, and retied the loops and put them back on. That would help to reduce the possibility of a broken girth strap while Mouse pulled. And he also decided to ease Mouse into it rather than slapping her on the butt. He hurried around to the back of the wagon and leaned his shoulder against the tailgate. Clucking his tongue, he ordered Mouse to walk as he put his weight behind his shoulder and pushed. Nothing happened at first, then the back wheel moved about six inches and stopped. He eased up, repositioned his feet, and shouted at Mouse to move as he pushed with all of his strength. Just when it looked as if nothing was going to happen, the wagon began to move.

But his happiness was short-lived. The Indians took exception to his efforts to move the wagon and Comanche war cries filled the air.

As Mouse continued to pull, Percy jumped into the wagon and scrambled forward to the Gatling gun. It was too dark to see much other than movement, but Percy thought that if the Indians were smart, they'd have surrounded the wagon to increase their odds. He grabbed the handle and started cranking as he walked a tight circle, swiveling the gun around as he walked, the wagon still moving forward. There were no warning shots this time — Percy was shooting to do as much damage as possible. He paused cranking as Mouse came into view in the sights then started back up once he was clear of his horse. He took a quick look to see if the wagon was clear of any obstructions, paused cranking, yanked his knife out, and cut the rope, freeing Mouse. Then he was back on the gun. He walked three complete circles, cranking the handle. He wasn't looking for specific targets, he just poured on the lead. On the third time around, he paused. His ears were ringing so hearing anything was out, so he swept his gaze around to see if the Indians wanted any more.

He saw several dead horses in the deepening gloom and assumed they once held Indian riders. Whether they escaped the gun's withering firepower didn't really matter to Percy. For good measure, he hurried back to the cannon, swung it around until it was lined up on the area where he'd seen the dead horses, adjusted the elevation a tad, then pulled the rope. The cannon roared, the wagon shook, and the muzzle blast stretched about ten feet beyond the end of the howitzer's barrel. And that was all Percy saw before he hurried back to the Gatling gun as smoke enveloped the wagon.

He hadn't really aimed the cannon and thought it more important to demonstrate the wagon's prowess rather than effect wholesale slaughter. As the ringing in his ears began to subside, he heard sustained rifle fire in the distance and assumed the Indians were on the run. But that didn't mean he was leaving the gun anytime soon. He checked to see how much ammo was left and thought he ought to open a new crate, but not yet.

Percy was still behind the gun when the last hints of daylight faded into darkness. And he remained there until he heard the calls from the returning men. Only then did he step out, although he didn't go far before he grabbed his rifle from where he'd stowed it on the wagon seat. "All clear?" he shouted into the growing darkness.

"All clear," he heard his father say as he rode into camp. "You okay?" Cyrus asked.

"Yeah. They all gone?" Percy asked.

"Think so," Cyrus said. "Wilcox is gonna ride a circle to see for sure. So keep that rifle o' yours handy." Cyrus pulled his horse to a stop and climbed down from the saddle. "You got coffee on?"

Percy smiled at his father's steady, unflappable nature. "Yep. Beans, too, if you're hungry."

Cyrus tied his horse's reins to the wagon wheel. "I could eat."

CHAPTER
49

While Percy was busy fighting off Indians, his mother, Frances, was busy rustling up supper for his children. It had been a long time since Cyrus had been gone this long and she was worried about him. She pushed the steaks around in the pan while she ruminated. Although still strong enough to outwork two men on a normal day, she knew her husband had his ailments. Hard not to live as long as they both had and not feel it in your bones. But it wasn't Cyrus's bones that had her concerned at present, it was the organ that resided inside that framework that worried her. A few days before he left, she noticed him rubbing his chest. He hadn't said anything at the time, nor would he, but she was concerned he was having chest pains. Not that there was anything they could do about it, but she didn't want him to start feeling poorly so far from home.

Frances forked the steaks onto three plates, added a scoop of mashed potatoes, poured gravy over everything, and carried the dishes over to the table. She didn't have much of an appetite and instead poured a cup of coffee and took a seat at the table. Amanda was in a good place after her mother's death and had recently struck up a friendship — or maybe more, Frances hoped — with one of Dan Waggoner's men who had come over during the branding. His job had been to cut out the reversed three-D cattle and then herd them back to the home range, but he'd spent the last two Sundays calling on Amanda with Frances acting as chaperone.

Chauncey still seemed indifferent to the whole situation and Frances didn't know if that was a defense mechanism that would eventually fall by the wayside over time or if he had difficulties expressing or understanding empathy. It did bother Frances some that both he and Seth ran off to the river to shoot pistols every chance they got. She didn't have a problem with them learning how to handle a weapon but did wonder if they were overdoing it sometimes. She couldn't remember if Percy went through a similar phase or not. Eli certainly hadn't and he still didn't have much to do with guns. Surreptitiously watching Chauncey saw through a piece of steak with his knife, Frances decided both he and Seth warranted closer observation. It was much easier to correct troubling behavior if it was caught early.

Franklin, on the other hand, was still openly grieving. He had periodic bouts of crying, but those had lessened over time. Although Franklin favored Percy, he had the inquisitive nature of his uncle Eli. Frances had answered more questions about death over the last two weeks than in her previous sixty-four years of life. The questions ranged from the afterlife to body decomposition and Frances was forced to consult a few of the books in her well-stocked library for some of the answers. She had zero concerns about Franklin's further development.

She did, however, have concerns about her own daughter Rachel. And they weren't worries about her development, because she was a mature woman with children of her own. No, what peeved Frances were her daughter's recent choices. She didn't know if there was something going on between Rachel and that Texas Ranger Leander Hays but he'd been lurking around the ranch on and off for two weeks. Although Frances hadn't caught them in any compromising situations yet, it just didn't pass the smell test. And it wasn't that Frances was a prude. She'd gone through her own brief period of promiscuity back in New Orleans prior to marrying Cyrus and she understood the butterflies-in-the-stomach feelings that came with new flirtations and shared mutual attraction. But Frances thought Rachel needed to look beyond that because the problems caused by an illicit affair significantly outweighed the benefits. She had seen it time and time again with her own parents, specifically her father, who was a serial philanderer who'd bed anything with two legs and tits. And it was a disgusting thing to see, and why her mother put up with it was a mystery and remained a mystery long after her death.

The more Frances thought about it, the angrier she became. "Amanda, keep an eye on your brothers."

"Where are you goin'?" Amanda asked.

Frances stood, carried her cup over to the wash bucket, and dropped it in. "I have something that needs doin'." Frances exited the house and made a beeline for Rachel's place. As she walked, she rolled a few ideas around in her mind in an attempt to predict how the upcoming conversation would go.

She knew her ability to control what Rachel did was long gone so she searched for a different approach, one that would allow Rachel to see the error of her ways. The key, Frances thought, was to keep the conversation low-key and not let it escalate into confrontation. Rachel had always been high-strung and somewhat volatile when prodded, and a shouting match wouldn't accomplish anything.

Frances stepped up on Rachel's porch and took a deep breath before knocking on the door. Without waiting for a response, Frances opened the door and stepped inside. Rachel was lounging on the sofa while Consuelo served supper to the kids. "Rachel, will you join me in a walk?" Frances said.

"Right now?" Rachel asked.

"Sure, unless I need to make an appointment to take a walk with my daughter," Frances said, her anger already bleeding into her words despite her own admonishments.

Rachel stood. "Well, if you put it like that, I guess I don't have much choice, do I?"

Frances was already kicking herself for letting her anger get the better of her. "I didn't mean for it to sound that way."

"No?" Rachel asked as she stepped around the sofa. She shoved her feet into a pair of deerskin moccasins and brushed by her mother on the way out the door.

Frances sighed, turned to follow, and closed the door behind her.

"Where are we walking to?" Rachel asked. "Shall we stroll by the cattle pens so that we might imbibe the aroma of fresh cow shit?"

"Hush, now," Frances said softly as she linked arms with her daughter. "I'm sorry." She steered Rachel away from the horseshoe-shaped array of homes and toward the river. "How's Seth doing?"

"Did you invite me on a walk to talk about Seth?" Rachel asked.

"That and other things," Frances said as they ambled along, in no hurry and with no real destination other than to put some distance between themselves and prying ears.

"Why don't we skip the *that* and get on with the other things," Rachel said, her angry undertone subdued, but there.

"In a bit," Frances said. They walked in silence for a few moments. Frances glanced over at the guest cabin to see a lantern glowing inside and that meant the current guest, Leander Hays, was currently in residence. The log cabin was small — one room — and had been the first home built on the ranch all those years ago. Situated closer to the river, it had been abandoned when the family expanded beyond its capacity. Frances had cleaned the place up and made it inhabitable again to accommodate cattle or horse buyers who visited or other guests who happened along.

As the sun slipped below the horizon, painting the sky with reds and pinks and purples, Frances knew she had to get on with it before it became too dark. "Have you had an opportunity to spend any time with our guest?" Frances asked.

"So that's what this is about," Rachel said, heat creeping back into her voice.

"It was just a simple question."

"No, it wasn't and you know it."

Frances sighed. "Okay, then, I'll rephrase my question. Is there something going on with you and that Ranger?"

Rachel stiffened. "That Ranger has a name. Leander Hays. And I'm a grown woman quite capable of making my own decisions."

"I realize that, Rachel. But sometimes those decisions have implications for others."

Rachel wrenched her arm free and turned to face her mother. "What is it you want to know?" she hissed.

"I want to know what is going on with you and that character Hays."

Rachel took a step forward until they were nose to nose. "We're fucking. Is that what you really wanted to know?" Rachel's low, angry words were dripping with venom.

"What about Amos?"

"What *about* Amos?"

"He's your husband."

"So what?"

"Does that not matter?"

"It might to you."

"But not you?" Frances asked, leaning forward until their noses *were* touching.

"Why do you care?"

The two glared at each other for a long, silent moment. Frances broke the stare and said in a low, angry voice, "I care about you and *your* family. What?" Frances said, poking Rachel in the chest with her finger, all pretense of a calm discussion obliterated. "You and your lover going to go off traipsing across the country? What exactly is your plan?"

Rachel took a step back. "That's none of your business."

Frances filled the void, taking a step forward. "It is my business," Frances said, emphasizing each word with a poke at Rachel's chest. "Everything that happens on this ranch is my business. And you need to quit this nonsense."

Rachel turned away and Frances grabbed her by the elbow and yanked her back around. "Don't you dare walk away from me."

Rachel shrugged. "It's my life and you can't do a damn thing about it."

"No?" Frances spat. "I can do something about it." Frances dropped her hand and stomped toward the guest cabin. "You just hide and watch!"

Rachel hurried after Frances and grabbed her arm, pulling her to stop. Rachel stepped in front of her mother and looked her in the eye. "Don't do something you're going to regret."

"Rachel, I have had a lifetime of regrets and one more is not going to make a damn bit of difference." Frances brushed past Rachel and stalked toward the cabin door.

Again, Rachel hurried past, turned, and put her hands on her mother's chest. "Stop this madness."

"I plan to," Frances said as she swatted away Rachel's hands and marched up to the door. She flung it open and pointed a finger at the Ranger, barely able to contain her rage. "I want you off this property right this damn minute!"

Rachel pushed past and entered the cabin, trying to get between Frances and Leander. Frances pushed her away and took a step forward, still glaring at the Ranger. "And if you're seen on the property again either I or my men will shoot you dead. And I don't give a damn if you've got a tin star or not." Frances whirled around and marched out the door.

CHAPTER
50

After standing the first watch, Percy had rolled up in his blanket and slept like the dead. The adrenaline rush of sudden battle and a day of constant worry had sapped him of any reserves of energy he might have had. Now with the first full rays of the sun breaking on the horizon, he sat up and rubbed his eyes. The odor of just-brewed coffee hung in the still air and, judging by the already-warm temperature, Percy knew they were in for another long, hot day. A new plan had not yet been formulated and he was going to suggest a change that two men remain in camp at all times. That was if they decided to stay here. He climbed to his feet, stepped away to drain his bladder, and returned to cinch on his gun belt.

It had been too dark for an accurate damage report so that was the first thing on his to-do list. They did know the Indians hadn't absconded with the mules and that was a relief. Percy grabbed a cup from the chuck box on the wagon and shuffled over to the fire. He filled his cup, took a sip, and took a seat on the ground. He looked over at Luis, who had the last watch. "See or hear anything?"

Luis shook his head. *"Nada."*

Luis, still sullen from the death of his friend, hadn't said much since they had buried Arturo. Not knowing Mexican customs well or whether there was a certain period of mourning, Percy assumed he'd come around at some point. Percy took another sip from his cup and gave a little thought to starting breakfast then decided he'd leave that job to Amos, who didn't seem to mind cooking. And Amos's food tasted better than his although, it could be that his dislike of cooking colored his opinion. He switched his thinking from cooking to the current situation when a shadow fell across his cup and he looked up to see Winfield Wilson strolling into camp, his rifle slung over his shoulder and an empty coffee cup in his hand.

"Where you been?" Percy asked.

Win propped his rifle against the wagon and refilled his cup. "Out lookin'."

"What did you see?"

"A passel of dead horses."

"No dead Indians?" Percy asked.

"Nope. Plenty of blood trails, though."

"How many dead horses?"

"Thirteen up close and another half dozen further out." Win nodded at the wagon. "That there cannon of yours did a number on 'em, I'll tell you that. Ain't never seen anything like it. Anyway, about the same on blood trails. Don't know how many Injuns were killed, but I reckon you lit into 'em pretty good."

"Where did you find the dead horses that were closer in?" Percy asked.

Win pointed to the area on the other side of the wagon and moved his arm in a semicircle to the left. "Shot the shit out of some junipers behind us, too, but ain't nothing dead over there."

"How many Injuns, you think?" Percy asked.

Win took a sip of coffee. "Too dark to see much last night and the tracks are too tore up to venture a guess. Wilcox'll have to look. But there was a pack of 'em."

"Which way did they ride when they left?"

"Whatever way they could get with you a-shootin' and us a-shootin', too. Them Injuns scattered like church deacons in a whorehouse when the lights come on." Win chuckled. "Beat all I ever seen. I reckon we'll know more when Wilcox gets back from scoutin'."

Percy heard a groan and he looked over to see his father standing up. He grabbed a cup and shuffled over to the fire. He poured coffee and said, "We have a plan yet?" He stepped out beyond the fire and took a piss.

"Waitin' on Amos and Isaac to get up."

"Well, wake 'em up. We're burnin' daylight," Cyrus said grumpily.

Percy picked up a couple of small rocks and tossed one at Isaac and the other at Amos and they began to stir.

Cyrus dropped the tailgate on the wagon and sat. "Well," he said, "I reckon every Injun within a hundred miles knows we're here now."

Percy looked over at his father, who was absentmindedly rubbing his chest. "I'm bettin' they knew well before last night. Your chest hurtin'?"

Cyrus immediately stopped rubbing. "Naw, had an itch. Damn skeeters. What we get for campin' so damn close to the river."

"You had as much say as anyone in choosin' where to camp," Percy said, stung by the rebuke.

"I know it. Don't get your feathers ruffled," Cyrus said. "How are we on supplies?"

Percy noticed his father was rubbing his chest again but didn't say anything. "I figure we can stretch it another three or four weeks. More if we can get some fresh game."

"Well," Cyrus said, "guess we ain't so concerned about shootin' no more."

Amos and Isaac shuffled over and filled their cups.

"Well, I reckon we're all here now," Cyrus said. "What's the plan?"

Isaac walked over and took a seat on the tailgate and Amos sat down next to Percy.

"Not everybody at once," Cyrus said. He looked over at Amos and said, "You cookin'?"

"I thought we was makin' a plan," Amos said.

"Ain't no reason you can't do both," Cyrus said.

Amos pushed to his feet and put a pan on the coals to warm before walking over to the chuck box. He cut off several pieces of bacon and carried them over and put them in the hot pan then returned to the wagon and started on the biscuits.

"Who thinks there's Injuns in the canyon?" Cyrus asked.

"We ain't covered all of it," Isaac said.

"We seen a bunch of it," Cyrus said, "and didn't see hide nor hair of any Injuns. Hell, far as we know, the redskins might not like campin' in the canyon."

"They camp down there," Percy said. "We rousted some Apaches out there back when I was workin' with the Rangers."

"That was might near twenty years ago," Cyrus said. "How do you know they ain't changed their thinkin' on it?"

"I don't. But I don't see any reason why they'd quit campin' down there." Percy pulled his knife and leaned over to stir the bacon.

Win joined the conversation. "After breakfast me and Percy'll ride down there and find out for sure."

"That'll work," Cyrus said. "But even if you do find evidence of Indians campin', that don't mean Emma was with 'em."

"Emma would have left somethin' behind for us to find," Isaac said.

"How do you know?" Cyrus asked.

"I just know," Isaac said. "She's a smart girl. And I'd bet my last dollar she left us somethin' to find."

"Even if she did, that ain't goin' to tell where she went," Amos said. He grabbed another pot, carried it over to the fire, and began dropping biscuit dough inside.

"It doesn't rain much out this way," Percy said. "If we know she was here at some point, we ought to be able to find their trail."

Cyrus took a sip of coffee, swallowed, and said, "Well, first thing I reckon is to figure out if Emma has been here." He turned to look at Isaac. "What d'ya think she'd leave?"

"A piece of her dress, maybe," Isaac said.

Percy didn't have the heart to tell his brother-in-law that Emma's dress was probably ripped off not long after she was taken. "Maybe she left somethin' else."

"Why not a piece of her dress?" Isaac asked.

"Well . . ." Percy said, stalling until he came up with something, which he did. "Indians would see it. That's why. It would have to be something less noticeable."

"Didn't think about that," Isaac said. He gave the matter a little more thought and then snapped his fingers. "Some of her hair. They wouldn't see that, would they?"

"Good thinkin'," Percy said. "Might make it awful hard to find, though."

"Not if you found where they was camped," Cyrus said. "If they was camped, that is."

"Won't know until we look, I guess," Percy said as he reached out and flipped the pieces of bacon over. "Going to take us four or five days to cover the entire canyon."

Cyrus stood up and arched his back. "I

don't know any way else to do it. Ain't goin' to do us much good to follow the Injuns' trail if Emma ain't with 'em."

Cyrus stood up straight and Percy noticed that he was rubbing his chest again as he looked off into the distance. Then he stopped rubbing and said, "Reckon a couple of us could do a little huntin' while Percy and Win are gone."

"We need to keep more than one man in camp. Too hard to watch everything with just one man," Percy said as he stood. He grabbed an old horseshoe lying by the fire and used that to pull the pan of bacon off the fire and he carried it over to the wagon and put it on the tailgate.

"Well, I don't think we're goin' to have to worry about it," Cyrus said. "Probably need Win or Wilcox doin' the scouting down in the canyon. Get too many people down there and it'll make a mess of everything."

Once the biscuits were done, Amos carried the pot over to the wagon and the chow was on. "Save some for Wilcox," Cyrus said as he forked out a biscuit onto his plate.

Once breakfast was over, Percy and Win saddled their horses and, after stocking up on extra ammunition, rode down into the canyon. The going was slow because they had no idea what they were looking for. It was like searching for that one fallen leaf in a forest of trees. And to add to the confusion it looked as if the canyon had seen plenty of action recently. They were just beginning the search and had already discovered two different places where the Indians, or someone, had camped. They'd searched both sites and had found nothing but a lingering foul odor from the feces and animal carcasses along with the ashes of long-dead fires.

"What are we lookin' for, exactly?" Win asked. "I didn't want to say nothin' in front of Isaac, but it ain't hair. It'd blow away, wouldn't it?"

"Most likely," Percy said. "Only thing I can come up with is maybe she drew something in the dirt."

"That don't make no sense, neither. It'd have to be somethin' that ain't goin' to wash away in the rain."

"I'm open for suggestions," Percy said.

"I ain't got none. I reckon we'll know it when we see it. Can't be clothes, though. The Injuns would have shucked those off right quick."

"You're right."

They rode in silence for a while, their eyes in constant motion scanning the ground and scanning for threats. It was obvious from the multitude of unshod hoof prints that the canyon was a popular place. And even though they hadn't seen any sign of an Indian camp from their vantage point on the rim, it appeared that the possibility of running into an Indian war party was much higher than either one of them liked. Percy was hoping that word of last night's introduction to the Gatling gun and mountain howitzer had spread. Nevertheless, both men had their rifles out and ready.

CHAPTER
51

Emma was exhausted, worn out — tired to the bone. The old squaws had been working her like a rented mule and if she failed to meet their level of expectation, she often received a beating via their hands, a stick, or whatever was handy. Her body was bruised and battered and, to add to her misery, she still hadn't adapted to the Indians' diet and her stomach was often roiling. And those were the agonies during daylight hours.

The nights were another type of horror altogether.

The worst part of it all was the isolation, the inability to commiserate with another human being. Emma was trying to pick up some of the Comanche language, but it was usually a word or two that described a physical object and nothing that dealt with the senses or emotions. There was a lot of pointing and grunting and that summed up

her social interactions other than the un-
wanted advances from the men. She had
hidden the knife in a safe place and had
dreamed of using it many times but hadn't
yet worked up the courage. And her body
ached enough as it was and the thought of
a more severe beating or worse was something she didn't want to contemplate — yet.
Not that she wouldn't get to that point if
the days and weeks stretched into months.
But she still believed a rescue was possible
and the sooner, the better.

After the Indians had broken camp and
left the canyon, they had been on the move
for many days and Emma thought, based
on the position of the sun, that they had
traveled in a northwesterly direction. Emma
didn't know the distance traveled in miles,
but she knew she was now a very long way
from home. The Indians had made camp
two days ago along a river bottom, the only
real body of water Emma had seen since
their departure other than a few small water
holes that the Indians must have been using
for years. It was the most inhospitable place
Emma had seen in her short life. The
uniformity — mile after mile after mile
without a trace of anything in which to mark
your progress — was mind-numbing and
monotonous. The Indians hadn't seemed

bothered by it. Emma didn't know what guideposts were used to navigate such a vast expanse of nothingness, but they did it with apparent ease. Emma was just praying the ever-present wind didn't wipe out their trail before her rescuers could find it.

Emma was brought back to the present when an old squaw whacked her across the back of the legs with a stick. Emma whirled around and tried to grab the stick from the squaw, but her grip was too strong. The woman sneered, yanked the stick from Emma's grasp, and hit her again, this time across the thighs. It was the same old hag who'd slapped her across the face, and Emma snapped. She stepped forward and shoved the old woman back, then took another step and shoved her again. The old squaw went reeling back with the second shove and she tripped over an undulation in the ground and fell flat on her butt. Emma pointed a finger at her and shouted, "No more!"

The squaw looked stunned and it took her a moment before she clambered to her feet. Emma didn't know what was coming next as the old hag approached, the stick still in her hand. But Emma was boiling mad, and she was ready for a fight if one came. The squaw outweighed her by a good forty pounds and was much stronger after a lifetime of hard work, but Emma was determined there would be no backing down this time, no matter the consequences. Even if the old squaw was someone who was important to the chief. Emma knew she didn't sleep in the chief's teepee because that was where she slept — or tried to when she was left alone.

The old hag walked up close until they were nose to nose, and Emma held her ground. She balled her small hands into fists and waited for the squaw to make the first move. They were now close enough that the impact from the stick would be limited unless the old woman was planning to poke an eye out. Instead, and to Emma's amazement, the squaw leaned over and placed the stick on the ground, stood up tall and placed both hands on Emma's shoulders, and nodded.

Well, shoot, just when I was really learning to hate you. Emma nodded back and the old woman smiled, revealing a mouth with only a half a dozen teeth. She patted Emma on the shoulders and nodded again before reaching down to take both of Emma's hands in hers. Hers were shriveled and callused and were much larger than Emma's. She squeezed both of Emma's hands and nodded for a third time, before gently releasing them. *Do I have to fight at every turn? Is this what the Indians expect of me?*

Emma smiled and the woman returned the smile before she turned and walked away. Emma didn't know if that marked the end of hostilities between them or if it signaled something else. Deciding the situation would bear watching, Emma was hesitant to read too much into it. If it meant the old squaw would quit attacking her, then she was all for it. She would not, however, turn a blind eye when the old woman was within striking distance.

Angel, whom she renamed Devil after that one brief interlude of peace in the tent, walked over and pointed at an empty water bag and grunted. Groaning, Emma grabbed the bag and headed toward the river. The one saving grace was that they'd camped closer to the water and Emma didn't have to lug the water bag as far. And she'd learned not to fill the bag all the way up. It was still enormously heavy, although, after scraping hides for days, she didn't think going after water was such a bad thing. It also allowed her an opportunity to enjoy some time alone. Although she'd been with the Indians for weeks, she was still watched closely and having eyes on her all the time was emotionally draining. She didn't know if the Indians thought she might try to escape or if there was another reason. Escape was the farthest thing from her mind after having traveled through that dry, inhospitable country.

As she walked through the camp, she spotted the two white boy captives who were learning to shoot a bow and arrow with Indian boys their age. Communication between her and the two boys was still strictly forbidden, but Emma could tell by watching they were still having a difficult time adjusting. That Emma could understand because it was the same for her. Her crying spells were less frequent and, to avoid a beating, occurred only under the cover of darkness. Thoughts of her family and life at the ranch invaded her mind constantly and it was a struggle to keep them at bay. Only through sheer will had she been able to keep going day after day after day, not knowing if or when she might be rescued. She didn't have any doubts that her father and grandfather were searching for her, but her long travels with the Indians made her better understand the enormity of their task. It was like being lost in the middle of the ocean and the only clue her father and grandfather had was that she was in there somewhere. The only difference was that trails were left on land, but they were far from permanent.

At the river, Emma paused to take a long look around before she slipped out of her dress and waded out into the water. Although she could have filled the water bag from the bank, she was hot and dirty, and the cool water was too tempting. As she drifted out into the middle of the river, she took a moment for another look around. She had seen Scar several times over the weeks and nothing had come of it — so far. It could be that Emma was always in the company of other people and he was waiting to catch her alone somewhere, thus her caution during trips to the river. Unfortunately, his appearance meant he hadn't succumbed to a nasty infection from her bite and, regrettably, all of his appendages remained intact.

After rinsing her hair, Emma scrubbed under her arms and between her legs, thinking that she'd kill for a bar of soap. From what she'd seen, the Indian women were frequent bathers as were a good number of the men. Of the men who refused to bathe, some were so raunchy that Emma would gag if she stood downwind of them. Thankfully, the chief had better habits than most of the other men, but there were times that Emma had to breathe through her mouth when he was near.

And as for the general state of Indian hygiene, Emma now knew that pulling up stakes to follow the buffalo was not the only reason the Indians moved camp so frequently. The last camp reeked so bad from feces, both animal and human, and harvested animal carcasses that Emma's eyes often watered. And she knew it wouldn't be long before the same happened at this camp. But she was hoping the Indians would stay long enough for her rescuers to catch up.

Emma swam over to the edge of a sandbar, scooped up a handful of sand, and used it to scrub her face and scalp. She had deduced that the bugs she'd seen in the buffalo hides were lice and, despite her best attempts, her hair was now infested. It was repugnant and she itched constantly, but there was little she could do about it. After dunking her head to rinse away the sand, Emma rubbed the water out of her eyes. When she opened them and looked across the water, her heart stuttered. Scar was standing on the bank, a sneer on his face. All thoughts of lice disappeared in an instant as she quickly scanned the river bottom, searching for an escape route or a place to hide. As she swam toward the opposite side, she realized her options were few. There was no place she could go where Scar couldn't follow. And she knew she couldn't outrun him even with a head start. Looking back over her shoulder, she saw Scar wading into the water.

Think, Emma! If she couldn't outrun him, maybe she could outswim him. Emma reversed course and swam back toward the middle of the river where the current was swifter. Turning with the flow, she began pinwheeling her arms, digging deep into the water as she raced downstream. She didn't waste time looking to see if Scar was following, she just swam with all of her might. And it wasn't long before she was gasping for breath. Already exhausted and worn down, her strength was fading quickly, and her pace slowed. And within seconds she felt his hand clamp down on her ankle. She had been stupid to think she could outswim him. She was too exhausted to mount a fight, and Scar pulled her easily toward the bank.

A momentary thought of drowning herself or him entered her mind, but he pulled her head out of the water so quickly she couldn't even formulate a plan. Grabbing her by the hair, Scar pulled her onto the grass and flipped her over. Just when she was about to scream, he punched her in the gut and the scream died in her throat. He slapped her across the face, stunning her, and then, using the forearm she had bitten, he pushed against her nose and mouth with all of his weight, instantly cutting off her air supply. Emma flailed, punching him in the face and torso, but he was too strong. When Emma was on the edge of blacking out, he pulled his arm away and she gasped for breath. Before she could recover, Scar punched her in the stomach again, lifted his breechcloth, and violently assaulted her, pinching and twisting her breasts until they bled.

When he finished, he stood and kicked her in the ribs before stalking off. Emma rolled over onto her side as tears ran down her cheeks. That pain inside of her which had diminished over time, was back and it burned like a hot coal in her gut. She put a hand down between her legs and could feel the sticky wetness of fresh blood. She watched as Scar disappeared among the trees and vowed to herself that his next attempt would be his last. She would bury the knife so deep in his chest that it would take two men to pull it out. Consequences be damned.

CHAPTER
52

It was deep in the night when Rachel rolled over from beneath Leander Hays's arm, fumbled for a match, struck it, and lit the lantern on the bedside table. She adjusted the wick until the tip was just visible above the brass lip and rolled back over to look at Leander, who was still asleep. She had mentally replayed the fight with her mother a dozen times, searching for a way out of the mess she'd created. She didn't believe her mother would actually shoot Leander or order it done, but she wasn't one hundred percent sure, either, especially as mad as she'd been. Her mother usually did not make idle threats and Rachel thought she might soften her stance now that the heat of battle was over, but she knew it wouldn't happen by daybreak, for sure. Her mother's only concession after the fight was that he could stay until daybreak, which was now quickly approaching.

Rachel watched as Leander's chest rose and fell, her mind jumbled with thoughts. Although Leander had fed her cravings, she was unsure what came next. She wanted him in her life but was having difficulty working out the logistics to make it happen. Her top priority was the welfare of her three children. And leaving them behind wasn't an option. She had no qualms about divorcing Amos, but it would be a drama-filled affair that would traumatize the children and send the entire family into chaotic disarray. That left option two, which was to pack up the kids and move to Leander's place. If Rachel anticipated a divorce would be tumultuous, she couldn't even fathom the pandemonium that would erupt if she tried to take the children away from the only home they had ever known. And it was the only home she'd known, too. She couldn't bear the thought of moving away from her parents and siblings. And the more she thought about it, the firmer her resolve.

Rachel's brain was on the verge of overheating. *What to do about Leander Hays? With a divorce unlikely and moving a definite no, what's left? An occasional illicit rendezvous to fulfill our carnal pleasures? That wouldn't really be fair to him, would it? But I really don't know what he thinks, do I? What if he was up for something* — Rachel reached over and nudged him awake.

Using his elbows, he pushed himself up against the headboard. "Why are you up?" he asked in a sleepy voice.

"Couldn't sleep. It'll be daylight soon."

"You think your ma meant what she said?"

"About shootin' you?"

"Well, yeah. Stayin' alive is kinda one of my priorities."

Rachel shrugged. "I don't know, but it's probably best not to test her right now."

Leander nodded and wiped the sleep out of his eyes. "About what I figured."

Rachel picked at one of his chest hairs. "How did you see this playin' out?"

"Didn't think that far ahead. You?"

"I asked first."

"That you did." Leander paused for a long moment and then said, "Seems like you're kinda attached to this place."

"Maybe," Rachel said.

Leander pushed a strand of hair off her face. "I don't know, Rachel. I can't wrap my head around much more than the next few days. I guess I'm not a long-term-thinkin' man."

"So, what? You just bed a woman and then move on to the next one?"

"No. To tell the truth, you're the first

woman I've been with since my wife died."

"Why's that?"

"Hadn't come across any women like you."

Rachel sighed, her mind more confused than ever. "What did you see happenin'?"

"In my line of work, I've learned to take it a day at a time. Like I said, I don't look very far into the future."

"So, you were planning on what? Just saying good-bye and riding off?"

"What do you want me to say? That I'd love to take you back to my place on the Brazos? I'm just a poor lawman, Rachel. I ain't got much to offer." He waved a hand at the cabin and all of the furniture inside. "My place is about half this size with about a tenth of the furniture. Think you would be happy with that?"

Rachel rolled over on her back and stared at the ceiling. "Worldly possessions aren't the foundation of happiness."

"No, they ain't. But it's a much easier thing to say if you can afford to buy 'em and make the choice not to. It's much different when a man doesn't have a prayer of being able to buy a nice feather bed or a new piece of furniture. We live in two different worlds, Rachel."

Rachel reached out and stroked his hip

413

while they lay in silence. Rachel eventually broke the silence and said, "I might not have a choice if my husband finds out about this. He might run me off."

"Then he'd be a fool."

Rachel rolled back over and fit her naked body against his. "You're a good man, Leander Hays," she said as she began stroking his chest hair again.

"I just don't see any way to make it work, Rachel. And it's not for a lack of wantin', neither." He ran his fingers through her hair. "I'm on the move most of the time, too. You'd be all by yourself down there. And that ain't fair to you when you have all of this family around here."

"So, we just go back to the way things were?"

"I don't think I can. I won't be the same man as I was before." He dropped his hand down and used his thumb to stroke her cheek. "I'll be a much different man than the one who rode in. And I have you to thank for it."

Rachel rolled over, turned out the lantern, and then said, "Show me how thankful you are."

CHAPTER
53

Late on the fourth day of searching the canyon, Percy and Win finally found the initials that Emma had laid out with stones. They now knew that Emma had been there at one point, and now the big question was — where did she go? Moses Wilcox had spent the better part of four days scouting out well beyond the campsite, or as far as he was willing to ride, being in the heart of Indian country. On his travels, he had found a slew of Indian trails and many false trails. He found a few that exhibited the telltale signs of travois use that indicated camp movement. The persistent winds and blowing sand made judging the age of the trail much more difficult. But through hours of study, Wilcox had narrowed it down to two trails, each going in different directions. If they guessed wrong, it would mean weeks of delay in rescuing Emma.

Now up at daybreak on the fifth day with

a fresh pot of coffee on, the men were debating the merits of each trail. One trail ran farther west and the other veered off to the northwest. Cyrus, Percy, and Wilcox were pushing for the northwest trail while the others thought the trail west was the answer. Technically, either Percy or Cyrus could pull rank and insist on their preferred choice, but both were hesitant to do so. They both thought it had to be a mutual decision or the entire outing would be threatened by dissension.

"I'm just goin' by what that Kiowa Injun told me," Cyrus said. "He made a point that the Injuns we're lookin' for might be camped up on the Canadian or further north on the Arkansas."

"How do we know the trail to the west don't end up at the Arkansas, too?" Isaac asked.

"We don't," Wilcox said. "But I followed it out about eight to ten miles and didn't see no bend in it."

"Why are you so hell-bent on goin' west, Isaac?" Cyrus asked.

"It'd put more distance betwixt us and them. Wouldn't that be what them rascals would want?"

"I don't know," Percy said. "Seems to me they'd stick to the places they know. And goin' west will be some hard travelin'. Water's as scarce as virgins in a whorehouse."

"All the more reason," Isaac said. "I bet them Injuns know where the water is."

"Let me ask a question," Cyrus said. He turned to Wilcox and said, "Moses, did you ride down for a gander at what Win and Percy found?"

"I did," Wilcox said.

"Are them Injuns that have Emma Comanche?" Cyrus asked.

"Yes, sir," Wilcox said.

"And you reckon you found the right trail?"

"I do." Wilcox pointed at the canyon. "Found a few horse tracks yonder that I found on the trail that wanders northward."

"Well, hellfire, why didn't you say somethin'?" Cyrus asked.

"I figured y'all'd get around to it somewheres in this here discussion. I reckon it's a might better for you fellers to come to yer own conclusions without me a-tellin' ya."

"And if it didn't come up?" Cyrus asked.

"I'da said somethin' fore we got too far off track," Wilcox said, sheepishly.

Cyrus shook his head as he looked at Wilcox for a moment. Then he turned back to the others and said, "We got us a plan. Load up."

Percy was ready to ride. The stench from the dead horses was already bad and another day roasting in the intense heat would have made the situation unbearable. They were loaded up and ready to ride within an hour. Percy spurred Mouse into a walk and a couple of hours later they left canyon country behind when they crossed the Canadian River. This was new country for Percy, who had never ridden this far north. A wide-open prairie, the sea of blue grama grass and buffalo grass extended beyond the horizon in all directions with nary a tree in sight. Percy thought it was some of the finest ranch land he'd ever seen. And then he finally understood why millions of buffalo had once called this area home. Although it was an astonishing sight to see, they would all be tired of looking at it by the time they reached their destination.

CHAPTER
54

Rachel had snuck back to her house under the cover of darkness about an hour before daybreak. Her mind was tangled with thoughts and the last round with Leander hadn't helped to make the picture any clearer. She lit a couple of lanterns and took a seat on the sofa.

The last few weeks had been the happiest she'd been in a long time. But she couldn't decide if that happiness resided with Leander or if he'd simply been the one who had scratched a long-lingering itch. And that thought led to another question — Could Amos fill that role again as he once had? Or was that something she even wanted? As she thought about that more, she decided the firm answer to both questions was no. Leander was kind, caring, thoughtful, funny, and an attentive lover, and Rachel knew that he alone was the reason for her recent happiness.

And now he was leaving.

Fresh tears sprang to her eyes as she stood and wandered around the house in a watery haze, her emotions swirling from anger to sadness to confusion, with no grasp of what the future might hold. She paused by the kitchen table, pulled out a chair, and sat. Wiping the tears from her cheeks, she forced her mind to go to a place she didn't want to go — Amos. She had no idea — not that she cared much — what his response would be to her betrayal. Knowing there were no secrets in such a close-knit family, she imagined his reaction would fall somewhere between extreme anger and utter despair. And knowing Amos, she thought the latter would be the most likely response and that would make the situation intolerable.

Consuelo stepped through the front door, ready to start breakfast. "You are back," she said when she saw Rachel sitting at the table. Consuelo lived in a small room that had been added to the back of the bunkhouse.

"What makes you think I left?" Rachel asked.

Consuelo stopped on her way by and stood, hovering over Rachel. "Señora Rachel, my eyes are old, but they still see."

Rachel nodded as she traced a deep scar on the table with her finger while her mind continued to whirl through an avalanche of conflicting emotions. "I figured."

Consuelo sighed, pulled out a chair, and sat. "Now you have mess to clean up, no?"

Rachel's only response was to nod.

"You are not the only woman who . . . who . . ."

"Cheated on my husband?"

"*Sí,*" Consuelo said. "Sometimes we go where heart leads."

"And the after?" Rachel asked.

"The hardest part."

"I know."

The two women sat in silence for a long time, until Consuelo nudged it along. "Señor Amos is good man."

"He is," Rachel said. "But he's also not sleeping in your bed."

"No, he is not. I have not had man in bed for long time."

"Do you miss it?"

"*Sí. Es más que sexo.*"

"More than the sex?"

"*Sí,*" Consuelo said, nodding. *"Mucho más."*

Rachel sighed, her eyes still drifting across the table. "And I assume your ears are working, too, and heard the argument between me and my mother last night?"

"*Sí*. Hard not to." Consuelo stood and said, "I make biscuits *tu amante puede tener para rastro.*"

"Please, Consuelo, I'm too exhausted to think in Spanish."

Consuelo put a hand on Rachel's shoulder. "I make biscuits your lover can have for trail."

"Thank you."

Consuelo made her way into the kitchen, where she put on a pot of coffee before starting in on breakfast.

Rachel glanced at the clock on the mantel and saw she had only about half an hour before dawn. She stood from the table and made her way out to the porch, where she took a seat in one of the rockers. It was already hot, though she didn't give much thought to the weather. As she rocked, she worked through the pros and cons again in her mind. When she was finished the pros came up a tad short, with the only two items being love and happiness. The second column, cons, had more items than she could remember. *How much weight should I give love or happiness?* She thought about that for a long few minutes, but decided probably not much, despite how she felt. She and Amos had been together for a long time and, if it wasn't love anymore, it *was* a life. And it wasn't all bad. He was good with the kids — most of the time — and he got along well with her family. *There is something to be said about that, right?*

She glanced at the guest cottage and saw a lantern flare to life. She pushed out of the rocker and walked over, feeling as if she were wearing lead shoes. In her mind she thought what she was doing was the right thing, but her heart and loins were still protesting. When she reached the door, she gave it a light tap and pushed it open to see Leander getting dressed. He stepped around the bed and wrapped her in his arms and her heart overrode her mind and she broke into sobs.

Leander held her until the sobs subsided and then he stepped back and thumbed the tears from her cheeks. "You're a special woman, Rachel."

"And you're a . . . special . . . special man."

"I don't know about that, but no more cryin', now, you hear?"

Rachel nodded as she wiped her eyes. Leander kissed her on the forehead and continued dressing. When he finished, he asked Rachel if she wanted to walk to the barn with him while he saddled his horse and she agreed. They walked in silence, each with their own thoughts. When they reached the barn, a few of the hands were up and about and they greeted both Rachel and Leander. Rachel didn't have the energy and offered a simple wave in greeting.

It didn't take long for Leander to saddle his horse and as he and Rachel exited the barn with the horse in tow, the sky to the east was brightening. "Consuelo made some fresh biscuits for you to take," Rachel said.

Leander nodded. He reached down and took Rachel's hand as they led the horse over to her house. "How do I get in touch with you?" Rachel asked.

"You sure that's wise?" Leander asked.

"I don't give a damn whether it's wise or not."

Leander chuckled. "You can send me a telegram to the Ranger post in San Antonio. Probably won't be back that way for a while, though."

"Okay." When they reached the house, Rachel went inside and retrieved the bundle of biscuits Consuelo had made and returned outside. She handed them to Leander, and he placed them gingerly into his saddlebags. "Ain't too hungry right now," he said, "but they'll keep." He turned around and Rachel stepped over for another long hug. And despite all the pros and cons, the lists, the recriminations, she couldn't help herself, and she whispered a suggestion and Leander nodded. They broke their embrace, and Leander walked around his horse and mounted up. He smiled at Rachel, turned his horse, and rode off the ranch.

CHAPTER
55

Frances had slept fitfully and had finally given up and climbed out of bed well before sunrise. She glanced out the bedroom window and saw lanterns lit at Rachel's house, indicating she wasn't the only one who had trouble sleeping. She felt a small twinge of regret for her actions last night, but not enough to rescind her ultimatum. After pulling on a robe, she shuffled into the kitchen, stoked the stove, and put on a pot of water for coffee. Percy's children were still asleep, and she was doing her best not to wake them. She needed some quiet time to think.

Sitting down at the table while the water heated, she wondered if her family was falling apart. Mary was dead, Seth was an emotional wreck, Rachel was acting like a harlot, and Emma was in the clutches of the savages who were known for terrorizing their captives. It was almost too much to think about. But those weren't the only things weighing heavy on her mind this morning. There were financial issues, too. If they missed making a cattle drive to the railhead in Kansas this year, their finances were going to be squeezed. That was not necessarily a new phenomenon. Money had been tight since Texas sided with the Confederacy and had only gotten worse when the carpetbaggers arrived from up north to wring out their pound of flesh. The Ridgeways had never owned slaves and did not choose a side in the war, but they were paying for it all the same. Frances sighed and stood, shuffling wearily into the kitchen. She dumped some coffee into the pot of boiling water and nudged it off the burner to steep.

Her right hip ached something fierce. And that, too, was not a new phenomenon. She now had so many aches and pains that it was hard to keep track of all of them. While the coffee steeped, she limped to the back of the house for another peek out the window. The lanterns were still lit in Rachel's house and she noticed that a light was now glowing inside the guest cottage. She wondered if her daughter was in there giving the Ranger a raunchy send-off. She wouldn't put it past Rachel and the thought flared her anger anew. Turning away in disgust, she limped back to the kitchen, poured a cup of coffee, and limped out to the front porch, where she sagged into a rocking chair. After taking a sip from her cup, her mind returned to Rachel. Frances couldn't put her finger on what it was that angered her so much about Rachel's dalliance with the Ranger, but she supposed it had more to do with Amos than her daughter's behavior. Amos was a good man and a good father. Yes, Amos was somewhat dull and extremely quiet, but he was still Rachel's husband — the one she'd vowed to love and support forever.

Frances did have to admit, though, that Rachel had been the happiest she'd been in a long time. But she knew that was often the case for any new relationship. It was only later when the problems and incompatibilities wormed their way into the romance that the initial giddiness faded into the background. And for a moment, she wondered if she'd made a mistake in ordering the Ranger off the property. Maybe it would have been better if he'd stayed around long enough for them to experience a period of hardship that might have reframed their thoughts about each other. As it was, Rachel would have only pleasant, satiated memories of her time with him and Frances knew, as time passed and the distance between them grew, those thoughts would magnify greatly in her daughter's mind.

But all of this thinking, Frances thought, was being undertaken with the assumption that Rachel would stay behind when the Ranger left. It was something she hadn't really considered because of the children. Lordy, her plate was already full looking after Percy's children and she couldn't fathom the possibility of taking care of three more children who would be utterly shattered if their mother left. She knew Rachel could be persnickety and temperamental, but she didn't believe, in her heart, that her daughter was capable of leaving her children behind while she ran off with another man. However, Frances also knew the allure of a new relationship — a new life — could have enormous pull. Deciding she needed to get a better handle on the situation, she pushed out of her chair and limped around the side of the house, to do a little spying.

She didn't want to confront Rachel and she knew another fight would erupt if she nosed into her daughter's business again. They would eventually patch things up even if it took a while. And once she deduced Rachel's intentions from afar, Frances planned to slip back home and allow Rachel a couple of days to cool off and to come to grips with her decision — as long as that decision was the correct one. If not, Frances aimed to set her straight and was mentally preparing for another fight that might escalate well beyond the knock-down, drag-out they'd had yesterday.

At the back corner of her house, she paused to listen. Hearing voices coming from inside the barn, she limped that way. When she arrived, she hugged the side and inched her way closer to the large rolling door. To her dismay, it had been pushed open only far enough for a person to enter, limiting her ability to see much of anything inside, even with several lanterns burning. She heard Rachel's voice and assumed she was talking to the Ranger although she couldn't hear what was being said.

After several moments, Rachel's voice grew closer and Frances scrambled backward, hoping she didn't trip over anything and blow her cover. A moment later, the door opened wider and Rachel and the Ranger exited. Frances held her breath and exhaled a few seconds later when she saw only one horse saddled and ready to ride. Waiting until they arrived at Rachel's house, Frances turned and crept back home.

Inside, she poured another cup of coffee

and took a seat at the table. She would need to start breakfast soon, but she wanted to reexamine Rachel's situation to see if she'd overlooked anything. Of course, it was possible that Rachel and the Ranger had picked a spot where they could meet up later and then take off for parts unknown, but that didn't seem likely to Frances. She just didn't think Rachel had it in her to leave her children behind. However, she would *not* be surprised to discover that her daughter and the Ranger had pre-selected a location where they could rendezvous later for nefarious purposes. And, after a little more consideration, Frances thought she might be okay with that as long as they were discreet, they picked a location far from the ranch, and they ceased the moment Amos arrived back home. The only problem she could see with that scenario, other than her probable inability to enforce such rules, was Rachel's safety as she traveled to and from. But, Frances thought, that could also act as a deterrent to the frequency of their liaisons and maybe, just maybe, drive a wedge into their relationship. It was something to hope for. She pushed out of her chair and limped into the kitchen to start breakfast.

CHAPTER 56

Abigail stood near the back window of her house, watching her sister and the Ranger in the dim light that washed out of Rachel's house. A saddled horse was nearby, and Abby assumed the Ranger was off to track down the nearest outlaw. Any other time in her life she might have been jealous, but since Emma's capture her emotional range had been stunted and now hovered somewhere between despondency and disheartenment. Her feelings of sadness were sharper than at any point in her life, including the burials of her two children who died much too soon. Emma had been a part of Abby's life for more than thirteen years and there had been much joy during that span and some sadness, too. But nothing like she felt now. The unknown ate at her constantly and her reservoir of tears had run dry long ago. In some ways, Abby thought, Emma's dying would have been preferable to the lingering uncertainty that was inescapable. At least with death, the outcome was determined.

Abby sighed, stepped away from the window, and shuffled into the kitchen. After pulling a cup down from the shelf over the stove, she filled it with yesterday's coffee she'd reheated and plodded out to the front porch. Tired of sitting, she leaned against a support post and stared out into the darkness. Rachel's house was out of sight so she couldn't spy on her sister, not that she really wanted to anyway. And that was the problem — she didn't really want to do anything other than curl up in a ball and deny her existence. But that was an impossibility with two other children to care for.

It had now been a month since Emma's kidnapping, and it felt like an eternity. Isaac had predicted before they left that they'd be gone a couple of months, but Abby knew that was a guesstimate at best and not anything she could plan for. She'd heard stories about families that had spent years searching for captured loved ones and she didn't know how they had coped day after day, year after year. A month had felt like a decade and Abby couldn't wrap her mind around Emma being gone for months, much less years.

Abby couldn't stand to think about it anymore. For all she knew, Emma was now with her father. She didn't really believe that but thought if she kept telling herself that it might soon be true. To take her mind off Emma, she stepped off the porch and walked around the side of the house, marginally curious to know what was happening with Rachel and the Ranger. She didn't have proof that anything was going on between the two although she had her suspicions. Rachel had always been impulsive, and Abby suspected they had been in the sack within an hour of his arrival.

Abby hadn't spent any time with Leander Hays although she did meet him shortly after he arrived and liked his looks. Tall and handsome with broad shoulders and a well-groomed mustache, Abby had thought if it had been any other time, she might have given Rachel a run for her money.

When she reached the back of the house, she discovered Rachel's porch empty and the horse gone. With no energy to cook, she decided to walk over to ask Consuelo if she would cook up some extra biscuits for her kids. She didn't make a habit of doing that but would if she had an argument with her sister because it pissed Rachel off mightily. She wasn't feeling spiteful this morning, just exhausted.

The roosters started crowing when she stepped up on Rachel's porch. She knocked on the door and pushed it open before anyone could answer. Rachel was sitting at the table, her head buried in her hands, weeping. Abby thought about turning around and leaving but instead, stepped over, pulled out a chair, and sat. She shot a look at Consuelo in the kitchen and shrugged a shoulder. Consuelo waved her hands at Rachel's back, suggesting Abby handle it.

"Leander off to apprehend some criminals?" Abby asked, making conversation.

Her sister lifted her head and wiped the moisture off her cheeks. "No. Ma ran him off."

"Do what?" Abby asked, momentarily taken aback.

Rachel ran her finger under her nose. "You heard me."

"How and why did Ma run him off?"

"She told him she'd shoot him if she ever saw him on the ranch again."

"Ma?" Abby asked, her voice incredulous.

"Yes, Ma," Rachel said.

"Why would she say something like that?"

"Why do you think?"

Abby rolled that around in her mind, trying to find the best approach that wouldn't appear confrontational. "Well, I suppose you could have been a little subtler about it."

"Why should it matter to her who I sleep with?"

"I don't know, but it obviously does."

"It's not like we were out screwing in the yard."

"I realize that. But how much thought did you give to the overall situation?"

Rachel cocked her head to the side. "What does that mean?"

"Well, you are married."

"Oh, so you're going to sit in judgment?"

"No, I was just making a point."

"No, you weren't. You want to know about my marriage? Huh? It's a piece of shit. How's yours?"

"This is not about me and Isaac." Abby could sense that Rachel was on the verge of exploding and who knew what would come out of her mouth if that happened? "Look, you're a grown woman capable of making your own decisions."

"You're damn right I am. Go tell that to your mother."

"She's your mother, too. Did you really think she would shoot Leander?"

Rachel shrugged. "She was hot enough last night that you could have lit a cigarette off her."

Now the picture was becoming clearer. "So, you two had one those type of arguments, huh?"

Rachel shrugged again. "She started it."

"Sounds like she ended it, too. Where did he go?"

Rachel turned to stare at something on the far wall. "I don't know. Home, I guess."

Abby didn't think that likely with Amos still away, but she didn't say anything, knowing her sister's short fuse. "Which is where?"

"I don't know. Somewhere down south on the Brazos."

Abby couldn't help herself. "Huh. So, you two spend a couple of weeks in the sack and then say *That was great, see you down the trail?*"

"What was I supposed to do?"

"It's not like you to give up so easily."

"Yeah, well, there wasn't much easy about any of it."

"Why did you start it to begin with?" Abby asked. "You had to know it wouldn't end well."

Rachel didn't answer and that angered Abby.

"You didn't give a thought to any of it, did you? Which is so like you. Dive right on

437

in without a care in the world and leave it to someone else to clean up the mess. And don't expect me to believe that you ended it. You didn't, did you?"

Rachel shrugged.

The slow burn of anger coursing through Abby's body flared red-hot. Rachel's most annoying tendency was to think only of herself. Abby stood and pushed the chair in, all thoughts of biscuits now gone. "Well, I hope it was worth it."

Rachel looked up and smiled. "Oh, it was. Every luscious second of it. I bet you wished it was you, huh?"

Abby looked Rachel in the eye and said, "I think Ma had the right idea but the wrong target." She turned and marched out of the house.

CHAPTER
57

Percy felt something nudge his shoulder and his pistol was out and cocked before he even opened his eyes.

"Easy," his father said in a low voice.

Percy looked up and it was so dark he couldn't see his father's face He sat up and whispered, "What's goin' on?"

Cyrus squatted down next to him. "Don't know. Thought I heard somethin'."

"Where's Amos? He had last watch."

"Don't know. I ain't seen him. It clouded up during the night and I can't see a damn thing."

Percy threw off the blanket, grabbed his rifle, and stood, the pistol still gripped in his right hand. "What did you hear?"

Cyrus stood. "A bump or a thump. Coulda been a grunt," he whispered. "Sounded like it was over by the wagon. Where was Amos standin' guard?"

"By the fire, the last time I saw him."

"Well, far as I can tell, he ain't there now. Fire's all but gone. There was just enough light to find ya."

"I'm goin' to walk over to the wagon," Percy whispered. "Where's your rifle?"

His father poked him in the side with his rifle barrel.

"Cover me."

"How the hell am I s'posed to cover ya?" Cyrus whispered. "We get out away from what's left of that there fire, and we ain't goin' to see nothin' at all."

"Okay, you woke me up. What do you want to do?"

"Don't know. Maybe get up behind the Gatling gun," Cyrus whispered. "If we hear anythin' else, them muzzle blasts will light 'em up like it's high noon."

"Don't know where the horses are."

"Don't matter. They'll haul ass soon as that gun starts, if the Injuns ain't already took 'em."

"Okay," Percy whispered. "Wake up the others and ya'll go over by the fire so I'll know where you are. Add on a little more wood so it doesn't go completely cold." He handed his rifle off to Cyrus and looked up at the sky to see if the clouds were going to pass anytime soon, but as far as he could tell it looked like they were socked in. He took a moment to get his bearings then put his left hand out and began walking slowly forward.

A little farther on he was hit by a thought — if they couldn't see neither could the enemy. Percy pondered that as he shuffled forward. If he was walking in the right direction and, if his recollection of locations was correct, he had about twenty feet to cover. Out of self-preservation, they kept the fire and wagon separated and the distance between them was usually twenty to thirty feet. With his left arm still extended, he began counting his steps, his ears attuned to the noises of the night. When he reached twenty-five steps, he stopped, looked back at the fire to judge his position, and then turned a slow circle with his arm extended. When he didn't hit anything, he wondered if he was off by a hundred yards or an inch. And there was no way to tell. He turned ninety degrees, took two steps, and hit wood.

Feeling his way, he climbed aboard the wagon, made it past the cannon, and finally arrived at the Gatling gun. He had to feel for the crank to know which way it was pointed and, once he was in position, settled in for the wait. He couldn't see the Indians attacking now, but first light was a different story altogether. But the more he thought about it the more he wondered. It didn't make sense that the Indians would attack them again, especially while they were camped on open ground with no cover for miles in any direction. Percy thought it more likely the Comanches would bide their time until they found the perfect ambush spot somewhere ahead. It made more sense for the Indians to wait for them and their horses to get tired at the end of a long, exhausting day and then strike. But he wasn't an Indian and didn't think like one. If they were stupid enough to attack here, the mountain howitzer would shred them to pieces before they could even get into arrow range.

Still on the gun when the eastern sky gradually brightened to announce a new day, Percy thought if an attack was going to come it would be soon. Now that he could see, he took a moment to make sure the gun had plenty of ammo. He counted five two-hundred-round magazines that were preloaded, giving him a thousand rounds to work with. If they were going to need more than that, he figured they had a good chance of ending up dead.

The sun continued climbing higher in the sky and there was no sign of Indians and no war whoops or banshee screams emanating from the distance. Sweat started at the base of Percy's neck and trickled down his back. Although the sun was low on the horizon and far removed from where it would be midafternoon, its impact was already being felt. And Percy knew it wouldn't take long to burn off the already-thinning cloud cover, which had been a curse last night but would have been a welcome gift later today.

The last attack had occurred later in the day when the location of the sun was irrelevant. Not so this morning. The Indians preferred to ride with their backs to the sun when attacking, making the sun's current position problematic. Percy pulled his hat down a little more, trying to block the glare. To assist, Wilcox rode a hundred yards to the north and was prepared to wave his hat if an attack appeared imminent.

Percy sat on the edge of the wagon rail and kept an eye on Wilcox. He glanced over at the fire and saw his father putting on a pot of coffee like it was another normal day. Percy didn't sense imminent danger and he was starting to believe it *was* just another day. He looked at Wilcox again and he was sitting easy in the saddle. Percy scanned the horizon for threats and didn't see anything. They might miss an invasion if the Indians belly-crawled through the high grass but there wasn't much of a breeze and Percy didn't see any unusual movement.

"Still ain't seen Amos," Cyrus said as he walked up.

"Unless he was resurrected during the night, he's gotta be around here someplace."

"Well, he ain't. You might as well get on down. There ain't nothin' out there."

"How do you know?"

"I know. We need to be lookin' for Amos. For all we know he coulda moseyed off to take a piss and broke a leg or got bit by a snake."

"Okay," Percy said. "Should we put Luis on the gun?"

"Naw. If the Injuns was a-comin' they'd already be here."

Percy climbed down out of the wagon and took a moment to stretch. It had been a long time since he had spent this much time not only away from home but also his feather bed. His back was reminding him he wasn't as young as he once was. After stretching, he placed his hands on the wagon and did three or four push-ups to get the blood moving. Looking under the wagon seat to see if he'd left his rifle, something caught his eye. He walked forward and stopped. Turning, he shouted, "Pa!"

Cyrus came hurrying over and Percy stepped around the nose of the wagon and kneeled down next to Amos, who was facedown on the grass. Percy put a hand on Amos's back to see if he was still breathing and found he wasn't. Cyrus arrived, short of breath.

"Oh hell," Cyrus said. "What happened . . . to him?"

There were no arrows or visible knife wounds. "Don't know," Percy said. "Need to roll him over." As the others arrived, Wilcox rode up on his horse and climbed down. Percy moved around beside Amos, grabbed his arm, and rolled him over. There were gasps when the cause of death became readily apparent — the right-front portion of Amos's skull was caved in.

"Injuns?" Cyrus asked.

"Don't think so," Percy said as he stood up. He took a moment to study the front of the wagon and found the cause. He pointed at the splash of blood on the far corner of the bed. "Remember, it was darker than hell last night. He must have tripped over the wagon tongue and hit his head." Percy looked at Cyrus and said, "That must have been the bump you heard."

Cyrus nodded. "Beats all I ever seen. All the dangerous things we done, and he gets killed walkin' around in the damn dark?"

"You sure it weren't Injuns?" Isaac asked.

"I'm sure. Look close and you'll see some of Amos's hair stuck there in the corner."

Cyrus pushed his hat back on his head. "Well, hell, we're two men down, now."

That was something Isaac didn't want to hear. He pointed at the wagon and said, "We still got that there cannon and that there Gatlin' gun. Those count for two dozen men."

"They ain't goin' to count," Cyrus said, "if we ain't got nobody to operate 'em."

"We still got people," Isaac said. "That's my girl with them savages. We ain't quittin'."

"Nobody said we was quittin'," Cyrus said. He took off his hat, wiped his face with his sleeve, and put his hat back on. "Well, hell, somebody grab a shovel and start diggin'."

CHAPTER
58

After finishing their chores, Seth and Chauncey saddled up their horses, slid their rifles into their scabbards, stopped by the river to grab the pistols and holsters they kept hidden in an old slicker, and took off, riding north into Indian Territory. They didn't have a particular destination in mind and Seth was keenly aware of what happened the last time he rode that way. And he would carry that mark from his previous visit for the rest of his life.

Once clear of the river, they paused to strap on their gun belts. Although both were the same age — twelve — Chauncey was the larger of the two and his holster and pistol better fit his larger frame. Seth, thin and lanky, looked somewhat ridiculous with his rig on, the holster running from his hip to his knee. But he didn't particularly care what others thought and he was determined to never leave home without his pistol ever again.

Although they didn't have a destination in mind, they did have a plan and that was to shoot something other than a can, or a tree, or any other type of stationary target. They wanted something that moved and weren't too particular about what it might be. Both carried a Colt Model 1861 Navy cap-and-ball, six-shot percussion revolver that fired a .36 caliber bullet. To make sure they had plenty of firepower they had preloaded several extra cylinders so they could just swap them out when needed. The pistols were heavy, a pain to load, and they were far from the boys' preferred weapon of choice, but it was all they had. They would much prefer to own one of the newly released Colt Single Action Army revolvers, or the Peacemaker, as it was better known, because there was no reloading involved. You simply popped a .45 caliber cartridge into the cylinder and let her rip. Both coveted one, but the twenty-dollar price tag was well beyond their means.

They rode toward a small creek, hoping to kick up a rabbit to test their shooting skills. Seth was a little concerned about firing from the saddle because, as far as he knew, his horse, Thunder, had never been exposed to close-range gunfire. But that wasn't Seth's only worry. Despite his bravado about riding into Indian Territory, he'd turn around and ride home in a heartbeat if his cousin made the suggestion. Which wasn't likely, knowing Chauncey. Seth had pushed for a hunt along the river on ranch land, but Chauncey had issued a dare, so here they were. And Seth was feeling dizzy because he was repeatedly turning his head one direction and then the other, searching for approaching riders.

"What are you lookin' for?" Chauncey asked.

"Just lookin' around," Seth said.

"You're scared, ain't ya?"

"I ain't scared. I'm here, ain't I?"

"You're here, but you're about to twist your head off your damn shoulders."

"Am not. I'm lookin' for game."

Chauncey laughed. "I ain't goin' to let anything happen to ya."

"I don't need you lookin' out for me."

Just then a rabbit darted out from a patch of high grass, and Seth was so angry, he pulled his pistol, cocked it, and fired without much thought. He had no idea how close the shot was because the instant he fired, Thunder reared up and Seth dropped his pistol as he grabbed for the saddle horn. He missed by an inch and he tumbled off his horse and slammed onto the ground, the breath crushed from his lungs. Chauncey sat his horse and laughed as Thunder took off at a dead run, making a beeline for the barn.

Seth finally caught his breath. He sat up and said, "Why didn't you catch my damn horse, asshole?"

"Hell, Seth, I couldn't have caught that horse if I'd had a rope tied to him," Chauncey said as he slapped his thigh and laughed again. "Damn, that horse's eyes was as big as dinner plates when he shot by me."

Seth stood up and dusted his pants off. He thought it lucky that he didn't have his pistol handy because he'd probably have used it to shoot Chauncey off his horse. He stalked around looking for his gun, found it, and jammed it into his holster. "I'm goin' home."

"Oh, c'mon, Seth. You didn't know that horse was goin' to rabbit like that." Chauncey was still chuckling when he climbed down off his horse. "I'll walk with you." He took off his hat and slapped his horse across the butt and shouted, "Git," and the horse took off toward the ranch. They walked in silence for a few minutes and then Chauncey leaned over and punched his cousin in the arm and said, "Maybe we can stop at the river and do a little shootin'."

Now on low simmer, Seth said, "Okay."

They had been only about three miles from the river when Thunder bolted, and it didn't take them all that long to walk back. Both were sweating profusely, but it was such a common occurrence that they hardly noticed.

"Think you could shoot somebody?" Seth asked.

Chauncey shrugged. "Maybe. Don't seem like that big a deal to me. I know my pa's shot his fair share and it don't seem to bother him."

"You don't think you'd feel bad about it after, I mean?"

"Well, I suppose I wouldn't shoot 'em unless I had a reason. Take them fellers that roughed you up. Would you have any doubts about killin' them?"

"No," Seth said. "And if Uncle Eli and Win hadn't killed them, I would have."

"So what's the difference, then?" Chauncey asked.

Seth shrugged. "I suppose there ain't one."

"There you go. I don't imagine shootin' a man is much different from shootin' a deer or another animal."

Seth pondered that for a few moments

451

and said, "Maybe. Except a man'll have kinfolk that probably care about him."

"So what," Chauncey said. "Kinfolk don't matter."

"They matter if they pick up a gun and come after you."

"I guess I'd have to kill them, too. I ain't thought much on it."

Another rabbit skittered out from under a bush and Chauncey pulled his pistol and shot it before Seth could even put his hand on his gun.

"That wasn't too hard, right?" Chauncey asked as he holstered his revolver.

"Well, the rabbit wasn't shootin' back, was it?"

Chauncey chuckled. "No, it wasn't. But a man ain't shootin' back, neither, if you kill 'im first."

CHAPTER
59

After burying Amos, it took Percy and the crew two weeks to reach the Arkansas River, where they lost the trail for good. During all that time, they saw no other humans. They had found some tracks that suggested they were being watched by Indians, but there had been no further attacks. Stymied, they had decided to camp by the river until Wilcox could find the trail again.

This morning, Percy was poking through their meager food supplies to see how much longer they could hold out. They ran out of coffee three days ago and used the last of the bacon yesterday. They had been hunting along the way and they had harvested several deer, but the meat didn't keep long enough to last more than a day unless they smoked it and no one wanted to take the time to do that. Of key concern was the lack of coffee. You didn't realize how much you missed it until you didn't have it. And it made for a cranky crew.

Situated where they were, out in the middle of no-man's-land, Percy had consulted a map and discovered the closest places to resupply were Dodge City, Kansas, 165 miles to the east, or Pueblo, Colorado, which lay 143 miles west of their current position. The map was an old one and it didn't show the locations of the newer army forts they continued to build, and trying to find one could burn through time they didn't have.

The reason there wasn't anywhere closer was directly related to the presence of not only the Comanche, but also the Apache, Ute, Sioux, Cheyenne, Arapaho, and a few renegade Kiowa Indians off the reservation in Indian Territory. These tribes controlled a great swath of land in the middle of the country that stretched from Mexico to Canada. And Percy, Cyrus, and the rest were now smack-dab in the middle of it all.

While looking at the map, Percy had also calculated the distance back to the ranch and found it was a disappointing 325 miles as the crow flies. If they pulled up stakes today and started for home, it would take them most of a month to get there. And that estimate was assuming they wouldn't hit any hiccups along the way, an unlikely scenario.

Percy also had some concerns about the wagon. Although it had been manufactured to exacting standards, it was beginning to show signs of wear after a month grinding across the rough terrain. Bust a wheel out here and they'd be in a world of hurt.

The one thing they still had in abundance was ammo. The Indians remained at a distance, carefully watching the crew's progress. It was frustrating, but Percy was hoping it would work to their advantage when word of the approaching beast reached the ears of Emma's captors. Percy thought the Indians would have taken a shot at stealing the mule team or their mounts, but their fear of the cannon and Gatling gun must have outweighed their hunger for horses.

Although the lack of food and the presence of an amalgamation of Indian tribes weighed heavy on Percy's mind, there was another, larger worry. And that was his father. Cyrus didn't look well, and it was apparent his health had declined during their long journey and there was still no end in sight. At sixty-four, his father had lived a hard life, as did everyone living along the frontier. Cyrus hadn't said anything about not feeling well, however Percy had noticed him rubbing his chest and left arm much more frequently. Percy wasn't a doctor and had never spent much time studying the ailments of the human body, but he was smart enough to know his father was in distress. And the sad fact that angered Percy the most was that he couldn't do a damn thing about it.

Percy closed the lid on the chuck box and walked over to the fire, where his father was sprawled out on the ground and leaned up against his saddle. Although they didn't venture too far from camp, Win and Wilcox were out scouting and Luis and Isaac took off downriver in search of game. A cool front had passed during the night, bringing a welcome change in temperatures. Camped under a massive cottonwood tree, Percy thought the morning would have been perfect if he'd only had a steaming cup of coffee.

"How bad is it?" Cyrus asked.

Percy sat down on his blanket. The thing he missed most was having a chair to sit on. "Well, it's not good," Percy said. "Looks like we're going to be living off the land for a while."

"Okay," Cyrus said. "Done that before. But I sure do miss my coffee, though."

"I hear ya."

The two sat in silence for a few moments, both staring at the flickering flames, each with their own thoughts. Percy shifted his gaze from the fire to his father. Cyrus was pale, and despite the coolness of the morning, perspiration coated his forehead.

Eventually Cyrus broke the silence. "We went about this the wrong way."

"How's that?"

"Wilcox might be a world-class tracker but he don't think like an Injun. We should have hired some of them Injun scouts up at Fort Sill."

"Not a lot we can do about that now."

"You're right there. But we could spend a year out here and never get a look at Emma. We're in Injun country now, and they've been travelin' these parts for hundreds of years. They know every waterin' hole and every little nook and cranny. It would take us damn near a decade to search it all."

"So what are you sayin'? You want to pull up stakes?"

"No, I ain't sayin' that. That's just some things I wanted you to ponder as this here search lined out. You might give a little more thought to startin' over in the spring with a passel of them Injun scouts."

Percy didn't like the direction of the conversation. "Where you goin' to be?"

His father ignored the question and continued. "The army ain't gonna tolerate these

Injuns runnin' wild much longer and besides, the buffalo's thinnin' out. Might be best to work through that Injun agent back at Fort Sill. You talked to Davidson, what'd he tell ya?"

"He said they were ready to mount a campaign to herd the Indians back to the reservation. He didn't say when, though."

"It's a-comin' soon. I can feel it. Too many white settlers wantin' their piece of the American dream. They got a name for it, but I can't recall it."

"Manifest Destiny," Percy said.

"That's it. Don't know why they had to put a title on it. We've been doin' it since we landed here two hundred and fifty years ago. The Injuns out here ain't got no concept of how many of us there are. Hell, you could put all the Injuns on earth together and they wouldn't fill up Saint Louie. And that's just one of hundreds of places like it."

"You're all philosophical all of a sudden. Is there a reason?"

Again, his father ignored the question. "With all the raidin' the Injuns been doin' down in our part of the country it's gonna put pressure on the army to do somethin'. And that might be the best chance to get Emma back. Even if you did find the right Injun camp soon, they're most likely gonna hide her somewhere. That's what I'd do if I was lookin' down the barrel of all that firepower you got."

Percy stood, angry at his father's repeated use of the wrong word. "Why do you keep saying, 'you'? It's how much firepower *we* have."

Cyrus waved his hand to silence Percy. "You understand what I'm tellin' ya."

"Yes, I understand. Do you wanna go home? Is that it?"

Cyrus started coughing and it took him a while to get it stopped. His eyes were watering when he looked up and said, "Naw. I want to get Emma away from . . . them savages, but I don't know . . . if we're goin' about it the right —"

Cyrus broke off when he was hit with another coughing fit. This one went on a lot longer before it finally subsided.

"You want some water?" Percy asked.

"Yeah."

Percy walked over to the wagon and grabbed his canteen, his emotions all over the place. He wanted desperately to find Emma and he was torn because he also wanted to get his father home as soon as possible. It was an impossible decision. He took a deep breath and walked back over to his father, pulled out the stopper, and handed him the canteen. Cyrus sat up but his hand was shaking so badly he struggled to get the canteen to his lips. Percy knelt down beside him, took the canteen from his hands, and poured a little water into his father's mouth.

"Thank you," Cyrus said as he lay back down against his saddle. "I guess my throat's dry."

Percy replaced the stopper and stood, his eyes welling up with tears.

"Best go check on the horses and make sure . . . the Injuns hadn't snuck up and stole 'em."

Percy looked down at his father as tears leaked out the corners of his eyes. "The horses and mules are fine."

"You can't see 'em from here. Probably down by the river. Best go check."

"Okay," Percy said. There were so many things he wanted to tell his father, but his thoughts were so jumbled he couldn't form a coherent sentence. All he could think to say was, "I love you."

"I love you, too, son. Now go see . . . about them horses."

Percy turned away as tears coursed down his cheeks. He yearned to sit down beside his father and hold his hand until the end, but he knew that's not what his father wanted. He was too proud. Tiny pieces broke away from his heart as he walked toward the river, his vision clouded with tears. His heartache extended beyond his father to his mother, who would be absolutely devastated by the loss of her husband. They'd laughed and loved together for more than forty years and for her to miss his final moments tore Percy up inside.

He found the horses and mules where his father said they would be, down by the water. Leaning against a tree, he watched them for a while as they grazed on fresh green grass. Lost so deep in thought, Percy lost track of time for a bit, the rhythmic chomping of the horses lulling him into a somber trance where images of his father's life played through his mind. He reached up and wiped away the last of his tears. He knew these weren't the last tears he would shed for his father and he knew his absence would be felt long after he was gone.

Sometime later, Percy made his way back to camp and found his father had passed. He kneeled down and closed his father's eyes for the final time. Percy wasn't much of a praying man and didn't hold much stock in churches and he didn't know any of the familiar verses. Instead, he said a simple good-bye, stood, walked over and pulled another blanket from the wagon, and covered his father's body.

Needing something to do to ease his mind, he returned to the wagon and pulled out the shovel and then stood and looked around for a long time, searching for the perfect place. With no high ground anywhere around, Percy studied the river and decided that under the leaves of a towering, two-hundred-year-old post oak tree would be the perfect place. He'd dig the hole and wait until the others came back for the burial.

Percy wasn't so consumed by grief that he forgot where he was. The spot where he wanted to dig was about a hundred yards away, and he thought that distance too far from the wagon. And if the Indians rode in along the riverbed and decided to attack, they'd be on him in seconds. He put the shovel back in the wagon, grabbed his rifle and a couple of ropes, and went after the mules.

Once he had the wagon hitched, Percy steered toward the large oak tree and parked in the shade. He took a few moments to make sure the Gatling gun was good to go and loaded the mountain howitzer then grabbed the shovel and started digging. The earth was soft and sandy from centuries of flooding and he wondered for a moment if he was making a mistake burying his father there. He didn't want the body to be washed out and exposed to animals, but he figured if he dug the hole deep enough there wouldn't be any worries. And he wanted to work — anything to take his mind off the loss of his father.

It took Percy three grueling, nonstop hours to dig the grave to his satisfaction. Although he was in the shade and a cool front had moved through during the night, he was drenched in sweat by the time he finished. And it felt good. It had been a long time since he'd worked that hard and it allowed him a chance to come to grips with the new world order. The ranch and everything on it, was now the responsibility of him and his mother and he was okay with that. It was as it should be. He just wished it hadn't happened so soon.

Percy climbed out of the hole and drove the wagon back to camp. Luis and Isaac soon returned with a freshly killed deer and both were shocked to learn of Cyrus's death. Percy took Isaac aside and they spent some time talking. Isaac's father had died when he was four years old and Cyrus had been the only father he had really known. Isaac, originally from San Antonio, had married Abigail when he was eighteen, and Cyrus had welcomed him into the family and treated him as if Isaac was his own son. Yes, his father could be a hard man, but Percy knew he had an extra-large soft spot for family.

Win and Wilcox rode in about an hour before sunset. They, too, were saddened to learn of Cyrus's passing. And they didn't arrive with good news, because they were no closer to knowing where the Indians were. It was like the Indians walked into a fog and disappeared.

They loaded Cyrus's body onto the wagon and Percy drove it down to the gravesite. Each man told their favorite Cyrus story, and each took a turn on the shovel and, as the sun settled on the horizon, they rode back to camp sullen and silent, each with his own thoughts.

CHAPTER
60

In the beginning stages of her captivity, Emma had worked extremely hard to keep track of the days but after a couple weeks she lost heart. The numbers nor what particular day it was didn't matter anymore. As a captive, the Sundays were just like the Mondays, and just like Tuesdays and on and on, until the days slowly bled from one to another with no differences whatsoever. Emma had also made it a point to talk to herself in English so she could remember, and even that had gone by the wayside. She hadn't spoken in her own language in a long time and the way it was looking, she might never again. To her, if felt like she'd been a prisoner for most of her life. The days were long, grueling, and monotonous. The only thing that kept her mind centered was thinking of all the ways to kill Scar.

He hadn't stalked her since the last time he so viciously assaulted her, but she'd seen him from afar and each time she had to suppress the urge to vomit. His constant smirk was always there either in person or in her mind. She knew she had to let it go or it was going to drive her crazy and maybe she could have if she'd had someone to talk to. Being a prisoner was one thing. But being a prisoner in a place where it felt like solitary confinement was soul crushing. She had picked up more Comanche along the way although it was such an awful, guttural language that there was no joy in speaking it.

There had been one interesting occurrence recently when the camp was visited by some Mexican traders. She knew they were Mexicans from overhearing their conversations in Spanish and that was all Emma knew about them. Big Nose had tied her up and kept her out of sight during the entire duration of their visit, which had lasted the better part of three days. And that might have been the one incident that put her over the edge — the total loss of any hope of ever being rescued. It was clear from that episode that the Indians had no intention of ever letting her go, and the only way it would happen was either by escape or by pressure from outside forces — specifically her father, grandfather, Uncle Percy, and all the others from the ranch. She had no idea if they were still searching for her, but it was something she silently prayed for every night. So far all she had to show for her efforts were more unanswered prayers than she could count.

Emma was so beaten down that she'd even lost the will to fend off the men during their nighttime advances. Although the number of incidents had tapered off some, Emma still felt dirty and humiliated after every encounter. She thought she might kill Scar and get away with it if she was smart about it, however, she had no misconceptions about doing the same to other males in the tribe. She'd seen the Indians when their blood was up. Another group of Indians had brought in a male Mexican captive who had apparently killed one of their braves and it had taken him three days to die after enduring the most horrifying tortures that one human could inflict upon another. It had been sickening to see and although Emma might one day be at the point where she'd welcome death, she couldn't bear the thought of being tortured to death.

Emma looked up at the sky to judge how much longer she'd have to scrape the hide before it became too dark to see. The

Indians might occasionally go without food for a day or two, but it seemed that they never ran short on hides. Those and horses were the tribe's trading currency and the old squaws were slave drivers. And there wasn't anything easy about any of it. The hides were heavy and hard for Emma to handle and if it had just been the scraping it might have been okay. Instead, the old squaws used a horribly tedious process that involved three separate stages of scraping in addition to washing, stretching, three stages of brine-tanning, then sewing, softening, thinning, and smoking. And each step in the tanning process often involved the use of water that had to be hauled up from the river. One hide could take a week to finish and they always had two dozen hides or more in various stages of finishing. It was exhausting and never ending. And if Emma wasn't working on a hide, they had her doing something every minute of every day from daylight to dark. Her arms had almost doubled in size since her capture and her chest and back muscles had thickened to the point where she imagined she no longer looked like a girl. Emma knew that hunters traveled great distances to hunt buffalo for sport and she hoped they killed them all, and soon.

As darkness settled over the camp, Emma set her scraper aside and washed up with water she'd hauled to camp in a water bag, which she now knew was a buffalo stomach. She hurried into the chief's teepee and sat down for the first time all day. If she had a favorite time in such a bleak existence this was it. It was too dark to work, and she wasn't allowed to cook — she guessed they were afraid she'd poison them even though she didn't know the first thing about poison plants — and she had time to herself. The chief was usually out consulting the elders or whatever it was he did, and Devil, who also lived in the chief's teepee, had cooking chores. The old squaw she'd fought and made up with had made her a new buckskin dress that actually fit, and that's what Emma put on as soon as she arrived back at the lodge. The dress was beautifully beaded, and Emma knew from the craftsmanship that her onetime enemy was now her dearest friend.

Emma heard horses approaching and she stepped out of the tent to see who it was. It was too dark to see much, but Emma didn't need a bunch of light to know that it was more Indians. She watched as one of them slid off his horse and walked quickly over to where the chief was sitting by the fire. There was a quick conversation and then she saw the chief stand. Something was going on and Emma didn't know if it had anything to do with her, but her hopes inched up ever so slightly.

Quanah Parker didn't really know why he was so surprised to hear Heap Big Guns and his wagon were only two sleeps away to the east. He knew it was going to happen and would continue to happen. They might go back home when the snows came but he knew they'd come back. Now the question was, what to do? Quanah walked out away from camp and ran through his options in his mind. They couldn't push much farther up into the mountains or toward the west without running into other brothers who were quick to take up arms. The only out Quanah could see was to pick a different trail and head back to the big canyon. They'd have to avoid the old man when he drifted back toward his stomping grounds, but that was fairly easy to do.

Or he could try to end it here by asking for a parley with Heap Big Guns and try to convince him that he didn't know anything about his young'un. The more he thought about that the less he liked it. The old man had the firepower to demand a look through the Indian camp and if Quanah refused, Heap could set up downriver, well out of arrow or rifle range, and rip them to shreds.

Whatever he was going to do he needed to do quickly. If they moved, the squaws could take down the camp and be ready to move at first light. And if he chose to parley, he'd prefer to do it while there was some distance between them. Then he ran through the old scenario of an outright attack again, trying to think of anything that would be different this time. But he couldn't think of anything. The new problem was the same as the old problem and that was their inability to get close enough to fight without massive loss of life.

And if they could escape again, he thought that maybe he would be able to put together a war party and go kill them all when Heap Big Guns returned. But that was something to consider at a later time. For now, the right decision was to move, and he returned to camp and announced that they were moving camp once again.

What Quanah didn't know — couldn't even fathom — was that the upcoming camp move would be their last of their own choosing.

CHAPTER
61

Percy and the crew had spent three more weeks searching for Emma with no luck. Then the weather had turned colder, and the north wind howled, forcing them to make a decision none wanted to make. With no winter gear and everyone shivering, Percy had called a halt to the search and they rode for home. The trip home had been long and uneventful and by the time they got to their present location, a day's ride from home, they'd been gone almost four months.

As they stirred from sleep, they went about their duties of saddling horses and hitching the team to the wagon in silence. They were all looking forward to a warm bed and their first cup of hot coffee in nearly two months. Percy put his foot in the stirrup and climbed aboard Mouse for the final stretch. He had debated about riding on ahead but decided that wouldn't be fair to the rest of the men. And a small part of him wasn't eager to break the news of his father's death and that had made the decision a little easier. However, he was eager to see his family with just a tad bit of apprehension about settling back into life with Mary and all the problems her illness presented.

Everyone was exhausted although they weren't so tired that they let their guard down. They all understood that they were still riding through Indian country and would be until they set foot on Rocking R property. Wilcox was hanging behind, keeping an eye on their back trail, and Win was ranging ahead a bit to make sure their path was clear. The last thing anyone wanted at this point was to run into an Indian war party. Percy elected to hang close in case they ran into trouble and he had to spring into action. Luis was driving the wagon and Isaac was riding shotgun, their horses hitched to the back of the wagon next to Arturo's, Amos's, and Snowball, his father's horse.

They were a silent group, everyone talked out from their long days of travel. And though they were miles and miles away from where they had been searching for Emma, the disappointment they all felt was still palpable. In fact, as they rode along, Percy was already thinking of next steps. He was planning to rest up for a day or two and then head north to Fort Sill to get the lay of the land. If the army was planning a spring campaign against the Indians, then he aimed to be a part of it. If his old friend was still in command, he didn't think it would be a problem and, if not, he would have to do some finagling. Not going was not an option. And if the army wasn't planning any action, Percy was going to mount another search and, this time, he was going to take his father's advice and hire the damn best Indian scouts he could find.

The timing was the biggest question for Percy. A search during the winter months would be difficult and cold, but it could also work to their advantage. It was common knowledge that the Indians were known to hunker down during the winters and that might make them easier to find. Waiting until spring presented another set of problems. With the spring rains, trails would be harder to follow, and the swollen rivers would be dicey to cross. The ideal time would be summer again, but that would mean Emma would have been held captive for almost a full year, an unthinkable proposition for Percy. The more he thought about the situation he realized he needed to find out the army's plans before he could make any decisions. So that would be step one in his plan.

By late afternoon they were within sight of ranch land and Percy's apprehension began to build. His mother was going to take the news hard and there was no way to soften the blow. Normally even-tempered and calm, Percy didn't know how she would respond to the news that her husband was gone. If that had been the only thing worrying Percy it would have been manageable. But he was deeply concerned about Abigail's reaction when they arrived home without her daughter. *Calm* and *even-tempered* weren't the words he'd use to describe either of his sisters and there was no way to predict what Abby's response would be. Her reaction could run the gamut from extreme anger to extreme disappointment and either one would cut Percy to the bone. As he was thinking about that, a new worry wormed its way into his brain — and that was Amos. He was going to have to tell his other sister that her husband was dead. And he truly didn't know what her reaction would be. The more he thought about it the more he realized he needed to talk to his mother first before Abby and Rachel discovered they were back. And the only way that would happen was to get there before the wagon rolled into the yard.

Percy nudged his horse toward the wagon and rode beside Isaac and said, "Grab your horse and we'll ride ahead. We need to talk to my mother first and then Abby."

"Not sure I want to," Isaac said. "Abby's likely to skin me alive for comin' home without Emma."

"Well," Percy said, "she's liable to do the same with me and she's your wife."

"Yeah, but she's your sister," Isaac said. "Might be better if she was to hear it from blood kin."

"So, you don't want to ride ahead?" Percy asked, his voice tinged with anger.

"Not really," Isaac said. "Why you got a burr under your saddle to ride ahead? Way I see it, the more people around when Abby finds out, the better."

Percy muttered a string of curse words under his breath. "You're really not goin' with me?"

"No, I ain't, Percy. If you think you need to ride ahead and tell her, then go on."

Percy couldn't see how it would work out the way he wanted it to without talking to his mother first. "I will," Percy said before spurring his horse into a gallop. Isaac's refusal to ride along angered him but didn't really surprise him. There was no doubt who wore the pants in that family. Percy knew Mouse was also exhausted, but he didn't have far to ride. A short while later he came to the road that led up to the houses and he slowed his horse to a walk. Holding Mouse to the side of the road, he used the main house as a shield for his approach. He was hoping Abby wasn't outside and spotted him first because he really needed to talk to his mother and, if she wasn't too devastated, enlist her help in dealing with his sisters.

He rode up to the main house and climbed down from his horse. He heard the squeal of the front door and turned to see his mother walking out on the porch. Taking off his hat, he climbed up the steps and wrapped his arms around his mother. Finally breaking the embrace, he stepped back. Frances leaned sideways to look around him and said, "Where's your father?"

Percy took his mother by the hand and led her over to the rocking chairs. "You better sit down, Ma."

Frances stood and stared at her son for a long time and then sagged onto the rocker. "He's gone, isn't he?"

Percy nodded.

"Was he killed by Indians?"

"No. He died peacefully." Percy took a seat in the rocker next to his mother. "I don't know what was wrong with him, but he was rubbing his chest a lot."

His mother nodded as tears began running down her cheeks. She stared at something in the distance for a long few moments and Percy held her hand as they sat in silence. Eventually, she pulled her hand free and wiped her eyes. "And Emma?"

"Couldn't find her, Ma. We searched and searched and never caught a glimpse of her."

"Abby will be devastated."

"I know. We ran out of supplies and the weather turned. I'm going to hire some Indian scouts up at Fort Sill and go back."

"Your father knew it would be a tall task," Frances said, her voice flat. "You need to rest up before you do anything."

"I'm afraid I've got more bad news, Ma. We lost Amos, too. He fell against the wagon one night and hit his head."

"I truly don't know how Rachel will react to that," Frances said. "We've had an interesting time." She took a moment to absorb all the news then reached out and took Percy's hand. "I've got some bad news, too."

Percy looked at her and said, "Mary?"

"Yes. She died shortly after you left."

Percy nodded. "How are the kids?"

"They're okay. Amanda went through a period of guilt but she's coming around."

"Guilt because I told her to give Mary all the laudanum she wanted?"

"Yes. But you did the right thing, Percy."

"I know, but I should have been the one doing it instead of dumping it on Amanda."

"It makes no difference. The result was the same. And Mary was suffering terribly."

Percy looked up to see the wagon turning up the road and sighed.

"Where did you bury your father?"

"Under a large oak tree by a river."

"He'd like that."

Percy pushed out of the chair and stood. "I guess I better go talk to Abby and Rachel."

Frances stood. "I'm going with you."

"Are you sure you're up for it?" Percy asked.

His mother thought about that for a moment, then said, "No. But what choice do we have? All we can do is carry on."

Percy and Frances stepped off the porch and walked around the house. Abby must have heard the wagon coming because she came barreling out of the house.

Abby, her heart racing a mile a minute,

looked up to see Percy and her mother walking toward her and she knew in an instant that Emma was still gone. It felt like the breath had been knocked out of her and she had to grab the hitching post to keep from sagging to her knees. Her heart was still racing, but now for a much different reason. Thoughts bombarded her like a volley of bullets and then they crystallized instantly into anger. She charged toward Percy and her mother tried to grab her, but Abby shrugged her off, stuck out her arms, and hit Percy at full speed, knocking him backward.

"Why are you here?" Abby shouted, spittle flying in the air. She stalked toward Percy and began pummeling him with her fists. Percy took it for a moment then reached out and grabbed her and hugged her tight, pinning her arms to her sides. That left her feet free and she began kicking her brother in the shins and stomping on his feet, anything to make him feel pain.

Percy looped a leg around hers and drew her legs tight to his body.

"I'm sorry, sis," Percy said.

"You're damn right, you are," Abby shouted as she used her forehead like a hammer and pounded Percy in the chest.

Percy squeezed her tighter, until there was

no room to move her head and that made her angrier, but she was completely immobilized.

"I'm going back, Abby," Percy said.

"You should have never left!" Abby shouted as she tried to squirm free.

"You're right," Percy said. "But we didn't have much of a choice."

"You had a choice," Abby shouted. "And you made it, didn't you?"

"I suppose you're right. If you want to hit me, go ahead." Percy freed her and stepped back, a pained look on his face.

Abby glared at her brother and balled her fists. She suddenly felt her mother's arms encircling her waist and, in the blink of an eye her anger was gone, and she broke into sobs. She looked at her brother and said, "I didn't mean . . . mean it . . . Percy."

"I know you didn't, Abby. I promise I'm going back to look for her."

Abby nodded and her mother held her while she cried. Eventually, she regained a small measure of composure. "Where's Isaac?"

"He's comin' with the wagon."

"He didn't want to ride in with you to tell me, did he?"

Percy decided not to answer.

Abby nodded at his nonanswer and allowed her mother to lead her up the porch steps and over to a chair as the war wagon rolled past on the way to the barn.

Percy felt like hell for letting his sister down and he was pissed at Isaac for not being part of the discussion. On the trip home he'd tried to think what they could have done different, but they'd done all they could.

He didn't have the heart to tell Abby that their father was gone and hoped his mother would broach the subject when she calmed down. He glanced over at Rachel's house and saw her stepping down from the porch. Percy walked up to her but stopped at a safe distance, having learned his lesson.

"I didn't see Amos ride in," Rachel said.

"That's what I wanted to talk to you about," Percy said. "You want to sit down?"

"Amos is dead, isn't he?"

"Yes," Percy said. "Sure you don't want to sit down?"

"How'd he die?" Rachel asked.

"Hit his head against the wagon one night."

"Figures," Rachel said. "I need to tell the kids." She turned to go back inside, and Percy grabbed her by the arm to stop her.

"There's more."

"Okay," Rachel said.

Percy stepped past Rachel and climbed up the porch steps. "You can stand if you want, but I'm gonna sit down." He walked over to one of the chairs and sat.

Rachel sighed, walked over, and took a seat on the edge of the chair like she was in a hurry to get somewhere.

"You don't seem too tore up about Amos," Percy said.

"Is that what you wanted to talk about?" Rachel asked.

Her attitude irked Percy and he decided not to sugarcoat it. "No. Pa's dead."

Rachel sagged back against the chair as tears sprang to her eyes. She sat and cried for a few moments and then reached out to take Percy's hand and gave it a squeeze. "I'm sorry, Percy."

"It's okay."

"Was he . . . was he killed by Indians?"

"No," Percy said. "He died peacefully."

Rachel nodded and wiped her eyes. "I love you, Percy."

"And I love you, Rachel."

"I'm sorry about Mary."

"Thank you. Are you okay?"

"Yes, but I need to go tell the kids about their father before they hear it from someone else."

Percy leaned over and kissed his sister on

the forehead and then pushed to his feet. "See you around, sis."

He stepped down off the porch and headed toward his house, eager to hug his kids.

CHAPTER
62

After a week to rest up and to check on things around the ranch, Percy was now riding across the river, on his way to Fort Sill, thirty-five miles away. He was still struggling with the loss of his father and probably would be for the foreseeable future. His purpose for going to Fort Sill was twofold. The first was to discover the army's plans for a campaign against Indians and the second was to see if he could work a deal with the Indian agent to sell the agency about two thousand head of Rocking R steers. The price per head he was hoping to get would be less than what he could have made at the railhead in Kansas, but it was much too late in the year to mount a cattle drive. And if he couldn't work a deal there, he was planning on riding over to see if Montford T. Johnson wanted to buy some mama cows to increase the size of his herd. Either way, he needed to sell some cattle to stabilize the ranch's shaky financial situation.

The problem with both schemes was that the buyer would be forced to overwinter the cattle and that would eat into the prices he was hoping to get. None of it was ideal, but it was what it was. And if he couldn't work a deal to sell some cattle, he'd have to explore the possibilities of selling some land, something he didn't really want to do. If he could hold on until the Indians were forced back onto the reservation, he knew land prices in the area would skyrocket. A thousand acres today might be worth a dollar an acre, but once the Indian problem was finally solved, Percy thought land prices might balloon to ten dollars an acre or more. Hence, his reticence to part with any land.

Tired of thinking about finances, Percy let his mind drift to his children. Franklin and Amanda were coping well with the death of their mother, but he couldn't say the same for Chauncey. Something seemed off about the boy, and he couldn't put his finger on what it was. He would have to keep an eye on both him and Seth, who, in addition to being roughed up and branded, was now dealing with the loss of his father, Amos. Percy hadn't yet put a stop to their frequent trips to the river to shoot because he remembered what life was like at that age. They were a long way from any neighbors, and the boys needed an outlet other than constant work. Before Mary's illness, she had taken up the mantle of teacher and had schooled all the children on the ranch and that had helped to keep Chauncey and Seth occupied. Now with her gone, the boys had too much free time, and Percy knew that could lead to all sorts of mischief. He made a mental note to talk to the Indian agent at the post to see if he had any leads on a teacher that would be willing to work for room and board. If not, he was going to have to find the means to pay for one. He was a big believer in education and had even contemplated going to college back East, much like Eli did later. Instead, he'd wandered through south Texas and wound up with the Rangers, which was an entirely different education altogether. So, finding a teacher was a must and he added it to a to-do list that was growing longer every day.

Percy had not met Amanda's suitor yet, but he was coming over Thursday for Thanksgiving. Percy was ambivalent about the holiday that would be ten years old this year, but it was nice to spend the day with family and enjoy some good food. With the loss of Cyrus, Amos, and Arturo it would no doubt be a somber day although Percy thought a day to reflect on their lives would be healing for all involved.

Percy spotted an Indian encampment ahead and adjusted his course to steer around it. If he had an interpreter, he'd stop and ask them about Emma's whereabouts and that thought spurred an idea to do just that. He would hire an interpreter at the post and spend a couple of days interviewing the Indians who were scattered around the reservation. If he could find a Comanche or a Kiowa who had traveled with Quanah Parker, he might get some insight into his group's movements. But then he wondered how willing those Indians would be to pass on factual information under the eye of their fellow tribe members. Would they talk more freely if Percy offered a pot sweetener like coffee and sugar or something else the Indians coveted? He decided the one person who could answer that question was his old friend Lieutenant Colonel John Davidson.

It was late afternoon when Percy rode into Fort Sill and he was undecided if he wanted to talk to the Indian agent now or wait until tomorrow morning. Bringing his horse to a stop, he spent a moment thinking it through. He wanted the agent to take a more active role in finding Emma and he didn't know how best to accomplish that goal. Having never met the man, Percy had no idea if he was the type of man who required a boot in his butt to spur him into action or if a subtler approach was needed. With those questions unanswerable without further investigation, Percy decided tomorrow would be better and he spurred his horse into motion.

Teepees dotted the landscape and several Indians lounged on the front porch of the agency building or in front of the trader's store. He rode across the large parade ground at the center of the fort and stopped at Sherman House, headquarters for the post commander. After climbing down from his horse, Percy pulled his rifle out of the scabbard to keep it from being stolen, wrapped the reins around the hitching post, and entered. The same desk sat near the door, but a different private was manning it. Percy gave the trooper his name and whom he wanted to see, and the man disappeared into the bowels of the building. He returned a moment later and led Percy back to a large office and Davidson stood, stepped around his desk, and stuck out his hand. "How ya doin', Percy?"

Percy shook Davidson's hand and said,

"Been a rough few weeks, John. How are you?"

"Been a rough few *years* for us." Davidson smiled and ushered Percy over to a couple of upholstered chairs arranged around a small table, and Percy sat. Davidson took a seat in the opposite chair and crossed one leg over the other. "What brings you to our lovely little piece of paradise?"

Percy took a moment to survey the office. Davidson's diploma from the U.S. Military Academy at West Point was framed and hung on the wall behind the desk. "A couple of things, John. I wanted to see you and then I have to talk to the Indian agent in the morning."

"Why do you want to talk to Haworth?"

"The kidnappin'."

"What kidnapping?" Davidson asked.

"Abby's oldest, Emma?"

Davidson uncrossed his legs and leaned forward. "Oh hell, Percy. When was this?"

"About four months ago. I've been all over hell and gone and never saw a trace of her. My father reported her kidnappin' to Haworth the last time he was here. Did he not pass the news on to you?"

"No, this is the first I'm hearin' about it."

"Why wouldn't he tell you, John?"

Davidson spent a moment thinking about

it and Percy could see his face redden with anger. Davidson stood and started to pace. "He was probably afraid I'd send out a patrol and stir up trouble. And I would have if I'd known." Davidson shook his head and muttered, "That son of a bitch." He paced in silence for a moment then returned to the main topic. "I get along with the Indians fine but not when they pull that crap. Who took her?"

"Cyrus heard from one of the Kiowa chiefs that it was probably Quanah Parker and his band."

"Figures," Davidson said. "Where did you look?"

"From here out to the Palo Duro Canyon then all the way north to the Arkansas River. Found out she'd been in the canyon at some point but no idea where they went."

"Did you hire any Indian scouts?"

"No, and that was our biggest mistake."

Davidson returned to his chair and sat. "They're damn near impossible to find even with a full complement of Indian scouts. About half the time we end up stumbling into them by accident. I'm certain they had scouts out and would have seen you comin' for days. And they can be packed up and gone mighty damn quick." Davidson lifted the lid of a small box on the table and pulled out two cigars and passed one to Percy.

Percy bit the end off, stuck it in his mouth, and Davidson lit Percy's and then his own. Percy took a couple of draws to get the cigar going then pulled it from his mouth. "The last time I was here, you mentioned the army might be starting a new campaign against the Indians."

Davidson took a deep draw from his cigar, blew out the smoke, and nodded. "They haven't got it all lined out yet. Sherman and Sheridan are raring to go but they have to get the folks at the Bureau of Indian Affairs to sign off on it."

"When do you think that'll happen?"

"Who knows. You can't get shit done until about a thousand people sign off on it. But I'm guessing it'll happen come summer."

"A fifty-fifty guess?"

"No, eighty-twenty for a campaign."

"Can I go with you to search for the girl?"

"You goin' to bring that war wagon of yours?"

"Of course," Percy said. "We took it with us when we went last time. Tangled with Indians a couple of times and then they left us alone."

Davidson took another draw from his cigar. "Can't say I blame them. Sure, you can go along, Percy. Hell, the more, the merrier. How old was the girl they took?"

"Thirteen."

"Think she can hang on another few months?"

"What do you think? You've seen what they do to captives."

"That's the hardest question to answer, Percy. But even with a few Indian scouts your odds of finding them are long. So, I don't know that you have much choice. From some of the preliminary planning I've seen, the army intends to put an end to the Indian problem once and for all. The plan is to send out five different army columns and then converge on the Indians' location. From here I'll lead my men west, and columns will move south out of Fort Dodge, northwest from Fort Griffin, north from Fort Concho, and east out of Fort Union. We're going to squeeze them until there's nowhere else for them to go. That'd probably be your best chance of gettin' the girl back."

"So, you think another trip for me and my crew in the interim would be a fool's errand?"

"I do, Percy. You might light a fire under Haworth's ass in the meantime to see if he can't work something out. He might be able to put some pressure on the recent parolees, Big Tree and Santana. They're Kiowas but they might as well be Comanches."

"What's it gonna take to light a fire under Haworth's ass?"

"Pressure. Hell, I'd send someone up from the ranch every few days. Doesn't have to be you. It might be a good idea to send Abigail up. Hard to ignore a distraught mother. Have Isaac bring her up and I'll put them up in one of the vacant rooms in the officers' quarters for as long as they want to stay."

"That's a good idea," Percy said.

"Or send Cyrus up for a few days. Haworth would be beggin' every Indian he saw about information on Emma, just to get rid of your father." Davidson chuckled, then checked the end of his cigar to see how it was burning.

"Can't send Cyrus, John. He died while we were out searching for my niece."

"Oh hell, Percy. I'm sorry." Davidson sat and stared at a thin wisp of smoke curling up from his cigar for a few moments then he looked up and said, "Indians didn't get him, did they?"

"No. I think his heart gave out on him. And we lost Amos and another one of our hands, Arturo, who was killed by an Indian when he strayed a little too far from the wagon."

"Damn, you have had a rough few weeks. What happened to Amos?"

"Fell and hit his head on the edge of the wagon on a really dark night."

"How did your mother and Rachel take the news?"

"Okay, I guess. My mother is a strong woman."

"That she is." Davidson stood, walked to a table behind his desk, picked up a bottle of brandy and two glasses, and returned to his chair. He pulled the stopper and poured a heavy splash of whiskey into both glasses and set the bottle aside. Davidson raised his glass and said, "To Cyrus and Amos."

Percy touched his glass to Davidson's, and they downed the brandy.

"Hell, I hate to hear that about Cyrus."

"I'm still trying to get over it. But he lived a long, full life and as hard as it is, we all have to go sometime."

"That we do." Davidson reached over, refilled the glasses, and handed Percy his.

Percy leaned over and stubbed out his cigar. "Are your wife and the kids coming down for Thanksgiving?"

"No. It's just too damn hard to get here. I'm going up to Saint Louis for a spell around Christmas."

"Come to the ranch. And you can bring your staff, too."

"Maybe," Davidson said. "I might need to stay around here and have dinner with the troops."

"Well, come if you can."

"I will. You stayin' tonight?"

"Yeah, if that's okay."

"Sure. We'll have supper in a bit then I'm going to try and scare us up a card game."

"Then I need to hide my wallet somewhere before you take all of my money."

"Last time we played it was you that cleaned me out. Want to walk over and talk to Haworth? Start applyin' a little of that pressure I was talkin' about?"

"Why not?" Percy said.

They finished their whiskey, Davidson stubbed out his cigar, and they exited the office.

Chapter
63

After a few days of mourning the death of her husband, Rachel Ferguson was ready to move on with her life. She felt bad that her children had lost their father, but things hadn't been good between her and Amos for a long time. Seth took the news hard and Rachel was worried Amos's death could push him over the edge of whatever precipice he imagined in his mind. She had asked everyone in the family to keep a close eye on him and didn't know what else she could do other than love him. Jacob and Julia appeared to be coping okay and she didn't have any real concerns about them going forward.

Although Rachel was ready to move on, she wasn't a crass fool who was immune to her family's expectations. With that in mind, she was carefully plotting her next few moves. Consorting with another man during a husband's absence might be considered scandalous but doing the same days after learning of that husband's death would be considered by most people to be horrifyingly wicked. And Rachel, who usually didn't much care about what people thought, didn't want herself or her family painted with that brush. So, the word she kept repeating in her mind as she saddled her horse was *discretion.*

Leander Hays had taken a room at a boardinghouse in a town — Wichita Falls — that had recently sprouted up west of the ranch. It was only an eight-mile ride and Rachel had traveled it enough over the weeks before news of Amos's death that she thought she could probably navigate it blindfolded. At that time, she hadn't cared much about the local gossip about her affair, but now she would have to be extremely careful in how she proceeded. Not having seen Leander since learning of Amos's death, he remained unaware of the current situation. To remedy that, she needed a way to discreetly pass on her plan to meet at a more remote rendezvous — somewhere well removed from the ranch and the town. In preparation for that task, she had written a short note telling Leander to meet her at the small creek north of town and had sealed it inside an envelope with his name on it. Her plan was to slip into the boarding-house unseen and put the envelope in his mail slot. How to ensure he found it in a timely manner was a problem she hadn't worked out yet.

After saddling her horse, she tied on a rolled-up blanket, led the horse out of the barn, and mounted up. The relationship with her mother was still strained so she had been relying on Abby to keep an eye on the kids while she was away, but she didn't feel comfortable doing that now at such a delicate time. Instead, she had crossed her fingers and asked Seth to keep tabs on his younger siblings while she rode out to check on a favorite stallion that had been looking sickly. Or that was the lie she told.

Spurring her horse into a walk, she plot-ted her next step. For her ruse to work, she'd have to ride east a bit and then cut back south before turning west for town and she had to do it without being seen. The task of being a spy was almost too much to manage and, combined with an unseason-ably hot day, she could feel a headache com-ing on. Both she and the horse were lathered up by the time they made the turn for town, and she couldn't remember a time when it had ever been this hot and humid in No-vember. Rachel glanced up to see the sky littered with white, puffy clouds and knew they could grow into storms if the heat continued into the afternoon.

When she reached the edge of the small town, she stopped her horse under a shade tree and surveyed the area, all thoughts of the weather now gone. The newly built boardinghouse was situated two blocks from the main street — the owner obviously imagining future town expansion. Wearing her short-brimmed sombrero, she pulled it down to better shield her face and walked the horse forward.

She rode up to the front door, climbed down from her horse, tied the reins to the hitching post, opened the door, and stepped inside, and ran smack into Leander, who was walking down the hall from his room. He opened his arms to give her a hug and she thrust the note into his hand and turned on her heel without saying a word. She could feel the heat creeping into her cheeks as she exited the building and remounted her horse. So much for best-laid plans, she thought as she rode out of town. She didn't think anyone saw her, but there was little she could do about it now if they had.

She reached the rendezvous point a few moments later and parked her horse under a shade tree and climbed down. She had been looking forward to rinsing her face in the creek to cool off, but she discovered it was as dry as a powder house. Someone had been cutting timber recently and she walked over to a fresh tree stump and sat. Having never lost a husband before, she didn't know if a certain amount of time had to elapse before dating again. If that was the case, what time frame would be acceptable? Two months? Six months? A year? Rachel didn't think she could skulk around in the woods for a month, much less an entire year. If it had been just her, she would have moved Leander in a week ago. But it wasn't and she had to consider the impact on her children.

She saw Leander riding in and stood to greet him.

He stopped his horse and looked down at her. "What in the hell was that? If we're done just tell me and I'll ride out of here right now."

Rachel didn't like his tone. "Do you want it to be over?"

"No. But you're actin' crazy."

"For a reason. If you'll get down, I'll tell you. Or if you want to ride on, then ride."

"Don't get your dander up," Leander said as he climbed off his horse. He stood in front of her and said, "I'm listenin'."

"Amos is dead."

"Who's Amos?"

"My husband."

"Oh." He rubbed a hand across the stubble on his chin. "Huh. That why you ain't been to see me?"

"What do you think?"

"How long's he been . . . d . . . gone?"

"I found out only days ago when my brother returned."

Leander took his hat off, hooked it on his saddle horn, and raked his hands through his long, dark hair, delaying. "Well . . . I don't . . . I'm sorry for your loss."

"He was lost to me long ago."

"That's a little harsh, ain't it?"

"Maybe, but it's true. I do hate it for my kids, though."

Leander waved the envelope in his hand. "What's up with this here?"

"Which part of 'only days ago' did you not understand?"

"Oh. Didn't think about that. Probably wouldn't look too good to see a new widow slinking around the boardin' house."

"You think? And I don't slink."

"Poor choice of words on my part." He tucked the envelope under his saddle and stepped forward until they were about a foot apart. "Can I hug ya?"

"Please."

He wrapped his long arms around her, and they hugged for a long time in silence. Rachel eventually looked up and kissed him on the lips. And that was the only spark they needed. She kept kissing him as she pulled him over to her horse, where she fumbled the blanket free. Leander took it from her hands, kissed her some more, then spread it out on the ground. They shucked off their clothes and Rachel pushed him down to the ground and straddled him. She reached down and slid him inside of her and started grinding her hips. She braced her hands on his powerful chest and stared into his eyes as she rocked her hips back and forth. She paused, leaned down, and they kissed for a few moments before she started grinding again. She found her rhythm and it wasn't long before both were spent. Rachel slid off him and lay down beside him, putting her head on his chest.

Leander ran his fingers through her hair. "What's next?"

"I don't think I'm done yet."

Leander chuckled. "Okay. Me, neither. After today, then?"

Rachel tilted her head up so she could look at him. "How much do you miss your place down on the Brazos?"

Leander thought about it for a moment and said, "Not much. But it's home, I reckon."

"How come you and your wife didn't have any children?"

"Well, it wasn't for a lack of tryin'. She lost a couple early on and lost heart, I guess."

"Do you like children?"

"Well, sure, I suppose. Ain't never been around them much."

"Think you'd like being a father?"

"Hadn't thought about that in a while, but I reckon I'd like it just fine. What's up with all these questions about kids?"

"Trying to decide if I want to keep you around."

"Well, hell, I didn't know I was bein' tested. Did I pass?"

Rachel pinched one of his chest hairs between her fingers and plucked it out.

"I guess that was a no?"

She rubbed the spot where she'd plucked the hair with her finger. "Still haven't decided."

"What exactly are we talkin' about here? What we been doin' all along?"

"More."

"You talkin' about gettin' married?"

"Eventually. We still have a little time."

"Time for what? I understand you gotta wait —"

She silenced him by placing her finger on his lips. She leaned up on her elbow and looked at him. "You asked me a question and you didn't let me answer."

"Which question? About time?"

"Yes. We have a couple of months before I start showing."

"Showing? Showing wha — oh hell, you're pregnant."

"I am."

"Hellfire, why didn't you tell me?"

"I just did."

Leander rolled over on his side so he could see her face. "I ain't tryin' to make you mad —"

"It's yours, Leander. I hadn't slept with Amos in a long time."

"Huh. Okay. Well. When's it comin'?"

Rachel laughed. "Not today. You can relax. My best guess is probably June."

Leander rolled onto his back and looked at the sky. "June, huh?"

Rachel hiked a leg over his and pulled herself on top of him again. "Could be July."

It was late afternoon before they dressed and rolled up the blanket. Leander rocked his head from side to side, trying to stretch out the kinks. When he dipped his head to the right, he froze. "How long does it take you to ride home?"

Rachel could tell from his tone that something was wrong. She looked around quickly, thinking someone might be approaching, and didn't see anything. "I don't know. Why?"

"Look."

She turned, followed his outstretched arm with her eyes, and just about peed her pants. A massive, nasty-looking thunderstorm that stretched so high overhead the top was obscured was lurking just to the west. "Which way is it moving?"

"Don't know. Come back to my room until it blows over."

She put her foot in the stirrup and threw her leg over. "Can't. My children are home alone."

"Surely they'll go to one of the other houses."

"Maybe, but what if they don't? I'll talk to you in a couple of days."

"C'mon, Rachel. That thing's throwing out lightning like crazy."

Rachel didn't wait to answer. She buried her spurs into her horse's ribs and he shot forward like a scalded cat. Anywhere else a thunderstorm like that wouldn't cause more than casual alarm.

But not here.

Here it could mean life or death. Home to some of the most violent weather on earth, a thunderstorm like that, here, could spin out a twister a mile wide that would suck up and destroy everything in its path. Rachel had seen it happen when she was a kid and you had to see it only once in a lifetime to know it was hell unleashed on earth. Rachel loosened the reins and let the horse run. She might kill the horse getting home, but she could always get another horse.

She was a mile from their rendezvous place when the skies opened up. It felt like someone had dumped a bucket of water over her head except the bucket was bottomless. She wiped her eyes once and then again, and then gave up. Her hat blew off and she hunched her shoulders in an attempt to keep the water from running down her back, but it was pointless. Lightning struck like bullets and the explosions of thunder reverberated through her body. A shaft of lightning hit a tree twenty yards to her left and the flash was so intense it was like being smashed in the face by a two-by-four. The booming thunder was instantaneous, and it sounded like a hundred cannons being discharged at once and the ground shook as if impacted by a rock the size of a house.

Unable to see, Rachel was forced to slow the horse to determine where she was, but the rain was too intense to take note of any landmarks. She spurred the horse back into a gallop, knowing she was going have to rely on him to get her home and she was praying the horse could see enough to know where he was going.

She turned her head to the side, listening intently for a roaring noise but couldn't hear much beyond the rain and thunder. The last time she'd seen a tornado, Rachel didn't have a point of reference to describe what it sounded like until she saw her first train roaring down the tracks. And that's exactly what it sounded like. Rachel's most immediate fear now was hail. She'd seen hailstones the size of cannonballs and if she got caught out in it, the stones would beat her and the horse to death. Her horse stumbled, fought for grip, and then started running again. Thinking that was almost a disaster, she pulled on the reins to slow him from a gallop to a canter.

Rachel knew that a twister in November was rare, but around here one could pop up any time of the year and as hot as it had been today, she knew she'd been foolish not to have kept an eye on the sky.

Pea-size hail began to pepper her, stinging her exposed skin. If it didn't get any larger, she thought she might be okay. But there were never any guarantees when it came to a thunderstorm as large as the one overhead. The rain tapered off a tad and Rachel glanced back over her shoulder to see an ominous-looking protuberance hanging from the bottom of a dark, rotating cloud and she knew if a twister was coming it would form there. The hail stopped and the rain lightened up some more and then the wind began howling as the immense thunderstorm sucked in an enormous amount of air, the inflows adding fuel to its violence. Turning back to the front she caught a glimpse of the outline of her parents' house in the gathering gloom.

Suddenly, hail the size of her fists rained down and it felt like she was being pummeled by a thousand hammers. She was in real danger now and she spurred her horse into an all-out run. The large hail stopped as suddenly as it had started, and Rachel sighed with relief. But with the hail gone so was the racket it produced, and that's when she heard the roar of a train and knew there weren't any railroad tracks within three hundred miles of the ranch. Stealing a glance over her shoulder, she saw the monster of her nightmares.

The horse was snorting and huffing as if he knew it was run or die. Reining her horse to the right to adjust her course, she was now three hundred yards from home and had no clue if she was going to make it or not. She ticked off a list of needed actions in her mind, knowing full well that the only way to survive a twister of that magnitude was to get underground and that meant the root cellar under her parents' house.

But she had to check her house first.

She flew by her parents' place, the horse lunging and stretching for every ounce of speed. When she came abreast of her own home, she pulled on the reins and squeezed her thighs and the horse locked his back legs and squatted almost to the ground. Rachel jumped off and raced for the front door as the horse stood and took off, running for his life.

Rachel yanked the door open and rushed inside, hoping her children had already taken cover. But she found them huddled together in the front room, terror etched on their faces. "C'mon, c'mon, c'mon," she muttered as she grabbed for hands, pulling them to their feet. The roar of the approaching twister was deafening, and she had to shout to be heard. "We've got to run to the cellar, okay?"

Three terrified faces looked back at her and then all three nodded. "Don't look. Just run. Go!"

Rachel let the kids run ahead in case one tripped and needed help getting up. They flew out of the house as if it was burning down around them. Ranch hands were pouring out of the bunkhouse and racing toward the cellar and she spotted her mother running for the underground bunker and she ducked inside and reappeared a moment later, waving her hands to urge the children on. And despite what she'd told the children, Rachel looked. The monster twister was at least a half-mile wide and was churning straight toward them, plucking smaller trees out by the roots and shearing off the tops of others, creating a vortex of dirt and debris. And the roar didn't sound like a train now — it sounded like a thousand trains. Rachel thought she had less than thirty seconds to get to the cellar and get inside. She turned and ran.

The winds were whipping and swirling, and the temperature had dropped twenty degrees as the air high up in the storm was pulled toward the surface. She saw Julia and Jacob disappear down the stairs, followed closely by Seth. Racing up to the cellar doors, Rachel was only a foot from her mother and still had to shout when she said, "Is everyone inside?"

Frances nodded and Rachel urged her mother down the stairs then ran down three steps and reached for the doors as the barn exploded in the distance. With the wind it was impossible to get the doors closed and she shouted into the dark interior for help. Eli came running, charged up the steps, and he and Rachel finally got the doors closed. He slipped a board into the two handles to keep the door from being sucked open and they hurried down the stairs.

With a dirt floor, the cellar was dank and steamy, and they sat, huddled together in the gloomy darkness. Conversation was impossible so all they could do was listen. And what they heard was otherworldly and hellish. The cellar doors began to vibrate and a few seconds later they started bucking and jerking and Rachel was afraid they weren't going to hold. If they blew off, they were dead and everyone in the cellar knew it.

After fifteen minutes of sheer terror, the cellar grew quiet and Rachel heard the heavy, frightened breaths of her family and the ranch hands. She stood and felt her way to the stairs. With her hand sliding along the wall, she ascended to the doors, pulled out the board, and pushed the doors open. Sunlight flooded the basement and Rachel didn't know if she could bear to go any farther. She willed her feet to move and she walked up the next step and then the next and her head cleared the opening and she looked around and sagged to her knees.

"That bad?" Eli asked as he stepped past.

Rachel stood and walked outside as the others began spilling out. Some sobbed, and some were too stunned to do anything but stare. Not a single structure was left standing. They had all been flattened and it looked like someone had detonated a thousand cases of dynamite. It was impossible to determine where each house had stood and the horses that had been in the corral were all dead, some flung hundreds of feet away.

Rachel turned in a slow circle and saw the massive monster plowing up the fields to the east. The utter devastation she saw was astonishing. That Mother Nature could create such an ugly, unruly monster was almost beyond comprehension.

"We certainly aren't accomplishing anything standing here," Eli said. "I suggest we start gathering up anything that is undamaged, if such a thing exists. And let's stack any usable lumber into a pile."

It took several moments for everyone to overcome their disbelief then they fanned out, searching for the things that would allow them to rebuild their lives.

CHAPTER
64

Percy had spent two days at Fort Sill, trying to gather information about Emma's abduction and stoking the fire he'd lit under the Indian agent's ass. The agent was now fully aware of the situation and what Percy's expectations were. And he'd had some success persuading the agent to buy some cattle. Not the two thousand head he was hoping to sell but he had agreed to buy a thousand steers, payable upon delivery. Percy was hoping they could round the steers up and get them started toward Fort Sill by the end of the week. Having accomplished that, he was now back in the saddle with hopes of making it home before dark.

One of the Indians he had visited with, through the use of an interpreter, was the same one his father had talked to, the Kiowa chief Kicking Bird. He had gotten much of the same information his father had, but he did learn something that amused him and that was the fact that the Indians had a name for him — Little Heap Big Guns. He assumed his father had been Heap Big Guns, but he hadn't asked.

Davidson had promised to send a runner Percy's way as soon as the army's plans firmed up. Percy wasn't expecting any news until spring at the earliest and he was going to have to tell Abby the bad news. He had also talked to several other Indians, again through an interpreter, to get an idea of what Emma might be experiencing during captivity. Some of it he would share with Abby and some he had no intention of sharing with anyone. But the overwhelming opinion had been that Emma would be assimilated into the tribe. And that's where things got a little sticky. As a young woman she would be expected to perform certain duties that her mother would find reprehensible. Percy didn't like it, either, but there wasn't much he could do about it. Anger wasn't going to help him find Emma any sooner.

The more he pondered Emma's probable mistreatment, the more he wanted to mount another search. If the weather held and they could get the cattle delivered, maybe he and Wilcox, along with a couple of Indian scouts, could ride out for another look. And if they took along extra horses, they would be able to cover a lot of ground in a hurry. There was both good and bad in leaving the wagon behind. It would allow them to travel faster and more covertly, but they'd also be without any real firepower. Percy wasn't really concerned about his own safety, but the original idea had been to use the war wagon as an overwhelming force to bend the Indians to their will. Without it, they wouldn't have much left to persuade the Indians that it was in their best interest to turn Emma over. Although the situation deserved further study, Percy knew the best bet was teaming up with the army. However, if Abby insisted on another search in the interim, he didn't know if he had the heart to say no.

By late afternoon, Percy was nearing the Red River and he was busy thinking of the things that needed to get done. Having struck out on finding a teacher, he was going to pass that task on to Eli. They had to get the steers rounded up and he figured that might be a three- or four-day job to find them all. The war wagon needed to be retrieved from the blacksmith's shop over in Wichita Falls and it also needed to be restocked with supplies. The ranch financials required a deeper dig to see if there were any savings to be had. And then he remembered that Thanksgiving was this week and that screwed up his hastily cobbled-together schedule.

He rode down into the river bottom and stopped to allow his horse a chance to drink. Once she had drunk her fill, he spurred the mare and she splashed across the ankle-deep water and he steered her up the bank. Trees lined both sides of the river and when he broke into the clear he reined the horse to a stop. He looked around to see if he'd crossed at the wrong spot, but he recognized several familiar landmarks so that wasn't it. Then he rubbed his eyes and looked again with the same result. He clucked his tongue to put the horse in motion and when he rode up a small rise his throat tightened, and a surge of nausea hit him like a cattle stampede.

The ground was littered with debris for as far as the eye could see, and where the five houses once stood was now an empty spot on the horizon. The pungent odor of rotten meat filled his nostrils, and he looked for the source and found it when he saw a pile of dead horses.

Out of habit he rode over to where the barn used to be and climbed down from his horse. Everyone was out picking stuff up and Percy couldn't take his eyes off the devastation as he walked out to his brother, who was pulling nails out of boards.

Eli looked up at his approach and said, "Welcome home, Percy."

"What the hell happened?" Percy asked. "Somebody come along and blow up every damn thing we had?"

"In a manner of speaking, if you want to include Mother Nature as one of your somebodies."

"Goddamn it, Eli. I don't have the stomach for one of your riddles right now."

"A tornado."

Percy turned his head and saw the enormously wide path the twister took when it left. "Jesus Christ."

"You are a tad late to be invoking the grace of God."

Percy shot Eli an angry glare. "Damn it, Eli, put a sock in it. Is everyone okay?"

"Okay? No," Eli said. "However, everyone who was alive prior to the storm remains alive today."

"When did it happen?"

"Late in the afternoon, yesterday."

Surveying the damage again, Percy saw the twisted hunk of steel that was once a Gatling gun that had been mounted in the main house and he mentally restructured his to-do list, moving the retrieval of the war wagon to the very top. Overwhelmed by the sight of it all, he turned back to Eli and said, "What the hell are we going to do?"

"The only thing we can do — start over."

■ ■ ■ ■

NINE MONTHS LATER

■ ■ ■ ■

CHAPTER
65

September 1874

Spring had been unseasonably wet and most of the rivers and creeks in the area had flooded and that, along with the devastation caused by the twister, had quashed any attempts to mount a new search for Emma. It had taken Percy two months to put together a deal for thirty wagonloads of lumber out of Dallas and when it finally arrived the incessant rain put them farther behind schedule. But when Percy, Isaac, and Luis had ridden away from the ranch at the end of August, progress on rebuilding was well under way. Eli was in charge of reconstruction and he'd hired several men from Wichita Falls and they were ripping and roaring. Even Leander Hays was busy working after being welcomed into the family when he had wed Rachel a few months before the couple welcomed their daughter, Autumn, into the world at the end of June. To cover the costs, Percy had convinced the Indian agents for both the Choctaws and Chickasaws to buy a thousand head of cattle each and that had put the ranch in better financial shape.

Indian raids on white settlements had continued through the spring and early summer months of 1874, but it took an Indian attack led by Quanah Parker against a group of buffalo hunters at a place called Adobe Walls out in the Texas Panhandle to spur the army into action. And that action came swiftly.

Following the plan that Davidson had detailed to Percy late last year, three thousand soldiers were quickly assembled and issued orders to disperse to five strategically located forts and the plan was to march five columns of troopers from five different directions to squeeze the Indians until they were all annihilated or surrendered. To aid the army, every Indian agency in the Territory quickly registered every peaceful Indian and confined them to their reservations, leaving the remaining Indians out on the plains as fair game.

In early September, Percy, along with Isaac and Luis, who was driving the war wagon, had ridden out of Fort Sill with companies from the U.S. Army's 10th

Cavalry and 11th Infantry, forty-six supply wagons, and a large number of Indian scouts, all under the command of Lieutenant Colonel John W. Davidson. After several skirmishes with hostile Indians and long days of travel, it was now late September and they were camped on Catfish Creek, 160 miles southwest of Fort Sill and only 30 miles southeast of where Percy had found Emma's initials arranged in stone on the floor of the Palo Duro Canyon. And not much had changed geographically during his absence, but what had changed was the army's determination to put an end to the Indian problem once and for all.

Davidson had joined his forces with Colonel Ranald S. Mackenzie's 4th Cavalry and units of the 10th and 11th Infantry and, because of his higher rank, Mackenzie assumed command. Although Percy had never met Mackenzie, he thought him somewhat moody, extremely intelligent, and intensely private. He had a long, dark, droopy mustache that obscured his mouth, and, like all cavalrymen, he was about five-nine and weighed somewhere around the 130-pound mark. And like Percy, Mackenzie had also earned not one, but two Indian names — Bad Hand and No-Finger Chief, after having lost the first two fingers of his right hand during the war.

To call the battles they were fighting a *war* would be a misnomer. There were no entrenched positions fighting off a frontal assault and no sustained long-term engagements. Most of the encounters had been running skirmishes that might stretch a few miles until one party called it quits. And there was no one location, the fighting stretching over an area that encompassed fifty thousand square miles. Within that vast open space were three thousand soldiers, hundreds of Indian scouts, a good number of frontiersmen like Percy, hundreds of supply wagons, and an unknown number of hostile Indians from four predominant tribes — Comanche, Kiowa, Southern Cheyenne, and Arapaho. And although the Indians might have originated from different tribes, they were all cut from the same cloth and were tough, rugged fighters who would just as soon kill you as look at you. And weapon type didn't really matter. It could be a bow and arrow, a lance, a gun, a knife, or their bare hands.

On the other side, the Ridgeway war wagon was badly outgunned by the army. They had brought out all of their shiny new toys, including new Winchester repeating rifles all around, several ten-barrel Gatling guns, a dozen mountain howitzers, and enough cannons to lay siege to the largest of American cities. The only problem with all of that firepower was that the army needed the enemy to stay in one place long enough to use it and that was the difficulty. The Indians would fight and run, fight and run, over and over and over again, preventing the hunters from ever grasping their prey. Not only was it exhausting, it was extremely effective — at least if you were an Indian. Several times army patrols had found themselves out of position or had outrun their supply train and were cut off by the Indians, forcing thirty or forty troopers to duel with hundreds of Indians.

Even though Percy had been in the area for a while, there had been no word of Emma's whereabouts. Nor had there been any sightings of her alleged captor, Quanah Parker, other than that one sighting at Adobe Walls back at the end of June. But Percy knew they had to be there somewhere. The key was finding him.

Late on the afternoon of September the twenty-seventh, two obviously excited Tonkawa scouts returned to the new camp in Tule Canyon and went immediately to confer with Mackenzie. Percy and Isaac moseyed over to listen in. It soon became apparent that the Tonkawa scouts had found a fresh trail that led into the Palo Duro Canyon. Percy heard Mackenzie ask something about winter camps and one of the scouts nodded. For Percy, that meant they'd finally found a large gathering of Indians. The order was given to mount up, and a short time later they were under way with four hundred soldiers and the accompanying artillery, including the Ridgeway war wagon. Percy rode beside his friend John Davidson as they traveled through the night.

At dawn, they reached the rim of the canyon and saw the Indian lodges spread across the floor. Mackenzie ordered the scouts to find a trail to the bottom and they soon did so. It was so steep the cavalrymen had to dismount their horses and lead them down single file. Percy asked Luis to park their wagon near the rim and man the gun in case it was needed. The howitzer would be useless once the battle began.

Davidson moved off to take command of his men, and Isaac stayed with Luis and the wagon, thinking he'd have a better chance of spotting Emma from a higher vantage point. Percy slid off Mouse and began the dicey descent into the canyon. Mackenzie, chomping at the bit, began the attack before Percy even reached the bottom. Melee ensued and soon Indian women and children scattered like rabbits escaping a collapsed den. Percy made it to the bottom and remounted his horse. With no defined job other than searching for Emma, he was unsure of his next move. That changed immediately when a bullet zinged off a rock right behind him. He pulled his pistol and rode into battle. The Indian braves mounted a small counter-attack to allow their women and children time to escape then they turned and fled. Percy was watching intently for any sign of Emma, but if she was in that mess of humanity, he couldn't see her.

Percy fired at a brave and missed as he rode into the camp. He heard a lot of gunfire but didn't see much in the way of results. Behind the camp, the canyon stretched on for miles and the Indians were streaming away from their village, leaving everything behind, including their horses. Percy hadn't been privy to Mackenzie's plans, but if it was to kill Indians, they were doing a miserable job of it. A few of the cavalry soldiers went chasing after the fleeing Indians and made halfhearted attempts to fire their weapons and it was then that Percy suspected Mackenzie's plan was much more complex than wholesale slaughter. And that was just fine by him. He holstered his pistol, turned Mouse, and rode up a small ridge for a better view of the retreating Indians.

By noon the Indians had all escaped and the temperature in the canyon was sizzling. Mackenzie ordered a search of the lodges and Percy didn't think there was much hope of finding Emma. He could have missed seeing her, but he didn't think both he and Isaac would have missed her. And he had no idea what Quanah Parker looked like and if he had been there, he was now gone.

Percy walked his horse over to the river and let her drink and spotted Isaac riding through the canyon. He stood in his stirrups and waved his hat to flag him down then dismounted. Once Mouse had drunk her fill, he led her into the shade of a cottonwood tree and waited for Isaac to arrive, which he did moments later.

"Damn, it's hot down here," Isaac said as he climbed off his horse.

"Hot up there, too," Percy said, nodding at the rim. "See anyone that even looked like Emma?"

"Nope. And I was looking through the field glasses you keep on the wagon."

"Well, hell." Percy sat down, stretched his legs out, and leaned back against the tree.

"How come they didn't try to round those

Injuns up when they was a-leavin'?" Isaac asked as he took a seat next to Percy.

Percy shrugged. "Best I can figure is the army has a plan. Even if they'd rounded them up what were they going to do with them out here in the middle of nowhere? Can you imagine trying to corral several hundred Indians for a month while we traveled back to Fort Sill? It'd be like herding chickens. It's a different story altogether if you force them to come in on their own. And at the rate those hunters are killing buffalo, it won't be long before they don't have anything to eat."

Later in the afternoon as the search of the lodges was still under way, Percy smelled smoke and stood to find the source. And that's when he knew his hunch had been right when he saw troopers piling the Indians' belongings into massive piles and throwing a torch on them. Percy and Isaac walked over for a closer look. Mackenzie hadn't just ordered the burning of personal belongings, he had ordered the burning of everything in sight including the teepees, the poles used to hold them up, the buffalo hides, war shields, blankets, and even a vast mound of buffalo jerky that the Indians had been relying on to tide them over for winter. While they were watching, Percy felt the ground shake, and he turned and saw a massive herd of Indian horses being driven up the canyon and as they passed, Percy estimated their number at close to two thousand. Notoriously hard for a white man to handle, he didn't know what Mackenzie had in store for them.

Percy saw Davidson riding through the canyon and waved. Davidson turned his horse and rode over. "I've been lookin' for you two. Grab your horses and follow me."

Percy and Isaac walked back to their horses and mounted up. They fell in beside Davidson and they rode deeper into the canyon. "Where are we goin'?" Percy asked.

"You'll see in a minute."

"Okay. How many casualties?" Percy asked.

"One private dead and a few others injured."

"And the Indians?"

"Three KIAs."

"What's that mean?" Isaac asked.

"Three Indians killed in action," Percy said before Davidson could answer. "Was that by design?"

"Partly," Davidson said. "One of the Kiowa chiefs fired a warning shot before we could get organized, so the Indians were already on the move."

"What's Mackenzie going to do with all those horses?"

"That's also part of the plan. He'll give a few to the scouts and plans to kill the rest."

"That's a shame," Percy said. "Ain't no other way to do it?"

"You want them?"

"No. Too damn much trouble."

"There you go," Davidson said. "Deprive these Indians out here a way to move around and they'll begin trickling into the reservations."

Percy looked ahead and saw one single teepee that was still standing, and it was being guarded by a couple of troopers. "Who's in the teepee?"

"Don't know for sure. That's why you're along."

Percy didn't want to get his hopes up and have them crushed again. "Is it a young girl?"

"If you consider young to be somewhere around fourteen or fifteen, then yes."

"I wonder why the Indians didn't take her with them," Percy said.

"There's a reason," Davidson said.

As they drew closer, a woman's sudden scream shattered the silence, startling both Percy and Isaac.

"What the hell are they doin' to her?"

Percy asked, spurring Mouse into a trot.

Davidson and Isaac matched him. "They aren't doing anything to her," Davidson said when he caught up.

Percy looked at him like he was crazy. When they reached the lodge a moment later, the three dismounted and Davidson held the flap open just as the woman began screaming again, freezing Percy and Isaac in place.

"Go on in," Davidson said.

Percy looked at Isaac and Isaac looked at Percy, neither wanting to be the first man through. Percy finally relented and stepped inside, and Isaac followed. The bottom of the teepee had been rolled up to catch a breeze and there was plenty of light to see and what they saw was a man kneeling next to a woman who was stretched out on a buffalo hide and who continued to moan and writhe in pain. Percy spotted a black doctor's bag next to the man's knee and assumed he was an army physician.

The man turned and waved them forward. "It's okay. If you'll confirm her identity, I'll step outside for a moment."

"Is she hurt?" Isaac asked as he took two tentative steps forward, Percy creeping along beside him.

"She's in some pain, however she isn't

injured. Please step on over."

After a few more tentative steps, Percy and Isaac stood and looked down at Emma's sweaty face and swollen belly. Both knelt down beside her.

"I'm sorry, Pa . . . and Uncle . . . Percy."

"Hush, baby girl," Isaac said as he sat back on his heels, stunned.

Percy turned and looked at the doctor. "How long has she been in labor?"

"Don't know for certain," the doctor said. "She was already in labor when she was found."

Percy leaned over and put a hand on Emma's forehead and looked her in the eyes. "You're a sight for sore eyes, Emma. We're goin' to take you home."

Emma nodded as tears leaked from her eyes. "I'd just about . . . given up —"

Her words were cut off when another contraction hit, and she screamed and then started huffing and puffing.

The doctor wiped her face with a damp rag. "Try not to push, Emma. We're not ready yet, okay?"

Emma nodded and groaned.

The doctor handed the damp rag to Isaac and said, "Just try to keep her comfortable and I'll be back in a moment." He touched Percy on the leg and nodded toward the entrance.

"What am I supposed to do?" Isaac asked.

"Talk to her. Comfort her."

Percy could tell by the look on Isaac's face that his initial shock was wearing off and anger was taking its place. "Tell her about —" Percy paused. He was going to suggest that Isaac talk about life on the ranch and her siblings, but he decided Isaac probably wasn't capable of doing that without mentioning the tornado, and the last thing Emma needed now was to know the home she knew had been obliterated. "Talk to her about how much you missed her."

Percy and the doctor stood, and they stepped outside and walked out of earshot.

After a formal introduction, Dr. Tom Miller asked, "How old is Emma?"

"Thirteen when she was taken, but I guess she's fourteen now. Is her age a problem?"

"Maybe. Keep in mind, I'm a field surgeon and not a midwife or an obstetrician, however I did study human anatomy. Her body is not yet fully developed, which means her bone structure also hasn't fully matured. Do you know what the pelvis is, Percy?"

"I do."

Miller cupped his hands and touched his fingers together. "Think of this as Emma's pelvis." He began moving his hands apart. "As a woman ages, the pelvis widens and usually reaches full width during their mid-twenties."

"So, what you're sayin' is she's gonna have a hard time getting the baby out."

"Precisely," Miller said.

"Why'd you tell her not to push, then?"

"Because her cervix is only partially dilated. Do you know what a cervix is?"

"Can't say I do."

"Think of it as the door to her womb. During childbirth that door opens ever so slowly with each contraction. Pushing before the door is open puts stress on the mother and child."

"That makes sense," Percy said. "When do you think that door'll be open?"

"Impossible to predict, especially with this being her first pregnancy." Miller was a short, older, distinguished-looking man with gray hair and his precise movements indicated his station as a skilled surgeon.

"Thank you, Doctor. If you need anything from me just let me know."

"Thank you, Percy. When she gets closer to delivering, I'm going to need some hot water."

"I'll get a fire started and round up a pot."

"Thank you." Miller turned, walked back

to the teepee, and slipped inside.

Smoke from the many bonfires hung over the canyon in the still afternoon heat. With it looking like they were going to be there awhile, Percy walked over and unsaddled Mouse and slipped the bridle over her ears. As Mouse moseyed off, Percy turned and saw Isaac angrily tossing the flap open before stepping out of the teepee. He spotted Percy and marched over.

Isaac jabbed his finger at the teepee and said, "We ain't takin' that thing home."

"Emma?" Percy asked, knowing full well what Isaac was referring to.

"No, not Emma. That thing inside of her."

"That thing is called a child."

"A savage half-breed is what it is. And I'll kill it if I have to. Them Injuns shouldn'ta done what they did."

"Agreed. But I don't know how much say you're going to have in the matter."

"What the hell do you mean? I'm her pa, ain't I?"

Percy was already tired of arguing. "And soon to be a grandfather."

"Fuck you, Percy. We ain't takin' that thing with us. You hear me?"

"I hear you. And if you talk a little louder, Emma will hear, too. Then what? If you aren't careful, you're going to drive her and the baby back to the Indians. Then *you* can explain to Abby why you came home again without Emma."

CHAPTER
66

Isaac had stormed off after their argument and Percy hadn't seen him since. Which was just fine as far as Percy was concerned. And if Isaac didn't settle down or listen to reason, he could hit the trail today by himself. He didn't know Emma's thoughts on the matter, but whatever they were they would likely change the instant she held the baby for the first time. If the baby ever came, that is. As the last of the light began to fade, Percy hadn't yet heard the cry of a newborn infant.

Dr. Miller stuck his head out of the teepee and said, "Percy, will you go and find a lantern?"

Percy stood. "I will, Doc. How is she?"

"We're getting there, but it'll be a while yet."

"Do you need anything else?"

"A canteen of water would be nice."

"Comin' right up."

Percy walked over to the war wagon that Luis had driven down earlier after finding an easier trail and pulled out a couple of lanterns from a box under the bed. He topped both off with fuel, lit them, grabbed a full canteen from under the seat, and carried everything back to Miller. Taking a seat by the fire, Percy stirred the coals and nudged the large pot of water a little farther into the glowing embers. At this rate, he might have to refill the pot a couple of times as the water boiled off. But with the wagon here, he had plenty of water at hand and wasn't particularly worried about that. He was, however, worried about Emma. He didn't know the intricacies of childbirth, but he knew there were a bunch of ways for it to go wrong.

A short while later, Isaac came slinking back to camp and sat down on the other side of the fire. Percy didn't say anything, not wanting to start another argument.

"How is she?" Isaac finally asked.

" 'Bout the same. Where's Luis?"

"Playin' cards with some of the army boys."

And that was the extent of their conversation. Percy had built the fire a few feet away from the Indian lodge and had cut the guards loose. He had some concerns about the Indians' sneaking back to steal Emma away again though he didn't believe it would happen until after the baby was born. She wasn't in any shape to go anywhere at the moment and probably wouldn't be for a few days, giving them a short reprieve from Indian worries. But after that all bets were off and they would have to remain diligent on the trip home.

Reaching behind him, he adjusted the placement of his saddle and leaned back against it, kicking his legs out. He listened to the murmuring coming from inside the teepee in between contractions and Miller must have said something funny because he heard Emma laugh. It was a pleasant sound to hear after worrying about her for so long. Percy had no doubt that her adjustment back to life among the family would be difficult and having a baby along would make it doubly hard. Every time she looked at the child she'd be reminded of her life in captivity and Percy knew that either resentment would build to unacceptable levels requiring some type of intervention or her memories would fade with time.

"Why'd they have to do that to my Emma?" Isaac finally said in a low voice so she wouldn't hear.

"Different cultures," Percy said.

"What's that mean?"

"What's right in one may be wrong in another."

"I'm still not gettin' your point," Isaac said.

"Okay, take dogs, for instance. The Indians don't have a problem eatin' a dog if they're hungry, but where we live, we wouldn't eat a dog if we were on the verge of starvin' to death."

"What's dogs got to do with what I'm talkin' about?"

Percy sighed, wondering what his sister had ever seen in the man sitting across the fire.

He liked Isaac, but Percy thought he lacked the curiosity needed to learn new things. For Percy, just getting by or doing things a certain way because it was the way it had always been done was unacceptable. Returning to the point he was trying to make, he spent a few moments thinking how to distill it into the most basic terms. "Let's do it this way, then," Percy said. "Do you walk up to every woman you meet and grab her by the hand and say *Let's go into the bedroom?*"

"Course not," Isaac said.

"Why?"

" 'Cause it ain't right."

"Exactly," Percy said. "In our culture that kind of thing isn't acceptable. And that's only because we've been told that, or we learned it wasn't the right thing to do. Now, let's say the people in, I don't know, say, Arkansas. Let's say all the people in Arkansas have always done it that way and didn't know any different. Do you believe they would think what they were doing was wrong?"

"Well, when you put it like that, most likely not."

"Why?"

" 'Cause that's all they know." Isaac thought about it a little more then said, "So the Indians didn't think what they was doin' was wrong 'cause that's the way they always done it?"

"Yes. What they did to Emma was unacceptable to us, but normal for them."

"I get it. Still rips my guts out, though."

"I understand. But, Isaac, you can't undo what's already been done. All you can do is accept it and move on."

Dr. Miller stuck his head out and said, "Percy, I could use that water now and I could also use an extra set of hands."

Percy and Isaac exchanged looks. "I can't do it, Percy. I can pull calves all day, but I can't do that."

Percy used a balled-up rag to pull the pot of water off the fire and carried it inside. It took Emma another hour to get the baby out and when she did, Dr. Miller did what he needed to do and placed the squealing baby boy on her chest. Percy knew this was the make-or-break moment. She'd either look at the child and talk to it or shun it outright. Percy held his breath and after a few seconds of staring at the thing on her chest, Emma picked the baby up and snuggled him to her cheek.

"I have some more to do, Percy, but thank you."

"No, thank you, Doc." Percy stepped out into the night. He looked at Isaac, who was still sitting by the fire, and knew his brother-in-law would simmer on low boil for a while yet. "It's a boy."

Isaac nodded. "Emma okay?"

"She's just fine."

ACKNOWLEDGMENTS

The first round of thanks goes to you, the readers. Thank you for taking some time out of your busy lives to read. I'm also a voracious reader and I believe books are the stabilizing foundation to a much gentler society, something we're in desperate need of. Feel free to contact me at timwashburn-books.com.

Thanks to my terrific editor and friend, Gary Goldstein. Thanks, Gary, for your guidance, the great conversations, and for the dinners and adult beverages we've shared.

A special shout-out to Doug Grad of the Doug Grad Literary Agency. Thanks for everything, Doug.

Thanks, Marc Cameron, for the great blurbs. If you haven't read any of Marc's work, I highly recommend it! You can't go wrong with any of his material.

Thank you, Steven Zacharius, for giving

us a place that writers can call home. Thanks, Lou Malcangi, for another amazing cover. I'm eternally grateful to all those who work at Kensington, including: Elizabeth (Liz) May, Lynn Cully, Lulu Martinez, Vida Engstrand, Kimberly Richardson, Lauren Jernigan, and Alexandra Nicolajsen. Welcome to the team, James Akinaka! You've already done some outstanding work.

A special thanks to two people who have made me a much better writer — my production editor, Arthur Maisel, and my copy editor, Randie Lipkin. You two are superstars.

Thanks to those who hold a special place in my heart: Kelsey, Andrew, Camdyn, and Graham Snider, Nickolas Washburn, and Karley Washburn. I love you all very, very much. Graham is a recent arrival and his name is on the dedication page — Welcome to the world, young man!

Also on the dedication page is Isabelle Kathleen Chandler, a recent arrival for my niece Andrea Chandler and her husband, Deke.

Thanks to my parents, Loren and Frances Washburn, and my brother and his wife, Daniel and Nancy Washburn. Daniel is tasked with driving my parents to book sign-ings and I can't thank you enough.

And lastly, to the woman who decided to share her life with me, Tonya. I love you forever and always.

ABOUT THE AUTHOR

Tim Washburn is the author of *Powerless, Cataclysm, The Day after Oblivion,* and *Cyber Attack.* A father of three, Tim and his wife live in central Oklahoma, deep in the heart of Tornado Alley. Tim Washburn is a member of the International Thriller Writers, the Authors Guild, and the Western Writers of America.

The employees of Thorndike Press hope you have enjoyed this Large Print book. All our Thorndike, Wheeler, and Kennebec Large Print titles are designed for easy reading, and all our books are made to last. Other Thorndike Press Large Print books are available at your library, through selected bookstores, or directly from us.

For information about titles, please call:
(800) 223-1244

or visit our website at:
gale.com/thorndike

To share your comments, please write:
Publisher
Thorndike Press
10 Water St., Suite 310
Waterville, ME 04901

CPSIA information can be obtained
at www.ICGtesting.com
Printed in the USA
BVHW070137111220
595440BV00001B/1

9 781432 881016